PURPLE BOTTOM CITY

BLANCHE KIRKENDOLL

Order this book online at www.trafford.com
or email orders@trafford.com

Most Trafford titles are also available at major online book retailers.

Printed in the United States of America.

ISBN: 978-1-4907-5280-8 (sc)
ISBN: 978-1-4907-5279-2 (e)

Trafford rev. 02/02/2015

 www.trafford.com
North America & international
toll-free: 1 888 232 4444 (USA & Canada)
fax: 812 355 4082

CHAPTER 1

When I first realized that there was something called life and you could make pretty much what you wanted with it, I wanted it all. Little did I know most of it was not good for me. Looking back on everything, I think I turned out pretty good. That is to say better than average. My mom always says that was because of my good upbringing. If only she knew a fraction of the things that I escaped from and the things that I escaped to and the pitfalls that I fell in and barely got out of, it wouldn't have changed anything. I lived life. All through high school I sported a 3.9 grade average. It could have been better, but between girls and sports it averaged out okay. Because of my physique and agility, most people thought that sports would be my choice. But no. During my sophomore year in high school, I knew that my life would be around something to do with rocks. I was a rock hound. The formation of the earth's crust was simply fascinating to me. During my junior year, NASA had invited me down to the Johnson Space Center to study some moon rocks and meteorites. No one had any idea what this did for me. It was doing this summer I was recruited by at least seven major oil companies in an apprenticeship position after my senior year. I know that this had something to do with my physics teacher, Mr. Orr. He always had great faith in me, and it felt good knowing that he had that kind of belief and respect for me. Plus, I had worked really hard to get where I was. I still had to make a decision whether I was going to go to college of my choice or to accept the offer that the oil companies had offered me. I was only eighteen. How could I make a decision like that? So I went straight to my uncle Willie. All Willie told me was I was the one who had to make the decision. But if I wanted his advice, the decision had already been made. The apprenticeship program seemed like the ideal solution. All I had to do was to choose which company, and I had to make that decision because in the long run I may build up some resentment against him if things didn't work out. But if I wanted his advice, the decision had already been made. The apprenticeship program seemed like the ideal solution.

He pointed out to me that I was an adult now and making decisions, whether right or wrong, was a part of being mature.

This was the first major decision that I had been forced to make on my own, and I didn't want to screw up. Those insecurities rose up to haunt me. But I knew even before I went to Uncle Willie that this decision was on me.

School and my apprenticeship went by in a flash, and before long I was well on my way. I was working at Atilla Inc. in Houston, Texas, as a geologist. It seemed as though God had made that job just for me. I worked more than ten years or more. I was happy at Atilla Inc. Promotions came steadily as I moved up through the ranks. Of course, there were mumblings and grumblings because of the promotions. Some resented him and some didn't because they knew that he was not given these promotions; he had earned them. He was not the product of some affirmative action program but because he was good at what he did. He knew what needed to be done and he did it.

One day came when someone higher up wanted him, no, needed him, to take over an ailing plant in Great Falls, Montana. He knew that he had heard or read about Montana before but couldn't place it because it was not on his list of places he would like to live or visit. Wherever Great Falls, Montana, was, it was in the wrong place.

Now, I can look back and ask myself some questions that I would not have dared to if things had turned out differently.

I can ask myself now because I am stronger in myself worth and many thing that I thought was impossible, I take a wait-and-see stance. Is there a place for everything and does everything have a place? Just because no one has seen it doesn't mean that it does not exist. If everyone is wrong and you are the only one right which of two is normal, or does normalcy join the ranks of the majority and even though you are right, no one cares?

At some point and place in my life I erased the words can't and impossible out of my vocabulary because many things that I had been told was impossible wasn't and can't had eloped with maybe. I have never heard or seen a body of water flow up steam. Just because I've never seen this happen does not mean that it is impossible. Somewhere in this world or out of this world this could be a common occurrence I leave my life up to fate? Naw, I don't believe in fate either.

I could begin this story with "once upon a time, there was this man . . ." but that would make it appear to be a fairy tale and everyone knows that fairy tales are not real. Also, "once upon a time" would make this story untrue due to the fact that it is impossible for something like this to happen. Then, there is can't. This could not happen because it can't be done. Would you call this an impossibility, or could this feat be achieved in an unorthodox way?

I was driving down Interstate 15 slightly exceeding the speed limit and humming an old Temptation song that was way off-key and feeling great just to be alive. I couldn't sing, and I never professed that I could only sing when I went to church and when I baked. Yes, I baked every chance that I got. I got that from my grandmother. It relaxed me and was sorta therapeutic in a way. When I baked, the neighbors would always benefit from it, and the children adored me.

I was living the lifestyle that many people dreamed about. I should have been happy. I was. Only, I had a feeling that something was missing and I didn't know what it was. I added this to my list of things that I wanted to find out later.

When I was twelve I began to compile an invisible list in my mind so that whenever I encountered something that I didn't understand but wanted to, or something I needed to find out about, I made a mental addition to this list. Whenever the opportunity would present itself, I would seek answers for these unasked and misunderstood items on my invisible mental list. At times the list became exceptionally long, but I never forgot what I had on my list.

This part of the country was new to Charles DeNero. He had transferred from Houston, Texas, to Great Falls, Montana. This was one move that he didn't want to make. He had been perfectly contended where he was and didn't have any intentions of moving anywhere, not in this century, anyway.

He glanced at his watch. He was making good time. He yawned, and water filled his eyes and ran down his cheeks. He wiped it away with the back of his hand. Those allergy pills had him drowsy.

The doctor had warned him of this, but he rarely did what the doctors advised him to do. He always thought that most doctors were arrogant and had a superiority complex and needed to be worshiped, and he would never show them the reverence that they expected. So what if he was drowsy? He turned up the volume on his car stereo, swore, and continued his journey.

The scenery was magnificent. There wasn't any litter along the road to mar the natural beauty of this pristine state. There were no billboards cluttering the majesty of nature with their rodomontade, as the state and its citizens always stressed.

Charles DeNero had been in Montana for five weeks, two days. Glancing at his watch added four hours and eighteen minutes. He didn't have anything against Montana; it was just that there so much space. Sure, Texas was larger than Montana, but the part that he frequented had many more people and all this empty space took some getting used to.

He had a 10:30 appointment and didn't want to be late. The loud music wasn't helping his drowsiness. He turned off the radio and rolled down the windows and began to sing. Surely, this would wake him up because he had been told that his singing could wake the dead. He began to belch out "I know an old lady who swallowed a fly / Now I don't know why she swallowed the fly, perhaps, she'll die." Abruptly, he stopped, because he didn't know the lyrics. He thought, no, that's not the kind of song to wake you up, that's the kind of song to put you to sleep. He smiled as he thought of his aunt Ella and what she had said about his Tchaikovsky CD. She said that it wouldn't wake you up or put you to sleep; it would drive you crazy long before any of that happened. I liked Tchaikovsky; at least there aren't any lyrics to remember. But right now is not a Tchaikovsky moment. He needed a more portent sound. Rap was not his cup of tea. He would rather eat grass than listen to rap. No way.

As his mind perused the crevices of his music memory, the sound of Chicago came crashing through.

He felt a little jolt. Yep, that was it. An older tune from the 1980s. Chicago's 25 or 6 to 4. He loved Chicago because they had that big band sound, and that guy made that guitar moan, dance, talk, pray, and cry. If that didn't wake him up, nothing would. As the sounds of Chicago surrounded him, his mind began to wander. He was thinking about his woman still in Houston.

She was everything that any man could ever want, and he was anxious for her to move to Montana. Phone calls and video chatting wasn't hitting it. He wanted something that he could hold, touch, smell, feel. Wait, was he being unfair wanting her to move here just to satisfy him? There weren't many jobs to pick from, and he wasn't quite sure how he was going to take to small city life. His new job would probably keep him quite busy, but what about Edye? Come to think about it, they had never discussed this. It had been too early. Just being away from her this short while made him realize just how much she meant to him. She was the arch in his smile, the salt in his tears, the love of his life; she was a part of him.

He was on his way back to Great Falls from Helena. He had been chasing ghosts for the past week and had came up empty. It seemed that he had been chasing ghost ever since he came here. Chasing company employees who had been ripping off equipment to the point of running the company into bankruptcy. He was nearing Wolf Creek when he started to reminisce about where he came from and where his life had brought him.

A smile creased his face as he thought of his fifth-grade teacher, Miss Hector. She would ask him why he always answered a question with why, and he would answer, why not? This would make her dentures clack and the class would sniggle, and this made her furious. Her huge breast would heave up and down like two pigs in a sack. It fascinated him because he wondered how she could breathe with those huge breasts attached to her chest.

He had no idea what made Miss Hector cross his mind. But every now and then buried stuff seemed to ooze through the cracks of his sealed reality, made a popping sound, and he'd wonder how many people are going through life living a lie and dragging along unwanted baggage that was chained to their necks by arrogant and uncaring people that they had looked up to for guidance.

Just listening to them talk made him angry. He could understand what they went through because it was still happening today, but not so openly. He couldn't change what they had gone through, but it made him more sensitive to the needs of others.

Everything that he had loved and grown up with was still in Houston, his friends, family, condo, and all of his favorite places he liked to frequent. The move to Montana was not one he relished. Sure, it was bribery. The promotion and huge raise was something that I couldn't turn down. Anyway, he felt that there were people that he had deemed more qualified for the job than he. But who was he to argue? If they wanted him, they got him and he would do the best job that he could do.

At Atilla Inc. he moved from the fourth to the third man from the top. Plus, he was the only single guy in the office with the exception of Ellen Forsithe and Christellen KeBent, but they were females. All the other guys were married and didn't want to uproot their families. Atilla had dangled an apple before him and he took a bite. That proverbial apple always got mankind into trouble. The raise and perks that came with the promotion and relocating were just too much to turn down.

Charles DeNero was a twenty-nine-year-old metallurgy engineer with a masters degree from MIT. He was six feet one inch in height and weighed one hundred seventy-eight pounds and was good-looking. As the women always told him. He had a honey-brown complexion and a head full of curly brown hair. The dimple in his chin and his wide sheepish smile was his ace in the hold. In his teenage years people told him that he was going to go far, but he never let it go to his head. He was always polite and seemingly easygoing. He had a personality that could make a stranger feel as though he had known them all of his life. But whenever the time came when he had to lay down the law, he did and did it well.

The blast from the horn of an eighteen-wheeler shocked him out of his reverie. Charles looked in the rearview mirror and noticed that the truck was driving too close for comfort. He slowed down to let the truck pass. The truck didn't pass and drew even closer. He became alarmed. What was wrong with this moron? He speeded up and the truck spew up. What in hell was this guy trying to do? At last the truck got in the passing lane, came up beside his car, and gave a blast of his horn. In the window there was a cardboard with a message on it. "Follow me!"

"Why?" He wanted to know. A rest stop was up a head and the truck drove in and stopped. A very pretty woman climbed out of the cab and came over to Charles's car. She was wearing a red cap with a John Deere logo on it. She took off her cap and shook her head, and a mass of fiery red curls cascaded down her back. I said nothing. I did nothing.

She came over to my car and said in a Midwestern drawl, "Just what does a girl have to do to get your attention?"

I answered, "Surely not by giving him a heart attack and scaring the hell out of him." His mouth was dry, and he needed some spit to swallow so he could talk. He swallowed hard and asked, in a tone that was laced with rage, "Are you crazy? You could have killed me."

"No. I wouldn't kill you. That would be a waste of a fine mankind."

I was still having saliva problems. My mouth was too dry. I swallowed again and said in a strained voice, "Where I come from, women don't do things like this."

"And, Sweet Pea, just where is that? You fine-looking devil."

"Texas."

"Texas. Maybe I should go there," she said bringing her mouth too close to my face.

I jerked my face away because her breath smelled like a sewer pit. I said, "Sorry, ma'am, I must be on my way."

"Too bad. We could have had a good time. Bye."

Charles nodded. She got in her truck and took off. She was gone and Charles hoped that he would never see her again. She was beautiful, but her breath could kill an elephant, and what a strange name she had, Alabama Detroit.

Charles decided that he would turn off his reminiscence channel and concentrate on the meeting that he was on his way to. He knew that his report would be favorable because some progress had been made. He knew that they didn't think he could change things overnight because things were in a bad way when he took over from bad management thefts and a host of white collar crimes and a healthy dose of I don't give a damn employees. A fourth of the employees would probably be gone before the first quarter.

Some had been out on sick leave for weeks, some for months, with all manner of trumped-up illnesses. Some had been caught fishing, putting a roof on their homes and in the malls shopping. One innovative employee had been caught commuting to Billings, where he had opened a small engineering firm while he was supposedly out on sick leave recovering from surgery to repair two ruptures in his back. When he got caught he said that he had no idea what I was talking about because he didn't have a business in Billings. He only went to Billings to see another doctor.

When I showed him the papers he had filed and a receipt of the money he had paid for a license and a copy of a lease he had signed for office space, he was still denying the allegations. I smiled a half smile seeming to agree with what he was saying as I continued to jot on a pad. Then, the other half of my smile emerged as I handed him a pink slip and wished him the best of luck in his new business. I left him holding the pink slip with his mouth gaping open.

The guy had gotten caught putting a roof on his house after supposedly getting injured by some drilling equipment. He had supposedly broken his thigh bone and severely bruised his side. Through his own investigation, Charles found that the man had someone else's x-rays. There had been absolutely nothing wrong with him except minor abrasions. This time his leg and thigh were broken and he had no insurance because I handed him a pink slip.

He had recovered equipment that had been stashed away for future illegal sales. Before he came, the plant was being run like a chop shop. All manner of oil-field equipment was being stolen and sold to the highest bidder. I was a geologist not a detective. I knew I was good with diplomatic situations, but I was no diplomat. What had I gotten myself into? I had made some enemies and no doubt will make more. It was just the way things were. I had to weed out the wheat from the tare, and I had a feeling that there would be a lot less wheat when I finished. After all no one told him that this was going to be easy.

There were some excellent employees at Atilla, and he had vowed that he would turn the company around in eight months or at least point it in the right direction. Now, he had to report on what progress that he had made. All that he knew was that he seem to be going in the right direction. Hard work never fazed him, but he wished that he had known how bad things were up here before he transferred.

Even with all the people who were angry with him, he had made some friends along with the enemies. One day he was approached by some of his coworkers; actually, he was their boss. They had invited him to go on a weekend camping trip. He tried not to act like the asshole that he had been hearing about behind his back, and said, "Sure." Later, when he got home he would kick his own butt for not saying no. Hell no. He had never been in the woods and really had no desire to go. The closest he had been to a forest was the Discovery Channel. He tried to calm his raging heart and to slow down his breathing and not faint. Then he thought, I can do it. They are no better than me. I am going to show them. Something good must be in this outing, but he just didn't know what. Right now he had to pee real bad. Chuckling to himself, he thought the very thought of camping scared the piss out of him.

The weekend seemed to happen overnight. Two days before the outing he had gone and bought a ton of camping equipment. He was nervous, scared, excited, and filled with great expectations, but he didn't know what he was expecting.

When they got to Charles's place he was standing beside the curb with enough equipment for all of them. He looked like he was moving. The guys got a good laugh at his expense. His ego was bruised. He picked up his equipment and started to go back inside. He was wondering why they were laughing so hard. Hell, he didn't know anything about camping. Besides, where he came from, black people didn't go camping. He started for the door, but Trevor stopped him. He threw his equipment in the back of Mike's Explorer, got in, and took off.

Charles had just about forgot the teasing because he was absorbed in the surrounding scenery. He sat looking out the window like a child, fascinated by all the woods. There were trees everywhere. He had never known that there were so many trees in the world. As they moved farther into the forest, the trees seemed to open up and let them pass through and close the pathway so that they could not return. He wanted to scream, but the others were laughing and talking and having a good time, and this seemed to ease his fears somewhat. He tried to fit in by joining the conversation. They were talking about fishing and lures, and he didn't know anything about either, so he sat and listened to what they were saying. A couple of miles into the woods they stopped. Everyone got out, stretched, and yawned. "Well, here we are," Mike announced to no one in particular. "Man, this seems to get better every year," he continued.

"Well, let's get clicking. I can't wait to feel the tug of a trout on my line," Dennis said as he let out a whoop.

Everyone was busy getting camp set up. Charles did what he could to help and not to get in the way. He stopped momentarily and took notice of his surroundings. He gasped. Never before had he seen such virgin beauty. Pure and unadulterated. The stream was picture-book perfect. The trees, the patches of cattails, the algae-covered rocks, the rippling sound that the water made as the sun's rays played hide and seek through the leaves. Charles was overcame with awe. He felt a tear cascading down his cheek. This place was so beautiful, so serene, so peaceful. For the first time in his life he had an experience that made him know and understand the biblical version of creation. A divine creation.

Not an accident, not a big bang. Being an engineer and a geologist, he could see that there had to be a divine plan to this creation stuff.

After his camping trip, Montana began to grow on him heavily, and he still didn't know blip about camping. But he was willing to give it a try. Yes, there were woods, many woods. There were plain, mountains, lakes and wildlife galore. The raw beauty and untamed spirit of things that was Montana and the inhabitant that was the overseer of these natural resource, changed a skeptic like me. It was fantastic. The air was so crisp and exhilarating it made you want to reach out, give God a hug, and tell him thank you.

He was making really good time. The sign read, Great Falls, 85 miles. Charles resumed his off-key melodies, but this time he was singing along with Chicago, mutilating their songs. He remembered the little old lady who swallowed the fly. He didn't know why she swallowed the fly, perhaps she'll die. Whoever wrote that song must have been on something that you can't buy at the drugstore. He made a note on his invisible list of things to do that he wanted to learn the lyrics to at least one song.

Up ahead there was some sort of commotion. He began to slow down, but he was still too far away to clearly see what was going on. As he got closer he could see an old model pickup truck and a beat-up Volvo. The guy driving the Volvo had a dead moose on the top of his car and it had slid off. Charles, being from the South, stopped and asked, "Can I be of any assistance?"

He didn't know why he had done that because he really didn't have the time and he was not properly dressed for moose anchoring. Besides, he had a meeting to attend and didn't want to show up smelling like moose shit. This was the first moose he had seen outside the Discovery Channel.

Everyone was absorbed in getting the moose back on top of the car. He watched fascinated. It was comical in a way. They would hoist it up on top of the car, and it would slide down the other side. I turned and walked back toward my car. One guy asked, "Hey, you in the fancy duds, do you really want to help and mess up your pretty clothes?"

Charles answered, "No. I was just getting a little sun."

He stared at Charles in a weird way and said, "Don't look like you need any to me."

They all stared at Charles. "Is something wrong?" He felt warm all over. They continued to stare, and Charles thought, This must be a staring contest and I'm it. The second guy spit out a wad of tobacco, and it landed on the toe of his worn boot. He pulled his pant out of his butt and rubbed the stubble on his chin and said something in a language he didn't understand. He must have said something funny because all of them cracked up laughing. Charles was getting really uncomfortable. He asked in a tense voice, "What in the hell are y'all laughing at? What are you'll staring at? Is there moose shit on my face, or have I sprouted horns?"

"Main, we seldom get to see a blackie round'er and we was thank to pare you wif what the white folks say aw is, you know. Them white folks still talk with a forked tongue You ain't nuthin' lack dat."

"Thank you very kindly, I think," Charles said. "Tell that to the white folks.

The first guy said to the guy next to him, "Hey, Pete, would you take a look at dis car?" Still digging in his butt, he said, "I bet this set you back many bucks." He smiled and exhibited a mouth full of rotting teeth. Charles thought, Just what I needed, a comedian in the middle of nowhere. Pete asked Charles, "What kin' o' work you do to get a car lack dis?"

Charles said softly, "Hard."

"No kidding, man."

"I am second vice president at Atilla, Inc."

"You hear that, Pete? He probably make more money in a week den we'um get in a year, and he is black."

Charles said, "You refer to being black like it's a disease." Then he turned and started to his car.

Pete stopped and said, "We don't get to see many blacks up here, and the only thing we'um get is off the TV. You know they say stuff like y'all on Uncle Sam payroll, you know, welfare. Plus, they say that y'all is dummer den us. No offense."

"None taken."

"Um, Pete Longfellow, dis is Little John and Spoon Redfeather."

Charles shook their hands, and it left his hand smelling like moose and stale tobacco. They resumed their laughter and conversation. Pete Longfeather spoke again, "Say, how can you help us anchor dis moose in your fancy clothes? You would not only smell like moose shit or have some on your face, you would be covered in it."

Little John added, "We been trying to anchor dis moose and I swear to God, it don't want to be anchored."

As they kept talking, Charles learned that they were members of the Blackfoot tribe. So that explained the unfamiliar language. Longfeather asked a question and made a statement. "You ain't from round dees parts 'cause ain't no blackies here. There is a few, not many."

Charles thought to himself, Thank you for sharing this much needed information with me. They continued their saga of trying to anchor the moose that didn't want to be anchored. Longfeather asked, "Just how can you help us?"

Charles said, "Why don't you put the moose in the truck?"

"Darn, why didn't I think of that? Thank you, mister."

I was thinking, There is one site you won't see in Houston.

Montana may not be on the edge of the world at all. Thinking of my recent encounter, I wondered if Redfeather could talk. Whenever you asked him something he grunted "un" for yes and "un" for no. In reality, Redfeather was big enough to carry the moose, Pete, and John all by himself.

The weather had been perfect when he had left the Indians and the dead moose. A few miles past the moose incident, a strange fog appeared. Actually he couldn't tell if it was smoke, fog, or what. You could look back and the weather was crystal-clear Montana style; now this. I drove into the fog thinking to myself that maybe this was some kind of smoke and not fog at all. What in the world—? Before I could finish the sentence a purple van or something I thought was purple was just there and just vanished. More strangely, the fog began to swirl like a thousand miniature tornadoes, and they were crackling with electricity. The purple van thing drove into the fog, and a gigantic lighting strike lit up the fog with white light and blinded me. It felt as though I was going down into a winding tunnel that was alive. Surely, this is one strange trip.

I inched through the fog following the van; at least I thought that it was a van. By this time I was no longer sure about anything. My engine stalled after the second burst of lightning. I tried to stop the car and get out but the car wouldn't stop and the doors wouldn't open. I felt like I was going to suffocate. I began to scream, but I don't know if I succeeded.

I don't know how much time had passed before I regained consciousness. When I woke up, my surroundings were completely alien. I rubbed my eyes thinking that when I opened them again everything would be normal. I opened them again and everything was still the same. Something was really weird because everything, everywhere, as far as I could, see was purple with the exception of me and my car. My heart was pounding in my chest, and I could hear my blood swishing in my ears. I was terrified.

Where was I? How did I get here? More important than all else, how was I going to get back to where I belong? As far as I could see there was signs of great destruction and no sign of life anywhere. I tried the car door again and it opened but I was too afraid to get out of the car. I looked at the ground and it emitted an illuminating purple vapor that crackled with static. For a minute I thought that it was moving. I wondered if there were any wild animals out there, or if this alien environment was the only thing I had to contend with. I kept hoping that none of this was real and any minute I would wake up and all this would be a bad dream.

I crawled into the backseat of my car convincing myself that if I took a nap, when I woke up, all of this would be something funny to laugh about. According to my watch I slept about two hours. When I opened my eyes, the purple stuff was still there. Just where was I? Why was I here?

Okay, Charlie, keep your cool. You are an intelligent man, you can figure this out. I wanted to laugh and I had to fight that little panic giggle building up in my chest. I was scared, but I wasn't quite ready to admit to that yet. Everything that was happening was against the laws of nature that I knew of, all of this destruction, all this purple. It was just too much. Come on, man, get to the bottom of this, I told myself. Actually, I wasn't sure that I wanted to.

I tried to rationalize the situation. Let me see, the last people that I had seen were those Indians and that strange fog. Then what else? At least my headache was gone, but something much worst had taken its place.

I got in behind the steering wheel and began to drive. I came across this semi clearing that seemed to lead into the woods and was tempted to drive down it because of its idyllic setting. A strong sense enveloped me.

I turned to get back into my car but something seemed to have a greater pull, urging me to go down this path. I did.

From the first step that I made this unseen force seem to grow stronger. It is true that this path had mind boggling beauty that made me equate this scenery with the path to the gate of heaven. It was breathtakingly beautiful. I had gone about a half mile down this path when the bouquet from the flowers seemed to overpower me, taking my breath away. I think that I fainted but I am not sure. Anyway, it was about ten minutes before I could safely breathe again. I dragged myself upright with much difficulty and looked around. There were dead flowers everywhere and the beauty that had lured me down this path had turned ugly and spit in my face. Only the trees with the interlocking branches were still unchanged. Again, I turned to go back, but I couldn't resist this unseen force that kept pulling me forward.

I turned and looked down this path pass the barrenness and ugliness trying to see what lie ahead for me and I couldn't see anything. Yet I couldn't go back.

Reluctantly, I stumbled forward wondering what manner of evil I had encountered. Surely this purple world had driven me insane, or maybe I was dreaming and there was no purple world. I decided that I was going to act like one would act when dreaming because you don't ever die in a dream and I had nothing to fear. But just suppose that I was not dreaming, then what? I didn't want to find out.

As I trod unwillingly down this ignis fatuus, I wondered how I was being controlled or was I being controlled if so by whom or what? Where was I going and why was I going there and what was going to happen to me when and if I got there?

He could not even manage to add these questions to his invisible list of things to find out about later because he felt like there wouldn't be a later. He thought, just listen to me, I seem to have given up without a fight. I am going to turn around and go back to my car and get the hell out of here.

He stopped and tried to turn around and couldn't. His feet felt like his shoes was made of lead and the only direction in which he could walk was straight ahead. His fears doubled and his mouth was dry. "God!" he prayed, Please help me."

He gulped down air too fast and became dizzy, and perspiration beaded his forehead. He sat down hard like he had been kicked by a mule. His head hit the ground and made a sound like someone had cracked a huge egg. He didn't move. He needed to think but somehow his mind was blocked and he couldn't. He bit his tongue, and the salty taste of his own blood brought back his sanity.

Perhaps his prayer had been answered, he didn't know. Damn, he thought, why hasn't someone written a book about "Things to Do When You Don't Know What to Do." There was far too many books about sex and people's lives that no one gives a flick about anyway. He never knew because sex was as natural as peeing, sleeping, and breathing. Everything plants and animals knew about sex and reproduction.

He stopped again because he had made up his mind that he was not going down this path another step. He turned his head toward the opposite direction because he was still unable to turn his body around. He had traveled pretty close to a mile. The path was narrowing and seemed more menacing. He felt like a fly trapped on fly paper. He was tired and thirsty and there wasn't anything he could do about it. What type of invisible entities inhibited this strange purple world, and why were they holding him captive?

He was standing in the middle of the pathway when a glass of purple liquid floated toward him. He gasped the glass into his hand and looked at it intensely. It looked wet. It smelled wet. Was it water? He sipped it. It tasted like water. But should he drink it? He was dying of thirst. Maybe his captors was reading his mind he had to be more careful.

Yet he could swear that something was communicating with him telepathically telling him that this is water and it was safe for him to drink. He took another sip; it tasted like water and he drained the glass and was still unsated. Another glass of purple liquid floated toward him, and without hesitation he drained it.

Now that his thirst was sated he felt much better. All he had to figure out now was how he was going to outsmart his captors when they could read his every thought. He remembered reading how slaves used to communicate in songs so that their massas wouldn't know what they were saying. He smiled. Maybe he would give it a try.

Before he could begin trying to outsmart his captors, he felt something or someone with great strength take him by both arms and literally drag him down the pathway, which grew more menacing, narrower, and darker the farther he traveled down it. It was useless to protest because whatever was holding him captive was much stronger than he was. Yet he struggled.

The idea of asking his captors why he was being held captive entered his mind, but before he could ask this question verbally he had the answer telepathically, "Because we can, you worm husk."

"Just who are you?" Charles asked in a small voice.

"Mute!" was all Charles heard.

For a brief moment all the beauty that had lured him down this path came back then disappeared again, leaving him alone with this entity.

He heard an answer in his head before he had asked the question, and it made his spine tingle, "We are not of his world. We could not survive on a world such as this. It's much too bright for our existence."

Charles was not amused. He had come so far down the path until it had became so narrow you had to turn sideways. He stopped and cried out loud, "I have had enough of this! Let go your hold on me now. Damn it."

He stood very still with his arms out stretched as silence permeated his surroundings. He closed his eyes as though he was expecting to see a miracle when he opened them again. Finally, he opened them and there was no sign of a pathway nor were there any trees with interlocking branches. The gloom and doom was gone. There was only a burned-out purple forest littered with burned trees, stumps, downed branches, and holes filled with weeds, debris, and water, and he was standing beside his car. What was going on? He was positive that he did not dream this. But if he was not dreaming, what had happened to the pathway, the trees, whose branches interlocked covering the pathway like a canopy? He looked at his car and wondered, How did it get here? He took a closer look at his surrounding and realized that he was back where he entered the pathway that was no more.

This was a dream, a nightmare, he concluded. None of these things really happened. Now that he was awake he could laugh about how scared he was.

Back in his car, trying to maneuver through this decimated place, he did smile. Even though he didn't have any idea where he was, where he was going, or when and if he got to wherever he was going, what would he find there. Little did he know how much this had already affected his life. Somewhere along the evolutionary link, the mind had built in bumpers to cushion the mind from shock that was too harsh for the conscious to handle without one going mad. A great example was how Charles could not accept the reality of the situation that he was in, so blaming it on a nightmare freed his conscience so that he could concentrate on his survival. He drove on.

Never in his wildest imagination had he ever imagined destruction on a scale of this magnitude, and he was sure that the atmosphere along with the destruction was detrimental to his all-around health. He sniffed the purple air and it had the pungent smell of decaying vegetation. He thought, This smell is normal, but the stagnant water was clocked in a purple mist that emitted an unfamiliar odor. He could still smell the poignant odor of sulfur that had followed him down the pathway. No, this can't be right because you can't smell in a nightmare, could you? Something is not right. Nothing is right!

He turned on his headlights because of the dark nature of this place, and purple shadows kept fading in and out. He turned his lights back off because it seemed to make a bad thing worse. The mist grew denser and the smell of decay began to smell like hot tar. He turned his lights back off. A thought popped in mind that made him smile and frightened him at the same time. He thought, This place is so scary and ugly until it didn't want me to see it. Then again, if it didn't want me to see it, it must be alive. Could it be? Naw. Charles, old boy, get a grip. Perhaps, but something alive is close by because I can feel it. This was not a comforting thought.

He had seen the TV series *The Twilight Zone* and all of the stories ended with the message that the possibility of this thing happening existed. But since he was having trouble trying to figure out whether he was dreaming or this was a realty, he felt like he was in the middle of the twilight zone alone, with an unseen presence that was evil. Right now he couldn't tell what reality was. What he did know was that now was not the time to give out or give up. Although he had no idea how he got caught up in this, he felt certain that there must be a way out. Think, Charles, think!

In his dazed and confused state he had unknowingly exited the low swampy land and found himself on a craggy mesa. He stopped and got out of his car and looked around as far as he could see. There was no sign of civilization. This place looked like a slew of H-bombs had hit it. Actually it looked more like it had melted than shattered. Surely, he must be the only thing alive on this eerie alien place. He couldn't tell if there had ever been life here. He smelled a sulfur compound. Damn! This place smelled funky.

He climbed back into his car and resumed driving to wherever.

As he inched his way down the craggy mesa, he tried to think of something that was not too depressing. Coming down off the mesa was a feat that exhausted every nerve in his body. He hit a hole so hard that he thought the car had broken into. He swerved and hit a bigger hole, so big his entire car fell in it. "Son-of-a-gun!" Charles swore through clenched teeth. He stepped out to see how much damage had been done and how big of a mess he was in. He was thinking that his tour in the National Guard would come in handy because he had plenty of experience getting vehicles out of muck. He bent over to pick up some poles and rocks to place them under the tires for traction. He hesitated because the rocks were glowing eerily. He dropped the pole he had picked up because it was burning his hand. He took a stick and pried a small rock out of the muck, and it glowed. He was a geologist and was familiar with rocks and never had he seen any like these. These rocks could move and he was sure that they were radioactive.

The ground wasn't muddy. He was stuck in supersoft dust, and those rocks were not going to be his savior. He had another fence to jump. He gathered sticks instead of rocks for traction. Finally, he got out of the mire and made it off the mesa.

By the time he got off the mesa, he felt positive that he was not on Earth. He didn't know how he got here but he wanted to get the hell away from here, and he didn't know how to leave.

When he was well on his way to who knows where, he remembered the time his father had taken him to Louisiana to go fishing. The haunting beauty of the swamp would always remain fresh in his mind. He wondered how nature could make beauty out of such a hostile environment. The cypress trees with the moss draped over their limbs and the stagnant water covered with algae were both beautiful and dangerous, and no one knew what lay beneath that green scum.

He remembered the alligator that he had seen. His dad, two of his uncles that lived in Oil City, Louisiana, and he had gone fishing on Caddo Lake, in northwest Louisiana. They were out in a boat on the lake, and he had his hand hanging outside the boat skimming the water. He had thought that it was a log floating in the water then his uncle snatched him back with great speed and force. He had no idea of what was going on until this beast opened his huge mouth. His father let out a yell that could curdle your blood. That was when I peed my pants. After that venture he had never wanted to go fishing or anything else that had to do with woods or the outdoors.

Woods was not a problem here. He would welcome some trees and animals, anything that would improve this dismal, depressing purple place. Anyway, that just goes to show you that beautiful things aren't always what they seem to be. Therefore, maybe ugliness may hold some redeeming powers also.

As he drove on, he felt like giving up because logic told him that if he had not seen any signs of life by now, there probably wasn't any. Then, he reckoned that if someone would land on Earth in one of its deserts like the Gobi or on one of the icy plains of Greenland or even the Arctic, they too could surmise that there wasn't life on that world either. Then again he could have landed in an ocean and could have swum for days and come to the conclusion that this was a water world and was void of land and civilization. Perhaps he had landed in a place similar to one of those places.

He drove on and decided that he would keep on driving until he ran out of gas or for some other reason couldn't drive anymore.

As he drove, he thought, If only I could find a piece of litter to let me know that civilization was present somewhere. He wanted to cry because he felt so alone. He thought this must be what its' like to be the last person alive.

After a feeling-sorry-for-myself break, Charles got back into his car and resumed driving. In a few hours he ran upon a sign that read, Purple Bottom City Road. There was an arrow pointing straight ahead. He was beside himself with joy. He prayed, "Thank you, God."

He felt better than he did when his uncle had snatched him from the jaws of that alligator. He patted himself on the back because he had found out that perseverance had paid off.

The road that he was on was graveled, but it was thousand times better than the one that he had just came through. Actually that was not a road but just something that he had driven through. He checked his gas tank, and it read three-fourths full. Evidently the gauge must have been damaged coming through no man's land. He knew that he had driven over three hundred miles and hoped that he would find a gas station soon. Aw, what the fuck, he thought. I probably wasn't going to live much longer anyway because he was positive he had been exposed to some very to toxic stuff. The tires on his car still glowed. Another forty miles down the road a sign read, WELCOME TO PURPLE BOTTOM CITY. Another five miles down the road there was an intersection. Constipation Avenue crossed Purple Bottom City Road. I thought, Now I'm getting somewhere. Maybe I'm not alone after all. I couldn't contain my jubilation. I crossed my fingers. Finally, I saw civilization. People.

There was something very wrong. But what was it? This must be a nightmare after all, and I can't seem to wake up. I looked at my watch and it said 3:45. As I drove down Purple Bottom City Road, it changed from gravel to asphalt to concrete.

As I passed people, they were looking at me as strangely as I was looking at them. I slowed down and asked a purple man, "Where am I?" He looked at me a full two minutes before he spoke. At first I thought that he didn't understand what I was asking him. Before I began to try to make him understand, he said, "You are in Purple Bottom City. Didn't you read the sign?"

I answered, "Yes, I did. But where is Purple Bottom City? I don't remember any place called Purple Bottom City. What state am I in?"

He answered, "I'm not a history teacher nor a tour guide, and I should be asking you these questions."

"Okay then, where can I find someone who could tell me this?"

He pointed down the road, "You probably could in the city." He left in a hurry.

That is one strange dude. I smiled to myself thinking that the man had looked like a chicken. Off to my left there was a store that looked like our Circle K Stores. I pulled up and got out and went inside. There was an old man and a pimply-faced teenager behind the counter. They stared at me and I returned their stare. No one said a word. The girl finally asked, "Vot do you want?"

I was still staring, thinking that they looked like chickens too. The girl asked again, "Vot do you want?" My voice returned from its state of shock and I asked, "Where can I get some gas for my car?"

"I don't know vot you ask," the girl said.

The old man began to speak, "We don't have gas anymore. We haven't had any gas in ages. But there is something that does the same job. Go down Constipation Avenue and make a left on Body Parts street, there is a place called Gill's Fill Her Up. You can get almost anything you may need there. "By the way, where are you from?"

I thought, finally I meet someone who had intelligence. I said, "I'm originally from Houston but I recently transferred to Great Falls, Montana."

"Just where is Houston and Great Falls?" the old man wanted to know.

The first thing that hit my mind was, Uh-oh, spoke too soon. Then I said, "I'll ask you a better question, "Where am I?"

"What do you mean where are you now? You are here."

"No. I'm talking about where is this place, this purple world. Where does this purple stuff come from?"

The man answered in a tired voice. "You will have to ask someone more knowledgeable than me. I just take things as they are. I ask no questions. I know that there is an answer somewhere, I just don't have it. I'm an old man now and I've lived all these years not knowing and it is not important to me anymore."

"I see," I replied. "Thanks for sharing this with me."

As I left the store I was still thinking how much these people looked like chickens or rather how much these chickens looked like people. Why was everything purple? There were purple trees with purple leaves, purple grass with purple weeds, purple houses with purple roofs, and little purple people chickens going and coming. Made me think of a little jingle that I had heard when I was in Texas. "I've never seen a purple cow and I never hope to see one, but I will tell you anyhow I'd rather see than be one." As I drove around trying to find out where I was, it was very possible that I may see one any minute.

As I was on my way to Body Parts Circle and trying to understand all that I had encountered, I was sure that this was the kind of stuff that Stephen King wrote about, all fiction and no facts. Where was old Stephen now? How would he handle a situation like this? Well, no matter. There's too much to find out about this place for me to think about Stephen.

I finally arrived at Gill's Fills Her Up. There were about ten other people with their strange vehicles. We checked each other out. One of the brave souls came over and rubbed his hand across my face and looked at his hand as though the color would come off. He repeated his action, positive that this time the color would come off. I was too shocked to react. Finally, he spoke. "Where did you come from with your skin that strange color?"

"I could ask you the same question. How would you answer?"

All the chicken people had stopped doing whatever they were doing and crowded around Charles, looking at him as though he was from another world. They were fascinated by him as he was by them. At first he thought that they were going to mob him. That thought vanished as quickly as it came, in an instant.

One of the guys in the group had elected himself to be the spokesperson. He held out his hand, and I shook it. He said that his name was Oscar Osana. He was a local know-it-all guy. He spoke, already knowing the answer to the question before you asked it. "You are not from around these parts, are you?" His voice had tone in it that played a jig on the nerves of my spine, and I wished that he wouldn't ask.

I answered, "No. I can't say that I am but, then again I don't know where around these part are. If I was from around these parts maybe I would know why everything is purple and I would know what had caused all the destruction that I encountered when I first arrived."

"Slow down, mister."

"Call me Charles," I interrupted.

"Okay, Charles, what did you mean about when you first arrived?"

"I told you. I have no idea where I am or how I got here. I was driving down the road on my way to a meeting. I drove into a foggy mist and I woke up here. But for a long time I thought that I was the only person living in this place." I stopped and caught my breath.

Oscar spoke again. "You must have come in from the Delta middle Section." He paused and continued, "How in the world did you get down there? No one ever go down there. It is forbidden."

"What is that?" I asked, thoroughly confused.

The nerve grinder resumed his narrative in that nerve-exploding tone. I felt like plucking his eyeballs out, but I also wanted to find out everything that I could about this place. About five hundred year ago the star that was closest to their planet went nova. A large portion of their world was decimated and would never be habitable again. A big part of it was at or near ground zero, and that is where he must have been.

Charles asked, "Just what is this place anyway?"

"This is Purple Bottom City," Oscar said. "Officially, Earth 111."

It was good thing that all my teeth were natural because they would have fallen out. "Say what!" I said much too loud. I knew that I had not heard him right.

He reiterated, "This is Earth. This purple world is Earth."

I suppose he spoke the truth because everyone else seemed to be comfortable with what he said. I was almost too scared to ask another question but I had to know. I said, "Come on now, I came from Earth and my world is not purple. Why is everything here purple?"

"That's a very long story but to make it short, the purple color is somehow tied in with the nova.

I said, "I see," because I didn't know anything else to say. I didn't ask anything else because I didn't want to hear the nerve grinder's voice again. I said, "Thank you," and proceeded to put some of the stuff that was used for fuel in their cars into mine.

I asked this chicken-looking person who was putting fuel into his car what the name of the fuel was. He looked at me as if he knew that I had not asked that question and said, "Gas." I thought to myself, Ha!

It really surprised me when I looked at my fuel gauge. I had a full tank this morning when I started out, and according to my calculations, I had driven at least fifty miles before I ended up here. Then, I had driven at two hundred miles afterward and I needed less than a fourth of a tank of gas. It was really remarkable. Kind of like running on air. I asked the chicken-looking person what kind of mileage he averaged. Again, he looked at me like I was the stupidest weirdo that he had ever encountered.

And he was having a hard time trying to control his temper. Finally, he said, "Anywhere from one hundred seventy-five to two hundred miles per gallon." Then he turned to me and asked, "Do you have any more dumb-ass questions you want to ask me before I go?"

I stood there with my mouth gaped open wondering if this was the truth or he was pulling my leg. Before I could speak again he asked, "What's with all these dumb questions? You are acting like you just dropped in from another world."

Before I knew it, I said, "I have. I think."

"Surely you are kidding," said the chicken person. "You must be the alien that everyone is talking about." He stood there just looking at me. Then he came over to where I was and said, "Gee, mister, I'm sorry. I didn't know." Then he rubbed his hand across my face, looked at it, and rubbed it again. "I simply do not believe this. It won't rub off."

I stood there listening to the chicken person and thinking how fast word got around in this place. What was he talking about when he said, I must be the alien that everyone was talking about? I was unaware that many chicken knew that I was here. In the mean time, this chicken person was trying unsuccessfully to rub the color off my skin. I said to no one in particular, "I'm going to start charging if anyone else should rub my face." Then I said, "If you are talking about my skin color, you are right, it won't rub off."

"I must be hallucinating. No. I must be really sick. I'm going to go home and lie down," the chicken person said as he was walking away. I have never seen anyone look as discombobulated as he was. Within five minutes I was facing fifteen chicken people. They were looking at me as if I were from hell. I should have said that they were looking at me as if I had sprouted horns and belched fire. I stared back. A couple came over and took my hand and licked the back of it and rubbed it with his sleeve. I just stood there because they were as alien to me as I was to them. With them coming as close to me as they were, I had the opportunity to check them out also. I knew that they were acting bizarrely, but what could I do? If I were they, I would probably do the same thing. As they came closer, I could see their hair looked like very fine chicken feathers. Purple chicken feathers. I rubbed my hand across one of their faces, and it felt like normal skin. My mind shifted into overdrive. This was someplace, wherever he was.

I sat in my car for a long time before I left Gill's Fill Her Up. I had to figure out what I was going to do next. One thing that I was grateful about was that everyone spoke English. Thank you, God, for small things.

I wondered if I should go to the authorities and solicit their help. No. I don't think so. I'll probably end up in a laboratory like guinea pig. But I had to do something. I needed to find me a place to stay and food to eat. I have some money, but I didn't think these chicken people would accept it. Thinking back for a few minutes, he remembered that Gill's Fill her Up had accepted it. But that cashier had looked dimwittedly and probably didn't know the difference. Anyway there was a decision to be made. Again he thought about his uncle Willie and wondered what he was doing. Enough of that; he had a real crisis staring him in the face, and something had to be done.

He put his car in gear and began to drive. He remembered that he had not seen any motel on his journey to wherever he was. And he thought that it was strange because there had been no billboards or any other advertisements. The only signs that he had seen beside the Welcome to Purple Bottom City sign were street signs. Surely there must be a motel or something similar somewhere in this place. He decided that he would keep on looking, perhaps he would luck up on something.

He continued to drive because driving would help him to concentrate on the problems at hand. First, he thought that he would free his mind of all clutter, and concentrate on the most pressing things. He tried, but to no avail. The clutter included, How did he get here? Why was this happening to him? Where exactly was he? How was he going to get back home? Had he lost his mind, or was he dreaming? Did he really see those chicken people? What had he done to deserve this? He didn't have the answer to any of these questions. Plus, the immediate emergency of finding food and shelter was occupying a great part of his mind.

Not only had he not seen any motels, he had not seen any fast food restaurants. He thought, I can always sleep in my car. Then again, he could just stop and ask one of the chicken people for directions or help. That would be a worst-case scenario. He glanced at his watch. It was 6:45 PM his time. If he didn't luck up on some food and shelter soon, he would have to jump-start plan B into action. Now, let's see just what plan B is. Damn it! He didn't have a plan B.

He thought about what the nerve grinder, Oscar Osana, had said about the dimensions. In a way it made sense. He could understand how this could be, but what he couldn't understand was why no one taught them about these dimensions and the other Earths. Why did he have to be on another world to find out about his world. He remembered that there were some people who had voiced these ideas down through the ages but the majority of the scientists ignored them. They claimed that these were just unproven theories and wishful thinking.

The odds were tied that if one of the chicken people had landed on his Earth, the government would have taken over and would have held him in captivity. He would have been poked, prodded, examined, and isolated all in the name of national security and science. He was grateful that the government of this world had not interfered with his arrival, at least, not yet.

CHAPTER II

It all began on the night of the senior prom when Ocena Heartburn and two other gentlemen under the high school stadium having a full blown orgy. As reported by the security guard they were doing it all, kissing, licking, sucking and fucking. When the security guard first stumbled upon them, Ocena stood up completely nude grated her pelvis vulgarly licked her lips sensually and laughed out loud. The security guard fainted. She laughed harder, came over, and sat down on the guard straddling his chest. She was still laughing when the guard came to. But by this time her other two partners in lust were long gone. While sitting on the guard's chest she made small hunching movements. This aroused the guard, and he tried to get up. As he raised his head, Ocena's long pubic hairs tickled his nose. She smiled sweetly and asked, "Baby Cakes, are you all right? Do you see anything that you may want to sample?"

The security guard didn't answer. Again he tried to get up but she still sat on his chest. She asked, "Do you know the doors of paradise are easily in your reach?" Baby Cakes.

The guard still did not answer. He swallowed nervously. Ocena kissed him on the lips and gently slid down his stomach. His lips burned like fire, but there was no flame. He trembled. When Ocena reached his pubic area, she encountered a lump. Again, she smiled shyly and said, "You naughty boy. What do we have here?"

The security guard heard himself speak in an unfamiliar, high-pitched voice, "Ma'am, will you please get off me?" Now that he had said it he felt like an ass because he didn't want her to move. She slid down his thighs, stopped, and rubbed her hands across his rock-hard erection. His pants felt damp and sticky. The strange voice came out of his mouth again, "Ma'am, will you please get off me. I have to report this."

"Really?" quipped Ocena, and she ran her hand inside of his pants, "And let all this go to waste?" It was hard for the security guard to move or talk, lust permeated his every cell. He couldn't tell his body that his mind was screaming no. With shaking hands he unzipped his fly. He could no longer deny his lust and passion. He kissed Ocena hard, and she kissed him back. The security guard had lost his inhibitions and let her have her way. He murmured incoherently, pulled off his jacket, and placed her on it and mounted her. He penetrated her and began to thrust. Every thrust was harder and harder. Ocena moaned, then everything was over.

After the lovemaking, Ocena slipped on her dress and slippers and said to the guard, "Okay, Tony. Let's go."

"What did you say? Where are we supposed to be going?

"You did say that you were going to report this, did you not?"

"Yes, sure, but that was before we became intimate."

Ocena was adamant. No, I don't want any special treatment, let's go. Because I really want to hear you explain how you got cum all over your pants."

"Man, are you sick or something? What kind of person are you?"

"Any kind that I have to be, Baby Cakes. What kind are you?"

"I'm the kind that believes that you would do exactly what you said you would do."

"Anyway, I think that I will pay Mr. Moses a visit."

"What?" the security guard asked in a strange voice. Why would you want to do a thing like that?"

"Do you think that I shouldn't?"

Tony was getting anxious because he realized what he had done. He was thinking of his wife and two kids. This job had been a godsend because he had gotten behind on his car and credit card bills when his wife became ill and this little moonlighting job came along just when he needed it most. Now, this little bitch was thinking about turning me in for something that she initiated. He wanted to strangle her right here and now. "Lord, what did I do to deserve this?" he prayed silently. He had no idea that Ocena was kidding, so he tried to reason with her. He said, "If you should go to Moses, you don't have to tell him the truth. Just tell him enough truth to make a lie more believable."

Ocena seemed distracted. "What are you talking about?'

"I'm asking you not to tell Moses about what really happened tonight."

"Really, wasn't that what you were planning to do to me? Looks like the spider got tangled in its own web," Ocena said in a remote kind of way.

"Okay. If that's what you want to do, go ahead. I won't try to stop you," the guard said with his voice rising.

"Well, I don't know but I'll ask him first thing tomorrow."

The guard was taken aback. "What are you talking about?"

Ocena nodded her head. The guard saw a couple coming their way and he knew why she had abruptly changed the subject. "I'll ask Daddy if he is going to hire any part-timers this summer." As the couple came closer, Ocena and the guard caught a whiff of marijuana smoke. He walked toward the couple, but they were so involved in what they were doing that they didn't see the guard until he spoke. "Hey. This is off limits to you. You'll have to turn back."

Before he could ask the boy what was it that he had, the boy swallowed a lit joint. He cursed, "Damn it."

I'll be a . . . a did you see that?" the astonished guard asked, "I don't believe that. He swallowed a lit joint."

"I think that you should take them to Moses," Ocena teased.

The couple took off running and they were in their car and gone before the guard had recovered from the shock.

"I can see that you are pretty swift on your feet."

"Aw, go fuck a frog," the security guard said as he walked away.

Ocena decided that she would pay Mr. Arthur Moses a visit just because he was there. First she would take a wee shower. She had everything that she needed in her locker. It never hurt a girl to be ready to rise to any emergency.

When she entered the ladies room, she was not alone. Actually, they were using the boys' locker room because the girl showers had monitors in them. There were six girls in there taking showers. She smiled. Each girl who was there knew what each one had been doing, and no questions was asked. There was not any dialog. Seeing the empty squirt bottles was a dead giveaway. These was the latest birth control devices. Just one squirt within eight hours and it was 100 percent effective.

Plus it was no bigger than a lipstick.

She had a quickie shower, lathered up once, and rinsed off. She applied fresh makeup, shook out her short feathered hair, put on her dress minus any underwear, and was off to see Arthur Moses. She was a pretty girl, and a lot of girls envied her, but no one ever bothered her. She got along with almost everyone. Those who didn't like her, who in the hell cared?

She looked as innocent and sweet as a newborn baby. The closer she got to Moses's office, the more excited she became. She knew that he was attracted to her because she could see the lust in his eyes whenever he looked at her. He always had to find some reason to touch her, but she was a no-no to him. She was going to find out just how far she could taunt him. She smiled wickedly and knocked on his office door.

"It's open," he said without looking up to see who it was that entered. Ocena just stood there and didn't say a word. Eventually, he turned around and was shocked to see her standing there. "Well, Miss Heartburns, what can I do for you?"

He immediately regretted asking her that question because she would probably tell him. She was tempted to tell him that he could do a lot of things to her if he wasn't so conscious of public opinion. But she said nothing. He asked. "What is it, Miss Heartburns?"

Ocena said, "I thought that I could talk to you about those nasty rumors that's going around about me."

"Nasty rumors? What nasty rumors are you talking about?"

"You know, the rumors about my morals."

"What about your morals?" Moses asked. "You know, they are saying that I'm a slut."

"Oh, those rumors. What about them?"

"They are not true."

"Really?"

"Yes, really. If God had wanted me to be celibate, he wouldn't have pumped me full of hormones that turn on all of those feelings and sensations that I'm supposed to suppress and ignore but scream out for fulfillment."

"Really?"

"Will you stop saying really?"

Moses had been having to restrain himself as she stood before him trying to make him believe that she was innocent. It was really playing havoc with his nerves and his patience was wearing thin. He said, "Ocena, why do you think that I care about your morals, your lifestyle?"

She looked at him unbelievingly, "You mean that you don't?"

"Why should I care one way or the other? Whatever I do or say is not going to have any effect. You are graduating this year and you'll soon be gone. So why should I get myself in a tizzy about your lifestyle?"

Ocena was taken aback. "Do you mean that you don't care?"

Arthur was dying inside because of all the pain that her action was causing him. He did not know how long he could keep up the charade. The Good Lord knew that he was so in love with this girl, this little teenager, and it was too big of a burden for him to bear. She caused him pain, mentally and physically. Yet he would not let her know this. He said, "Ocena, what if I told you that I did care? Would that change anything?"

This question caught her off guard. She hesitated before she answered, "To be honest, I really haven't really thought about it. But I suppose I could change some."

"For me?"

She smiled, "I would do a lot of things for you."

"That remains to be seen," Arthur said as he tried to contain his emotions.

This was not going to be as easy as she thought it would be. She wondered what she should do next. This was more than she had anticipated. He asked her point-blank, "How much would you be willing to change for me?"

Again, she was at a loss for words. She tapped on the desk nervously. Then, looked at him as she asked, "How much would you want me to change?"

"Enough not to cause me any problems in the future."

"Me causing you problems. Just how am I causing you problems?"

"If I have to answer that, I will have my answer."

"Now you are double-talking me. I don't know what you are talking about."

Moses said, "Forget I said that. The situation is hopeless anyway. Why would I ever expect anything from you? Because you are calloused in matters of the heart. Just tell me why."

"Tell you what, I'll answer that as soon as I return. Nature calls and I must go to the comfort station." She exited.

Moses could feel a migraine coming his way. How much he despised those things. Closing his eyes, he could see those familiar red and silver stars exploding everywhere. He could feel something in the back of his eyes trying to suck his eyeballs through a straw. He could feel the little demons attacking the inside of his eyeballs with ice picks and at the same time his stomach felt like a roller coaster. But that pain behind his eyes was a son-of-a-bitch. His doctor had given him some medicine to combat the pain. He opened his desk drawer, opened the pill bottle, and took out two pills and went to the water fountain to swallow them. The pills was mostly for stress and Oceana gave him a lot of stress. He closed his eyes waiting for the pills to kick in. He was thinking, Man, I really do feel ill and Ocena sure played a part in bringing this on. He prayed, "God, please help me," then wondered if God was listening. When Ocena returned from the comfort station and reentered the room, he guessed that God had answered, no.

Moses stretched out on his lounging chair and began to reminisce. He was twenty-six years old and most people thought that he was not old enough to take on the responsibilities of being a high school principal. But this was his second year and he had been doing fine. He was a gifted person and had graduated from college at the age of eighteen. He had three degrees in education but never used the doctor part because it made him sound old. He had always wondered why people called gifted people nerds. He wasn't only gifted he looked good too. The teenage girls always said that he was a vision to be hold. His toasty purple complexion and short curly hair, two shades darker than his skin made him look like a Klingo. At least that what he thought. His six feet one height and his one hundred seventy-eight physique was perfection personified. He worked out four days a week and he looked good. Nothing that even resembled a high school principal. Half of the girls in school were in love with him and he knew it. Only Ocena Heartburns held his heart in captivity, but he would never admit it.

So far his reputation had been exemplary. He lived the kind of life every mother would want for her son. He had an intellect of the genius status, so why couldn't he handle Ocena?

How many times he had contemplated quitting his job because of her. Something had to be done. But what? That is the hard part. She was like a thorn in his side, and it was festering. His headache had subsided some. Maybe he will live until the morning. He wanted to forget that tonight ever happened. The thorn in his side moved a little. Moses moaned. He tried to appear normal but was unsure of what normal was. He just wanted to go to sleep. Then he noticed that Ocena was back. "So you are back," he said flatly.

"Yes, I can see how much that excites you."

"You were supposed to answer a question when you returned."

"Okay, refresh my memory. What was the question?"

In a strained voice he said, "Tell me about your orgy tonight."

Ocena felt as though the earth had moved under her. She felt like someone had punched her in the stomach. "What did you say?"

"I said, tell me about your orgy tonight."

"Where did you hear this lie?" she said in a scared voice.

"Lie?" Moses said.

"Lies," she repeated.

"Why would someone come in here this time of night just to tell me some cockamamie story about you having an orgy under the stadium?"

"Because it turns them on," she said nervously.

"This is not the place or the time for this because I don't see anything funny."

"How in hell am I supposed to know why some jackass tries to make himself look good at my expense."

"I take it you are denying this."

"Absolutely."

Moses was trying to remain aloof as he turned to face Ocena. Very softly, in a steaming voice, he said, "Hell, Ocena! What are you trying to put over on me? What kind of crap are you smearing now? All of the disruptive things that you do look as if you are deliberately trying to hurt and embarrass me." His voice turned icy, and he spoke the remainder of the words in a deep voice very slowly, spitting out each word like an ice cube. "This is one big pile of hockey. Don't you ever tell the truth?"

"This is the truth. I don't know what it is that you want me to confess to."

"So, I suppose Reggie is lying. Is that right?"

"Reggie!" she said in a whisper. "So he is the rotten brain mother who told you this and I bet that he doesn't have anyone to back up his lies."

"Be careful with your choices of adjectives and nouns. You sound like a rummed-up sot. Anyway, he said that a security guard saw the whole thing."

"A security guard, huh! Did he put a name to this guard?'

"What difference would a name make? Lord, girl, if you wanted to do it, why do it in public? Dammit, Ocena, can't you see that you are tearing me to pieces."

"Nothing is going to come from this."

"It amazes me how you say that so confidently."

"Oh, it's not hard to do. Because me and the security guard made a deal. I promised to give him the fuck of his life and he promised not to tell the truth."

"No, you didn't," Moses said shocked.

"Oh yes, I did," Ocena answered as she got up and locked the door. Chuckling to herself, she said, "I bet many cherries will be picked tonight."

"What are you doing?"

"I'm locking the door, Baby Cakes." Most of the girls in school referred to him as Baby Cakes. He didn't like it but what was he supposed to do about it? Now here stood this teenage vixen threatening him. Moses thought, I'm in a hell of a fix because he had no idea how to handle this situation and he did not need Ocena here making a bad situation worse. He decided to take a direct approach. He asked, "Who was you with tonight?"

She looked at him shocked. "I know that you did not ask me what I thought I heard you ask me."

"Yes, I did and I want an answer."

"Not from me, you don't."

Moses's voice boomed. Ocena jumped from surprise. He said, "Ocena, I don't have time to stop and pin the tail on the donkey. I've got to get this straightened out once and for all."

"Didn't I tell you that the security guard wouldn't say anything?"

"Yes, you did. But now is not the time for me to start trusting security guards, so spill."

"I'm not going to tell you anything," Ocena replied. Then, she changed her mind and said, "Okay. I'll tell you about the orgy thing, but I'm not going to apologize and I'm not going to say that I'm sorry because that would be a lie. I may be a slut but I'm not a liar. To me the sexual experience is normal and natural. God made it that way. Besides, I've always wanted to make love out under the stars and in the woods. To be one with nature. Rolling on a carpet of leaves and straws with the damp smell of decaying leaves and straws penetrating your senses and pollen attacking your sinuses and perspiration tickling down and mixing with nature's carpet. Just rolling, banging and being one with nature. Just like Adam and Eve. Can't you just imagine little twigs snapping from the weight of your bodies as they rise and fall to the natural rhythm of nature? Much like the day Eve gave the apple to Adam. Hell, I could get my jollies from smelling that raw natural scent."

"Come on and get real, Ocena. Don't you know that the ramifications from this can be very, very messy? Especially if the media get a whiff of it."

"You wouldn't dare," she bluffed.

"Try me," Moses challenged, "the ball is in your court. Now what are you going to do with it?" For a long time Ocena had nothing to say. This was revolutionary all by itself because the time never came when she didn't have anything to say.

Moses continued, "I don't trust that security guard. He may or may not keep his word. I need some reassurance really bad and right now I don't have any idea where I am going to get some. Like I've said, this is not my day to start trusting security guards. Now cut the crap because we have a very serious problem here and you are acting like you've returned from a Sunday School Convention. Don't you care any?"

"No!" she shot back. "I don't give a damn! You sanctimonious asshole. As long as you are banging away with me in your mind it's okay. Just because you don't have enough guts to act like the man that you claim to be. Don't go around trying to stop those who act and react and don't just fantasize like someone that I know. I'm a slut and a disruptive element in your life. One that you can't get rid of fast enough. You see, I've got your number, you are my sex machine, and any of your bottom I push, I turn you on and you can't stand it because you are too scared to treat me like the woman that you love. Why won't you make love to me like I know you want to?" She got down off the desk that she was sitting on and stood up behind him and began to massage his neck and shoulders.

.

It felt heavenly. He was tempted to give in to the relaxation but could not give in to the feelings that this brought on. He took her hands into his and thought, She has such pampered hands. He kissed the palms lightly. "Baby, now is not the time for this." He stood up and began to pace. She began to pace in sync. Whenever he would turn around she would be there blocking his way. She put her arms around him and kissed him lightly on the lips. This annoyed Moses. Abruptly he stopped, pushed her out the way, and asked, "Why are you trying to drive me insane? Playing havoc with my emotions?"

Softly she said, "So you do have emotions. Could one of those emotions be love especially for me? Arthur, my love, you worry too much when there's really no reason to despair. Remember, I told you that nothing is going to come of this. I promised the security guard that I would let him in my cookie jar if he got rid of the crumbs."

Moses looked at her as though he had never seen her before. "Just what are you talking about? What does a cookie jar have to do with this?"

"Oh, naïve love of my life, don't you know anything? To be blunt, sweetheart, the goody-goody-two-shoes security guard promised to forget most of what happened tonight if I would fuck him. Period."

A shocked Moses came back to the present, "You can't be serious." He repeated, "You can't be serious. This just can't be." He could not stop thinking about the ramifications that could spring up from this festering situation.

Ocena ran her hand up his thigh. He began to protest but not soon enough. Amazed, she stood with her mouth slightly open. "So what is this, Mr. I Am So Important Man?" Moses couldn't say anything, he just stood there with a silly grin on his face, looking guilty as he really was.

Didn't you say a short while ago how important this task before you was and you didn't have time for this?"

Uncovering his erection, Ocena stood back and smiled. She said, "Just look at this. This is ridiculous."

Moses still didn't speak. His grin looked as if it was painted on. "You sorry pitiful man." Ocena smiled wickedly. "Don't you want to donate this to me, Baby Cakes? I promise that I'll take good care of it."

Moses stood motionless, he and his silly grin. He was thinking, There is no way I'm going to screw this girl in this office tonight. He was trying to convince himself that he could control this primitive urge. He will not give in.

Ocena lightly squeezed the bulge in his pants. He tensed and gaped. "Is something wrong?" she asked knowingly.

He didn't answer her for fear that she would hear the passion in his voice and convey all the raw lust that he was fighting so hard to control. She pushed his chair away from the desk. It rolled effortless, as she faced him she could see that he had a pained look on his face. Her heart quickened. She could feel his pain and simply could not help himself. She had bewitched him and held him spellbound.

He didn't want to be a slave to this eighteen-year-old vixen. Surely, he was addicted to her just as certain as a wino is addicted to his wine. His face and eyes spoke simultaneously. They were pleading, Please don't let this happen, God. Please help me.

If there was ever a man who needed sex, it was Arthur Moses. She unzipped his pants and he didn't protest. All of his pleases and don't were drowned out by the rhythm of his blood swishing past his ears telling him that he had lost the battle. He was head over heels in love with this girl and didn't want to do anything to hurt, her but things had already gone too far to turn around. Besides, she was doing everything she could to make this happen. He prayed again, Please, Lord, forgive me for what I'm about to do.

He was drawn to her and was putty in her hands. She said, "Darling, I have a feeling."

"What kind of feeling?" he murmured in her hair.

"I really don't know just a feeling." She let her hand glide over his erection. He stood up and dropped his pants in a pile on the floor. He was in a hurry. His throbbing phallus stood up and seemed to bow, saying thank you for setting me free. She wanted to laugh because his penis bowed upward as if beckoning for her. It didn't really matter to her because she was going to give it the ride of its life.

She sat straddling his lap and slowly sat down on his penis. She would rise up and sit down. This steady rhythm brought Moses to an exploding climax far too soon. He held on to her, burying his face between her luscious breasts. "Baby, I'm sorry," she heard him say.

She responded saying, "It's okay, my love, I understand."

When it came to Ocena, Moses was a weak man. As she held his head between her breasts she exclaimed, "I've got it."

Moses didn't move or say anything; he was too weak. Finally, he murmured, "Got what?"

"The answer to our dilemma."

"And just what is that?"

"I'll tell them that I was about to be raped and the security guard misunderstood what was going on. I'll tell them that was why the other disappeared."

Moses sat quiet for a while. Finally, he spoke, "That may work."

"Sure it will," she said jubilantly.

"Not so fast," Moses cautioned.

"What now?" she wanted to know.

"I said that this may work. Not that this is a sure thing."

"Baby, I know that it will work." She kissed him passionately, blowing in his ears and nibbling at his breast. His breast was extra sensitive. Whenever she sucked on his breast, he would get an instant erection. He could not help it. She ran her hand across his penis and it was ramrod straight, except where it bowed upward and hard as cement. It seemed to be grinning, glad that it was up to par once more. Ocena felt it too. She smiled and took it in her hands. It was throbbing and pulsating and ready for whatever came next.

Ocena lay on the sofa and beckoned to him with her finger. He came over and rolled her on her back and admired her beautiful body. She had beauty without trying. He caressed her thick patch of pubic hair and rubbed the fine feathers on her purple butt. It was velvety smooth. He caressed her clitoris, and she moaned with pleasure. He gently increased his pace of caressing, and she came. He didn't stop. She came again. This pleased him. He felt good. He positioned her on her hands and knee, mounted her from behind, and penetrated her. She called God's name; this was a bonus. He began to thrust. Every thrust was harder and deeper. Ocena moaned in lust; he moaned in pleasure.

"I love you. I love you, my darling." He meant it. He told her that he would search the corners of the world for her if she would ever leave.

The intensity of their lovemaking grew like the cadence of jungle drums. Faster, louder, faster. Boom! Boom! Then exploded. Perspiration and the juice from their lovemaking glued them together in sin. Shortly, they parted. That was when that guilty feeling slipped in and rapped on the conscience of his mind, stirring up the very things that he had tried so desperately to bury. He looked at her lying on the sofa. Her firm breast jutting toward the ceiling and her flawless skin covered with perspiration. He felt another erection coming on. Darn, he thought, did his desire have no end when it came to her? They made love again and lay spent in each other's arms. After a while she put on her dress and heels, kissed him on the eyelids, and left him lying on the sofa. That muscle that had given them so much pleasure was lying on its owner in the same way, like an old wet dish rag.

Ocena was about three blocks from her house when she realized that she had left her purse in Moses's office. She knew that she had to go back and retrieve it. She prayed that Moses would still be there.

It would really be a disaster if someone would find it there because that would be something else that she would have to explain. Ah, she saw that Moses's car was still in that camouflage place that no one would notice unless you were actually looking for it. She parked beside his car and entered the building from behind, being very careful not to be seen by any security guard because she had had her fill of them.

She made it and slipped into Moses's office as quietly and quickly as she could. She spotted her purse and started to pick it up. When she turned around, she was face to face with Moses. "You're still here? Why don't you go home?"

"I was just fixing to do that," Ocena answered. "I suppose everyone else has already gone."

"I noticed a couple of cars still in the parking lot."

Moses spoke to her harshly because he feared that what had happened earlier would be repeated. Somehow he had got to get her out of his system, and it seemed like the harder he tried, the deeper she dug in, and it hurt. Even worse, Oceana was aware of this.

He looked at her with guilt written all over his face. They both began to speak at the same time. She smiled, "You go first."

"I really don't know what to say," Moses said with his eyes cast downward, still unable to face her.

Ocena took his hands and kissed the palms and said, "There's nothing to say except that you love me. We didn't do anything wrong. It was normal and natural and you were wonderful."

"You do know that if this got out I'll be ruined."

"Not to worry, my sweetheart, I won't tell a soul."

"I just wish that I could feel as positive as you. Physically, I feel good enough to soar, but mentally, I'm a basket case riddled with apprehension."

"What happened tonight was beautiful and I will always cherish the memories. So stop worrying and go home. We can't change anything that's already been done."

"So true," he answered. "but we must assess the damage control and I really don't know where to start.'

"Damage control?" she stated flatly. What do you mean damage control?"

Before Moses could answer, he heard voices in the corridor. "Sh," he cautioned. She had heard them too.

The voices sounded familiar. They thought that everyone had gone except them and two security guards. You could hear their conversation clearly. It was Mary Piti and Sally Cornelius, two of the chaperons at tonight's prom. It was ironic that these two women were selected because they were so different. Piti was a straight-lace spinster with eighteen hundred morals, and Sally was a modern woman and in tune with the way the world is now. Pati was saying to Sally, "The prom tonight was surely different than when I was in high school."

Sally answered, "Yes, I know what you mean."

"No, I don't think that you do. Let me see, I must be at least twelve years older than you. This is your third year of teaching."

"Hum," said Sally, "you talk like you grew up with the dinosaurs."

"I don't mean like that. It's just that half of the girls in there tonight didn't have on any underwear and most of the remainder had on those thongs things."

"How do you know this?"

"You can tell me that you didn't notice."

"Yes, I noticed some, but I can't—"

Pati interrupted, "There were many bare cats in there tonight. Take my word for it. Did you see Rosetta Chestbone? She was on her period and pantyless."

Sally stopped. "How do you know this?"

"When she was dancing with Willie Elbow, she bent over, and with that mini dress that wasn't any better that a t-shirt, you could see her Tampax string. Well at least she won't be screwing tonight," Pati finished.

"You are sick," Sally said. They both started laughing, not because it was funny but because laughing would beat crying tears of sorrow.

Patti said, "I wonder why do they do it."

"I could give you an answer, but I don't think you would like it," said Sally.

"Go on," Pati urged.

"Well," began Sally, "I can say that it is not because they are immoral. They have moral and values, but somehow they got misplaced. Then again they look at us and don't like what they see, us lying, conniving, backstabbing, corruption, and God knows what else. Everything that we are telling them that are supposed to be bad for them and that they are not supposed to be doing, are the very things that we live by and are too phony to realize it. They are rebelling. Things need to change. I mean everything.

"The preachers tell us not to do this and that but they are doing it every chance that they get and they explain their actions by saying God knew that we was going to do these things, that's why he said that he would forgive us. The truth is, God said that he would forgive us provided we ask forgiveness and atone for them.

"We steal, rob, lie, screw around, and are too busy making a living until we forgot to make a life. The love and attention that they can't get at home, they go and find it elsewhere. They want to be accepted and loved any way that they can. Be it sex, drugs, crime, gangs, disorderly conduct, or just plain rebelling. They are looking for attention, and love and acceptance in all the wrong places."

"One thing that you said was right, and that was I wouldn't like your answer," Piti said as she pushed open the exit doors. Their conversation continued but was no longer audible.

Ocena looked at Moses and started to feel uncomfortable. "I guess you heard that."

"Yes, I did. And we are living proof that she is right."

Ocena stated, "I don't know why I feel so drawn to you. I . . . aw, forget it."

A silence blanketed the room. Moses stood at the door holding the knob like a scene frozen in time. The silence was so deep you could almost hear time passing by.

Ocena looked at Moses, Moses stared at the floor, seeing nothing. The sound of his blood passing by his ears could be heard. He could hear his pulse beating as clear as drums in a Fourth of July parade. He thought that he could hear the voice of his first love, calling to him, who had been killed when she along with a group of her friends went hiking too close to Zone XY-20. It seemed as if they were trying to tell him something but was too far away for him to hear it. His complexion turned ashen. "What's wrong with you?" Ocena asked.

Moses heard her, but she sounded very far away. He could not respond. She crossed the room to where he had seem to have frozen, caught him by his arm, and called his name. "Arthur, Baby Cakes, what wrong with you?"

Moses could hear her and feel her holding his hand, but he was still unable to respond. She became alarmed. "Arthur, what is wrong with you?" she said, her voice rising. She led him to the sofa and sat him down gently, like you would a sick person. Concern, love, and dread flooded her emotions. Maybe he was having a heart attack or maybe a stroke. She didn't have the first idea what was wrong. She cradled his head against her shoulder and gently held him and prayed. As she prayed, tears filled her eyes and spilled down her cheeks. She desperately wanted to call 911 but she didn't want to have to try to explain what she was doing there that time of night. She lost track of time and didn't know how long they had sat there. When she felt Arthur began to stir he looked up at her and saw the tears in her eyes and mucus hanging from her nose to his face. "Hey, what going on here? Why are you still here? What with all the tears and snot?"

Ocena was beside herself with gladness. "Arthur! You are okay!" she exclaimed.

"Sure, I'm okay, why wouldn't I be?"

"You mean that you don't remember?"

"Remember what?

"Something happened to you and I was so afraid."

"Girl, what are you talking about?"

"I'm trying to tell you that you were completely out of it. You couldn't move or talk. I thought that you were having a heart attack or something."

"Really? Tell me more."

"I don't know how to describe it. I just knew that I was really scared."

"Well, as you can see, I'm all right now, so you can go home now. I'll be leaving soon myself."

Ocena looked at him with tears and snot still on her face and asked, "Are you sure that you are okay? I could drive you home."

"Sure, I'm good. Go home."

After Ocena had gone, Arthur sat a minute trying to understand what she was talking about. He had experienced something, but he couldn't single it out. This had happened before or something similar, but he had never realized that something serious could be going on and he had not imagined it. Once his doctor had asked him something similar, but again he had no answer. This made him feel very distressed, but he was unable to do anything about it because he didn't know what it was. Anyway it was late and he was going home.

On the fourth day after the prom rumors began to surface. There were at least four occurring simultaneously and all were about Ocena Heartburns. People were saying very nasty things about her.

Some were true; most were not. Any thoughts about the possibility of them being mistaken and damaging someone's reputation didn't matter. The ball was going downhill and the momentum was increasing.

The churchgoing women were the most pronounced gossipmongers. They put on airs like they were angels and had never done anything wrong in their wretched lives. They carried themselves as though they were sinless, guiltless, and perfect; and whatever they said had been okayed by God himself.

These people were too refined to call someone a slut to their face, but behind closed doors, among others of their kind, their conversation were intense as laser. Their scrutinizing of Ocena's morals occupied a great deal of their daytime activities.

In reality not one of them had any room to talk about anyone else because of their own behavior behind closed doors and in dark corners in smoky places. Ocena knew about their unscrupulous trysts because a guy who was trying to come on to her told her about how they paid a select number of younger men to do dirty sexual things to them. He even told her about how he had seen old lady Gussie, the one with the great dame, would get down on her knees and let the dog do things to her. Sometimes when Ocena would pass by she would giggle and ask about Jerico's great balls of fire.

Old lady Gussie never spoke back because she wasn't sure if she knew her secret or not. She certainly had no knowledge that Ocena knew about her deep, dark secret, or did she?

Two weeks had gone by before Moses heard about the gossip and rumors. He was on the verge of panic and had not a remote idea how he was going to respond to it or was he going to respond at all. He broke in perspiration just thinking about what this could do to him. His ashen color painted him guilty. He had been alone when he first heard about it and was thankful about that because it took him a while to rectify his composure after that major shock. But finally a sense of normalcy crept back into his now retched existence. He had to think of a way to combat the fallout from this bomb that he had set off. Of course he could deny that it had happened, but that would be a lie and he was not about to make a confession. Ignorance about the whole situation was his best bet.

"Damn!" he swore, "I told Ocena that she couldn't trust that security guard. Now, just look at the ramifications that he was facing just from getting a little bit of pussy."

In his heart he could not deny what had happened and he could not deny that he had wanted it to happen and had dreamed many times what it would be like when it did happen. And he had been right on the button. At least he should've waited and not done it in his office at school. Too late for all that now.

It was no use, he was guilty as sin and should turn in his resignation immediately and leave town. God, what a disappointment he had been to himself, his profession, his community, and especially to those who had looked up to him as a role model. How he hated the description "role model." Some role model he was. All those mothers and fathers who had wanted their sons to grow up and be like him would probably shoot him in the back with poison darts. After all, he had turned out to be just another Once upon a Time or another Used to Be story.

He wondered how can I possible go out there and face my faculty and the students body? He thought, if I had a gun I would end it all right now. Naw, I could never do that. I'm not that desperate. I know that I can't sit here in this office all day waiting for everyone to leave. He threw his hands up in resignation. The phone rang. It startled him out of his cogitation. It was Ocena.

He snapped, "What do you want?"

"Don't go and blow a gasket. I've got to talk to you, but by the way you answered the phone. I suppose that the rumors have reached you."

"You suppose right. I can't talk to you now."

"Okay, I understand. I'll drop by later. I can straighten this thing out. Have a little patience. Bye." She hung up.

He got up from his desk and walked over to the windows. As he gazed out the windows, his mind was racing in turmoil. He decided that if anyone should ask him anything about the rumors, he would feign surprise and shock, then lie like the devil. Then he resumed his duties as principal of Purple Bottom High School No. 14.

The remainder of the day was uneventful. When he was leaving his office, he noticed a couple group of teachers and students talking. They stopped abruptly when he passed, and they pretended to not notice him. He couldn't wait for the day to end, but he didn't know why because that wouldn't assure him that tomorrow and the days to come would be any better. But today seemed to have lasted thirty hours, and relief flooded him when the day was done.

He had been home exactly eighteen minutes when he heard a faint knocking at his door. Reluctantly, he opened the door, and there stood Ocena, the very last person in Purple Bottom City that he wanted to see. She didn't wait to be asked to come in. When he opened the door she barged in. He closed the door and faced her. He could see that her face was contorted, her eyes were red, and she was seething with rage. She spoke in a whisper, "You were right."

He just looked at her and she continued, "That despicable security guard just couldn't keep his mouth shut. But I'm going to get him if that's the last thing that I do. I'll get my dad to run him out of town on some trumped-up charges."

"Hold on a minute. Who told you that the security guard said something?"

"What are you talking about? Who else could have, who else knew?" Moses caught her by the shoulders and said, "Now, listen, love."

Ocena smiled and said, "I like it when you talk dirty to me."

Moses said, "What?" Never mind that. Now listen. From parts and bits of gossip that I've heard, it was Reggie down at the pool hall bragging about how many times you and he had done the wild thing and how you couldn't keep your hands off him. He never saw us doing anything. When he stopped by my office and told me about the ordeal under the stadium, he just made most of it up when he saw you talking to Tony. He asked Tony where you were going in such a hurry and Tony told him that you were going to see me, and he asked him if you were going to bang me like you had banged the others. That's as much as I could find out eavesdropping."

"I'm going to kill him. I don't mind too much what they say about me because it's part of the game I play. But when they start on you, that's another thing altogether."

Moses held up one hand with the palm facing outward telling her to stop. "Now, what have I done this time?"

"Nothing. It's just that you are letting your emotions cloud your senses. We must think this through before we speak or make irrational decisions. You and I know that we are guilty of sin and we can't blame this on no one but us."

Ocena stood looking very hard at nothing. Then she turned and looked at Moses as if just looking at him she could tell him what she wanted to say without speaking. She realized that she couldn't communicate with him telepathically, so she said in a small voice, "No. You are wrong. It's my fault. I shouldn't have come to your office because I came there for one purpose and that was to seduce you."

Moses turned to her and said, "You did what?"

Ocena's sass had returned and she answered, "That's right. I came to your office to seduce you because I had been waiting for months and I could never get you alone long enough to do it until the night of the prom. Now you are standing there looking at me like I'm Medusa, but I dare you to tell me that you didn't want it as much as I did."

He sat down resigned because he had nothing to say. She sat beside him and continued her narrative. "I've known for quite some time that you wanted to do the same thing to me but you were morally tied because your conscience would never let you and I knew that if I didn't initiate things nothing would ever happen. So I did it."

Moses sat with his head in his hands saying nothing and doing nothing. She sat beside him saying and doing nothing. They sat like that for a long time. Finally Moses cleared his throat and stood up.

He said, "I can't believe that I fell for that. Just to think that I have jeopardized my career, my reputation, my entire future. I just can't believe I was that gullible. I know that the board of education will be calling on me any day now and what can I tell them, plead insanity?" I don't have a prayer for defense. He had never felt so tired and trapped and defeated as he did right now.

Her heart ached as she realized how lost and helpless he looked. She stood up and put her arms around his neck and said, "I'm going to make sure this thing doesn't sully your reputation if it's the last thing I do."

Moses looked her in the eyes and said, "Don't make things any worse than they already are."

"Baby Cakes, you just sit back and watch me make magic happen."

"Don't ever call me Baby Cakes again, ever. I really hate that."

She went by the agency that employed Randy, the security guard that had lied on her, and asked where he was. They wanted to know who she was because they didn't give out that kind of information to just anyone. She told them that she was Randy's first cousin and her mother, Randy's aunt, had just had an accident, and since she practically raised Randy she was asking for him. They didn't think that she would make it. For emphasis, she let a single tear run down her cheek.

The receptionist told her that Randy was on duty at Bones and Crosstires Processing Plant, out on Sneezing Lane. About four miles outside the city limit.

She glanced at her watch. It was 3:15 PM. She had time to work her magic. As she drove, her mind was pregnant with thoughts of what she could do to Randy, and not any of them were good or legal. As she slowed down to make a left turn off Runs Road to Sneeze Lane, she bit her lip. When she reached to get a tissue, she noticed that she was gripping the steering wheel so hard her hands had blanched. She thought, I've got to cool it before I blow something. That lying snake Randy is a piece of dead meat.

Sure she was guilty and so was Arthur, but that didn't give anyone the right to go around broadcasting lies about it. Millions of people screw every day, and it was no one's business but theirs. No one is going around sullying their reputations.

She was about a mile from Bones and Crossties when she noticed that she was still gripping the steering wheel. She inhaled. Girl, you can handled this. She took some deep breaths, and it made her feel dizzy, and her face flushed. She had to be more careful. When she got to the plant she pulled up to the guard shack and asked to speak to Randy. What was his last name beside Motherfucker? It had something to do with a leg or foot. No. It was Brokentoe. No. It was Legbone. She said that she wanted to speak to Randy Legbone and it was urgent. In about five minutes Randy appeared. When he saw her a smile erupted across his face. He spoke cheerfully, "Hi, Ocena, are you looking for me?"

Ocena smiled sweetly and said, "Yes."

She led him to her car out of hearing range of the guard's shack. He said, "Hi, babe, couldn't get enough of me, huh?"

She felt like puking. How dare he speak to her like he knew her, calling her Ocena and babe. "Shut the fuck up, you low-down mangy rat.

I just came to tell you that you are not going to get away with your filthy lies, and this is not a threat."

He was taken aback. He saw fire in Ocena's eyes, and the sweet smile that had caressed her lips was gone and her face had turned to stone. She told him that he was coming with her and that she had already cleared it with his boss. She told him that his aunt had been in an accident and wasn't expected to last through the night.

What are you talking about? I don't have an aunt that lives here."

"They don't know that. Now, if you don't come with me I'm going to camp out at your house. Because you are going to pay for lying and sullying the reputation of a man like Arthur Moses."

"So this is all about your boyfriend."

"You slimy little sewer rat, you darn well know that you never saw us making love anywhere, then you go and spread a vicious lie like that. What kind of person are you? Don't you have any scruples?"

Randy's grin froze. "What are you talking about scruples. What is a scruple? Now, you listen to me, I didn't go spreading lies about y'all. I only told two people that I thought that Moses was banging you. I never said that I saw you doing it."

"You liar!" Ocena screamed under her breath. "You had no business saying something like that to anyone. You just opened Pandora's box."

"Who is Pandora?"

"She is someone that you can't go and spread lies about. But I wish that you could."

"I'm sorry that I ever said anything."

"Now you are saying that you are sorry. Just what good do you think saying you are sorry going to do? Everywhere you go you can hear someone talking about Arthur and me like we are world-class sluts. Now, you think that saying you are sorry is going to fix anything. Right now," Ocena said as she locked eyes with Randy. Arthur's mood and his outlook on his future seemed as dark as a thousand midnights of sorrows. "And you say that you are sorry. If I had a gun I would kill you with a smile on my face."

Randy looked down at his hands like they had turned to snakes, but he was afraid to look at Ocena. He cleared his throat three times before he tried to speak to see if his voice still worked. He started to say something like he didn't think that what he had said would grow into monstrous proportions but his voice was six octaves higher than normal, and he knew that Ocena was going to say that it was true. He didn't think so.

As she fought with her emotions she demanded that Randy tell her the name of the two guys that he told the lies to and where they lived. He agreed to do that because he was really afraid of Ocena. He had never seen anyone who was so driven with rage. One thing that he was thankful for was she didn't have a gun.

Two days later Moses got a visit from the school board. He called Ocena and told her. She told him not to admit to anything because there were no witnesses. The security guard, Randy, was just bragging and lying and she was going to see the two guys that he was bragging to. This revelation didn't make Moses feel any better because he knew in his heart that they were guilty. How can you deny a lie especially when that lie was the truth but the one that told the lie didn't know that he was telling the truth? He was too worried to be angry.

His meeting with the school board climaxed with his job still intact because of insufficient evidence. They had found only rumors. Nothing concrete. They would notify him if something else came up.

He felt as lonely a the stars. He didn't feel like waiting until the axe fell. He felt like going home and packing up his belonging and not coming in the next day or perhaps never again. He went home and decided to get drunk and thought, just let someone report this. Ocena called and wanted to come over, but he didn't want any company. She came over anyway and he was glad she hadn't listened to him because he needed someone to talk to. They embraced, and Moses said, "I guess it doesn't matter what we do anymore since I probably won't be your principal much longer."

She kissed him on the lips and said, "Don't let despondency get you down. We both know the truth. It's up to them to prove that we are lying. There were no witnesses."

"But why do I feel so guilty?"

"That's because we are guilty."

"Don't remind me," said Moses. Then he held on to her really tight and kissed her like never before. Ocena stepped back, looked at him, and asked, "What was all of that about? You've been drinking," she accused.

"Uh-huh. And I'm going to make love to you and get funky drunk."

She smiled. "At least half of your plan sounds good, but you can put the other half on hold."

"Meaning exactly what?" he asked after kissing her again.

"Baby, leave the booze in the bottle. I know how painful things are right now but you don't need the booze because you've got me and you'll have me because I love you without limits."

He buried his face in her hair and said, "I love you, Cena."

"I know," she said as he picked her up and carried her into the bedroom.

One week later Moses had to reappear before the board of education. Ocena was there with him, plus she had brought along Randy and his two cohorts. When the board asked him how he pleaded against the alleged charges of having sex with a minor who is also a student under his guidance.

He answered, "Not guilty."

"Is there any way that you can prove this?"

Moses looked at Ocena and answered, "Yes, I can."

"Okay, Mr. Moses, you have the floor."

Moses first called Ocena as a witness and she said, "It is an absolute lie. I have here those culprits that perpetrated this whole messy lie present and you can question them yourself about why."

All three of the guys testified that there wasn't any truth to any of the rumors and they were just that, rumors. Randy testified that he only said it to impress the guys down at the pool hall, and he didn't know how it had spread so fast and far. It had never crossed his mind that someone's reputation was at stake, and he was very sorry.

Ocena's statement had bite to it. She said, "I don't think that the school board had been efficient because you've casted him as guilty before you had any facts. You were ready to feed him to the lions before he was dead. You accused him of having sex with a minor. I am eighteen years old, a fully grown woman. And being a woman, I don't think that sex is dirty or illegal. God put it here for us to enjoy. He made it feel good so that we would have it often, that was one way to make sure that the races would be continued. I bet there is not one of you here who hasn't engaged in an illicit affair. You don't have to admit it because that's just the way life is. If any of you should say that you haven't, you will be lying. One thing about many grown-ups is that they take the Bible and try to twist and shape its teaching to fit their own twisted lives. They get their kick trying to put down the younger generation by forcing their twisted morality and laws on them. Laws that they don't adhere to. I think that the whole community owes Mr. Moses an apology because everywhere you go someone is saying derogatory things about both him and me. They may say what they want about me. But Mr. Moses, a man who has proven that he is an honest, all-around-outstanding citizen who has put the interest of your children and grandchildren and their education above any personal gain."

Someone asked," Isn't it true that you are in love with Mr. Moses?"

Ocena answered, "You are trying to make notes on an idea. First, it's none of your business. Secondly, even if I am, it's still none of your business. But for your records, I will make love to Mr. Moses whenever I choose. We are both adults. Any more questions will be channeled through my attorney, the Honorable Betty Gramp."

She got out of her seat and exited the room. The room became eerily quiet. Shortly, someone said, "Well, I guess that's that. Mr. Moses, you have our sincere apologies. I'm sorry about the mix-up because you are doing a great job. I wonder if Miss Heartburns will ever know how right she really is." They shook hands and left.

CHAPTER III

*S*ujusoe spotted Charles driving around like he was from the land of the lost. He had an expression on his face that made him look like an idiot. He stood on the curb and flagged him down. Charles looked at him, trying to figure out if he should stop or not. He slowed down and took a good look at him. Sujusoe said, "Hi, how are you?"

"I don't really know. How are you?" Charles answered.

"Just fine. You look like you are a wee bit lost. Can I be of any assistance?"

"That depends on whether you can tell me where I am?

"Sure. That's easy enough. You are on Indigestion Avenue in Purple Bottom City."

"Yes, I know that much because that's what the sign read. What I really want to know is where is Purple Bottom City?"

"What do you mean, where is Purple Bottom City?" Sujusoe asked puzzled.

"I mean what state am I in?"

"What state? You are not in a state. This is Purple Bottom City. Period."

"Well, can you tell me what country I'm in?"

Sujusoe smiled because he had never seen anyone as confused as this man was. He answered, "I keep telling you P U R P L E B O T T O M C I T Y. Period. "Period. What?"

Shaking his head in amazement, he said, "Let's start this conversation over. You are in Purple Bottom City. Purple Bottom City. It's not a state or a country, it is a world. You may say a planet. Now, does this answer your questions satisfactorily?"

"A world!" Charles said. Fighting the whole idea that he was really in another world. He knew that something was not right about this place, but another world? He was more shocked than ever.

"I can't believe what you just told me. You did say world?"

"That's right."

"A world like a planet, like Earth?"

"Exactly. In fact this is Earth, at least it was Earth sometime back."

"Now I am really confused. Am I alive or dead or what?"

"Of course you are alive and everything that you see is real. I know that you want to know if you are seeing things. You are not seeing anything that is not normal in this world. I am purple just like everything else here is purple."

"Well, how in hell did I get here from Montana?"

"I don't know. I can't even make an educated guess. By the way I'm SujuSoe Suju," he said, offering him his hand.

"I'm Charles DeNero."

SujuSoe said, "Well, Charles, let's go somewhere where we can sit down and try to figure something out. Want to take my car or use yours?"

"You ain't no queer, are you?"

"Besides being purple and having a few unusual feature, no. Let's go get something to eat and talk about your predicament."

Rubbing the stubble on his chin and feeling the growing pang in his stomach, he said, "That sounds real good because I haven't had anything to eat in a while. I've been trying to figure out whether I've been dreaming or this was real. I am starving. But first I wanted to ask you something, and please don't be offended."

"Ask away," SuejuSoe said.

"I don't know how to ask this without sounding like a moron."

"Ask. Ask," SuejuSoe urged.

"Okay then. Are these chicken people or people chicken or what?"

SuejuSoe grinned and said, "A little of both. But that's another long story."

What else was going to happen next? Charles wondered as he put the car in drive and accelerated. Trying to navigate was complicated. The traffic signals were all purple, and he didn't know when to go or when to stop. SuejuSoe came up with a working solution. Their signals had only two lights; both were purple. So SuejuSoe told him when one light was on you can go, two lights means stop.

"Okay, let's get started." Then he asked, "Do you know how I got here?"

"To tell the truth, I don't have a clue and most of what I'm going to tell you came down through the ages. Passing from one generation to the next. Most of my family were historians from my tenth generation down, and they have a lot of it stored in the Graveyard Library. I can take you there the next time I commute. I, too, am a lawyer and a historian and one of the Graveyard people."

"One of the what people?" Charles asked.

SuejuSoe grinned in amusement, "That's another long story."

"Okay. While I'm on a roll, tell me why everything is purple. I never knew that there were so many shades of purple."

SuejuSoe looked at Charles and took a deep breath. Without waiting for an answer, Charles said, "Yes, yes, that's another story." Then he asked him to turn left and go down Runs Road because there was a place that was still relatively the same before the nova happened.

As they drove down Runs Road, Charles was stunned. "How can this be? How can anyone get used to all this purple?"

SuejuSoe was saying something, but Charles missed it all because he was so engrossed in these strange surroundings. The next thing that he heard was SuejuSoe saying, "Turn left."

They were in the parking lot of a place that looked a lot like a 1970s eatery back on his planet Earth. SuejuSoe said, "This place shouldn't shock you so much. This is the Chickpeo's gift to the past. They kinda left it this way as being a part of the mostly lost history of this world. But the purple stuff is here also.

"That purple stuff is everywhere," Charles said. "No. It is not in the Graveyard."

"Graveyard?" Charles asked puzzled.

"There is another world beneath this one. But I'll explain this later," SuejuSoe explained.

As they entered the cafe and bar called the Left Over Purple Place, Charles said, "They really rub it in."

They was seated in a corner booth where they could see anyone who came in. The Chickpeo who ran the place was friendly enough. Someone gave then a menu and they ordered spaghetti pie and coffee. Charles shook his head and asked SuejuSoe, "How can I drink purple coffee and eat purple spaghetti?"

"One sip at a time and one fork full at a time."

Charles continued, "This can't be real. Any minute I am going to wake up and laugh about this preposterous dream."

SuejuSoe said to a bewildered Charles, "No. That will never happen because this is not a dream. This is real. Better get used to it."

"Pinch me," Charles said to SuejuSoe. "Pinch me real hard. Please, God, let this be a dream because if it's not, I'm afraid that I'm going mad."

"No such luck," SujuSoe said as he took a sip of the purple coffee. Charles closed his eyes really tight and took a sip of the purple coffee. He bolted upright and opened his eyes. "Is there something wrong?" SuejuSoe asked.

"This stuff tastes good. This is really good. I've never tasted coffee this good before."

"All the food and everything else taste better and is better for you than anything in the Graveyard.

"I don't know why so don't ask me. My advice to you is to roll with the punches and don't let anything surprise you. That's the name of the game."

"Well, SujuSoe, let's get started."

"One thing before we get started, where did you say you came from?"

"Great Falls, Montana, USA, planet Earth."

"Really?" SuejuSoe asked. "Which Earth?"

Charles shot back, "Which Earth? Earth."

SuejuSoe saw that he had his work cut out for him. He explained to Charles that according to their history files there are five Earths. Each is in a different dimension. Currently, they were on Earth IV. But there exists an Earth 1, Earth 11, Earth 111, Earth 1V, and Earth V. Each of these Earths is separated only by dimensions. Each Earth is on a different plane. Some are more advanced than others, some have mastered the technology of traveling from one dimension to another at will. They were just trying to perfect the technology when our closest star went nova and we were forced to go underground to survive. But that's another story."

When SuejuSoe had finished his narrative, Charles remembered what the "Nerve Grinder," Oscar Ocena, had told him at Gill's Fill Her Up.

During that time he really didn't believe what he had said. Hearing more about it didn't make it any easier to believe. Ah, their dinner had arrived. He thought that he was going to be sick eating purple spaghetti. It was just plain hard for him to put a fork full in his mouth. To his surprise it was delicious. They ate with relish.

Shortly, they resumed their conversation. Charles wanted to know if SuejuSoe was from the Graveyard since his complexion was not quite as dark as some of the other he had seen and he did not look as fowl as some. "Yes," SuejuSoe answered. "I commute three times a week. Somehow, we haven't figured out why the Graveyard people began to mutate every time they come topside. Our scientist have tried for years to find out why this happened and to find an antidote. Sadly, they are still searching. So let's get this long story started before I start mutating. I don't want to scare you any more than you already are," he said, sopping up spaghetti sauce with a piece of garlic bread. "So where do you want to start?"

"How about the beginning?"

SuejuSoe began his narrative from the history files and folklore. "Once upon a time our world was identical to yours, planet Earth 111, in another dimension, we are told. The closest star to our world, Earth 1V, was going nova. It had been having drastic upheavals in its atmosphere for some time. They knew that this was going to affect our world and did everything that they could do to prevent as much damage as could be and to save as many lives of our citizens as we could. Abandoning the planet for a man-made planet was out of the question. The technology was not that advanced. That would have been suicide. We did have the technology to build underground cities, and this could be done before the star went nova. They worked day and night to complete this task, building factories, farms, homes, and just about everything that they would need for survival. A real world one and one half miles under the Earth. There were already trained people who knew what had to be done to maintain this underworld. So from this underground world of twenty-five thousand people to a world of two million.

"They didn't want to overpopulate and overpopulation would always be a concern. They stockpiled everything that they could and programmed their factories and farms. Specially trained workers provided the remainder of what they needed. Artificial light, heat, atmosphere, sewer plants that recycled everything, nothing was spared. This world worked. But in the beginning they had their trials and tribulations. We have lived under the ground for over four hundred years, and anyone who was born in the Graveyard wouldn't know that it was artificial if they weren't told differently.

"Above the ground, where we are now, this planet was desolate. Over 40 percent of this planet was useless, a nuclear dump. The people that survived went through a long period of mutation. The planet itself went through a period of mutation. It was lopsided, thrown off its axle from the impact of the nova. The whole shebang should've exploded into a billion pieces, but somehow it didn't. A great part of it melted and the soil became hard as granite. It seemed our savior was a dark star. A star no one had ever seen before or since. A star that turned our once-yellow sun into a purple maze with a plethora of beneficial assets."

Charles shifted in his chair, asked for another cup of coffee, and settled back for more of SuejuSoe story.

"You know the part of this story that gets me the most is every time I come from the Graveyard I began to mutate. But when I return I revert back to my normal self. Out of all the many things that we could mutate into, why a Chickpeo? The first time I came out of the Graveyard and began to mutate, I panicked. I wanted to scream. I wanted to cry, but I thought that my tears would be purple and I just couldn't tolerate purple tears. So I began to walk, trying to see what else would happen. I said to myself, there has got to be an explanation somewhere. So I came up topside more and more often and again whenever I returned, I would revert. So I began to confer with the doctors topside and the Graveyard explaining to them what was going on. They began research trying to find an answer. As of today, there is no answer.

"There was a doctor in the Graveyard named Yunk Kneecap who was studying the purple world and its inhabitants. In his studies he discovered that all babies were asexual at birth and did not began to become individualized until ten weeks. He also discovered that the Chickpeos were immune to most viruses that causes colds and other childhood diseases. Although they had been exposed to massive radiation not any of them had developed cancer. There weren't any cases of heart diseases, arthritis, or mental illness on record. In fact their IQs were 50 percent higher than norm; he couldn't find any reasonable explanation for this. All the Chickpeo doctors credited this to that wonderful whatever it was that made everything purple.

"People in the Graveyard often suffered from respiratory problems, and Dr. Kneecap was adamant in his search for an answer. Things became quite serious when many Graveyard people came down with pulmonary distress and the only cure that was available was to take them topside where they were permanently cured. A lot of the Graveyard citizens didn't want to go because of the mutations. But after they found out the mutations would regress once they returned to the Graveyard, they came in droves. Eventually a hospital was built topside especially for the Graveyard people.

"One thing Dr. Kneecap found was that the Chickpeos who visited the Graveyard did not mutate. Their purple color and chicken features remained with them no matter how long they stayed. Many of the Graveyard citizens treated them with contempt."

Charles was listening to SuejuSoe talk, but other things were on his mind. He asked, "Why does anyone want to get rid of the purple stuff? It seem to be more beneficial to the people and doesn't cause any harm. They should embrace it for all the good it does."

"I don't have the answer to that."

"I think that all the energies that are going into research for getting rid of the purple stuff should go into something that really could benefit everyone.

"Something like what?"

"Oh, I don't know. Something like getting rid of all of the violence and I would say pollution, but you don't have any, thanks to the purple stuff."

SuejuSoe sat upright like the proverbial light bulb just came on in his mind. "I've got it, we could sell it to the Graveyard."

"At what price would the citizens of PBC have to pay? If you could get rid of the purple stuff, how would it effect its inhabitants?"

"You know that does give one something to think about."

"What can I say?" said Charles.

SuejuSoe looked at Charles like he was totally lost. He asked him, "What was we talking about before you sideswiped me?"

"Some stuff about traveling through the dimensions."

"Yes. I was telling you about the history of our world. Shall I continue?"

"Why not?"

SuejuSoe began where he left off. "My grandfather said that there were worlds out there that the imagination cannot fathom. He went through two dimensions of other worlds, and if he had stayed one minute longer he would have vaporized. He went to another dimension on a seventh plane. This was a gaseous world. Life on this world cannot be identified or recognized as life as we know it. Life was all around him and he did not recognize it. It was not tangible. The life-forms on this world were like bubbles in a pepe pop but much larger. This life-form was so advanced that they didn't need physical bodies. They did not need dialogue. Their communication was pure energy, and they could reproduce by thoughts alone. All he saw was swirling bubbling gases but he knew that someone or something there was communicating with him. Even saved his life. He had called them Ozzies because oxygen and hydrogen were lethal to them. As we seek life on other worlds we must think of other forms besides carbon-based. We would never recognize this as a life-form, only gases. But they did provide an environment where he could survive long enough for him to pass through their dimension.

"There is a place on your world where there are numerous springs and geishas sprouting. When that area cools down somewhat, this is believed to be a permanent portal to travel the dimensions. Something like a wormhole.

"Fact of the matter is, almost no one is aware that a lot of your most advanced breakthroughs in medicine and technology come from visitors from Earth 1 and Earth 11.

"You would not believe that a John Kennedy was an exchange from Earth 11. Even though you think that he is dead, he is not. His replacement from Earth 111 was killed in his place. He is alive and well on Earth 11 and is totally unaware that people on Earth 111 think that he is dead. There are others who have been switched and are not aware of it. I think that there is a binding unwritten law that people who die a natural death cannot bridge the dimensions. When you visit our library you will find a revelation that will greatly shock you. I'm telling you this so that you can prepare yourself in advance.

"On your Earth, Earth 111 there are uncertainties about many things. The explanation that has been given for these phenomena leaves much to be desired.

"The god people from other worlds were real. They lived on Earth 111 for many years. They built the pyramids, the sphinx, and most of the superstructures that can't be readily explained. They taught the Egyptians how to perform brain surgery and the basic principles of modern medicine. The god people from other worlds also inhibited the south country teaching the Incas. When a meteor shower initiated a colossal earthquake and the continent of Atlantis sank, the god people feared that this would happen again. This prompted them to abandon this planet. The people of Atlantis had the technology to bridge the dimensions and many escaped to other worlds in other dimensions."

Charles was spellbound by what SuejuSoe was telling him. He had a look on his face that would rival the second coming. He couldn't began to excogitate what he just heard as the conversation of a sane person. No way!

SuejuSoe spoke to a seemingly invisible person saying, "I know that what I've just told you sounds like the ranting of a crazy person, and I know that you are wondering why I'm not locked up somewhere and I'm certain that you think that you didn't wake up in a mad world that is purple, you woke up in a purple world that is mad."

Charles decided to play along with this weirdo. After all, he did say that he could prove it. He will darn well have to show me proof. "Okay, now tell me about this purple stuff." He thought, Just let him explain that.

"The purple stuff." SuejuSoe started, "Well, that is weirder than what I've just told you."

"Naw. That can't be," Charles said, "nothing can top that."

"That's what you think." He beckoned for the waitress and ordered more coffee. "So where do you want me to start?"

"At the beginning always worked for me."

"Now, let me see just where the beginning begin." SuejuSoe thought more than said. "The day of the nova all five Earths were lined up and a dark star entered their path. When the star blew, for about two minutes all five Earths were in the same dimension and took on the characteristics of the dark star and of each other. Since the dark star was in the exact vertical position with an unknown dimensions and Earth 1V and the inhabitants of this dimension was mostly fowl in form. It was during these two minutes when they shared the same dimension, all the inhabitants who resided above the ground on Earth 1V mutated taking on the characteristics of a chicken. When the star blew, the chicken people were the results. I don't know what happened to the dark star.

"When the fires were finally out, the fallout from the explosion blanketed the planet and blocked out the sun. It cast black and orange shadows over everything. That along with the radioactive fallout mixed with acid rain caused a purple haze to engulf the atmosphere. The sun could not penetrate this haze as you can see, and presto! Purple happens. When this happened and for causes no one knows our sun never completely set again.

"Since all this happened centuries before I was born, I am relying on oral, written, and guesstimated records. Plus, about two hundred years ago some land was being cleared and a steel drum was unearthed containing some type of records of the day of the nova. These records was meticulously kept even though the author knew that his death was eminent. After his death, other survivors recorded. In a way this is the best record we have of events during and after the supernova.

"These events did not affect the inhabitants of the Graveyard because no one came topside for more than four hundred years. They feared that everything was gone. When someone finally got up enough nerves to venture out of the Graveyard, they wore heavy bulky protective suits. The first thing that they noticed was that everything was purple and that there was life. Now as to the rest of the story, I really don't know. Period."

Slowly coming out of his self-imposed trance, Charles said, "You know, that is the story of stories. It might be right up there with the creation. It sure beat the hell out of the parting of the Red Sea. I wonder just how many have lived to tell a story like this? Yup, that is one story for one to believe," Charles said mockingly.

"You asked me to tell you this and before I began I told you that it would be hard to believe but you wanted to know anyway. Now, you mock what I've told you and want to know more. What do you take me for?"

"Cool it, man. You must admit that story is as hard to believe as it is to swallow a pill as big as an egg."

SuejuSoe said as he got up from the booth, "I'm going home. You can talk to whomever you want to find out about Purple Bottom City."

"Come on, man, I didn't mean to offend you. You must admit that story is as hard to believe as it is to tell. I certainly didn't mean to imply that you were lying. It's just that the story is so different than anything else that I've ever heard."

"Is it stranger than you ending up here?" Charles grinned, "No. I can't say that it is."

SuejuSoe said, "I'm going to the can. I'll be right back."

While he was gone, Charles sat thinking that all this had to be true because it was too far out to be a lie. Then he wondered what his fate would be in this strange purple world. He shrugged his shoulders and decided that he had enough to think about right now; he would think about some of this at another time.

There were approximately fourteen chicken people in the cafe beside them, and they kept watching every move that they made, trying to hear every word that they said. Occasionally, they would look at them and immediately turn away pretending to be unaware that they were listening. SuejuSoe took the toothpick out of his mouth and grinned, saying, "I think that they think that you are one strange dude."

"Oh yes," said Charles, "but not anywhere close to what they look like."

They both chuckled. Everyone head turned toward them. Charles finished his beer and asked SuejuSoe if he wasn't ready to go. SuejuSoe said that he was, and both stood up and left the booth. There were seventeen pairs of eyes watching their every move. Charles would turn and look back just for the hell of it and again all seventeen pair of eyes would instantly turn away instantly. As SuejuSoe was paying their bill, Charles heard someone say, "I wonder who in the hell is that?"

Someone answered, "I wonder what in hell is that."

Charles spoke out loud to no one in particular, "And so do I."

Outside a crowd was gathering. It was the Terrible Toilet Papers. They were neither a vicious nor a violent gang. Just noisy. In fact most people liked them. Even the vicious, low-down mean gang like the Stomach Cramps and the Rumbling Guts gave the Terrible Toilet Papers respect. They sometimes called them the Choirboys. Every member in this gang was a professional martial arts expert. Most of them were barely out of their teens but had endured years of training in the arts. The Terrible Toilet Papers were a godsend, and because of them people felt safer and the aged and disabled was far more grateful than most because they performed chores for them that they were unable to do for themselves and they did them without pay.

They had names like Joe Toe, Charles Cheeks, Michael Elbow, William Legbone, Marion Headache, Tony Wrist, LaSalle Earlobe, Glen Legbone, and William's first cousins, Brian Thighbone and Scott Charmin, the leader. The Stomach Cramps and the Rumbling Guts combined were not a match for them. So they respected and feared them, and the citizens were delighted and very glad to have the Terrible Toilet Papers and their leader Charmin, who was indeed charmin'.

When SuejuSoe and Charles left the Left Over Purple Place, Charles seemed to be spaced out. SuejuSoe looked concern and asked, "Are you all right? Do you need medical attention?"

"No. I'm okay. Sometimes I think that I'm my own worst enemy." He sneezed so hard until it got everyone's attention. He seemed to be allergic to purple pepper.

SuejuSoe helped him get his allergy pills and gave him some water. After he had taken the medication he sat in the car looking weak and strained, waiting for the medication to kick in. No one spoke or moved.

Outside the Terrible Toilet Papers were playing tiddlywinks with pepe pop tops and they had a captive audience. The Purple Place seemed to get more crowded by the minute. The lot was full and the disturbances were minimal. The Stomach Cramps were guzzling down beers and pitching popcorn into each other's mouth. Everyone knew that this placidity would not last long because the Stomach Cramps could act like civilized people only for a short while.

Charles said to SuejuSoe, "Are you okay enough to leave?"

"Yes. I think so."

SuejuSoe volunteered to drive because he didn't know just how okay Charles was and time was running out. The Terrible Toilet Papers had already left and the Stomach Cramps had invaded the place.

They were playing chicken. Two guys on a motorcycle would drive straight at the other to see which one would lose their nerves first. "Woe," said Charles. "That was close. I'm sure that we should be on our way like now."

"Ditto," said SuejuSoe as he was buckling his seat belt. "Ditto fast."

Charles looked back and witnessed the Stomach Cramps doing their thing, acting like the uncouth morons that they were. Screaming, spitting, and destroying everything that they could. No one with the exception of the Terrible Toilet Papers would stand up against them. As they turned the next corner the police had arrived. The police often responded to the disturbances but did very little to help.

"That was pretty close. These things are almost the same everywhere you go. One thing about living in the Graveyard is there isn't any violence. Minor spats were just about as bad as they got. There was only one prison in the entire place and it was occupied with people who broke the laws of conservation and recycling and rarely domestic disturbances. There were minor things like spitting in an unspecified place. This could land you in prison for six months. Throwing away unsegregated trash, like putting plastic with paper and putting plastic with vegetable waste. If someone threw out unsegregated refuse you could land in jail for five years.

Charles was thinking here he goes off again to lullaby land. No one cared what happened to garbage. All they wanted was someone to pick it up and haul it off to a land fill. Surely, he must see this place called the Graveyard, it sounded like a fairy tale. He chuckled to himself. In his world you could piss in a public fountain and twenty people could witness this but if no one reported it nothing would come of it. Now he is telling me that you could go to jail for mixing up your garbage. Far out! During his summation he thought that he had heard SuejuSoe say something. He turned and asked, "Did you say something?"

"Yes, I did."

"I asked would you like to go to a meeting with me tomorrow evening?

"What kind of meeting?"

"The kind that you'd probably be really interested in."

"Really?"

"Yes, really," said Suejusoe.

CHAPTER IV

When Charles and SuejuSoe left the Purple Place they drove around so that Charles could get a better view of this purple world. The view to Charles was unsettling. Never before had he seen so much purple. He had no idea that something unreal as this could exist. SuejuSoe talked and Charles listened.

"Hey. Check this out. Purple teenagers in purple swimwear swimming in purple water under a purple sky in purple daylight. You can't get any weirder than that," Charles said to SuejuSoe. "Man, I think that I need a potent drink real bad."

"We had a couple of beers less than an hour ago," SuejuSoe reminded him.

"You must be hearing in purple too. I said that I needed a strong drink. I didn't say that you needed one."

"My apology. I guess we will stop somewhere and get you that drink. There's a place about four blocks away. We'll go there."

"I didn't mean to sound so crass, but this place does things to me that my mind has a hard time processing."

"That's okay. I won't hold it against you. When I first came out of the Graveyard it was very hard for me to maintain my sanity, but somehow I did. I can't imagine how all this is affecting you."

"I really don't have the vocabulary to express how this is affecting me."

SuejuSoe pulled up in the parking lot of a place called Candie's Store. Charles looked at him like he was an idiot. "What . . . why are we going into a candy store? I need a drink, not candy."

SuejuSoe spoke in a calm voice, "Let's go in."

He knew that he would ask the proverbial question, why, and the next word Charles spoke was "Why?"

"Because I asked you to," SuejuSoe answered.

Reluctantly Charles followed SuejuSoe into Candie's Store. Inside there was a medium-size crowd.

There were slot machines, crap tables, roulette wheels, and a bar like none other that he had ever seen. It was shaped like a great colon with stools running along and around it. The sight of this made Charles forget why he had come to this place. He turned to SuejuSoe speechless. He was waving his hands and moving his lips without words coming out. He was acting like he was having a stroke. SuejuSoe burst out laughing. This brought Charles back to the reality of this purple world with the colon bar and the purple polyps, veins, and constipated turds. When Charles could talk, his words came out deliberately slow, and each was piercing. "I am dumbfounded. I never knew that my shock could be shocked. Is there any end to this?"

"I can't answer that because I don't know. But I can tell you this much, when I first ventured topside from the Graveyard, I had one major shock after another. Everything up here was strange and new to me. Every time I thought that I couldn't see anything stranger, I kept topping myself. I finally got to the place where it didn't matter anymore and decided to find out everything that I could about how and why these things were the way they were. Today, I am still in the learning process."

"You certainly straighten me out. I must be a total asshole thinking that I was the only one who was experiencing these mind boggling occurrences."

"Let's sit down at this big gut and have a couple of strong ones to numb my acute reaction to my ending up in this purple world."

"I can agree with that. Only let's sit at a table. This big gut does something to me."

They walked over to one of the kidney-shaped tables and sat down. A waitress wearing a top hat and a see-through top seemed to materialize out of nowhere. She wasn't beautiful but was pleasant to look at. She asked, "What can I get for you, gentlemen?"

65

"Oh, I don't know. I'm new here, could you get me a menu of your beverages," Charles said as he pulled his chair up to the table.

"I'll be right back," said the waitress, and she left. She returned with a long list of drinks. Not any of them sounded advertising. There was a bloody rum punch, a bloody mary, pepe pop and rum; there was a belch-a-minute beer and a list of something on the rocks. There was poop and scoop on the rocks and a hot hemorrhoid punch and a volcano blue bottom. There was pepe pop on the rocks and a list that seemed to go on and on. I asked the waitress what she would recommend. She asked me what kind of mood I was in and I told her adventurous. She gave me a teasing wink and said, "I've got exactly what you need, a Volcano Blue Bottom."

I looked at SuejuSoe and he said, "Don't ask me." I asked the waitress, "What is in that?"

She answered, "You don't want to know."

I looked at SuejuSoe again, and his face was blank, then said mostly to myself, What have I got myself into now?

In a very short while the waitress returned. She gave us our drinks and gave me another one of her winks and said, "If you need anything else, I'm Funky Freda." I nodded and she left.

I took a sip of my drink and thought, "Not bad." But that was before I swallowed. When that drink hit my stomach, my face broke out in a superheated sweat. My tongue and mouth belched fire and my teeth did a skeleton dance. I sat straight right up trying to maintain control, but that Volcano Blue Bottom had erupted. Everyone in the Candie's Store clapped and whooped up a storm. Tears and backslapping abounded. I stood up but was unable to speak because my intestines were still erupting. Freda came over and tears were rolling down her cheeks. She tried to talk between breaths, "Mister, I hope that you are not offended and I hope that you will forgive me, plus, I hope that not much damage was done. I've never seen anyone react behind a drink like you did. You've made my day worth getting up for."

I just stood there, the heat in my face and guts was abating somewhat. I looked at SuejuSoe and spoke in a voice that I didn't recognize. "What do you have to say?"

"Nothing," he answered, and didn't say anything else.

I smiled sheepishly at Freda and told her that I wasn't offended and I didn't harbor any ill feelings. Cheers and whoops took the place of the tears and laughter. When they heard that drinks were on the house, there were more cheers. No one questioned Charles's appearance because he had not mutated; they thought that he was from the Graveyard. They didn't care, they were having a good time. After that Volcano Blue Bottom had stopped erupting, he was having a ball even though he was the butt of an undefined prank.

The good times didn't last long. The Candie's Store which was often called the Pot Gut Palace was invaded by one of the local gangs, the Rumbling Guts. Their leader, Scab Malock, was schizo. You never knew what he would do. He wasn't mean low-down and nasty; he was just mean and low-down and insane. But to make things worse, he was the chief of police's son.

The Rumbling Guts were a motley, unkempt group. Their membership grew steadily. When the elite and the moderate elite escaped underground because of the supernova, those who were denied entry had to learn how to survive anyway that they could. This was the birth of many gangs including the Rumbling Guts. Because food was scarce and many were hungry for long periods of time, the Rumbling Guts seemed to be a natural realistic name for many, thus the name.

Those who had survived the heat, fallout, and radiation had to face starvation, illness, being killed, and a host of other postapocalypse maladies. Medical supplies were minimum and mostly limited to those left in hospitals and drugstores that had survived the explosions and fires.

Almost all of the medical community was safely underground and the only medical came from medical school dropouts and doctors and nurses who had been suspended for some reason and didn't qualify for the Graveyard. There were medical personnel who stayed behind because their families were not qualified for the Graveyard. These people did whatever they could to help the sick and injured. They too were facing the same hardships that everyone else was facing. It was during this time the Rumbling Guts were viewed by many as next to angels. They helped many to find food and shelter and helped many ill and maimed. They also provided protection to those from others who were willing to kill to survive. Many desired their presence because it made them feel safer. That was then. Down through the years when civilization and reconstruction and reinvention began to change the way they had to live, things began to change. Most of the other gangs died out and the remaining did an about face. People began to fear the ones that they had once looked up to.

They were on a fast track to becoming a public nuisance. So the survivors began to mutate. Most thought that they were sick until they realize that everyone was mutating. They began to accept their fate and rebuild their world.

The Rumbling Guts was like sitting on your butt after a massive bea attack. Whenever they showed up, it was painful. During the last ten years the Guts membership had regressed to uneducated, uncouth, and unemployed hoodlums. Everything that was wrong with anything was blamed on the purple atmosphere blanketing their world.

SuejuSoe let all these thoughts invade his mind as they sat sipping a milder form of a Volcano Blue Bottom. He seemed to have forgotten about Charles. Charles didn't think much about it because they thought that the drink had done a number on him. He was feeling good and watched SuejuSoe trying to figure out what was going on with him.

He decided to leave Suejusoe with his own little demons. Besides, these chicken people seemed to know how to have a good time. And after all he had been through, he wasn't sure if he had enough sense left to have a good time. But he was willing to give it a try. Maybe, he thought, that this was the after effect of the Volcano Blue Bottom. Even if it were, he didn't want to waste precious time. Lately, the way his luck was running, he may end up in another world. He said to SuejuSoe, "I think that I will go and check out the slot machines and get to know these chicken people. They seem to be friendly enough." SuejuSoe nodded and watched Charles walk away.

SuejuSoe couldn't understand why he was being bombarded with these "in the beginning" and "once upon a time" flashbacks. He couldn't stop the thoughts from flowing through his mind. It was like being in college studying for an exam. Just about everything he had read or seen about Purple Bottom City flowed through his memory, and it puzzled him.

Those who survived the nova had taken shelter wherever they could find it. Many were fried because their shelter was grossly insufficient. Every city sewer system, cave dug inside hillsides, and basement was crowded with those seeking refuge. And the cities and roadsides reeked with the stench of the dead and the dying. There were body parts decaying beside people who were too ill and too weak to move. Some survivors were so desperate to survive until they tried to eat the dead. Needless to say this hastened their demise. There were mass graves everywhere. No one worried about contaminating the Graveyard population because burning the dead was the utmost emergency.

Since approximately 40 percent of the landmass of the planet was destroyed and 20 percent of this was uninhabitable, space was critical. Homes had to be built. The food chain had to be reestablished; law and order had to be maintained. There was a critical need for medicine and medical facilities and personnel. Normalcy was a long way away. Yet the survivors took on the seemingly impossible task. They had to find a way to operate farms and factories. Schools and churches had to be built. First and foremost they had to find out if the planet would be habitable. Would it be able to maintain its orbit? Would it be able to sustain a population, or would it go uncontrolled out of orbit and burn up? Questions that needed answering and there seemed to be none.

The stench of death was everywhere except in the deepest darkest shaded areas of purple. These areas seemed to have a life of their own. People who resided close to these areas healed quickly. Food would grow in these areas that could be safely eaten.

It was ten years after the nova before the people realized that the purple haze that covered their world was not going away. Eventually they began to realize that this haze was beneficial. Instead of hiding inside on beds and pallets, the sick were taken outside. The haze seemed to have a healing power of its own. As word of this got around, needless to say, streets, rooftops, empty lots, and everywhere one could lie or sit on was filled up with the sick and injured. At least 90 percent were healed or greatly improved. New ideas from the minds of the less elite medical community began to take shape. The less elite scientist began to work on products that were derived from this purple haze. They discovered many useful products.

This began a boom within itself. If you were to feed animals concentrated nuggets of this purple modified food, they thrived and their flesh was tastier and more nutritious. The taste improvement was 50 percent or more. When farmers fertilized their crops with this, their yield was a 160 percent improvement and a double increase in yield.

The Chickpeos created a serum with the purple haze that had the ability to increase their wisdom and knowledge. It also gave them the ability to concentrate megapower beams to parts of the body and heal it without medicine or surgery. In a lesser concentrated form it brought one's IQ up 25 to 40 percent. It was a surefire way to guarantee the survival and the advancement of their world.

The need for schools, churches, and medical facilities still needed to be addressed. Since the top educators and most other professional had gone underground, ideas on how to accomplish this had to come from virgin minds This was an unexpected bonus for them. Because before the nova their schools had left a lot to be desired, the students were failing, the teachers could not maintain discipline, and there were massive dropouts. With a new school board and new teachers they could start over at the beginning. Plus, with the power of the extract from the purple haze that could enhance one's IQ, things were coming up roses.

Not all of the Chickpeos benefited from this formula called Rocket Star PJ40. You had to have an IQ of at least eighty-five; otherwise, you made it anyway that you could. Those graduating from medical schools and schools of scientific knowledge had superb minds and found cures for many maladies.

The citizens of Purple Bottom City were approaching a period in their lives that had yet to be defined. Their knowledge and advancement was at a far greater pace than anyone could predict. Growing pains were rampant, and somehow they had to find a way to harness this overflow for useful purposes.

The knowledge that the Rocket Star PJ-40 caused was bewilderingly complex. It was too much too soon to be processed accurately. Yet they managed the best that they could. Who would have thought that too much knowledge would become a problem.

For many years after the nova no one had given names to anything. There were numbers and letters and codes. These seemed to work well enough for everything until people started coming topside from the Underground City. They walked up to a Chickpeo and poked him in the side. The Chickpeo looked at this monster and asked, "Are you a problem, or a dream or a smartass with a problem and no dream."

The citizens from the Graveyard were amazed that this chicken-looking thing could talk, but more outstanding was that it was purple. Naw, this couldn't be. Perhaps they was experiencing mass hallucinations. The people from the underground thought that everyone that had not taken shelter in the Underground City had been killed. Now before them were strange-looking chicken people and a beautiful city that was functional and rivaled anything that they had in the Graveyard. And they talked.

They tested the air and found that it was safe to breathe, and they removed their protective suits. They did this in a hurry. In their eagerness to explore this purple world they didn't consider that they were visitors and they were odd-looking to the Chickpeos. The Chickpeos watched them in fascination. They thought their visitors were strange indeed.

As the Underground City citizens shed their protective garments, they talked nonstop. Asking questions. Hardly waiting for an answer before asking the next. It was only a short while before they noticed that their questions were not being answered. Abruptly, they ceased their chatter and questioning and noticed that their audience had begun to dissipate. One spoke up calling out to those dissipating and those who were contemplating dissipating, "Wait."

They halted and looked around. "Please don't go. We really would like to talk to you."

"About what?" someone asked.

"About your survival, your existence and . . . and . . . this purple."

"From what I've been told, none of you cared about us during the nova. You wanted nothing to do with us."

"I know what you are saying is the truth, but we had nothing to do with that."

"So you think that you can just show up here after leaving us down here to perish? Do you think that you can speak a few words and all will be forgiven? You have got to be crazy."

"If you will listen I can explain."

"I don't want an explanation."

The citizens from the Underground City were totally thrown off. They had never dreamed that they would find life, yet he found a city teeming with life of an advanced nature. And he had never experienced such hostilities. None of it was his fault. He tried once more. He ran to catch with the hostile Chickpeos. Now that he had caught them he did not know what to say. He began, "Please, sir, just listen to me for two minutes and if you decide that you don't want to hear anymore, I'll go."

The Chickpeo stopped, turned around, and in a commanding voice said, "Speak."

The abruptness of the Chickpeo father startled the Underground citizen. His mind was totally blank, but he had to think of something soon before his last chance to make a connection with this Chickpeo's expired. In desperation he began asking questions about the purple haze and trying to come up with an acceptable reason while many were denied refuge in the Graveyard City.

He wasn't doing a very good job because the Chickpeo started to leave, then stopped, turned around, and gasped, "What is wrong? Why are you acting like that?"

The Chickpeo laughed and turned the Graveyard citizen around so that he could see his reflection in the plateglass window. Then he laughed harder.

The Graveyard citizen had begun to mutate, taking on the feature of a chicken.

When the Underground City citizen finally understood what was going on, he began to scream. "No. No. No."

Other Chickpeo began to gather around trying to see what was happening. When they did see what was happening, they cheered loudly. This left only one recourse for the Underground City citizen and that was to run. Run as fast and as hard as possible and get back under the ground. The other Graveyard people who had not taken off their protective suits followed, leaving the Chickpeos rolling with laughter.

Charles had returned to the table with SuejuSoe and found that he was still spaced out. He tossed a coin on the table and said, "Here's a penny for your thoughts."

SuejuSoe did not respond. Charles tossed another penny on the table. Again, there was not a response. Charles waved his hand in front of SuejuSoe's face. He jumped. "What . . . say . . . Charles, man, do you have some type of problem?"

"No. Do you?"

"What do you mean?"

"You were so out of it a minute ago, I could have bashed your head in and you wouldn't have noticed."

"I guess I was sort of out of it. My mind was on a history tour of some sort."

"How about filling me in?"

"You wouldn't be interested. Let's get out of here."

"And go where?" asked Charles.

"Anywhere."

The noise outside was getting louder. SuejuSoe asked Funky Freda what was all the commotion was about. She answered, "I don't know but I'm going to find out."

She went to the door and saw that the Rumbling Guts and the Stomach Cramps, another local gang was starting up a ruckus. The Stomach Cramps leader was named Ass Hole. His was the most violent gang around. They were nasty, mean, low-down, and dodo dumb. They would start a melee if someone would step in their footprints. Every one of them had done time at some point in their lives.

Freda told Charles and SuejuSoe that the Cramps and the Guts were trying to start something and things may get out of hand soon. "So my advice to you would be get out of here while you still have time and please take the back door."

SuejuSoe was ready in an instant. Charles hung back. He began, "What's with all these gangs? I haven't been here eight hours and already I have encountered two gangs. Now I'm faced with two more. This is ridiculous. Everywhere I go, gangs follow me around, and I've had enough already."

SuejuSoe urged Charles to go on. Charles was adamant. "No."

Everyone in the place was taking the backdoor exit. The din outside doubled. Charles still wouldn't move. There was a terrible noise. Then, there was none. The Terrible Papers had arrived like the cavalry did in the old Western pictures. They came around the corner honking and yelling twice as noisy as the other two gangs combined. As mean, nasty, and low-down as the Stomach Cramps and the Rumbling Guts were, they respected and feared the Terrible Toilet Papers. It was widely known that they were peacekeepers because when you had the Stomach Cramps and Rumbling Guts you surely needed Toilet Paper. That was a necessity.

Charles was puzzled. "Someone please tell me what just happened? I was getting ready for the fight of my life and now it is quiet as a tomb."

"The Terrible Toilet Papers showed up." Freda whispered. "And just who are the Terrible Toilet Papers?

"They are a peacekeeping gang. All the other gangs are afraid of them."

"Halleujah!" Charles exclaimed, "I need to meet them and to congratulate them."

In a booth not far from where Charles and SuejuSoe were sitting, Wester'C Ulcer sat sipping his drink and trying his best to ignore the commotion going on outside. He was working on some papers for a meeting that he was going to tomorrow. He was also eavesdropping on Charles situation, and he too felt like congratulating these young men.

He left his table and came over to where they were and introduced himself. SuejuSoe was already acquainted with Wester'C, and he introduced Charles DeNero, his newly found alien friend. SuejuSoe explained to Wester'C that Charles was an alien who found himself in this world after a strange incident occurred on his world. He was kind of his guardian since he bumped into him on the street. Charles smiled as he shook Wester'C's hand. He told him to excuse him for a minute because he wanted to meet the Terrible Toilet Paper gang members. Wester'C went with him because he had heard of them but had never had the chance to meet them.

On their way to meet the Terrible Toilet Papers, Wester'C asked Charles, "Did I hear Mr. Suju say that you were an alien?"

"Yes. You did, and I am. New to this world since sometime this morning. I haven't got over the shock of it and probably never will."

"My goodness, we must talk about this soon. I've never met an alien from another world. I have a million questions to ask you. I must say that you don't look like a Chickpeo, nor do you look like a spook. That is slang for the citizens of the Underground City." Wester'C reached for his hands again and grasped them saying, "Man, this must be my lucky day. I've met a real alien and I'm going to meet the members of the Terrible Toilet Papers." He pumped his hands again.

When he let go of Charles's hands he looked at them as he saw something alien also. They were almost outside where the Terrible Toilet Papers were and someone had announced that the Honorable, Dr. Wester'C Ulcer was present and wanted to meet the members of the Terrible Toilet Papers. The small crowd that was left stood aside and let them pass through. When they came face to face to the gang members, he was shocked to see that they were so young to have earned such a reputation as crime fighters. He guessed that they were from age seventeen to twenty-five. Some had not yet begun to shave. They stood off by themselves, and Wester'C walked over and offered them his hand. They shook it and exchanged pleasantries. He praised them for their bravery and courage and introduced them to Charles DeNero, the newest and only alien in town.

Tiny, a member of the Terrible Toilet Papers, let out a whoop, "You don't mean the alien that arrived today, do you? I've heard of him."

"Yes, I am he. I am from another world," said Charles as he offered him his hand.

Tiny took it and shook it. Then he examined it, rubbed it, and tried to taste it. Charles withdrew his hand with a jerk. "Just what are you doing?"

Tiny tried to explain in his teenage broken voice, "Sir, mister. I'm sorry, I just got carried away. I never seen or met someone from another world before, and I have always been fascinated by them. At least what I've read about them. I'm sorry to say that you don't fit the bill of aliens."

'Say what?" asked Charles.

"First, you don't look like an alien. You look more like a toasted spook, and you don't taste like milk chocolate."

Charles voice went up an octave, "Say what?"

Tiny's voice was barely audible, "You don't keep up with the latest in alienology magazines, do you?"

"I have no idea what you are talking about."

"I can see that by the way you are talking. Really, sir, I'm not trying to be unreasonable, not smarting off. I have more than just have more than a passing interest in alien life-forms. You see I'm going to study it when I go to college."

"It's all right," Charles said, "I'm not offended. You see, I too am new with being an alien and I don't know the proper alien protocol. I came out here to congratulate you and the members of your elite squad on the excellent job that you are doing keeping the peace. You all are so young to be crime fighters and you are to be commended."

Wester'C and SuejuSoe agreed with what Charles had said, and the Toilet Papers took it all in stride. They said that they didn't consider it crime fighting; they thought of it as doing what was needed to be done especially when there was no one else to do it. They were modest in accepting a compliment and didn't stay around too long before they left. They had complimented Charles on how well he had handled the way the young crime fighter, out of the blue questions, came at him.

Charles shrugged his shoulders like it was no big deal, and he did it all the time.

Wester'C said, "Guys, I really hate to part with you right now, but I was preparing myself for a meeting first thing in the morning. I simply have to reconnect with you as soon as I can. There's too much I need to know about this. I feel like postponing our meeting. All this is so new and interesting. Can y'all pencil me in around 10:30 tomorrow morning? I may bring someone with me."

Charles started to protest saying," I don't know. I've just got here. I don't have any place to stay. I don't have any clothes. I'm just not in a meeting mode."

"Oh, man. I hadn't thought of that. Mr. Suju, do you have any of this covered? Because if you don't, Mr. DeNero can come with me, that is if it's all right with you."

"We hadn't discussed it. But what do say, Charles? Is it all right for you to hang with me or do you want to go with Wester'C?"

"I'll stay with you since I've been with you almost as long as I've been here. I feel like you are my only friend in this world."

"I'll see you guys tomorrow," Wester'C said, getting into his auto.

SuejuSoe pulled up to his apartment and they exited his auto. He said, "Shall we go in?"

Charles followed him in and looked around thinking, So this is how inhabitants of another world live. Not bad for chicken people. He immediately chastised himself for thinking like this. He was grateful that someone had befriended him. He was as alien to him as he was to him. Instead he said, "This is not at all what I expected."

"Just what did you expect?"

"I really didn't know what I expected. Everything here is new. I guess I was comparing ever thing with what I am used to."

"Don't sweat the little stuff. You have a lot of things to overcome and come to grips with. Come on and I'll show you around."

Charles took the short tour through the apartment and thought that it wasn't too much different than a regular apartment. If he had to stay here a little while, he guessed that he could manage. SuejuSoe asked, "What do you think?"

"I think that I can manage."

"Good, let me see what can I do about clothes?"

That Charles thought was going to be problem. They were not built the same. Wester'C was a better candidate as far as clothes were concerned. Maybe they could go to the Graveyard and pick up something. Listen to him talk about the Graveyard, just like he know something about the Graveyard. He knew nothing about nothing.

After looking through his closets SoejuSoe agreed with Charles that they would probably have to go to the Graveyard to get him some clothing. But in the meantime they would have to make do. He did have a sofa that he could sleep on, and that was good.

*****

Wester'C had dual citizenship, and he wanted it to stay that way. He remembered how his parents had perished in the Graveyard. It had been fourteen years since he had first emerged from the Graveyard, and he would never forget how traumatized, scared, and excited he had been. There was no way he could've prepared himself for what he would and did encounter. To the best of his knowledge, everyone had perished during the nova. It was amazing to see cities functioning and advanced civilization abound and serious technology at work. It really freaked him out when he saw that all the people of this world had the features of chickens. But most of his amazing discovery was after a short period of time topside, he too began to look like they did.

So this is what the real world is about? he said to himself. It always weighed heavy on his mind ever since the first time he exited the Graveyard why there wasn't an antidote for this mutation and what all this purple stuff was about. What had happened to this world? His work was cut out for him.

Wester'C drove into the parking lot of a modern building that had more than its share of glass. The glass reflected the puddles of water and the lights from the streets like huge jewels. He walked faster. As he passed a double glass door, he espied his physique and thought, Life has been good to me even though I just crawled out from under the ground.

He entered the outer office charged with anticipation. He heard voices in the conference room and thought, They have started without me. He opened the door and walked in. Bojo jumped off the corner of the massive desk that dominated the room and mockingly announced, "The Honorable Dr. Wester'C Ulcer."

Some people clapped and whistled like he was a celebrity. This embarrassed him and made him feel self-conscious. He put his hands in his pocket and gazed at the floor.

Time passed slowly. Political meetings were boring and slightly productive. They were trying to find a candidate to run for the governor and the president. SuejuSoe and Ocena were their first and second choices, but they wouldn't commit. SuejuSoe thought that Wester'C and

Ocena should run because he wasn't especially interested in running for any political office.

While they were debating on who were going to be candidates for governor, across town another meeting was taking place. The Chickpeos were trying to select some of their people to run for the same offices. They felt like they should be in charge of their world because it were them that had survived hell, high waters, winds, plagues, fires, and starvation and rebuilt their world. The Graveyard citizens only recently began to emerge from their underground city. Who was more qualified to run their world, their own people? Wasn't it them that had saved the Spooks when they were all dying with respiratory illness? Wasn't it the Spooks who thought that they were not good enough to save and were left to perish? Yes. Yes.

Now, Miss Heartburns was okay. But Wester'C Ulcer and SuejuSoe Suju, with their so-called dual citizenships were no way going to be candidates.

At the political meeting across town, SuejuSoe slapped his forehead with his palm and said, "Hey, I almost forgot. I want you to meet someone, Charles DeNero. And does he have a story to tell."

"Charles stood up, grinned nervously, then said very politely, "Hello."

"Will you tell your story to these guys?"

"No. I don't think so. This is one of those occasions where once is enough. But I would like to get as much information as possible to take back with me. That is if I can get back home."

"What is he talking about getting back home?" Bojo asked.

"You won't believe the answer." SuejuSoe said shaking his head. "Y'all are being mighty mysterious 'bout this K'Narf said.

"I'll leave it to you," SuejuSoe said, "Charles, you have the floor."

Charles stood up, looked around, then sat back down. "What's the matter now." SuejuSoe asked.

I want to get back from where I came from and if I were to continue, y'all wouldn't understand and its personal."

"Try us. We are a versatile bunch," K'Narf chipped in.

"No, I don't think so," said Charles.

"Listen," K'Narf said, ":Are you going to tell us or are we going to beat it out of you." Charles teased, "My aren't you guys hostile."

"You don't know just how hostile we can be." Bojo added.

"All right, you big bad boys, I'll tell you but you better not laugh. Okay."

"Shoot," Bojo drawled, "I'm aging fast and I don't want to be putting my teeth in a glass at night 'fore I find out."

"Me too," K'Narf added, "I can feel my bones popping and creaking."

"Cut the crap, guys," SuejuSoe said, "Don't be a total asshole."

"Too late," Jelly Belly blurted out. That happened a long time ago. Y'all was born that way."

"Let me get out of here," Charles said, walking to the door.

"Pray tell me just where do you think you are going?" SuejuSoe asked, stopping in front of Charles, blocking his path to the door. "You don't know shit about this place."

Charles answered, "I know one thing, the shit in here is much deeper than it is out there."

"Don't take anything these dunderheads say seriously. I think that they have brain damage. Come back and tell your story," SuejuSoe coaxed.

Charles began to speak, "I don't believe that these gentlemen are ready for this. I can see in your faces that you've made up your minds not to believe anything that I may say, and I don't need this provocation. I've already got enough to contend with."

"No. Go on. No one is trying to judge you. Isn't that right fellows?"

Charles continued, "I'm not from around here. I don't know why I'm here, but there is one thing that I do know, and that is I want to get back to where I came from."

"Okay, I'll take the bait," quipped K'Narf. "Just where did you come from?"

"I came from a place called Earth."

Someone began to sniggle. "Yes, so are we. So what else is earth-shattering news?" K'Narf said nonchalantly.

"Just let him finish," SuejuSoe snapped.

"Chill, man, I'm cool," K'Narf retorted defensively.

Charles continued, "I can easily see how you may question what I'm about to tell you. If I were you, I'd do the same thing. But with the help of Mr. Suju, I've found out that I'm from a place that used to be identical to this one before the cataclysm. Only now your world looks exactly like this place to me. A place out of my world."

"That is one story to be told. Now, tell us what we can do to get you back home."

"I don't know myself, but I've been told that you are experimenting or rather tryin' to perfect a method to travel through the dimensions."

"Yes, I've heard some rumors about this but as far as I know they were just rumors," Bojo said. "I thought that was a long ways off in the future."

"We've come much farther along than most people realize," SuejuSoe announced. "But none of this is public knowledge. So I'm going to take him to the Graveyard tomorrow to see what we can dig up."

"Yes, it's amazing. Actually it's just about, you know . . . kinda like a fairy tale."

"Fairy tale nothing!" Charles exploded. "This is a nightmare."

"Why doesn't something extraordinary ever happen to me?" Jelly Belly said. "I think that I could get a zing out of it. It always happens to the other guy."

"I promise you," said Charles, "it will scare the hell out of you."

"I can't began to imagine the terror that you must have gone through," K'Narf said, shaking his head.

"No. You couldn't," snapped Charles. "You cannot began to know what I've been through. How I was scared shitless. How my tongue was so swollen with fear I tasted panic. I was not sure if I was alive or had gone to hell without dying. Have you ever been so scared that you wanted to take your own life rather than face whatever came next? Have you ever cried blood for tears? When I woke up in this strange place, this strange purple appeared where nothing seemed familiar, then the first living creature that I see was a chicken man. I thought that I was hallucinating, but when I shut my eyes and opened them again, he was still there. That's when I cried. I thought that my tears were purple as they rolled down my cheeks. I took my finger and tasted them and they tasted like blood. When was the last time your heart fell down in your pelvis and bounced back so hard it ended up in your throat rendering you speechless?

"When was the last time you were driving down a road and everything was normal then in the blink of an eye you ended up in an alien world where everything that you had been taught was impossible was the norm. I had never ever considered nor even imagined a complete world that was entirely purple inhibited by chicken people."

"That's Chickpeo," Bojo corrected.

"Whatever," Charles paused and continued. "When have your eyes seen thing that your mind couldn't register."

Charles voice began to rise as he continued to speak. "How can you expect me to understand or accept the reality of your world? Tell me now how many of you can end up in a place like this and maintain your sanity?" A big tear rolled down his cheek, and he wiped it away angrily then continued. "Tell me!"

Everyone in the room was deathly quiet. It was like time had stopped and they were inside a time frame. It was quiet enough to hear your blood swishing as it passed your ears. No one moved. It seemed as eternity had passed and at long last Charles cleared his throat and said, "I would like for someone to tell me something."

"Something like what?" asked Bojo.

"I want to know where in hell did all this purple come from?"

Everyone burst out laughing. "You know as much as any of us about this purple stuff. It was here before I was born and probably will be after I am gone," said K'Narf.

SuejuSoe spoke in an uncertain voice, "Well, what did I tell you?"

Bojo spoke apologetically, "Hey, man, I'm really sorry about what I said earlier. I had no idea this stuff sounded like something out of this world."

"It's okay," Charles said as he sat on the plush leather sofa. "I probably would have reacted the same way if someone had laid this on me."

"I think that this would be best because SuejuSoe have more clout than the rest of us. But if there is anything that the rest of us can do just say it." Bojo said.

"I want to know what does clout have to do with a situation like this?"

"Nothing," answered Bojo.

"Well, why would anyone bother to bring it up?"

"I want to know are we going to make any decision tonight or are we going to help . . . or . . . or."

SuejuSoe finished, "Do y'all want to vote on this matter, or does everyone agree that we have an emergency?"

Shrugging his shoulders, Bojo said, "That's cool with me."

"Okay, when will we meet again?"

"Can't say," said SuejuSoe, "I'll have to get back with you guys later."

"Okay by me," said Bojo.

Arthur Moses and Jelly Belly said in unison, "me too."

As they were leaving Ocena spoke up for the first time, "Mr. Suju, Mr. DeNero, what I want to say is that ever since I heard your story I guess that I've been in shock. I suppose my wee mind still haven't or maybe it can't register what you've said but I want to let you know that my heart goes to you."

"Why, thank you, Miss . . ."

"Heartburns, Ocena Heartburns. If there is anything that I can do for you, just let me know." She smacked Arthur Moses lightly on the lips and blew into his ear, "See you later, sexy thing."

And she left, leaving only Charles, SuejuSoe, and K'Narf.

Charles asked, "Where do we go from here?"

"Back to my place," SuejuSoe answered. K'Narf said "good night." And he was gone.

Charles smiled shyly and asked SuejuSoe, "Are Ocena and Moses an item?"

"Yes and no," SuejuSoe answered.

"I don't get it," said Charles, "how can you say yes and no?'

"You know, it's a low-down dirty shame the way those two behave. They get engaged, break up, get engaged again, break up, and so on. They agree on most things, but when it comes down to a commitment, neither one can stay still long enough to tie the knot. When he is ready, she is not, and when she is ready, he is not, or they are both busy. It's sad because Moses has been in love with her since she was in high school."

Charles smiled; he was thinking about Eidas Sirron. Now that was a woman. Just thinking about her had his penis in the first stages of erection. He wondered how could she have this kind of effect on him a world away. Yep, it made him feel good all under too. SuejuSoe looked at him as though he knew what he was thinking about. He smiled too. "Thinking about someone pretty special?" he asked knowingly.

"Yes," said Charles, "very special."

They didn't have to say anything else; they knew how the other one felt. It felt good.

Both Charles and SuejuSoe were quiet as they was driving home. There wasn't any reason for words. They were on the same plane and didn't need to speak; they communicating mentally.

When they arrived at SuejuSoe's place that he often referred to as the coop, he opened the door and he and Charles entered. Charles whistled softly, "This is great. You Chickpeos do know how to live."

"Excuse me," SuejuSoe said, "I'm not a Chickpeo. I'm from the Graveyard."

"Sorry, I goofed, but I'm new at this."

"No offense taken. Anyone who have been through what you have has every right to goof up. Do you want a drink to wash down some of the crud that you heard tonight?"

"I would love one as long as it is not a Volcano Blue Bottom. What do you have?"

"The usual stuff, scotch, bourbon and gin."

"Yes, sure. A gin and tonic will be fine."

"You do know that all of it is purple."

"I wouldn't have it any other color," Charles kidded. He looked around SuejuSoe's living room and admired the décor. "Did you decorate this yourself"?

"Hell no," SuejuSoe said, laughing. "I can't even tie my own shoelaces straight."

They both laughed. Charles seemed to be handling the predicament that he was in okay, but there was something about him that wasn't there before his abduction, that is, if he was abducted. This made him feel like he was defeated before he had begun to fight. He wasn't sure what this feeling was all about and didn't know how to go about handling it. He was trying desperately to rid himself of this dreaded feeling that he felt was only afoot behind him. Unconsciously, he felt that it would catch up with him and what had endured before would have been a duck's walk. He did not tell anyone about it after; all he was a man, a real man. Not a chicken man.

SuejuSoe turned out to be a great host, and he went beyond the ordinary to make Charles feel comfortable. Yet when they woke the following morning, that dreaded feeling was still lurking just out of reaching distance.

SuejuSoe was already up and eating toast and jam and purple coffee. "Morning, Charles. Pull up a chair and help yourself."

Charles pulled up a chair, sat down, and poured himself a cup of coffee.

"How can you be so cheerful this early in the morning?" Charles asked as he took a sip of his purple coffee. Before SuejuSoe could answer, he exclaimed, "Damn! This coffee is delicious. What kind is it?"

"Purple," SuejuSoe answered.

"No, really, I'm quite serious. This is the best coffee that I've ever tasted."

For a minute Charles was jubilant, pushing aside that dreaded feeling, but he knew that it wasn't far behind.

"You want an answer to that? I think that it has something to do with this purple stuff."

"If I ever get back home I want to take some of this purple stuff with me. I could make a billion dollars."

"You really think so," SuejuSoe said more than asked.

"You bet. I am serious. Where I came from, people would pay a mint for this."

"I guess that you will have to take some back and find out." Then he added, "Today we are going to the Underground City and see about getting you homeward bound."

"That sound as good as the bells in heaven."

"What?"

"Homeward bound. That sounds heavenly. I never knew that I could miss Montana so much."

"That is something yet to be determined. My advice to you is not to go and get your hopes too high."

"I know that you are right, but I just can't help it."

"We will find out something pretty soon, or our trip to the Underground City could be unproductive, and remember that I said could be."

*****

At 8:30 AM, they caught the Mole train to the Underground City. Charles was ecstatic. He could not ever imagine ever doing something like this. They were going fifty miles per hour underground. There weren't any signs or signals to look at. The train was computer controlled and ran on air rails. It didn't need a conductor and made only one stop and that was when it reached its destination, Underground City. The ride was smooth, and if he knew what to expect at the end of the ride it could have been relaxing. In about twenty minutes they had arrived. Every time Charles thought that he had seen the most strangest thing in the world, something else would show up. But then again he was not in his world.

Underground City was another world altogether. If he had thought that Purple Bottom City was eerie, strange, and unique, he had been grossly erroneous. This place took the prize. It was beautiful. There was trees, green trees, grass, green grass, streets, houses, downtown office buildings, and shops. The people were normal people like he was only everyone was the same color. There were cars, small cars of many colors. There was an exact orderliness about everything.

Charles was awed. How could they do this? There were schools, factories, and homes. With the wonderment of a child, Charles asked SuejuSoe, "How did y'all ever manage to accomplish all of this and maintain it so efficiently?"

"You'll have to ask someone else because I don't know. I only live here part-time."

"I love this. Where are we going to go first?"

"We are going to my apartment and pick up some much needed papers. But in the meantime don't spit anywhere."

Charles looked at SujuSoe with puzzlement on his face, shrugged, and said, "Lead the way; you are my personal guide."

"Bet ya, let's go," SuejuSoe said as they boarded the tram. The ride to his apartment was a short one, but the effect the ride had on Charles was major.

He was excited, and everything amazed him. He looked at things as if they were new, yet he had lived with all of his life, things that on Earth was ordinary like trees and houses. They looked the same, yet something was different about them but he didn't know what it was.

Maybe it was because everything was two miles under the ground. To him this was awesome.

The more he saw, the more he wanted to see. This was amazing. Real streets with traffic lights, office buildings, people. Now this was strange. He thought that he had imagined it before, but this was something that needed an answer. He would ask SuejuSoe later. All of the people was the same color. Only the visitors from the top side were different; they were purple.

The citizens of Underground City were neither white, black, brown, red, or yellow. It seemed that all of their colors had been blended together and the end product was the color of the citizens of the Underground City. A bronze tan.

SujuSoe explained to Charles that the purple Chickpeos were only visitors and rarely stayed longer than three to five days.

The citizens here had to mix and interbreed the races for hundreds of years. They did so because when they first inhibited this city, blacks had built up antibodies against a virus that killed many whites and other fair-skinned races. Then they found that the whites and other fair-skinned races had built up an antibody that was deadly to blacks and other dark-skinned races. Then they discovered that if they should interbreed with each race this would protect all races. Thus, we became a new race altogether.

Yet we are vulnerable to diseases that the Chickpeos harbor."

"Well, I'll be damned," exclaimed Charles. "You don't suppose that I'm carrying a deadly virus that I may pass on to you."

"No," SuejuSoe answered. "About one hundred years ago someone came up with this debugging chamber. Let me see, yes, it was called the CU-STUZ. They built this chamber and every citizen had to go through it to be debugged. At first this made a lot of people sick. Many died. So the people revolted and wouldn't go through them anymore. Something had to be done. They worked on the chamber and found that it had been killing off the white cells, leaving the immune system wide open for anything that came by.

"It took a while but they finally perfected the CU-STUZ, but the people still wouldn't go through the chamber. They were desperately determined to find a way to debug these people without them knowing what was going on. One day they came up with the idea of placing chambers in places where everyone would come to sooner or later. They had perfected the chamber so that it took less than a minute to work.

"When one would walk through the chamber, a blue light would come on for two to three seconds, and by the time it would take you to walk through would be debugged. These chambers were set up in schools, hospitals and shopping centers. Eighty-five percent of the people were immunized and had no idea that they were.

"Son-of-a-gun," Charles said through clenched teeth. "Did this create any problems like you know the same people kept getting zapped over and over/"

"No because the machine was programmed so that people who had already been debugged would reflect the invisible rays. This way no one would get ODed.

"My, my, y'all thought of everything. What did they do about the 15 percent who were not immunized?"

"They were eventually rounded up and quarantined. All who would not volunteer to be immunized would have to spend the rest of their lives in quarantine. So I guess that you can imagine how that turned out."

"What will they think of next?"

"You are about to find out things that turn your eyes backward," Charles repeated, "son-of-a-gun."

When they reached SuejuSoe's apartment, upon entering it surprise once more. It was small, super compact but it had everything that one would need. Things were so cleverly designed until six hundred square feet seemed like the state of Texas. Well, maybe that's overstating it a bit, but it seemed huge. Everything was either built in, pushed down, or could expand and reverse. By the time SuejuSoe finished pushing buttons, flipping switches, and turning knobs the whole place had been transformed as though it was magic. Charles was speechless. To think that they had the technology to do something like this. All the furniture was the same color. A stereo the size of an egg carton and could disappear with the turn of a switch. The bathroom tub could fold up like an accordion. When you walked in the front door there seemed to be a plush armchair but mash a button it would become a regular size couch. Amazing!

Charles had noticed on his way over to SuejuSoe's apartment that dome shape that protected the city also served as a sky. I would have never noticed it if he hadn't said something about it. The artificial sun was so close to the real thing until he would have never known that he was two miles under the ground had he not experienced it.

When he had first heard of the Graveyard or rather Underground City, he did not know what to expect especially since he had seen the purple chicken people. He had tried to imagine living in a coffin but could make nothing of it. This was not a mausoleum. He wondered if Underground City had a graveyard or did they recycle the dead. Mentally he put this question on his invisible list of things to find out about later. But in the meantime he continued to explore this fascinating place called Underground City, affectionately call by the Chickpeos, the Graveyard.

In the back of his mind Charles was thinking that if he would be unable to return to his beloved Earth it would not be too bad living down here, but it would take some getting used to. First, he would have to find him a sweet little thing and he had seen some fine babes down here.

To think of this now was not the thing to do. He had some serious work cut out for him. So he better get down to it. SuejuSoe voice jarred him out of his reverie. 'Say, Charles, where is your mind? Are you still with me?"

"Did you say something?"

"Yes, I did. What have you been thinking about?"

"I'm sorry. My mind has been, well, you know . . . I was just thinking . . . you know about my predicament and my . . . options. At the present time I don't have any options and you already know this place have blown my mind. I don't know what to think of first."

"Well, I can," said SuejuSoe. I've got what I needed so let's boogie on down to the science institute." On the way to the science institute, Charles noticed how neat every house and yard was. All of the lawns were lush and green. There wasn't any trash anywhere. It was picture-perfect.

He thought that this was so unreal until it gave him an uneasy feeling. It looked like it was staged for his benefit. He longed to see something that wasn't perfect. He wanted to see Purple Bottom City.

All of this perfection had him feeling like he was in the second stages of insanity. He thought about those guys back in Montana with the moose. That was real. He missed things like that. He thought about the Chickpeos on the topside. Their behavior was natural. The place was natural with the exception of being purple and cloudy with purple chicken people. He began to compare the two places.

There were fumes from cooking, exhaust from factories and cars and people just hanging out. So far he had yet to encounter anything that he could equate with normalcy. This place was more like a serene painting rather than a real place. Like a bowl of waxed fruit.

He made another entrance on his invisible list of things to ask about later. Where was the living taking place down here? This place seemed as peaceful as a graveyard.

"Gone on another trip?" SuejuSoe asked.

Charles answered with a question, "Do you think this place is messing with my mind?"

"How do you mean?"

"You know, I'm here in this place and I desperately want to get back home. Yet I keep thinking not about going home but comparing the Graveyard with Purple Bottom City."

"It could be shock."

"I suppose that it could be shock. Lord knows that I've been shocked a mammy since I've been here."

"Maybe you should slow down some. I still think that you have not had all the shocks that you are going to get. I know that it is still in the morning, but I think maybe you should have a stiff drink."

"Whatever you say," said Charles as he paused in rolling his neck and looked out the window. What he saw brought on more tension. He said to SuejuSoe, "Well that didn't take long."

"What are you talking about?"

"You just said that I had more shocks in store," he said, pointing outside of the window, "and there it is." Outside they were passing a farm, another picture-perfect place. The pasture was filled with cattle that looked like they were groomed every day. The pasture was immaculate; it looked like it had been painted a lush shade of green just the day before. There were an astronomical number of calves and there weren't any flies or cow patties anywhere. In a pen next to the pasture there were about ten bulls having sex with an artificial heifer contraption. The thing didn't look like a helfer anyway you looked at it. It was crude looking, but it didn't matter to the bulls because they were going at it full speed. Everything else was precise and orderly except that crude heifer.

Across the road was a huge poultry farm and processing plant. I have never seen neat chickens before. In a pen beside the chickens were turkeys. There were more turkeys than I could count. All picture-perfect. Farther down the road we passed pens filled with ducks and geese and a pen filled with assorted fowls. Everything was clean and neat as the White House lawn. There weren't any smells and very little noise and no waste.

Charles was getting more and more perplexed. He said nothing and added to his invisible list of things to find out about later. About three miles down road number 10 there was a large, beautiful, and immaculate complex. It was gleaming white and beautifully landscaped. The artificial sun made it sparkle like a diamond. A sign read, UNDERGROUND CITY'S ADVANCED SCIENTIFIC COMPLEX. A thought ran through his mind that maybe he was dreaming about all of this and none of it was real. He was still in Montana. He wished that he knew for sure.

As they entered the parking lot, Charles felt relieved. That super subcompact car had done a number on him. He wished that he could have driven his car but that was out of the question. Besides he came down here on the Mole train. They exited the car with great relief, did a body stretch, and walked down the picture-perfect path that led to the picture-perfect building complex. They entered the building. Inside the walls and all the furnishing was white. The floor was white marble with black veins in it. Everything looked as if no one had been there before.

SuejuSoe stopped and asked the receptionist where he could find Dr. Wannabelax. She came from behind the desk and escorted them to the third door down the hallway. She rapped lightly on the door. A voice inside said, "Enter." She left them and returned to her desk. Her heels made a rhythmic beat as she walked down the corridor.

SuejuSoe and Charles entered a small reception room. No one was there except them. He called out, "Is there anyone here?"

A voice from an adjoining room said, "Yes. Come in."

As they entered the room, they saw this child-looking person busy at a massive computer. SuejuSoe cleared his throat and asked, "Where can we find Dr. Wannabelax?"

Stopping what he was doing and standing up to his full five feet five frame, he turned and faced them speaking in the cracking voice of a boy-man and said, "Gentlemen, your search is over."

SuejuSoe's mouth was agape. Somehow he stammered, "I . . . I . . . we . . . Well I must be looking for your father."

SuejuSoe and Charles looked at each other and stood there with a blank look on their faces. Wannabelax asked, "Is there something wrong?" It was his time to laugh but he didn't. He said very politely, "Please don't be embarrassed, most people react to me that way. I'm afraid that you do have the right Dr. Wannabelax since my father is a colonel in the Underground City military. Now, how may I help you?"

SuejuSoe cleared his throat and said, "This is Charles DeNero, the man from another planet, Earth 111. We discussed it briefly on the phone."

"Yes, I've heard a rumor or two about this," Wannabelax said as he shook their hands. "How may I help you?"

Charles blurted out, "I want to know if you can help me get back home."

Even as he spoke, Charles was thinking, This is little more than a child. How can he help me? He had a feeling of dread and felt that he was losing his mind.

Dr. Wannabelax noticed the change in Charles face and asked with concern in his voice, "Is there something wrong that I can help you with besides getting you back home?"

Charles had to use restraint to keep from yelling, "How in hell can a kid like you help me? How did you ever get here in the first place?" but said nothing.

Dr. Wannabelax offered them seats and they sat down. He spoke in the same crackling voice of a boy-man. Noticing that I can't believe this expression on their faces, he began, "First, I don't want you to let my age fool you. It's true, I am very young, but I'm more than qualified to do what I'm doing.

"I finished high school at the age of nine. By the time I was fourteen I had two doctorate degrees and two masters degrees. Besides, I've been doing this most of my life, which I know is not a long time. Now, is there anything else that I can do to ease your misgivings, or would you prefer to see someone else?"

"Is there anyone else?"

"Sure there is." He picked up a phone and said, "Will you please come into my office?" Two men and one woman entered. He introduced them. "Gentlemen, these are Dr. Hal Dalbuctill, Dr. Sydney Torwell, and Dr. Kay Cleadermeeks."

They exchanged greetings and shook hands. Charles thought, Now this is more like it. These doctors, at least the two men looked like they were learned and respected. Heck, one of them had gray hair. The woman looked like she was in her thirties. She must have finished high school at the ripe old age of fourteen.

Dr. Wannabelax's teenage voice interrupted Charles's thoughts. He was saying, "Gentlemen, all of these doctors are qualified to help you. You are free to choose."

"But you are the one in charge, why would they want one of us?" Dr. Dalbuctill asked.

Dr. Kay Cleadermeeks added, "Yes, that's correct and he is over this entire Advanced Science Complex. He was the one who initiated this whole project. In other words, he is everybody's boss."

Charles thought, If I get another shock, I may have the big one. SuejuSoe said, "Add me to that list."

They stood there with a smile painted on their faces, looking like idiots. SuejuSoe broke out of his state of egg on my face mold and said, "Since my appointment was with Dr. Wannabelax, we will stick with him."

Wannabelax asked, "Are you sure?"

"Yes, sure," they said in unison.

"Well," Dr. Wannabelax began in his boy-man voice, "Mr. DeNero, will you please tell me what has already transpired?"

Charles began telling about how he was driving down a highway in Montana when out of the blue this strange sparkling fog came out of nowhere. He told him about what he believed to be a purple van with pulsating lights, and how these lights seemed to hypnotize him. The next thing that he knew, he woke up in the middle of nowhere, and that nowhere was completely purple. He was not really sure yet of whether or not this was real or he was simply having a nightmare, one that he couldn't wake up from.

"Did you experience any physical symptoms during the time you were in the fog?"

"Yes. There was static, a lot of static. I was perspiring and my heart was pounding."

"Did you have any problems with spots before your eyes?"

Charles tried to recall what had happened. Come to think of it, there were little tornadoes swirling around everywhere."

Dr. Wannabelax smiled, "That was going to be my next question. How many did you see?"

"I don't know. A lot of them. Too many to count."

"Would you say that there was more than twenty?"

"Definitely. There were hundreds."

"Hundreds," Dr. Wannabelax echoed with a puzzled look on his face. "Sure," said Charles.

"This is very interesting. I've never heard of hundreds before now . . . let me see." He pulled his chair up to this enormous computer and began pushing buttons. The screen lit up in an eerie green, then became white. Wannabelax typed in some numbers and watched. He typed in an equation; it appeared on the screen. He added more equations. He kept this up for twenty minutes or more. Charles and Suejusoe watched in fascination. They knew that they were educated intelligent people, but what they were seeing on the screen of that computer was alien to them as the hieroglyphics of the ancient Inca and Egyptians. It did not faze this twenty-one-year-old doctor. He sat at that computer for at least thirty minutes pushing buttons, entering equations and occasionally pursing his lips.

Abruptly he stopped and stood up like he just remembered that he had left the water running in the bath tub. He exclaimed, "Darn! How could I have missed that? He smiled as if he just remembered that he did turn water off. "Yes. That's it."

SuejuSoe and Charles looked at each other. They had nothing else to do besides watch Wannabelax and they sure didn't know what he was doing. Shortly, Wannabelax resumed his work at his computer. Again, silence permeated the room. The only sound came from the keyboard of the computer and graphs on the screen. About ten minutes later, Wannabelax looked up from the computer and spoke, "Uh-huh, I can't believe this. I've never seen this before."

They did their little unrehearsed eye contact game. "Did you say something?" SuejuSoe asked. "I'm sorry but I was talking to myself. I don't know how to put this so that you will understand it."

"Is this uh-huh something good or uh-huh something bad?" Sujusoe asked.

"I'll have to add something to it to make it good and I'll have to take something from it to make it bad. But now it is in the uh-huh stages," Wannabelax answered.

Charles sat on the sofa watching Suejusoe and Wannabelax having a discussion ways beyond SuejuSoe's understanding. Still he listened occasionally and nodded his head saying he understood.

On the sofa Charles began to perspire and feel faint. He loosened his tie and unbuttoned his collar button. He was feeling very distressed. That deja vu that had been following him around seemed to intensify. He was filled with perspiration. His tongue felt like it was too big for his mouth and has rendered him speechless. That feeling of dread raised its ugly head, and this time it had brought along a companion, panic. The panic was unmerciful. His heart pounded so hard until he thought that his chest would explode. He thought that he heard someone call his name. It sounded alien and very far away as if it was floating across the universe like distant thunder. He felt the thunder rattle his frame. He heard someone talking to him but he could not understand what they were saying. Thunder echoed off his shoulder. He heard his name called again. This time the thunder answered in a muffled voice, "Uh-huh." He sat there, his face a complete blank, staring straight ahead with eyes as blank as the mask that was his face. He seemed to be looking at something that he alone could see.

SuejuSoe looked at Dr. Wannabelax not knowing what else to do. He sniggled nervously and said to Wannabelax, "He's probably in shock, but who could blame him? Poor chap, he has been to hell and had to stay because he didn't know how to leave. Shit fire! If it was me I'd probably be in a state much worse than this."

Dr. Wannabelax was thinking that of all the knowledge that he processed he was dumbfounded about this. He didn't know what to say or do, so he didn't say anything and did nothing. He stood there looking dumbfounded.

The voice that Charles thought that he heard was someone talking to him, but he couldn't understand what they were saying. He felt thunder grabbing his shoulders again. This time he realized that it was not thunder but SuejuSoe shaking him by his shoulders calling, "Charles, Charles, hey, man, what's going on with you? Charles, answer me. Say something. Say anything."

That mean old-man panic was after SuejuSoe now, bumping and grinding on the fringes of his sanity and he fought diligently to maintain control.

Charles began to respond to SujuSoe's voice. It still sounded far away and alien. He turned to look at him. His face was still blank, but his eyes had begun to move. This time Wannabelax spoke. "Mr. DeNero, are you all right?"

Charles didn't say anything for a full minute, then he spoke, "Why are y'all looking at me like that?'

"You mean you don't know?"

"What is it that I'm supposed to know?"

"You freaked out on us. You were spaced."

"Really, what were you doing at this time?"

"Do you mean besides being scared to death? I was trying to resuscitate you."

"I don't know what caused me to do that and I'm glad that you guys brought me back. All I can say is thanks."

"I think that you should be checked out by a doctor. I mean a medical doctor," Wannabelax said.

"I was going to say the same thing," SuejuSoe said, "You went out like someone flipped a switch to the off position."

"You are looking at me like I have sprouted horns. But come to think of it I was feeling quite ill. I thought that I heard someone calling me but they was too far away for me to answer. Then, this weird feeling came over me. I felt like I couldn't catch my breath and I can't remember after that."

"Do you feel up to riding?"

"What do you mean?"

"I was thinking that we could leave."

"No way," Charles said adamantly. "We haven't found out anything about why we came down here for." He turned to Wannabelax, "Have you come up with anything to help me?"

Dr. Wannabelax said in his immature voice, "At the present time I have nothing but possibilities. It's going to take some time to work this out. Remember, you came and dropped this on me like a ton of bricks, but there is hope."

Charles said in a strange voice, "I see."

Wannabelax added, "As soon as I come up with something positive, at least more than I have already I will get in touch with you."

"Yes, sure, I know all about this. I've heard it before," Charles said in a voice heavy with defeat.

SujuSoe added, "We need to get you to a doctor and get you checked."

"Why waste my time and your money seeing a doctor? Anyone with the brain of a monkey knows why I am reacting this way."

"I know what you are saying, but it darned on me that maybe your symptoms could be the results of something that you encountered from your transition from your world to ours or maybe the results of the purple stuff that you had to contend with. Plus, do you suffer from allergies?"

"I agree with Mr. SuejuSoe. . . I forgot your name."

"My first name is SuejuSoe and Suju is my last name."

"I must say, that is an odd name. Is it family oriented?"

"As a matter of fact it is. My ancestors were Japanese and American Indian so I am told."

"I see," Wannabelax said. "As I was saying, I concur with Mr. Suju. It's better to be on the safe side.

"Okay. You have told me what was on your minds. Now, I will tell you once more. I feel fine. Now you can continue your pursuit in finding me a way to get back home."

Wannabelax spoke up, "You've already given me all the data that I needed to work with and I can do the rest without your presence."

"So you are telling me to get lost."

"Yes I am, but in the nicest way that I know how."

"Let's go," Charles said to SuejuSoe.

As they exited the door, Wannabelax called out, Don't forget to let a doctor check you out."

Charles murmured, "And fuck you too."

"Did you say something?" asked SuejuSoe. "Naw. Let's go."

Once outside they walked to the car in silence. SujuSoe was sore because he thought that Charles had insulted him. Charles was sore because he felt that he had been the scapegoat of some joke that he had no memory of. They rode in silence.

As SujuSoe drove, Charles looked out the window at the picture-perfect scenery along the way. The perfection of this world was driving him mad. He felt physically ill. Then he thought that once upon a time he imagined that this was the way heaven was going to be except everything would be white and gold. He silently prayed, Please, God, don't let this place be my personal hell. Please, God, deliver me from this madness. And, God, please give me the strength to maintain my sanity.

That small prayer seemed to comfort him a little but he was still stunned by the artificialness of this place. It would make him feel much, much better if he could see something out of place. A piece of trash, a loud noise, some smoke, someone sitting on the ground. The more he thought about it, the more nostalgia tugged at his consciousness. His heart ached severely, and he could feel scalding tears building up behind his eyes, threatening to spill down his cheeks. He fought hard to maintain control but was failing miserably. One tear cascaded down his cheek he wiped it away angrily, but to no avail. Another followed and another. He began to weep, and huge tears like raindrops ran down his cheeks, silently and abundantly.

SuejuSoe glanced at Charles and saw the sadness and defeat frame his face as the silent tears flowed down his face. He felt a wave of compassion for his newfound friend sweep over him. He cried also.

Both began to speak at the same time. "I'm sorry," they said in unison.

"You go first," SuejuSoe said to Charles.

Defiantly, Charles wiped his tears away with the back of his hand. "If you had any idea how I feel, you wouldn't make dumb insensitive remarks about my sanity."

"What dumb insensitive remarks are you referring to?"

"That stuff about me being spaced out."

"Charles," SuejuSoe said patiently, "I only told you what did happen. I neither added nor subtracted from it. If I offended you, I am sorry, and I apologize. If you can't accept my apology, that's a problem you'll have to deal with. I will help you any way that I can, but I'm not about to put up with any accusations of any kind from you. Now, do you understand what I'm talking about?"

Charles shrugged his shoulders and said, "I guess."

"I guess my ass. Either you do or you don't."

"Since you put it that way, yes. Yes."

"Do you still hold it against me for trying to save your wretched life?"

"Nossa, masser."

"Cut the crap. I can't imagine the emotional roller coaster that you are trying to contend with, but you already know that I have your survival and sanity at the top of my list of important things to do. I am not your enemy, so put it in a sock."

"I said that I was sorry. What more do you want, me to sign something in blood?"

The remainder of the trip was in silence. No one spoke a word. Each was fighting his own personal demons.

Charles closed his eyes and tried to blot out the unrealistic scenery. The acid taste of disgust bubbled up in his mouth. He had decided that if he wouldn't get back home, he could never live in a place like this; it would drive him insane in record time. The hope of getting back home was the only reason that he had not already gone mad. It had came to him what this place reminded him of was wax and plastic animation.

He asked, "Suju, does any of this stuff bother you?"

"What stuff?"

"You know, the quietness, the neatness, the perfection. How everything work on a time schedule. No surprises, no excitement, no nothing to make life challenging or enjoyable," Charles said with a profound sadness in his voice.

Suju thought for a minute before he spoke. Then he said, "I've never thought of this before. I suppose that it doesn't because this is all I've ever seen. I don't have anything to compare it with except the topside. People down here in the Graveyard at least most people think of the Chickpeo as rejected mutants. Needless to say, they have never been out of Underground City. They have heard wild tales and ugly rumors about the outside world but have never seen it."

When they first built this place, only the elite and those with advanced education were allowed to enter. Only a few average workers were admitted as servants and factory workers. What I'm trying to say is no."

"Do the three days you spend on the outside of the Graveyard have any effect on you? Because it is more normal even with the Chickpeos and purple stuff."

"My excursion to the Purple Bottom City are refreshing, and what the people down here don't understand is that the Chickpeos are not dumb, stupid, ignorant, or low-class. They are afraid to go to the topside because of the mutations. Sure, they would revert to their normal self once they returned to their world. But some were desperate enough to overlook this and stay topside and completely mutate because they felt the same way that you do about the Underground City. They live productive lives and don't have any regrets."

"When the Graveyard was first built, how did they go about selecting who could live there and who couldn't?"

"You do ask some tough questions. I can only answer that by relating to what have been told down through the ages. I cannot swear to any of this being actually factual. But I'll give you my best shot."

"The nova was approaching so fast that there was not enough time to evacuate or time enough time to test everyone so they chose by admitting just about all rich people because they could but their way in. They choose the top scientist, mathematicians, medical personnel, teachers that had a masters degree or higher. They chose people in highly skilled professions and people who were specially trained in building, waste, and water management. Others got in through other means. I can't say, but these people was chosen worldwide from all nations. They were serious when it came to recycling and maintenance because in the Underground City everything is recyclable. It is against the law to spit on the streets. Any trash anywhere outside is forbidden. A fine plus a mandatory jail sentence is automatic. There is no plea bargaining, parole, no nothing but pure jail time.

"I'm not bragging but the crime rate is less than 3 percent. In a city of two and one half million people, that is not just excellent; it is superb.

"I know that you think that we have gone a bit too far, but it was and is still necessary. For a very long time Purple Bottom City was still Earth 1V. Things were almost identical to your Earth 111, but after the nova it was uninhabitable. We had to use all of our resources, and to be able to do this we recycled everything.

"It worked so well and we kept improving it until it was down to an art. Underground City is completely self-sufficient.

"Illness is almost nonexistent. Many illnesses that are prevalent on the topside do not exist in our environment. When the refugees from Earth 1V first settled in Underground City, they were scared to breathe the air. When Underground City was in the experimental stages many people became ill and many died because the air was being improperly filtered. Instead of purifying the air the disease carrying germs were multiplying as the unsterile air was being recirculated. The air became so saturated with diseases 35 percent of the inhabitants died.

"Now the air is 98 percent pure, free of all disease-carrying germs and viruses. Then those who were left thought that 2 percent would get them.

"I know that the day that we went to the Science Institute made you feel like you had lost your sense of reality because it was spotless and unnaturally pristine. What you didn't know was that beneath the ground, under the fertile farms, were filters to recycle everything that hit the ground and to purify the air."

"You don't say," Charles said unbelievingly.

"I do say and there is more."

"These machines keep germs and diseases out of our world. Do you know that out of a population of more than two and one half million people we have only three six-hundred-bed hospitals. It is believed that the Chickpeos brought in these germs by commuting back and forth."

"If they believe this, why do they let them commute?"

"Don't ask me."

"Who else can I ask?" Charles inquired.

"Did anyone ever tell you that you are one nosey son-of-a-bitch?"

Charles answered in his most refined voice, "I am not nosey. How would you react if you just popped from your world to another world in another dimension, so I am told. A world that is stranger than anything that I could ever imagine."

"Hang it on a tree, man."

"You know, for an alien, you are okay," said Charles.

"Say what? I am not the alien, remember? You are."

Charles proclaimed. "Yes, and that make me feel so happy."

This conversation ended when SuejuSoe and his beloved putter-scooter pulled up in the parking lot of a tall building called the Beck Tower. They entered and took the elevator to the fifth floor. There was a strict building code that a building could not have more than six floors because of the bubble that enclosed Underground City.

They entered room 1509. On the door a gold plaque read, M.P.C. Ltd., Marketing, Planning Consultants. He entered the room still thinking about how the Graveyard people thought the Chickpeos was dumb. All the things that he had seen proved that these people have worked wonders and created miracles. To think of them as dumb was a grave mistake of monstrous proportion. Only if they could see how they took this decimated world and brought it back to life. A life prosperous and almost as normal as his own world. When he compared both worlds he decided he would choose Purple Bottom City over the Underground City any day. PBC, as real even with the purple everywhere and the people looking like chickens, playing. Now that he remembered, he had not seen one child in the Graveyard. He had to ask SuejuSoe where the children were. He would add this to his invisible list of things to find out later.

They entered the room and most everyone was sipping coffee that had been laced with brandy. He was thinking that they could skip the coffee and give him straight brandy. He really needed it. He deserved it. He had been patient long enough. He needed a double brandy. If he didn't get back home soon, he was going to become an alcoholic. K'Narf saw that desperate look on Charles's face and, while reading his mind, poured him a double brandy. "Here, take this you look like you can use it."

"Thank you. You must be a mind reader." Charles swallowed it in three gulps and gave the cup back to K'Narf. This time he filled it with coffee and laced it with brandy. He spoke, "So, how have you been faring in our alien world?"

"Okay, I guess. You know as weird as this purple world is, it is more real than that perfect world in the Graveyard. If I can't get back to my world I'm not going to live in the Graveyard. I repeat, I'm not going to live down there in that plastic place and eat cardboard food. I'll go mad in one week and I'm stretching that."

"I'll tell you something, I'm going to show you the other side of Purple Bottom City. Just tell me when you want to go."

"The way that you are asking me that maybe I shouldn't go. Nothing personal," Charles said.

"Are you a yellow belly scaredy-cat?" K'Narf teased.

Charles began to laugh and this caught K'Narf off guard. He didn't know what to do or say. SuejuSoe eased the tension somewhat, asking, "Mr. Charlie, what's so funny? I want to laugh too."

"Just a private joke, that's all."

As they sipped their laced coffee K'Narf gave an update account on their political progress.

"First, I'm going to tell you a funny joke because it is written somewhere that is the way a boring meeting should be opened. Here's a funny joke."

"Skip the joke, K'Narf, I want to go home and make love to my wife," Bojo said. "You don't have a wife."

"Well, I'm going to look for one."

"Wishful thinking never gave anyone a thrill."

"Yes, but there's a first time for everything."

"That's true. So get clicking."

"If you insist. Our last meeting was cancelled because of our newfound alien friend, who I see, is in our presence tonight. Hello, Mr. DeNero." Charles nodded and K'Narf continued, "We still haven't settled on a candidate. .Donations have been coming in and our coffer is growing. Our indecision is going to cost us votes if we don't do something soon. The lieutenant governor and the mayor are supposed to meet with us Tuesday. We are going to find what is causing the turmoil over in the Wasgreen community. They have reported several bodies out by Zone 30J. It looked like they had been victims of some type of religious ritual. There is an under cult of supposedly coven growing in numbers and it is reportedly a strong believer in the occult. The Rumbling Guts are mixed up in it some way. They reportedly are going to get someone to run for governor on an independent ticket. It is supposedly so that the spirits would send them someone who is guaranteed to win," K'Narf finished.

"Well, I'll be. What is going to happen next?" Bojo said. "Calling in the occult means that they really do mean business. But I don't think that some spooks need to be feared."

"As I was saying, we really need to agree on a candidate. The people in the Graveyard are not wasting time worrying about who is the best person to run this side of the world. They think that we are too simpleminded to drive a pig down the road with a steering wheel in its butt. So we must prove to them that three plus three doesn't equal five. All they need is somebody that they can control. A yes man."

"Just how are we going to show them that the answer to three plus three does not equal five?" Bojo asked, throwing up his hands.

"Hey now, don't let this get out of hand. It seems like everybody want to rule the world. But we know that this is impossible. Our problem stems from our lack of organization. We must get organized before we can ever attempt to make headway. So let's get this done tonight. So we all agree?"

Yeses were in unison.

K'Narf began speaking in his universal language. Ocena always said this because most of the time no one knew what he was talking about. "First, we need a chairperson, a treasurer, a secretary, and of course a candidate that is committed. You know, someone that have the betterment of this world first place on his list of important things to do. Not someone who will use this as a stepping stone to higher and better places. I nominate Wester'C Ulcer."

Someone seconded the motion.

"Just hold it a minute," Wester'C interrupted. "I can't run because of my already many obligations. Plus, there is my practice to think of. I didn't go to medical school all those years to throw my passion away and take up politics."

"Okay, then who do you suggest that we should nominate?" asked K'Narf.

"How about Mr. Suju?" Wester'C suggested.

"Not me," Suju interrupted. "I have obligations too."

K'Narf rubbed the back of his neck and said, "I can see why we can't make any progress. But I do know someone who is both qualified and is willing to run. Matter of fact, they are here, Bill Elbow, better known as Bojo, and Miss Carrie Blister."

"This is great. I don't know how I forgot about them. They are indeed perfect. The only thing we have to decide on now is which one are we going to choose," said Wester'C.

"Let's do this thing scientifically," said SuejuSoe as he searched his pant pocket for a coin. He pulled out a quarter and said, "Heads it's

Bill and tails, it's Carrie." He tossed the coin into the air, caught it and announced, Carrie Blister."

"This is all wrong," said Jelly Belly. "There are two openings and we need two candidates. I don't see why we can't get one of them to run for president and the other one for governor."

Everyone looked around the room as though it just occurred to them that Carrie was not present. A gross oversight has been in the making because she should have been here. SuejuSoe asked, "Did anyone bother to notify Carrie of this meeting?"

No one answered. "See what I mean? We have to get organized. I see that there are several key people missing that should be here. Didn't anyone notify them?"

No one answered. K'Narf said, "We can't relive the past so let's begin again. Let's finish getting our officers in place. We need a chairman, a secretary and everything else. This way everyone would know when and where we are going to meet. We need a treasurer and a PR person. Are there any volunteers for any of these positions?"

"Jelly Belly, you could be our PR person since you are already a media biggie," K'Narf suggested. "I can be of use as a treasurer if it's okay with you guys."

"Okay with me," SuejuSoe voiced. The rest agreed with him.

"Now we are getting somewhere. I nominate SuejuSoe as chairperson."

"I've already told you that I have too many obligations already. I nominate Wester'C Ulcer."

"Sure, I'll be chairperson," Wester'C said to a stunned committee.

K'Narf wiped his face with the back of his hand and said, "I never thought that I would live to see this day. This is a surprise, but a welcome surprise. Is there anyone who object to Wester'C being chairperson? I didn't think so. We need a secretary. Who will be our secretary? Will someone please volunteer to be secretary."

"What about Ocena?" Bojo blurted out.

Ocena spoke up, pissed off. "Every time a position of secretary comes up you name a female. Why does this happen? Because men are nincompoops. I may have served but I won't just because you people are sexist. So go get someone else."

"I guess that y'all heard that. She really told you off," said K'Narf. "Y'all!" someone blurted out.

"Yes. Y'all," Ocena confirmed as she got up and left the room.

"I think that the lady had spoken. But we still need a secretary. I need some nominations." Pissy Dean had been sitting in a huge leather chair doing nothing and saying nothing finally he spoke up, "What about Mamie?"

"Personally," Mamie said, "I feel the same way Ocena does. Whenever the word *secretary* come up you equate it with a female. I should tell y'all where to go and what to do when you got there. But I won't. I'm too dignified to do that. So for the sake of the future of our world, I will, but I'll have to make some adjustments to my work schedule. But I think that I can do that since it is only for ten months."

"Okay, we have a secretary, a treasurer, a PR person, and an uncommitted candidate, plus a committee chairperson, and we got all this done in one night's work."

Everyone was comfortable with the selections and the meeting was adjourned until Tuesday, when they would meet with the Lieutenant governor and the mayor.

SuejuSoe and Charles stayed behind and tidied up after everyone had gone. He informed Charles that he had to spend the next two days in the Graveyard and he wanted to know if he would go with him or stay in PBC. He decided to be reckless and go to the Graveyard with him.

They had to hurry because the next Mole train, the name that the Chickpeos called the train that ran between the Graveyard and Purple Bottom City, came along in the next twenty minutes. If they had missed this one they would have to wait another hour before the next train came along. Before the Mole train arrived they both realized that coffee and brandy did not take the place of food, and they were hungry.

Charles announced, "My appetite is ravenous. I could eat creation off the cross."

"I'm going to challenge those very words in a short while. But I will warn you, the food in the Graveyard is different than the food in Purple Bottom City."

"Different, how?" asked Charles.

"I don't know how to describe it for you to understand. All I can say is, it's different. Do you remember how the countryside looked, picture-perfect, artificial."

"Yes."

"The food here looks and tastes the way it looks. The Chickpeos wouldn't touch this stuff with a bulldozer scoop."

"That bad, huh?"

"After you've tasted the food, I wouldn't feel bad if you spent the next two days in Purple Bottom City."

"I think that I'll stick around to see what happens."

"Great! Be my guest. What's mine is yours as long as you need it. Let's go eat."

They pulled up to a fancy-looking restaurant and got out. A valet took the car, and they were ushered into a restaurant that looked like it belonged in heaven. Charles nudged SuejuSoe, "Are you sure we can afford to eat here?"

"Cool it, man. It's not as expensive as it looks."

"That's a good thing, I think," said Charles. Then, that uneasy feeling bombarded him again making him feel like he was losing his mind or perhaps he had already lost it. Damn! he thought, this is weird. He fought hard trying to suppress this unnatural emotion. SuejuSoe sensed that something was wrong.

He asked, "Is there something wrong?"

Charles lied. "No. Everything is cool."

A hostess floated toward them like a specter and ushered them to their table. They were given a menu and asked did they want anything from the bar. They choose a gin and tonic cocktail. Charles was amazed at everything he saw. "Wow. I couldn't afford a salad in a place like this back home."

He lied.

Shortly, a perfectly groomed waitress returned with perfect drinks on a perfect tray. He was thinking that he was topside with the Purple Bottom City Chickpeos. SuejuSoe was trying hard to make small talk as they waited for their dinners to arrive. Charles was listening halfheartedly. He was busy trying to maintain his sanity.

When the perfect-looking food was served by the perfect-looking waitress, his mind was still trying to make two plus two equal five. He couldn't continue to think about that at this time; he would have to think about that later. He saw SuejuSoe swallow a pill of some sort. This puzzled him somewhat because he offered him one also. He declined. SuejuSoe said, "Okay, don't forget, I warned you."

"Warned me about what?" Charles asked, puzzled. When he took a sip of his drink he almost retched. "What! What's in this drink?" A smile toyed at Suejusoe's lips. "What's so amusing?" Again Suejusoe offered Charles a pill. "Naw, I don't want a pill. I'm going to call that waitress back and order me another drink."

"It won't do any good," Suejusoe said.

"My drink tastes like skunk piss. How does yours taste?"

"Fine," Suejusoe answered.

"Let me taste yours," Charles requested. He took a sip of Suejusoe's drink an had the same reaction."Damn. Man, what is wrong with your taste?" This stuff tastes like skunk piss too." Charles was enraged.

He decided to eat his dinner. He spit it out instantly. He looked at Suejusoe and asked, "How in hell can you eat this stuff? It tastes like cardboard."

"It tastes okay to me."

"Something must be wrong with you."

He smelled his food and it didn't have any aroma. It looked so delicious. Suejusoe took another bite and ate it. Charles was wondering how he could eat this crap. Suejusoe laughed hard. Charles was getting super pissed.

"What do you see that's so funny?"

It began to sink in what he was laughing about, that pill. "Okay, what part did I miss?"

"All of it. I mean the whole thing," Suejusoe answered.

"All right, I'll bite, what was the pill for?"

"I forgot to tell you, no I did tell you the food down here was different than the food in Purple Bottom City. Didn't I?"

"Well yes, I suppose you did. Again I'll ask you what was the pill for?"

"Flavor. That pill makes the food taste like it looks. Can you imagine what a steak that comes from cows that are fed on cardboard fortified with artificial vitamins mixed with toasted weeds and recycled human waste would taste like? Without waiting for an answer, he continued, "No. You can't either. But you have experienced something that you don't want to repeat. All the inhabitants of UGC haven't ever tasted any other food to compare their food with. This is all they know. Only those who have ventured to Purple Bottom City have experienced other flavors so that they know what real food tastes like.

"It got to be so bad until they had to come up with something so that the people could eat the stuff. Go ahead and try one and see what the different is like."

Charles was past being skeptical now that he had tasted the cardboard food. It was something he did not want to do. Being the adventurist that he was, he tried it. The pill did make the food taste much better, but he no longer had an appetite. Cardboard food was not one of the things that he craved. He asked Suejusoe to order some fruit and he'll wait until tomorrow when he would be in Purple Bottom City and get something to eat." Suejusoe asked, "Are you sure?"

"Sure, I'm sure."

"No wait," Charles answered. "What's wrong with the fruit?"

"One word, waxed."

"Damn!" Charles almost screamed, "Wax? Please don't say that word again. Is there anything down here that's real? No wonder no one down here gets sick. Flavored, sterilized styrofoam is the perfect food for the perfect people who inhabit this perfect place. I'll be damned again. I've got to get out of this place pronto."

That strange unreal feeling came over him again. Why is this happening? He was perplexed. Maybe it was because he was not of this world. He knew that at least he had been told that this place was an exact copy of the Earth that he came from it was just not purple. He knew that he didn't want this feeling to return. He made another entrance on his invisible list of things to ask about later. He was going to ask Dr. Wannabelax.

His appetite was gone so he could skip dinner. Tonight he was going to get pissy drunk. So drunk that he would forget about food and so drunk that he wouldn't care what he was eating.

When they arrived at Suejusoe's apartment once again this metamorphosis took place. As he pushed buttons, flipped switches ad turned knobs the apartment was transformed to a state-of-the-art residence. Suejusoe asked Charles, "Do you still want a drink?"

"Uh-huh," Charles answered, "I need many drinks. I deserve them after all I've been through. I've never drunk this much in my entire life. If I don't get home soon I'm going to be a serious alcoholic."

"I didn't want to be the one to tell you what I told you before, I told you so."

"Then why are you doing it?"

"Aw, man, have a drink on me."

"Only if you insist."

"I insist."

Suejusoe gave Charles a drink. He sipped it and remarked, "Not bad. Where did you get this? Surely not from here."

"Can't you see what color it is. I managed to smuggle some from Purple Bottom City without getting caught."

"What do you mean, without getting caught?

"It's illegal to bring things like liquor and food stuff and mostly any household products down here."

"Why?" Because it could upset the way the recycling process takes place."

That strange, unreal real feeling came over him again. "Why I this happening to me?" He was perplexed. "Maybe because he was from a different world. He knew at least he had been told that this place was an exact copy of the Earth that he came from, but he really didn't really know this. All he knew was he didn't want that feeling to return. He made another entrance on his invisible list of things to find about later. He would ask Dr. Wannabelax."

His appetite was gone, so he could skip dinner. To night he was going to get pissy drunk that he would forget about food and eating. Damn, damn, damn, what a crock of shit. This Graveyard is a real Graveyard. Where things that look alive but is actually dead."

When they arrived at Suejusoe's apartment once again this metamorphosis took place. As he pushed buttons, flipped switches and turned knobs the apartment once again was transformed to a state of arts residence. Sujusoe asked, "Charles do you still want a drink?"

"Uh-huh," he answered, "I need many drinks. I deserve them after what I've been through."

"I didn't want to be the one to tell you I told you so.

"Then why did you do it?"

"Aw, man, have a drink on me.' "Only if you insist."

Suejusoe gave Charles a drink. He sipped it and remarked, "Not bad, where did you get this?

Surely not from here."

"Can't you see what color it is. I managed to smuggle some from PBC without getting caught"

"What do you mean not getting caught?"

"It's illegal to bring things like liquor, food stuff and mostly any household products from down here."

"Why?"

"Because it could upset the way things are ran down here. The way they recycle things. They know approximately how much waste should be processed everyday and when it's more than they have calculated somebody is going to pay. I know that you think that we've gone too far but it was and is necessary. As I said, Underground City is totally self-sufficient. By the way, I certainly must show you our man-made Oceans and lake. They have been stocked with every fish of every kind even sharks an whales. I know what you are thinking, it is picture-perfect all the way down to the sail boats and on the horizon. The way I understand it is they tapped into the ocean on the top side, Purple Bottom City, and channeled the water flow, fish and all to our underground seas that is five hundred to eight hundred square miles."

"Do tell." Charles said as he poured another drink.

"It's true," Suejusoe continued, "When Underground City was built, it was to be permanent and self-sufficient. No one ever thought that anyone on Earth 1V would survive the nova and if anyone did survive they would not have the tools or the intelligence to rebuild."

"You don't say," murmured. Charles Perplexed by Charles attitude, Suejusoe asked, "Do you want to hear this or not?" Again Charles answered, "No fooling."

Suejusoe realized that Charles was not listening to anything that he was saying. He said, "By the way the stuff you ate for dinner was snake and frog guts."

"I suspected that."

Still perplexed, Sujusoe said, I know that I'm not the world's greatest conversationist but I'm nowhere near the bottom either. If you want me to shut my mouth I will do just that. Thank you very much."

Charles had no reaction to Suejusoe's outburst. Suejusoe poured himself another drink and began to sing. He always sang when he was pissed. "Mama, Mama, Mama there's far too many of you to cry. Brother, brother, brother, there's far too many of you to die. We've got to find away to bring some loving here today, what going on?"

"You missed father, father, father, we don't need to escalate. Picket signs, picket lines, don't punish me with brutality. Come on and talk to me so. you can see, what going on?"

Suejusoe said, "You don't say. When did you rejoin the present time and age? Now let me hear you sing it if I'm doing so bad."

Charles chuckled and said, "I can't carry a tune in a wheelbarrow I know the lyrics to this one song but I seriously main almost all the others. There's this one song I've been trying to learn the words to but for a long time. So far I still don't know them, so I make some up."

"What's song is that?"

"It's not just one song, it's all of them. My favorite song is, I Know an Old Lady Who Swallowed a fly But I Don't Know Why, She Swallowed the Fly Perhaps, She'll Die. Then she swallowed a spider a rat, you know she kept swallowing stuff. Before I die I have promised myself to learn the words to that song."

Suejusoe looked at Charles like he had sprouted horns. "This is unbelievable. Man why would anyone want to learn a song like that?"

"What do you mean a song like that. I like it very much."

"To each his own finally make some sense." Suejusoe mumbled. "Did you say something."

"No not really. I was just rearranging the clutter in my mind. No biggie." Charles exclaimed, "I don't want to talk about a funky old song anyway.

Suejusoe began by saying, "I can only tell you what our history books and folk lore says."

"You've got my undivided attention, so shoot."

"My mama always told me to begin at the beginning." Charles stated.

"Okay," began Suejusoe, "Our world used to be a seemingly ideal place to live in, that is if you was the right color. Only three things blotted our world, we became too civilized. We were where Earth 111 is right now. We had an abundance of food in one land and in another land there was next to nothing. People threw out more food in a day than other people got in one week. We had democracy in some lands and monarchy in other and just plain hockey in others. Things began to really deteriorate when became too civilized. All of this happened so subtlety most people was unaware that it was happening.

Our world was made up of many diverse races. Little by little everyone was at war and our personal freedom was taken from all of us in the name of progress and freedom, all in the name of democracy. Let me tell you how this happened. First they created a world of impoverished people. Anyone who was not of the white race was considered an underclass. But of course no one would come out and say this. It was just the way things were. They never had much freedom to start with anyway and it took extraordinary means for these people to become citizens and overcome their oppressions and their oppressors. They were locked up in prisons, many were sent to foreign lands to fight for the very freedom that had eluded them in their homeland. Can you imagine someone risking their lives for people who despised them. But they didn't have a chance to refuse and if they did they faced prison and death. Ever since the great war, before people of color had rights, they were undermined. In the first place these rights were on paper and were not enforced down through the ages. The undermining was the welfare system and government handouts. It took away people's desire to become independent. It crippled more people than all the others combined. It took away people's pride, self-respect, self-esteem, self-worth and left them living in a gray zone. A zone where every step that you took forward you'd take two steps backward. Some tried to break out of this, but it was like being in a maze and not being able to find the way out."

Suejusoe said jubilantly, "Just let me point out that there is no welfare in the Graveyard, there are no handouts." Out of desperation, hopelessness, and plain hatred, many turned to a life of crime. Then they were labeled sorry, lazy, dumb, and gullible. This kept the prisons jumping. This kept the man in power. This gave people who were supposedly to be against crimes and violence lucrative jobs at the expense of other people lives. They would set up worthless and ineffective committees with grand-sounding name and all the good that they did was sounded good on someone resume.

Before the cataclysm happen all of the things that we had taking for granted drastically changed.

They would build more and more prisons only to be filled to capacity. The politicians would brag about how they were putting all the criminals in jails to make our streets safer and our cities safer for the citizens.

The ages of the major criminals were getting younger and younger. Death row were filled to capacity. Some criminals were on death row for fifteen years. The law-abiding citizens, the taxpaying citizens already laden with taxes are taxed more because they would take some sorry, no-good bum and give them a life that was better than the ones whose taxes are supporting the criminals.

Yes, the criminals were living better than the taxpayers.

"This type of thing is happening on Earth 111 as we speak," Charles added. "We are so civilized until the criminals have more rights than their victims. If you shoot someone after they have raped your wife and daughter and robbed your home, you are at fault if you shoot the son-of-a-bitch."

"Bull manure!" exclaimed Suejusoe. "It get even worst. If this criminal should fall on your premises, he can sue you."

"This remind me of something that happened about ten months ago. This guy was in the process of robbing a bank when he turned too quickly and lost his balance and broke his shoulder. He was able to sue the bank for negligence. What a pail full of manure," he said, shaking his head in disgust.

"Hold on," Suejusoe added, "it gets even dumber. We were too civilized to kill someone who for no apparent reason got a gun and started shooting at everyone they saw. It is because society had deprived him of the necessary means for him to learn to live in civilized society. Yet I can run a stop sign and get a hefty fine plus jail time."

"I know what you mean. The way I see it is the lawbreakers have more rights than the lawmakers or should I say the law abiding citizens. But in my wildest imagination I never knew that this had happen someplace else," Charles said.

"I think this civilization thing has gone too far. But you'll never see our lawmakers do anything to correct these matters 'cause it would put them out of a lucrative job and clip their reign of power," Suejusoe said, despondence in his voice. Then he added, "We need to make the punishment fit the crime. It had to be harsh, humiliating, public for all to see. They should be made to feel the pain and fear and helplessness that their victims felt. How would they react if they knew that if they would commit a crime they would face dismemberment of a leg and an arm or even castration? And all of this would be done in public without the benefit of anesthesia. How would they would react if they were in prison with two meals a day and soup would be one of those meals. How would they react if, while in prison, the only TV program that they could watch was in black and white and documents about the weather, the Bible, and the early lives of the ancient people of the Earth, and they would have to watch it standing up?"

"I'll bet my last dime that most people will think that we are insane to even think of something like this."

"I don't want your last dime, you cheapskate, but your last hundred dollars and I'll bite. No penny ante for me," Charles said jokingly as Suejusoe came back to his narrative. "People elevate the rights of animals above those of humans or Chickpeomen."

"At least until crime slaps them in the face with all of it ugliness and crudeness, the people who make the laws will go on playing God with the lives and welfare of the human and Chickpeo races."

Then they will cry for more policemen and more jails. Not one of them will stop and think or realize that this is not going to work they don't seem to understand that this is not the answer. With all the prisons we already have crime continue to escalate. Enough of this already, I see we have wandered off course," Suejusoe said with a tiredness in his voice. Charles realized it was not tiredness but the sound of resignation. Then he spoke up trying to uplift his spirits.

"Well, the meeting that you took me to sounded promising. I'm glad that someone sees the truth, as ugly as it is. If you all should get your candidate in office, it seem like a good start in the right direction. Even all your opponents have had some good-sounding words. I don't know if there is any substance to them. Anyway, when I get back home I'm going to try to implement some of these ideas even if I did stumble upon them with my unscheduled and unsolicited visit."

Suejusoe looked at his watch and announced, "It's almost three thirty. I think we should call it a night. A substitute for sleep has not been invented."

"Yes, I'm either tired or drunk, both feel the same to me. If you will just stretch out this accordion of yours, it's taps for me."

*****

Jelly Belly, aka, Jon Dexter Dimple, had been attending a meeting with the Conference Media Association. CMA had recessed one hour for lunch. He had skipped lunch to meet with Baxter Pinkie, a media biggie from Forest Garden Enterprise. He had hinted at a possible position for him, and it sounded like something that he should give his utmost consideration.

Nature was calling and he had to answer. He entered the men's room and couldn't believe what his eyes had exposed his mind to. He was not seeing this. He closed his eyes and opened them again, and it was still there.

There were three guys who were so into what they were doing that they were unaware of his presence. What was he supposed to do? He did not know. Because he was not sure that he was seeing this. He closed his eyes again and rubbed them with the back of his hands, then opened them again seeing that his purported mirage was still viewable. He attributed it to the fact that he had not been sleeping well and he was in fact hallucinating. Yes, that was it. He closed the door and entered the men's again. He stopped and took a good look to prove to himself that what he was seeing was real and not the by-product of last night's party.

No such luck. There were three guys so into what they were doing that they were totally unaware of his presence. Looking closely, he did not recognize two of the participants, but the third guy was none other than our illustrious senator, Roy Cavity.

This was one sight that you would have to see to believe. Then you would still have doubts. Senator Cavity had his penis in guy number two's anus banging away. Guy number two was sucking on guy number three's penis. All of them has their pants down to their knees. What a sight! I had seen something similar to this in an X-rated movie, but I never thought that anyone did this stuff in real life. I cleared my throat and snapped a photo. Nothing happened. I snapped another picture and cleared my throat again. Still no one acknowledged my presence. They could not move because they were experiencing an orgasm like one I had never seen. Roy had a look on his face that was a cross between pain, pleasure, and torture. I snapped another picture.

Slowly they seemed to realize someone else other than them had witnessed it all. You should have seen how quickly they pulled up their pants. To me it should have gotten in the book of world records. I was preparing to make a speedy exit myself because I thought that I was going to be history. They looked at me in astonishment with a splash of guilt painted on their faces, as if they were wondering what I was doing there. Two of the guys made a hasty exit, and our senator shrugged his shoulders, turned, and slowly walked out of the door. But before he left he made his fist into an imaginary gun, pointed it at me and said, "Bang! Bang! If you relish your life you will give me that camera."

That was when I forgot that I had to pee. I left with the speed of an Olympic sprinter. I couldn't wait to tell someone, but not just anyone, about what I had walked into. Another plus was I had it on film. This was a media event. I did a victory dance and took off.

Wester'C was the first person that I could think of to call. I was feeling too jubilant and needed to share my discovery with someone. I really wished that I could go to the station and put it on the airwaves, telling everyone, but I knew that would not be too cool. I had to use restraint. I did. I went over to Wester'C office barging in without notice.

Wester'C receptionist looked up as he entered the office. She gave him a warm smile. He smiled back. She knew who he was because he was a very popular DJ, plus he and her boss were friends and spent a lot of time together. In her sweet little girl's voice she asked, "Is there something that I can do for you?"

He answered, "Is the doctor in?"

"I'll check and see." She buzzed Wester'C office.

"Yes, Miss Ella."

"Doctor Wester'C, Mr. Jelly, er, I mean there is a Mr. Jon Dimple here to see you."

"Okay, send him in, I have a few minutes to spare."

She nodded to Jon, "You can go in."

He got up and entered Wester'C office. "So what have pumped up your adrenaline to the critical stage? It must be humongous."

"If you only knew. Man, if only you knew."

"If you don't tell me, how am I going to find out?"

"Okay, but you better sit down first."

Wester'C said, "If you hadn't noticed, I am sitting down. Now, if you don't want to end up in an emergency room, I suggest that you tell me what has you so fired up."

"Well open your gizzard and digest this. I was attending this media workshop at the Scenna Towers Hotel and had to go to the john. When I walked in I couldn't believe my eyes. Right before my eyes there were three guys getting it on. One of them was our own hypocritical senator, Roy Cavity. They all had their pants down to their knees just banging and sucking away. It took a full minute for them to realize that I was there. Man, I'm telling you, I've never seen or heard of an orgasm of such intensity."

Wester'C was shocked, "I know that I did not hear you right, so tell me again."

"There is no need to," said Jelly Belly. "You heard me right the first time."

"Do tell. Have you been smoking those funny cigarettes?"

"Believe it, Wes. I have pictures to back up what I'm telling you."

"Did you say that you have this on film?"

"Yep! Sure do," said Jelly Belly. "Right neeto," patting his jacket pocket.

"Well what are you waiting for? Get your butt home and develop those pictures. I'll be there in about an hour."

"Hot diggity dog, yes. God has smiled on us today."

After Jelly Belly had gone, for a minute Wester'C sat trying to make some sense of what had just been told him. He smiled to himself knowing that this was going to cause a scandal of monstrous proportions. He would call Pissy Dean, K'Narf, and Bojo and ask them to meet them at Jelly Belly's place. He told his secretary to get in contact with Arthur Moses, Bill Earlobe, Carrie Blister, and Ocena Heartburns and relay the same message.

When everyone got to Jelly Belly's place comfort was something to be desired. It was not that his place was too small because it was large for one person's occupancy. It was congested because he had wall-to-wall and floor-to-ceiling shelves filled with hundreds of CDs and audio tapes, videotapes, cameras, audio- and video-recording equipment, and at least six stereos. He had a huge sixty-inch triple-screen TV, a computer, and equipment that took up another fourth of the room and a coffee table made out of conch shells and bits of coral reef.

In the right corner upon entering the door there was a custom-made aquarium four feet wide and six feet high filled with a variety of tropical fish. Standing beside the aquarium was a yo-yo lamp and a huge ceramic cobra standing upright in a striking position. There was a genuine purple bearskin rug laying in front of a huge fireplace. Scattered upon this rug were more CDs and tapes.

Jelly cautioned everyone to beware of the equipment because some of it were pretty sensitive and expensive. He offered beer and coffee to everyone who wanted any. Some sat on his very masculine comfortable sofa and chairs and some remained standing, checking out Jelly's tools of trade as they speculated about what was to come.

Wester'C asked Jelly Belly to tell them what had transpired. He began his narrative, "I went in to the men's room at the Scenna Towers Hotel and found—excuse my language, ladies, but I know of any other way to put this—Roy Cavity had his you know what in another's man's you know what and that man was sucking on another man's you know what, and I've got pictures to prove it."

"I don't believe this," K'Narf said.

"Me neither," said Carrie.

"Enough already," Wester'C exclaimed, "show us the pictures."

Jelly Belly went into the bathroom, a room that also served as his dark room and was as congested as his living room. He took the pictures down off a line he had them drying on and took them outside. He gave them to Wester'C who took the pictures and examined them closely. He shook his head in disbelief and disgust. He said flatly, "I just don't believe this. I see it and I still can't believe it."

"Hey, hand them over," said Moses, "Let me take a look-see."

Moses looked at the pictures and whistled softly, "Sweet mother of Jesus."

Reaching for the pictures, K'Narf said, "They can't be that bad."

The pictures were passed around to everyone present. Shock, disbelief, dismay, and many other nouns were used to describe the photos.

K'Narf had poured himself a cup of coffee, took a sip, and exclaimed, "Bojo, what in the world did you put in this coffee? It tastes like wood."

"What are you talking about? That's plain old gourmet coffee. I guess your taste buds are not as refined as you thought."

"My taste buds? This coffee tastes like it was made from wood chips."

Jelly Belly called out, "Hey, has anyone tasted this coffee?" No one answered. "See, what did I tell you, no one wanted any of this steeped wood chips brew."

"Man, how can you complain about coffee at a time like this? I'm going to prove that you are wrong so that you can shut your flap. Carrie, come taste this coffee."

She came and he poured her a cup of coffee and gave it to her. He said, "Here, taste this."

"Why, what's wrong with it?"

"Please just taste it. Jelly Belly said it didn't taste good."

Carrie took the cup and took a sip and her face seemed to freeze. "What's the matter?" inquired Bojo.

"I don't want to be impolite," she said, "but this coffee tastes like, what can I say, wood shaving that is used for landscape."

K'Narf began to snicker in a very annoying way and said, "Discussion is over."

Bojo fumed, "You people just have undeveloped taste buds and cannot appreciate the finer things of life. You are a bunch of losers."

Wester'C called out, "What's so hellfire important that you all are discussing?"

"Absolutely nothing," said a disgruntled Bojo as he joined Wester'C.

"I really want to know."

"It's the coffee. It tastes awful."

"Let me taste it."

Wester'C took a sip and spit it back in the cup, "I can see that you all have never tasted coffee from Underground City. "Bojo, how did you get this coffee?"

I think someone played a prank on me when I was down there doing an event. Maybe someone put it in one of my equipment bags."

"Don't you know that it is illegal to take anything from the Graveyard?"

"No. I had no idea. I won't ask why."

"Just don't do that anymore you could go to prison for a long time."

"Since you told me what could happen to me, I will ask why."

"Because, it is illegal to transport anything from the Graveyard. They are a self-sufficient world and they recycle everything, and if their recycling load exceeds their projection they know that something is amiss, and they start investigating. They have a method that can trace everything and where it come from and it is very accurate."

"That is vital to know. Plus, I can see what made the coffee taste the way it did, recycling. Now I wonder how they eat their food?"

"That's all that they know and they are used to it. Only a few of them have tasted anything else, only those who have ventured to Purple Bottom City."

"Okay, we have gotten to the bottom of the undrinkable coffee and a small history on Underground City and its recycling and food supply. Now, let's get back to the business of Roy Cavity. "What in the world was Roy thinking? No, he must not have been thinking."

For a moment it got quiet that it was eerie. Everyone had seen the picture and couldn't seem to gasp the significance of the why.

Finally, Bojo said, "What did I tell you? Huh! I got the real lowdown on him. Huh! Huh! I should take these down to the TV station and the news paper. Huh!"

"No, no, no, we can't do that. That will be the worst thing that we could do," Wester'C said.

"What then?" asked Bojo.

"We need to talk to Roy."

"Why?" asked Prissy. "What do you think he's going to tell you?"

"I don't know. I don't even think that he will talk to me," answered Wester'C. "Then why go through this charade?" Prissy asked.

"Because," he answered, "if it were me, I would want to talk to someone and either admit it or deny it."

"All right then, let's go," Jelly Belly said. "We can all go in two cars.

When they got to Roy Cavity's place he was gone. "What now?" Pissy Dean wanted to know. They called Roy's office and was told that an emergency had come up and he had to leave town pronto. "I know," said Wester'C.

When they left Roy's place, Carrie and Bill went to the Pot Gut Palace. When they entered, the first person that they saw was Suejusoe and Charles DeNero. They went over and spoke to them. Bill said. "Hi, Charles, Suejusoe, I thought that you guys was in the Graveyard."

"We haven't been back long. We just stopped in to get a bite to eat before we called it a day," said Suejusoe.

"Man," said Bill breathless as if he had been running, "did you guys miss it?"

"What did we miss?" asked Charles in a sober voice.

"Man," Bill said in the same breathless voice, "we just left Bojo's place and man you wouldn't believe it."

"I won't know what I wouldn't believe unless you tell me," Suejusoe said, slightly annoyed.

"Bojo was at this media convention workshop and had to go to the men's room. When he walked in, he said. "Do you mind if I sit down? I feel foolish standing up talking about this."

Suejusoe nodded. "Go on, please have a seat."

Bill sat down and continued his narrative. "Anyway, when Bojo walked in the door of the men's room he could not believe his eyes. Standing just outside the urinal were three guys—how can I put this— I'll just say it. These guys had their pants down to their knees and were getting it on."

"Get out of here," said a surprised Suejusoe.

"Hold on a minute until I get back. I've got to go tell Carrie that I'll be back in a few minutes."

During the time that Bill was gone, Suejusoe and Charles sat dumbfounded. Bill came back still animated and announced, "I'm back."

Charles said, "I don't think that we heard you right, would you mind repeating what you said?"

"Yes, you did. You heard me right and I'm not kidding but the best part of it is yet to come. Our Honorable Roy Cavity had his penis up one man's ass and another man was sucking on you know another man's penis."

"Heck, Bill, where do you get these wild tales, you sound more like Pissy Dean. You should become a fiction writer."

"You think that I'm making this up?" asked a bewildered Bill. "Listen, Bojo has pictures to prove it."

Sujusoe said, "You are serious. I can't believe this."

"I can," said, Charles. "The people in the higher echelons of government and sports tend to do these abnormal, unthinkable things quite often. They do these things because they think that they have enough clout to get away with them."

"But having an orgy in a public toilet is stretching things a bit far," said Suejusoe.

"Naw," answered Charles, "They happen more frequently than you can imagine."

Suejusoe asked Bill, "Did you say that there were pictures?"

"Yes, Jelly Belly and Wester'C have them."

Suejusoe said mostly to himself, "I shouldn't be too surprised. Roy got appointed to that position because the governor was banging his sister."

"How do you know this?"

"Bojo, dear Bojo, I know a lot of things that the average person doesn't know," Suejusoe said in a nonchalant manner. I guess that our calling it a day will have to be put on the back burner. I have got to go see Bojo."

"Charles, you are sitting there like this don't faze you at all. You are acting like something like this happens all the time," said Bill.

"Don't make me out to be diabolical. It's just that I've lived through enough scandals so that it don't shock me anymore."

"In my world, Earth 111," Charles answered, "everybody was trying to screw someone in power for one reason or another. I don't mean it literally, you know what I mean to say."

"No. What are you saying? For one reason or another?" asked Bill.

"Some people do things for publicity, money, or just plain meanness and jealousy and to ruin someone's life for good."

"I can see where you are coming from. I never would have thought of that."

"It's a common thing where I come from," said Charles.

"Yes. I can see where you are coming from," said Suejusoe. "Anyway as soon as I eat I'm going to pay Bojo a visit to see those pictures."

"Do you think that he would mind showing them to us?"

"Oh no. Not at all," said Bill as he went to find Carrie.

Charles and Suejusoe arrived at Bojo's apartment unannounced. Bojo let them in and said sheepishly, "I guess that you've heard about the pictures."

"Yes. Would you mind showing them to us?"

Bojo yawned and said, "Excuse me." Then he said, "No, not at all."

Then he exited to go get the pictures. He returned and gave them to them to Suejusoe. Sujusoe took the pictures and looked at them for a long, long time then gave them back Bojo and said, "My, my, my. Do these pictures tell a story."

Charles took the pictures, looked at them, and said, "I've seen such graphic photos before and for them to be taken in a public restroom. Those guys certainly were not resting."

"I can't leave this place even for a short while before these Chickpeo's start acting like uncouth morons. I've seen enough. What was Roy thinking about?"

"From the expression on his face he was reacting to a primitive urge, not thinking," said Charles. "You are right about that," Suejusoe said.

"Bojo, thanks for showing us the pictures. I'm going home now but I will see you tomorrow."

"Okay."

Charles and Suejusoe left Bojo place astonished, "How could someone let themselves get into a situation like that?" asked Charles.

"I don't have an iota of an idea," said Suejusoe.

As Charles and Sujusoe were driving home Charles sat quietly for a long time. Sujusoe asked, "Is there something wrong? You are so quiet."

"No. Not really," Charles answered. "It just that I've been here for a while and how long did you say that you were topside before you began to mutate?

"At least four hours. Why?"

Charles was fighting the idea of him becoming a chicken person. Because to him there was only one thing worst than being stranded on this strange purple world and that was becoming one of them. He said to Suejusoe, "I've been here for five days and nothing has happened to me."

"I can see that and I've thought about it, but I don't have an explanation."

So far he had not mutated, not even a little. He was extremely grateful for this. He thought maybe he shouldn't be so happy about mutating because if he could not get back home and had to stay here forever, he didn't want to look like a freak but he didn't want to turn into a purple chicken person either.

He wasn't about to give up all hopes of getting back home again. He reasoned that if God made the Earth and the heavens and ruled over them, then if he had enough faith, God would get him back home just like he got him here. He asked Suejusoe, "Is there any way that you could find out? Mind you, I don't want to mutate, it's just from what you've told me I was just wondering."

"I don't know the answer. I've thought about it and the only thing that I could come up with was that you are from a planet that have a yellow sun."

"I can see that you've been doing some heavy thinking."

"Always have, always will."

Charles looked at Suejusoe and thought how much more he looked like a professional athlete than a whatever he called himself. He didn't fit the mold of what a lawyer was supposed to look like, and another thing, women were falling over themselves to get to him, and he had almost no reaction. What was this, a man or a Chickpeo? He preferred to pine away for a woman that he couldn't ever have, and always took things too seriously. Everything. He had also noticed that when he was in Underground City he acted like he didn't belong. In Purple Bottom City he was forceful, a leader. Knowledgeable and always on the cutting edge. He wondered why he maintained his dual citizenship when it seemed like he only stayed in Underground City like it was an obligation. One could easily see that when he came topside to Purple Bottom City he lit up like a neon sign.

Charles decided that he was not going to get involved in the lives of the inhabitants of this strange world because he had enough problems of his own and couldn't do anything for them.

After a week had passed and no one could find Roy, someone leaked copies of the pictures to a rag magazine. Things exploded. When they hit the airways it was like someone had the A-Bomb. If Roy couldn't be found before this happened, he surely wouldn't come out of his self imposed exile now.

Tongues were wagging. This was a major scandal and it got major attention. The XXX-rated pictures in the rag magazine made people ask why and the B-Tan news used them for a centerfold.

Nothing had ever captured the attention of Purple Bottom City like this since the evangelist Rev. Joe Stumptoe was caught spending donations on enticing young girls from twelve to sixteen to have sex with him. He ended up with syphilis and had infected six of the girls, plus three of the girls ended up pregnant. Those mothers could have murdered that man with a smile on their faces and singing. Instead they kept him in solitary confinement to protect him from becoming a victim of their wrath. But Roy had been so vocal about homosexuals. He had called them shit maggots and said that all of them should be herded into a pen and tattooed on the forehead with "fag.' Every chance he got he said something derogatory, plain low-down, and nasty, making many Chickpeos who were also prejudiced against homosexuals change parties in support of him. Yes, he was a big man yesterday, but just look at him now. The same woman whom he had paid to give him an alibi when his parents were killed he also paid to be his companion when he was out in the public so that people would not know his sexual preference. Roy fought hard against being gay. He thought if he didn't give in to his urges they would go away. He tried to have a normal sexual relation with his paid companion but it was perverse, perplexing, and awkward. It wasn't worth the effort. He would leave filled with embarrassment and shame. He would feel loathsome and disgusted, and he despised himself because of this demon who had taken over his life.

As if he had no will of his own, and a force he couldn't reckon with, he was drawn to men. Roy blamed his sexual perversions on his parents, and he was glad that he had killed them and he wished that he had done it sooner because they didn't deserve to live for doing this to him. He thought, if ever there was a God, why did He let this happen to him? What had he done to deserve this? He knew some gays who wouldn't have it any other way and were happy with their lot. He couldn't understand why it was bothering him so much. Why couldn't he just accept what he was and go on with his life? Why had he listened to his parents fill his head with all this negative crap? Now he was a prime candidate for the loony bin. When he was having sex things were okay. It was only afterward when he felt so dirty and vile. No one but him knew the magnitude and the strength of his doomsday demons, and he couldn't do anything about them.

When legislation was in session, he couldn't concentrate on the matters at hand. He would sit mentally undressing the men and having his way with them. He remembered the day when he ejaculated and had to spill coffee on purposefully trying to cover up his stained pants. No one, absolutely no one, could imagine the shame he felt. He went to his hotel room and didn't return to session. He feigned a migraine for two days.

He knew people were talking about him but he would neither confirm nor deny rumors about his sexuality. He would go on as if he didn't know what they were talking about and go out more with his paid companion acting like he was straight.

He couldn't understand why it mattered so much to other people about his sexual preference. It was not a crime. He may not be very good at his job but that was not a crime either. People constantly harassing him was a crime. He had just found out that some members had formed an unofficial committee to bribe his paid companion to tell the truth about their relationship. Now he had to contend with this. He couldn't. His best bet would be to get out of town, and that's just what he would do. Damn that reporter. Damn him all the way to hell. He hastily packed and left.

*****

Charles had been hanging with Suejusoe like another shadow. He had been exploring and trying to find out the secrets of Purple Bottom City. There was so much to investigate, so much unexplainable so much he wanted to know and didn't know how to go about finding out. Scientist from where he came from would kill to find a place like this, so similar to their world, yet so different, so alien. An outside laboratory, and an eternity such for answers. They were saying that the purple stuff was very much responsible for their increase in knowledge by elevating their IQ to twenty to 50 percent higher than it was before the nova. Something in the purple stuff made their food taste outstanding and super nutritious They knew that it came from the purple stuff but didn't know why. The citizenry had the features of a fowl and you could easily tell that were not human the way he was. Their main feature was the fine, down like feathers that was on their purple butts. He knew a couple of people on his Earth that has a red vein on their forehead that looked like the beginning of a cock comb. They also had lips that puckered like a chicken beak but they were soft like our lips. These minute features made them look like chickens and officially dubbed them the name Chickpeos.

This place was a storehouse for scientific research. He wished that he could bring a team of scientist here to sturdy this world. But why would he do that? Because he don't know how he got here, and had no idea how he could get home. Perhaps if they could come together, they could compare notes and maybe come up with some answers.

That dreaded feeling invaded again, leaving him confused and super anxious. He couldn't find out while this haunting feeling kept after him. It always made him feel very uneasy. His grandma had always told him just because no one had seen or heard it didn't mean that it wasn't so. Don't ever be afraid to dream or think things that other people are afraid to admit to. A lot of people believe, but their thoughts and actions are ruled by the majority. He could hear her laugh her weird little laugh. He always laughed not because what she said was funny but because of the way she sounded when she laughed.

He had learned a lot from his grandma. He wanted to say that he had not learned anything from his mom, but in reality he actually did. He wouldn't say that it was anything good but it was certainly useful. Her lifestyle and the things that she had put him through taught him a lesson that he will never forget.

He wondered if he would ever see any of his loved ones and friends again and he wondered if Edias Sirrom was thinking about his disappearance. He felt sure that she loved him. God! He wished that he could get a message to her. She was supposed to move to Montana in a month. What was she thinking about? He would try telepathy. "Eidi," he always called her, "I hope that you will get this message."

"Baby, I love you and I'm not there because I don't want to be. I'm not there through no fault of my own. Honey, I'm trying my best to get back to you so don't give up on me."

He had no idea whether or not he had made contact but in his mind he felt that he had. It was all he could do. "God, please help me. I won't make any promises, please help me just because you love me and I'm on a world where there is not much that I can do for myself. You promised that you would watch over me and I'm depending on you now." Then he added, "Lord, I'm truly thankful that I'm not an alien on my world because there is only one place that's worst than that and that place is hell. Amen."

Charles gazed up at the purple sky and noticed that all the stars were surrounded with a wide purplish golden halo. He wondered why everything on this world made him wonder. How desperately he wanted to go home, and once he got there he didn't ever want to go away again anywhere unless had at least a 95 percent chance of returning. One thing for sure, he was not an adventurer. Oh, well one more day has passed and how many more were there left to go? Sadly, he walked out in the eerie Purple Bottom City night, back into the more comforting atmosphere of Suejusoe apartment.

Worlds away, Eidas Sirrom sat up in bed as if she had been hit by lighting.

As he entered Suejusoe living room he thought that if he was back in the USA of Earth he would never be the same. Matter of fact anything that he had learned, heard, saw, felt and thought about everything from now on would be different.

He had experienced things that anyone on Earth could only dream about or see in a science fiction movie. But even they could not feel, taste, or experience how it really was. He decided to spend most of today in the Purple Bottom City library trying to find out all that he could. Then, he may hop a Mole train to the Graveyard to see Dr. Wannabelax and see what he had found out. First he must tell Suejusoe of his plans. Suejusoe fussed over him like a mother hen. One thing he could say about the Chickpeos was that they were caring and passionate being.

Inside, the library was gigantic, unlike any that he had ever seen. There were rooms for computers I could guess about two to three hundred and all of these computers operated by thought command. I sat down at a computer and put the ear phones on and pushed the on button and all type of personal information covered the screen. My name and everything about me down to my blood type and sexual preference covered the screen I said, "Far out." the computer answered, "I know."

I was getting all kind of feed back until I learned how to control my thoughts. Never had I realized how much I was thinking about home.

I spent the greater part of the day in the library with the computer and I will be forever grateful that a Chickpeo sitting two desk down showed me how to operate it. It had given me a pet name, "Yarlie Q" for Charlie's questions. It amazed me how all the information about myself could be on a computer screen when I was from another world. I just had to ask. The computer told me that every thought that I had and all the information that was stored in my brain was scanned the moment I had asked for personal data. I thought, wow! I am not going to do that again. It was truly spooky knowing that there was a machine that could do something like this. I didn't find out much more than what Suejusoe had already told me but, I did find out something that I couldn't believe, the tales attributed to lore and mythology was in fact, true.

As I was leaving I scanned the shelves for books titles and the selection was massive.

*****

On the Mole train back to the Graveyard I tried to think about what I was going to do if I could not get back home. I wanted to know what kind of job I could get, and where I would live? Not in the Graveyard, that's for sure. I needed clothes because all I had was two sets. I could not think of all my clothes being purple thank the Lord for Underground City there was color and variety. I could shop where the dead folks abided. I only hoped that their clothes were not like their food.

He decided that he would talk to Suejusoe about this tonight. It would take his mind off spending the next two days in the Graveyard. Maybe he was prejudiced but he always thought that the Graveyard was for the dead and it was repulsive for him to stay there for one night.

When he got off the Mole train he went directly to Suejusoe's place. He had left some material about the Underground City's history for him to look over. He poured him a drink, and he did not forget the flavor pill, officially known as "Ysorta."

He sat in the recliner and began to read. As he read, the unbelievable became believable. In developing Underground City, the appearance and the natural functions of the outside world were duplicated as much as possible to be natural. What does this mean? It means that they had to create an artificial atmosphere, sun, moon, snow, fog, and clouds. These were operated by a computer. The controls were set so that the sun came up each day and set each evening at the same time. It'll be announced by the news media or you could pick up a weather schedule at a local store, and there were no slip-ups. The seasons were also computer controlled. Clouds and artificial thunder were also computer controlled.

In the summer it never got hotter than eighty degrees. In the winter, complete with artificial snow, it got no colder than thirty degrees. There were three weeks of snow, and one of these weeks was dedicated to the birth of the legendary Jesus Christ. Charles took a big gulp of his drink and murmured to himself, Well what won't they think of next? This place gives me the heebie-geebies. It is so perfect that it's unreal, planned out by the smartest brains in the world.

He wondered if people sweated down here or if it was illegal, like spitting on the ground. The next day was Friday. They were due back in Purple Bottom City Saturday. Suejusoe had a wedding to attend, and he asked him would he like to go with him. Since he had nothing better to do, he said yes.

The bride was one of his associates' niece and the whole thing would be one big gala.

On the day of the wedding everyone was in a jovial mood. No expense had been spared. Inside the chapel it looked like there had been a diamond storm, everything sparkled. The colors was candle light and iridescent. There were amyst candles and roses sprayed with iridescent. The iridescent reflection in the crystal chandeliers sparkled, sending miniature rainbows everywhere.

Everyone was sitting, waiting for the ceremony to begin. A hush came over the guest when the music of a heavenly harp began to play softly. The wedding party wearing candle light, still purple, came down the aisle, and the flower girls lined the isle with iridescent flower petals. There was a strong smell of roses and honeysuckles permeating the air. After a short pause, a harp began to play "Here Comes the Bride." The people began to stand.

The bride came down the aisle looking angelic as her train, supported by four other members of the wedding party, ran from the altar to midway the isle had iridescent petal of roses bordering it.

The music stopped and everyone sat down. The minister finished the marriage vows and asked, "If there is anyone who object to this wedding, speak now or forever hold your peace."

Someone from the audience cried out, "No! This marriage cannot happen. I am the one who should be standing there, not her. This woman is a slut and is marring for someone to take of her."

Then the best man said, "Yes, we are in love. This is true. I cannot let my best friend marry this slut because we are in love. We made love only four hours ago." He turned and gave the bride a passionate kiss. The bride fainted and the wedding guest looked as if Satan had just made his live appearance. No one spoke a word. The groom got angry with the best man and punched him out. A third person from the audience began to speak, "These two don't love each other, this marriage is a sham to cover up the fact that we are going to keep our affair going and use this marriage as a cover-up."

The minister looked at the bride crumpled on the floor. A couple of the wedding guest tried to revive the bride. Then, the guest began to talk.

The minister asked for everyone to be calm and to please remain in their seats. No one seemed to pay him any attention. "Please, please, remain calm and keep your seats." The minister reiterated. The roar was reduced to a few whispers and murmurs. "Please, everyone, shut up," the minister shouted.

Order was restored and everyone was wondering what was going to happen next. The bride had regained consciousness, and the wedding party was somewhere in the back of the church. The minister went to talk to the bride and groom and their families about the outcome of the almost wedding. He found the two mothers in shock and the fathers were yelling at each other and making threats. "Come, come now," said the minister. "I'm sure there is a solution somewhere."

"Butt out!" both of the fathers said to the minister.

The minister asked, "Didn't either one of you see this coming?"

One yelled, "My daughter ain't no slut."

The other one yelled, "My son ain't no fag."

The minister hesitated before he spoke again. "I see. So let's go back some and try to find out how this happened."

The bride's mother dabbed her eyes and asked the minister to dismiss the guest. She looked at her husband with tears rolling down her cheeks and asked, "Why? Why? Why?"

He looked at her with sympathy and said nothing; he didn't know anything to say.

The mother acknowledged that her daughter was two months pregnant. But she thought that it was for the groom. The groom swore that he had never had sex with her. She agreed that it was true. She was pregnant by the best man and she loved the groom. "What about this Reggie guy from the audience?"

The groom spoke up, "Pop, I'm not gay. I tried it with Reggie. I only did it with a guy a couple of times. I didn't like it and I told him that and I told him not to get hung up on me. When I told him that this was not going to happen again, he got angry and told me that he was going to fix me if I ever tried to marry that rotten cunt whore." He was referring to Tina. "Pop, I do love Tena and I don't care if she is going to have another, I mean a baby that is fathered by my best man. I still want her to be my wife."

Paul's father said, "I see."

The minister said, "I see. What about the wedding? I've done over sixty weddings and this is the first time that I've asked the question if there's anyone here who objected to this wedding, and someone did. I am going to inform the guest. Wait a minute, I must talk to the bride."

The bride acknowledged that she had an affair with the best man and she was indeed pregnant with his baby. "He engineered the whole thing. When he found out that he would never be able to father children, he thought, What the heck. He couldn't have children, and it would be my first time surely nothing would happen. As you can see we both were wrong. I still want to marry Paul, that is if he would marry me." The best man lied to me; he wasn't sterile at all, he is gay and would not be a threat to our marriage."

The minister wiped his face with a handkerchief and sat down. He said, "I need me a drink."

"That'll make two of us," Paul's dad concurred.

"No, that will make three of us," Tina's father added, then continued, "is there going to be a marriage or not?"

Tena and Paul looked at each other, smiled, embraced, and said, "We do and yes."

The minister said, "By the powers vested in me, I pronounce you husband and wife. Congratulations, Mr. and Mrs. Liverspots. You may kiss your bride."

"Thank God, that's settled," said Tena's father.

The minister returned to the guest and announced, "The wedding is over. You are free to attend the festivities." Then he thought, those young people have many mountains and rivers to cross. They have had a very bad start and I pray that they will get the strength from somewhere to make their marriage work. But right now, he really did need a drink.

At the reception the guest had already began to gossip. This was not a surprise to anyone present. Tongues were bound to wag.

The decorations at the reception made the decoration in the chapel seem bland. It was magnificent. All the crystal and the iridescence was complimenting each other. There were glittering, rainbows and flowers everywhere. The food was served banquet style. The silverware, crystal, punch bowl, and candles all blended together with the iridescence to make a picture-perfect paradise. There were hors d'oeuvre trees, rivers made watercress, and avocado dip. Anti pasto made in the shape of wedding bells. There was food and champagne galore. But most of all there was whispering and gossiping.

The two mothers tried to appear cordial and act normal while a major catastrophe was happening and never could make the connection.

Charles looked at Suejusoe and didn't speak a word, but he could read his face like a book. With all the whispering going on, everyone had something to say, and all of it was bad.

I don't know how he made it through that charade, but it was over; both mothers had to leave. One ended up in the hospital emergency room in shock. When the newspapers hit the stands the next day the newlyweds left town. The wedding had made the front page: "DID IT HAPPEN? HOW COULD THIS BE?"

The wedding of the century turned out to be the fiasco of the century; the presses had to render overtime to keep up with the demand.

*****

When Charles and Suejusoe returned to his apartment, they poured themselves a drink and sipped it in silence. Eventually Charles spoke, "I have been too many weddings but, I've never heard of anything remotely similar as that wedding and to have witnessed one in a lifetime is more than enough for me. I've have never heard of or seen anything like that where I came from."

Suejusoe grunted, "Me neither."

"That was a sight to behold and remember for a lifetime."

"You said it."

"Actually, what happened to me was historical, but there wasn't anyone around to witness it."

"Uh-huh." Suejusoe sat like a manikin, looking straight ahead, not moving.

Charles said, "Tonight, I'm going to blow your brains out."

"Yes, that would be nice."

Charles exploded, "Man, you haven't heard a word that I said. I know that I don't rank among the top ten who's-who in conversation, but I do think that you could at least be polite enough to pay attention or tell me to shut the fuck up."

"I'm sorry, man. Something else happened today that I can't stop thinking about. I got this letter today from my brother and I can't stop thinking about what he said and I'm trying, without success, to figure out what's what."

"I didn't know that you had a brother. What does he do?"

"He's a media jockey and a damn good one. People who have been in the business for years could take lessons from him. He's that good."

"Does he have a name?"

"Yes. His name is Nate Suju."

"Now that's one hell of a name. It sounds like Japanese in my world."

"Yes, he is named after my great grandfather."

"What did the letter say that is troubling you so?"

"Here, you can read it for yourself."

Charles took the letter and began to read it.

Dear Suejusoe,

During my years as a well-known announcer in a mediocre populated area, I never knew that the people that you work with and for were so absentminded. Racism played a big part of the reason why I was dismissed from my duties. My absentminded manager didn't realize that I did not need to be there to work as a professional announcer and I could go else elsewhere. I can and I did. Why must I suffer to the point that in order to fulfill my dream of becoming Underground City's most beloved and most popular media personality? I have to be knocked in the head and fired. The truth is I resigned. The benefits sucked and weekends off never happen.

I was doing the work of three people, and when I questioned this in-house slavery no one wanted to listen. They just stood around scratching their butts until break time arrived. They are assholes and most talk behind by back anyway. I could be wrong about some of them, then I could be right about all of them. I am really disappointed about the way things out and then again, I'm happy. A double whammy. The biggest disappointment is when someone was wrong and I pointed it out, and no one stood by the right side of things.

What we call assholes in this society mostly affect those who have treated others without respect or proper tone of language.

No one may know why I would compose such a letter. This letter is not a cry for help or hatred, but a painful cry of sweet freedom.

WARNING!

The following paragraphs are not meant to offend those of the Underground citizens. I would not consider this letter to be one that hates but one of understanding in order to know a person you have to know their history.

You will also have to include the history of events that have derived from both worlds, Purple Bottom City and the Underground City, and further explore the mistakes that have been by all points of view. The truth is that the Chickpeos's or the purple people's point of view has not been important until the Goolies wanted to invade Purple Bottom City.

The Spooks and the Chickpeos have been at each other's throats ever since before the cataclysm and the day they walked out of the Graveyard. Ever since then the Spooks was known blood suckers and advocates of slavery. Racism still exists in the Graveyard. From choosing who were to live and who were to die. Screening who would get to live in The Underground City before the closest star went supernova. As if only educated and rich people were fit to live.

The real salt of the Earth people were expendable except to work to keep them alive. How those that survived and prospered are still held in contempt just because they are mutated and purple. The Spooks are forever trying to sabotage their positions. Well, are you the one that is two faced and back stabbing or is it them?

Scientist actually take the time to find a cure from deadly viruses and even researched ways to duplicate genetic backgrounds of dinosaurs, after all of the research would not you suppose that someone would research a genetic code which could define stupidity and racism?

I know that I've lost you somewhere but keep on reading, I'm sure that you'll find something interesting.

This started back when the world was young. The newly found land needed developing and this needed muscle power. Fact two will explain the history of slavery and how it applies to this present day scenario. As you know as painful as it is to remember a people that was diversified before we all became purple our ancestors were brought here by slave traders, today's term, account executives, to be used and mistreated any way that the spooks choose. Some of them could not stand the sight of an ugly wooden tooth Spook ordering purple slaves around so many of them fled. Some of them were captured, tormented and killed by the hot unbearable breath of a screaming toothless Spooks. The reason why I say purple slaves is because there were no pictures or recollection of my knowledge of any Spooks serving on plantations. Correction, there were some Spooks but they were called Masser. Many of us said mother-fucker but they thought that we were talking in our native language. Masser was often used by the purple Chickpeos, translation was, asshole. The following may or may not be true but it gives you something to think about.

As painful as it is to remember if you belong to one of these races, you will have to begin speaking and acting like you are not racist and make the people who hate other races feel uncomfortable and vile. As painful as it will be we have to just sit back and laugh about it. I'm glad to have informed you. A donation for this effort will be greatly appreciated.

Go with God's Grace,

Until I get pissed off again.

*****

NOT FOR GOVERNMENT USE! And if you are guilty of having a part in this, I hope that you are offended.

Your brother,
Nate

"What do you think?" asked Suejusoe. "It sounded as if I wrote that."

"Say what?"

"That sounded like an essay on the history of my country."

"You don't say. I didn't know that your world suffered the same as ours. At least the world that that once was. You know this make the universe seem much smaller."

"It was correct all the way down to the slave trade and the Massa. Sorry, I meant mother-fucker."

They both laughed at the humor and the irony of it all. Plus the accuracy of it all. Suejusoe said, "God must have made five Earths so that if one or two screwed up he would still have some to fall back on. So far, three was at strike two and ball three."

"Sure, but tell me something, what is a black person?"

Charles starred at Suejusoe for a full minute, then asked, "What did you just asked me? Because I know that you didn't ask me what I think that you asked me."

"Are you thinking about when I asked you what is a black person?

"Yes, my dear friend Suejusoe. Look at me and tell me what do you see?"

"That's easy. I see you."

"No. Describe me."

"You are about six feet tall more or less. One hundred and seventy pounds. I guess some would call you handsome, but what can I say? A dapper dresser and articulate."

"Is that all you see?"

"Yes. What more is there?"

"Lord, I never thought that I would see the day come when someone would not know what a black person is. My friend, I am a black person."

Suejusoe looked at Charles in disbelief and shook his head, "No, that can't be. You are not black."

"Yes, I am. The last time that I checked, I was."

Suejusoe was really confused; he kept saying, "I don't understand. In our history books, persons who had thick lips, nappy hair, and wore hardly any clothes was called eccentric earthlings. They had black skin. You don't possess any of these traits."

Charles answered, "Perhaps not, but we are one and the same. Actually, black is not a color any more it is a state of being."

"I need a drink. My life is not turning out the way that I thought it would. All of these years I thought that I was knowledgeable and I really didn't know anything at all. I don't feel well." Charles smiled and asked, "Does it bother you that I'm black?"

"No. I can't say that it does."

"Well don't bother about it."

"If our history records were so wrong about a black person, what else can they be wrong about?"

"Don't worry about it. People wrote the history records. People are known to err."

"I know what you are saying, but it still makes me wonder. I've always thought that history was facts; now this makes me wonder what else is not right."

"I've told you not to worry about it. You are opening up a can of worms. Purple Bottom City doesn't have enough fish to eat. I'm sure if you look deep enough you will find many things that are inaccurate. All the facts are not there, something was taken away and something was added. That is the way of the world."

"I've always took pride in being accurate and factual."

"Keep on doing that. I'm sure there are some others doing the same thing and one day the whole truth will come out."

"It still don't feel right trying to build a life on a lie."

"Don't think of it as a lie; say misinformation. Doesn't that make it more bearable?"

"I guess."

"Just think, all this came about because you didn't know that I was a black person."

"All I have to compare what you are saying is nothing. I'm not saying that you are wrong, all I'm saying is that the jury is still out."

"Take your time. You have until the portal is ready and I'm homeward bound."

CHAPTER V

*T*he next two weeks were historical. The portal was finally ready for testing. It was brought topside and reassembled. Just what or who they were going to use for a test subject was yet to be found. But that came in second. The Spooks were too chicken to leave the Graveyard to give the portal a test run. They set up a remote control system and did it from Underground City.

Charles was so anxious to get back home until he volunteered to be the test subject, but they turned them down. They needed a humanoid or rather a Chickpeonoid to be used for a test subject. They needed someone that was intelligent enough to report where they had been and what they had seen. It was agreed that they would use someone that resided in the XOZ-30 Zone. These was not really Chickpeos nor human but once upon a time they were before the mutations. The most important thing about them was that they could communicate.

These mutants were closer to being an alien that Charles. All of them were so dark purple that they looked black to Charles. They had larger feathers that gave off a more eerie glow than the regular Chickpeos. When they talked it sounded more like a clucking hen, but you could understand what they were saying.

They didn't associate with the other Chickpeos. They lived their lives among themselves. The closer you got to ground zero, the more grotesque the mutations became. Most wouldn't come out until night because sunlight was their enemy. It would sear their feathers and leave huge running sores that never healed.

Many didn't have legs or arms. Some had too many legs and no arms; they scooted around on their purple bottoms. Some had arms and no legs, they crawled on their bellies. Some had all their legs and arms on one side. No one approached them. They lived their entire lives alone. No one knew if they were violent or dangerous; no ever got that close.

The radiation level was too high for anyone to go there unsuited. The only ones out there were the ones who were too grotesque and weren't accepted anywhere else. The government had declared XOZ-30 Zone uninhabitable, and it was against the law for anyone to go out there. Only scientists, with the government's permission, could go out to this otherworldly zone, and only for a limited time, not to exceed ten hours per month. The XOZ-30 Zone was mostly swampy. Not only were the inhabitants mutated, the animals that resided were grossly mutated. The vegetation had mutated along with everything else.

This seemingly otherworldly zone held many secrets, but they were safe because only a few scientist looked for them.

Many of the twisted, misshapen inhabitants of the XOZ-30 Zone were the descendants of the elite and very elite. These were those who choose to ignore their impending doom. Their reluctance to leave their worldly possessions was pure lunacy and beyond understanding of the masses. Their possessions were their god. Their possessions were their lives.

To see the destruction of this paradise that the very rich and the filthy rich ones lived in was more depressing than any other place in Purple Bottom City. They had ignored all warnings of the impending nova. They were far too busy enjoying the finer things of life. Their refusal to go underground created other problems. Most of them were young adults, and their parents were reluctant to go underground and leave them to face destruction alone. Neither time nor the lack of time fazed them. They partied day and night. The smidgens of older people who refused to go underground looked more distressed every day. They somehow hoped that their presence would delay their day of reckoning. They also knew that facts bore surety that the nova was a sure thing, and their small underground shelter would not protect them from the nova. Some of them didn't go because they didn't think the underground bubble was going to work and they were going to get blown out of the sky anyway. No one partied for three days before the nova. They stayed in their underground bunker, and this is what they had been reduced to.

They found a couple of Chickpeos before they reached the XOZ-30 Zone that was not a hazard to be around and was willing to undertake treatments for their conditions once they got back, but they would have to live in special housing for eighteen months for treatment and their children could begin at once. They agreed to this but wanted to make sure no one was trying to put anything over on them.

Scientists from Purple Bottom City were present because they had helped build the portal. Dr. Wannabelax had sent one of his assistants topside to monitor the test launch as he viewed things on a screen in Underground City.

The test subjects were extremely nervous and were given a mild sedative before entering the portal. The plan was to travel to other dimensions and return with some proof that they had been to another world. That seemed easy enough to do. Both subjects entered the portal at the same time. They were fitted with control belts so that they could get back from wherever they ended up. Their coordinates were programmed into a computer built especially for this purpose. A button was pushed and energy rays began to circle around the test subjects. Three separate energy rays were revolving around the test subjects, creating a hypnotic effect. They hummed as they made a figure eight that circled them. This circle went faster and faster and in less than two minutes the test subjects were gone. Where? They had to wait at least twenty minutes before they could find out if the portal was working and if the test subjects were still alive.

Fifteen minutes went by. Tension began to mount. The scientist and observers was trying hard to act like they weren't worried but it showed in their faces. Sixteen minutes, seventeen minutes, eighteen minutes passed, with each minute seeming an hour long. Charles thought that he was going to faint. Nineteen minutes. Everyone was holding their breath. Twenty minutes, and nothing. Dr. Wannabelax's colleague, Dr. Collin Skintknees, was extremely anxious, "Where were the test subjects? Did something go wrong?"

Dr. J. B. Jawbone was livid. "This was not supposed to happen." He entered the code that was to rerun the last program hoping that it would trigger the return sequences. Nothing happened.

Wannabelax, who was watching the test in Underground City on a monitor, was frantic. Immediately, he pushed the abort button hoping that by aborting the mission the test subjects would immediately return from wherever they were. He pushed it again and a faint electromagnetic reading was recorded. A full minute passed. The reading became stronger. As he posed to push the button again, one of the test subjects appeared in the portal.

They could not get him out of the portal until after two minutes had passed. They had to give his molecules time to reassemble before they could remove him.

"Can you speak?"

The test subject answered, "Yes."

"Do you know the whereabouts of test subject B?"

"No. I haven't seen him since the beginning of the test."

Dr. Jawbone was adamant; he kept asking the same questions. "What did you see?"

After about the tenth time, test subject A, whose name was Method Way, answered, "Yes. I saw something. Darkness, total darkness."

"Were you ever on a solid surface?"

"I can't recall ever being on a solid surface or any other surface. It was like that dream of falling down a well. Only this well reeked of burning sulfur."

Dr. Jawbone's eyebrows shot up. "Burning sulfur?"

"Yes," Method Way said.

All eyes and ears had tuned in on Method Way. No one noticed when the portal began to beep again. Dr. Wannabelax had noticed and informed Dr. Jawbone. Dr. Jawbone looked at the monitor on the portal like he was seeing it for the very first time and had no idea why it was beeping. The beeping stopped and there was a thud. All eyes forgot about test subject A and focused on the portal. Test subject B was in the portal, but he didn't look like he was alive.

Dr. Jawbone and his assistants removed test subject B from the portal; he reeked of burning sulfur. He had a heartbeat and a pulse and was alive, but just barely. The medics were working on stabilizing him when he sat up and began to talk. He was speaking in an unknown language. All eyes turned to test subject B.

Dr. Jawbone was staring at subject A and stopped when he heard beeping from the portal. He turned his attention to subject B, whose name was Baul Baam. He was talking nonstop about something that no one understood. Dr. Jon Jawbone was shouting, trying to get test subject B's attention. That didn't work. He calmly slapped Baul Baam as hard as he could. Baul Baam instantly ceased talking. He looked at Dr. Jawbone and all the others as if he was seeing them for the first time. Then he spoke in a language everyone could understand. "Will someone please tell me what is going on?"

That outburst caused a silence so deep that the piece of world that they called home must have lost thirty seconds. Before test subjects A and B began the test, they could speak only with difficulty. Now they were talking unknown languages and chattering like the best of them. Dr. Jawbone looked at test subject B in shock and with his dogged persistence he asked, "Tell me what you remember."

"Remember about what?"

"Everything that you remember while in the portal. Traveling through the dimensions. Things that you encountered, things that you felt and smelled."

Test subject B looked at Dr. Jawbone, then the others, and repeated, "Will someone tell me what is going on?"

In a condescending voice, Dr. Jawbone asked again, "Do you know who you are?"

"No."

"Do you know why you are here?"

"No."

"Tell me, what is the last thing that you remember?"

Test subject B began to narrate in the unknown language. Quickly, Dr. Jawbones interrupted, "What language is it that you speak?"

"I don't know."

Dr. Jawbone was perplexed. He asked Baul Baam, test subject B, "How could you possibly learn another language in twenty minutes?"

Test subject B did not answer. He was out cold. The medics took him to the special care unit where there were top doctors and state-of-the-art and equipment. Speculating about what had just transpired, Dr Jawbone contacted Dr. Wannabelax. "Say, Doctor, what do you think about what just happened?"

Dr. Wannabelax began in his immature voice, "Right now I'm at a loss about almost everything. Everything that I had planed turned out different than it was supposed to. I've got to go back to step one and try to trace where things went wrong. So you can see, I've got my work cut out for me. I'm going to get back to my lab and try to find out what didn't go right."

In the infirmary test subject B was in a deep dark sleep, the sleep of the unconscious. He slept for fourteen days. During this time the scientist in Purple Bottom City and Underground City worked from dusk to dusk trying to find out what had gone wrong with the portal test. According to them nothing remotely similar to what happened should have occurred.

Test subject A had experienced something so horrifying, so shocking until his wingtips had bleached, and the worst part of it was he couldn't remember one thing associated with the portal test.

As Dr. Wannabelax researched and backtracked, he thought that he had found the answer to what had gone wrong. He did not set the monitor for a specific time, and when the test subjects exited the portal they were just out there, somewhere, in space. The monitor should have been set to a specific time and place. They didn't have a space map and only guessed about the dimensions. Sure they had gone somewhere, and encountered something not of their world, and he would give a kidney and his right leg to find out. First he had to find out how to map a trajectory for the dimensions that he had always heard about and scientists had taught about, and all of them believed in as much as they believed in morning and night.

He flipped the switch on his supercomputer, and typed in an equation and asked the computer a question. "What happened to the test subjects in the portal?"

After a minute had passed the computer answered, "You need to check your configuration and reconfigure the energy levels of the atoms in relationship to the specified nucleons that as far as we know exist only in dimensional zones."

"I see," said Dr. Wannabelax to himself. "I've got to find out the relationship of specified nucleons that only exists in the zones that we call dimensions. That shouldn't be too hard."

He went to work figuring out the measurement of the dimensions, then reconfigured the energy level of all sides. The dimensions seemed flat on all surfaces, but that was where the answer lies. The surfaces aren't flat; they seemed to be flat if the configuration was wrong. They are pleated like little tents are gathered. Bang! You are in another dimension. It was almost like making a half turn and you are light years away. You are in the dimensional zone.

Wannabelax heard his beeper go off. Someone on Purple Bottom City wanted him right when he was on the edge of finding out what went wrong. He shouldn't answer, but he did, "What is it?" It was Dr. Jawbones. Jawbones felt exceptionally jittery. "Mr. SuejuSoe and Mr. DeNero have a reaction of some sort."

"What are you talking about?"

"They were speaking in the same unknown language that the test subjects were talking in when we found them."

"When did all this happen?"

"About five minutes ago."

Dr. Wannabelax heard in the background, "If I'm out of line just tell me so."

"You're out of line," test subject B said.

"Seriously," Suejusoe continued, "Charles, will you please tell me what is going on?"

"Nothing," Charles answered flatly.

"But I heard you all speaking in an unknown tongue."

"I don't know what you are talking about."

"You have to. Come on, Charles, this is me. You can tell me anything."

It was if someone snapped their fingers and the spell was gone. All three were normal again and had no recollection of talking in a strange language.

Suejusoe had not noticed the change. He was adamant, "Tell me what is going on with you."

"SuejuSoe," Charles said, patiently, "I know that you already know Baul Baam and Method Way, and we were just talking about—"

"Yes, I know," SuejuSoe interrupted. "What I want to know is where did this strange language come from and when did you learn it?"

"Man, you sound like a broken record. I keep telling you that I don't know what you are talking about."

"Don't lie to me. I've seen you and heard you talking in this language, and it was more than nothing. "For the last time, SuejuSoe, I don't know what you are talking about. So let's change the subject and get something to eat."

"My appetite is gone. I'm going home."

"Suju, wait. I don't understand what's going on either. Stay and talk to me."

"Why?" asked an angry SuejuSoe, "so you can tell me more lies?"

They were out of range for Wannabelax to hear. He turned back to Dr. Jawbone. "Just what is the meaning of this?"

"Can't you see that all of them were speaking in an unidentified language and neither knew what it is nor remember ever speaking it? Mr. SuejuSoe was accusing the other like he had no part in it when he did. What happened to their memory? They were only standing close to the test subjects, and whatever happened to them seemed to have rubbed off on them. This is getting stranger by the minute."

It does seem to be getting stranger, but right now I'm in the middle of finding out what went wrong with the test subjects and the portal and I will have to get back to you later."

Dr. Wannabelax hung up abruptly. That was something new for him, because he had always been patient to a fault. Maybe things were affecting him two miles under the ground. No, he thought. Now is not the time to become delusional. A small chill ran down his back; it surprised him. Again he said, "My, that's never happened before. Let me get back to work before something else happens." He resumed his work on the equation. He typed in the equation that he thought was going to give him the answer to the dilemma of the portal to the dimensions. He was feeling elated because this had to be the one. As he was waiting for the answer, he drink a grape soda. While he sipped his soda the computer screen turn a orangey green. He sat his soda down and turned to the screen. Something huge must be coming up because I can't remember ever getting a screen this color. Wannabelax felt weary; this was something new too. The computer screen turned black and red. Dr. Wannabelax was trembling. What did this mean?

There was a big pop and a screeching sound. The screen had turned into a big black round thing that grasped Dr. Wannabelax's head between hands unseen. He fainted. He didn't know long he was out. When he came to, the maintenance man had pulled him up against a desk and was giving him CPR.

He was trying to ask him what was going on but he was unable to speak. He keep gasping but nothing came out. The maintenance man called for help and gently laid him on the sofa. The paramedics were there in five minutes.

They took him to Mercy Medical Center, one of the Underground Three hospitals. All the time Dr. Wannabelax was trying to talk but couldn't say a word. His face looked like it was frozen in horror. After being examined by the doctors, who couldn't find anything physically wrong with him, their diagnosis was extreme stress. He needed to be admitted for a few days to find out what brought this on so suddenly. Once again he tried to protest but he couldn't talk. He was admitted.

They had run every test on him that they could and found nothing wrong, only that his pulse and his blood pressure had elevated. His blood pressure had risen to stroke level. This worried the doctors. They monitored him closely because they had found nothing that could be causing these symptoms. After three days he began to talk. He asked the very question that he had been trying to ask ever since this happened. "What happened?"

Dr. Lenora B. Sensor, his neurologist, said, "I should be asking you the very same question. Now, I would like an answer."

"Why should you be asking me? All I remember is sitting down at my computer running some equations and . . . and . . . and . . . ."

"And what?"

There was no answer. He began screaming, and screaming like someone had dropped him into hell three quarters of the way before pulling him up.

He was given a sedative to keep from going mad. Dr. Sensor was at a loss about what was going on.

She had guessed that something had scared this young man so severely he couldn't get past it before it happened. He began to scream again. His sedation was doubled.

Dr. Sensor left word that if he should wake up screaming again, they should give him another sedative and call her. She went to her office and called Dr. Wester'C Ulcer.

"Hello, Wester'C, this is Dr. Sensor."

"Well, Lenora, this is a surprise. I know that you wouldn't call me out of the blue unless you've been stumped."

"I'm glad to talk to you too. I didn't forget that you always get to the heart of things. Could you come down here like right now?"

"What kind of booger bear have you let loose?"

"I'm not all sure. That why I need you."

"The earliest that I can get there is first thing in the morning. Will that be okay?"

"It will have to be. Oh, I didn't tell you who the patient is. It is Dr. Wannabelax."

"No. Don't tell me that! Dr. Wannabelax is one of the smartest and sweetest personalities that I've met. I just might come tonight."

"No. Tomorrow morning will be fine because I have him so sedated he probably won't wake up before then.

"See you tomorrow." And he hung up the phone.

Since these were his three days in Underground City, getting up early and going to the hospital early wouldn't cause him any hardships. He got up very early, and walked to the hospital. In the early hours of the morning, things seemed to be more peaceful unless a crises was going on. That was the life of doctor. He walked down to Dr. Sensor's office and lightly knocked on the door before he turned the knob and was surprised to see her napping on the sofa. He walked over and kissed her on the forehead.

She yawned and said, "Good morning, and I do mean good morning. Why are you here so early?"

"After you told me who it was, I started to come last night. Why are you still here?"

"I never got the chance to go home. The sedation didn't work. He woke up screaming at the top of his lungs as if he was being tortured by an unseen entity."

"That's an unusual description. Why did you say an unseen entity?"

"When I finally got him calmed down again, I examined him and he had pressure marks on his body that was made with hand or suctions unknown."

"Lenora, I've got to see these marks. If he is sedated, I can't start a relapse, can I?"

"I can't say yes and I can't say no, because I've never witnessed anything like this before. We can give it a try. Because if we can't find out what is causing this and get him calm down without putting him in a drug-induced coma, he is going to lose that beautiful mind and perhaps his life."

"What are we waiting for? Let's go."

The walk down the corridor calmed both or their nerves somewhat. Upon entering the room, Dr. Wannabelax was lying propped up with pillows looking like a small boy asleep.

Seeing him looking like this tugged at Dr. Wannabelax heartstrings. Compassion was overflowing in his heart for this young man. He careful lifted the sheets to examine his body. The first bruises covered his face, and bruises were found on his chest and abdomen. There were fresh bruises on his thighs and back. He called Dr. Sensor over and asked why these were so new. She exclaimed, "I don't know. Perhaps this was what woke him up the last time."

"You know, I think that you may have something going on with these invisible attacks. I think that I'm going to stay in here with him until he wakes. I want to see what happens."

"Be my guest. After all, I did call you. You can fill me in later. I'm going to catch me some z's." Dr. Sensor exited the room, and Wester'C tried to find a place where he could sit close and observe Dr. Wannabelax. Poor little fellow he didn't deserve this. Now let me see if I can catch this invisible demon. He sat down on a small sofa next to a nurse who was watching Wannabelax.

He asked the nurse what had been happening lately. She replied, "He had been resting and has not had any problems, but that could change any minute."

Wester'C thanked her for her input and continued his surveillance. Around 10:00, Dr. Sensor came into the room and the patient had awakened. He looked around the room and saw all the people who were watching him. Dr. Sensor and Dr. Wester'C approached his bedside, and Dr. Sensor took his hand and asked him how he was doing. He replied in a small voice, "I'm good."

She asked, "Do you remember anything that has been happening to you?"

"I don't think so."

"Are you in any pain? Have you seen or heard anything unusual or heard any strange voices?"

"No. I don't think so."

"Do you remember who you are?"

"I'm not sure."

"Come on, give it a try"

"Am I a doctor?"

"Very good. Go on."

"Now, I remember, I'm Dr. Wannabelax. I am a scientist. I was working on a project trying to a misplaced person back to his world. A Charles DeNero. I was working at my computer when something big black and scary came out and attacked me and ouch, ouch, ooo, ooo."

"What seems to be the matter?"

Wannabelax began screaming and convulsing. Dr. Ulcer and Dr. Sensor tried to hold him down to keep him from hurting himself. His strength had increased more than sixfold, and they were no match to hold him down. A noxious odor permeated the room and made Dr. Sensor sneeze really loud. Suddenly everything returned to normal. This made everyone wonder what happened. Dr. Wannabelax was no longer cringing in pain; the noxious fumes were gone. Dr. Wannabelax had a message; he didn't know if he had heard it or felt it. It said, "Stop poking around where you don't belong."

He didn't know if he should tell the doctors or keep it to himself. He decided to reveal the message and pray that no one would think that he had lost his mind.

He cleared his throat and said, "Dr. Sensor, Dr. Ulcer, I was given a message during all the turmoil. I don't know if it was verbal or telepathy or if I simply felt, it but the message was "Stop poking around where you don't belong." What do you suppose that mean?"

"I can't say," said Dr. Ulcer, "but I intend to find out." Then he turned to Dr. Sensor and said, "I am more inclined to believe that we have an entity at work. But how does one fight something that he cannot see? Tell me again what you were doing when these attacks began."

"I had typed in an equation that I felt would give me the answer to what went wrong with the portal test. Then I asked the computer what went wrong. The computer's screen began changing colors that I've never seen before. It turned a deep red and black and pain engulfed me and that's the last thing I remember."

"How are you feeling now?" asked Dr. Sensor.

"I'm feeling great. Ready to go back to work. I admit that I'm feeling a bit apprehensive, but I'm sure it will go away soon. I really want to find what is going on with the portal."

Dr. Ulcer said, "What do you think, Dr. Sensor?

"I still think that it's too early to let him go, he may still have a relapse. I think that I may keep him another forty-eight hours to see how things go. Is that okay with you, Dr. Wannabelax?"

"Under the present substances I agree somewhat."

"Good. Now we can all rest easy."

Meanwhile in Purple Bottom City, test subject B had woken up. Physically he was normal as he ever been, but emotionally and physiologically he remained a mystery. Even after he had returned to his house he went around like he was all alone in an hostile world. The language that he had spoken when he came back from the portal test had yet to be determined. A break in the case came one day when test subject A went to see test subject B at the infirmary. The visit was normal with the exception that they both communicated in the same unknown language. But when they talked to others they would speak in the normal language of Purple Bottom City.

Whenever someone would ask them what they were saying, they would abruptly stop talking. This went on for about two months. One afternoon Charles was sitting in the Pot Gut Palace waiting for SuejuSoe to join him. But before SuejuSoe arrived, the two subjects came in and saw Charles sitting alone at a table and walked over and joined him. Charles was pleasantly surprised. They asked Charles if they could sit down a minute to talk. Charles obliged. They were sorry that the portal had failed and he could not get back to his world. Within five minutes test subjects A and B began to speak to Charles in that unknown tongue. The amazing thing about this was that Charles knew what they were saying.

SuejuSoe entered and came over where they were sitting and witnessed this spectacle. He began to speak but decided against it because the conversation seemed too intense to interrupt. Momentarily they noticed SuejuSoe. The conversation abruptly ceased. SuejuSoe spoke, "Hi, how are you all?

They all replied in unison, "Fine, and you?"

"I'm okay," SuejuSoe answered. Then he asked nonchalantly, "Why are you so serious?" No one answered. Again he spoke, "If I'm out of line, just tell me so."

"You are out of line," test subject B said.

"Seriously," SuejuSoe continued, "Charles, will you please tell me what is going on?"

"Nothing," Charles answered flatly.

"But I heard you speaking in a strange language."

"I don't know what you are talking about."

"You have to. Come on, Charles, this is me. You can tell me anything."

It was as if someone had snapped their fingers and the spell was gone. All three were normal again and no one had any recollection of talking in a strange language. SuejuSoe had not noticed the change. He was adamant. "Tell me, what is going on with you?"

"SuejuSoe," Charles said jubilantly, "I know that you already know Baul Steve and Metor Maan. We were just talking about—"

"Yes, I know," SuejuSoe interrupted. "What I want to know is where did this strange language come from and where did you learn it?"

"Man, you sound like a broken record. I keep telling you that I don't know what you are talking about."

"Listen, I've seen you and heard you talking in this strange language and it was a bit more than nothing. If you don't want to tell me, you don't have to lie about it."

"For the last time, SuejuSoe, I don't know what you are talking about. So let's change the subject and get something to eat."

"My appetite is gone, I'm going home."

"Suju, wait. I don't understand what is going on either. Stay and talk to me."

"Why?" said an angry SuejuSoe, "so you can tell me more lies?"

"When did I lie to you?" Charles asked with sincerity.

"Why do I even bother?" SuejuSoe sat back down. "Okay, talk."

"What do you want to talk about?"

"I want to talk about the portal test. I want to know when you and the test subjects got to be so chummy."

"Honestly, SuejuSoe, I don't know anything about any alien language. Really, I don't know anything about what you are talking about."

"I see. Then we have nothing to talk about," SuejuSoe said as he prepared to exit.

SuejuSoe left Charles sitting at the table with his mouth agape. Charles had begun to worry that something was wrong with his friend. He did not understand the accusations he heaped on him and that deal about the alien language was the strangest of all. Somehow he had to find out what was wrong. He had to find out what was troubling his friend. If only he knew where to begin. Well, since he was already here he may as well eat before he embarked on his journey to find out what in hell was going on that could make people act so weird.

Charles left the Pot Gut Palace determined to make sense of SuejuSoe's accusations. He arrived at the apartment and found him sitting in the dark, pouting. He spoke, "Hi." His greeting was met with a brooding silence. He continued his narrative, "Okay, I give up. What do you want me to do?"

"I knew it!" he answered jubilantly. "So let's start with the conversation I overheard at the Pot Gut Palace." He murmured, "I just knew you were holding out on me."

Charles turned on the lights, and SuejuSoe could not help but see the bewilderment that shrouded his face. This made him acutely aware that things were not as they seemed. He began to speculate that maybe Charles didn't know what was going on. But how could this be possible? There must be an unseen demon at work.

He turned to Charles with a sympathetic pose. He didn't want to alienate him because already had serious problems that had intensified since the failure of the portal. He had no idea what or how his alien friend was faring and he felt guilty about the way he had reacted. Charles didn't deserve the wrath of his frustrations. If only he knew how to handle this diplomatically. But he didn't know zip about being diplomatic. "Charles, suppose I told you that I believed what you told me but I don't understand any of it."

"I can believe and understand that you mean that."

"Don't you agree that something is amiss about the whole situation?"

"I can believe that."

"Well, how do you suppose we can get to the bottom of this dilemma?"

"That's something that I can't tell you," Charles answered with resignation in his voice. "I just wish that none of this ever happen and I would be back in my world contented."

"But it did happen and we have to find a way to deal with it."

"Yes. Right."

"I know that it's hard and no one ever wrote a book on *How to Deal With Something No One Ever Had Dealt with Before*."

"If I ever live through this, I just might write that book."

"But in the meantime what shall we do?"

"I don't know."

An idea began to take shape in SuejuSoe's mind. But in order for it to work, Charles must not know anything about it. He decided to plant a bug on Charles so that when and if he should meet again with Baul Steve and Metor Maam he would hire someone to follow Charles everywhere without his knowledge and to videotape his every move. Now that this idea had been conceived he had to conceal it from Charles.

Charles looked at SuejuSoe with a puzzled look on his face and asked, "Is there something wrong, or did you decide not to grill me over hot coals any longer?"

SuejuSoe somehow managed a smile as he looked at Charles. He was thinking that it was not going to be easy keeping him in the dark about his plans. He said, "Naw, I didn't change my mind, the coals went out."

"Now what?"

"Nothing. I've decided to leave this alone until tomorrow, because I have the granddaddy of headaches."

"That sound like a good idea but I need a drink first. Today has been a trying one for me also." SuejuSoe took a sip of his drink and said, "Charles, you know, you and me both need a woman."

"Sounds like a good idea to me. Do you have someone in mind?"

"Personally, I would like to make it with Ocena."

"I know that I didn't hear you say that because I didn't know that you had a death wish."

"Why do you say that?"

"Because the way Moses looks at her, he would kill a dead snake for her."

"I see your point and it is well taken."

"I'm sure that you have the hots for someone else other than Ocena."

"Perhaps. But have you ever watched her walk or stoop over? She can make a dead man cum."

"My advice to you is go stand on a corner and watch her walk by and have two or three orgasms. That way you will get to live."

"Point well taken. Now how about you? You've been celibate since the day you arrived."

"Add a month to that. Actually, I'm not at all comfortable with the females here. They are not exactly what I am used to."

"Bull shit! The Grave Yard is teeming with women who don't look like chicken. Anyway, when you turn out the lights, it's all the same."

"Yes, but you have to turn the lights back on again. Then again their stuff might be like everything else down there, all show and no substance. Or do you have to take a pill before you can feel anything? I don't know if I'm allowed to sweat or fart or ejaculate and not recycle it."

"I can see that you are not a spook lover. Actually, it's not that bad."

"I think that it would be like screwing a ghost."

"Now that we've discussed our lust let's try to get some z's."

Early the next morning SuejuSoe was busy trying to get someone to bug the places where Charles frequented most. He hired a private detective to tail Charles everywhere he went. He was determined to get to the bottom of whatever it was that was going on. It took him two days to find someone suitable for the job. The man turned out to be a woman. But they seemed to hit it off immediately.

She would report to him everyday even if she didn't have anything significant to report. On the third day she hit the bull's eye. Charles met with Baul and Metor at a public park. She walked past where they were sitting and seemed to trip so that she could plant a bug under the bench. She stood up and continued onward until she was sure she was out of earshot. She doubled back and came within range where she could clearly hear what was being said but she remained out of sight.

She managed to tape most of their conversation. Later on that afternoon when the trio vacated the park bench, she revived the bug.

That night she met with SuejuSoe at a coffeehouse. The taped conversation was played. They were speaking in the same alien language, and they could not understand any of it.

SuejuSoe was extremely confused. What in the world was going on? The next three days the trio met again. This time they met in a cafe out on Runs Road. She was dressed as a teenager and came by their table sniggling and acting like a typical teenager. She had a dollar worth of quarters in her hand and accidently dropped two. Laughingly she bent over to retrieve them and planted the bug under the table. She got up still acting like a teenager and apologized for her clumsiness, went into the ladies room for a short time, came out, and left.

Their conversation was in that strange alien language again. Toward the end of their meeting to the best of her knowledge it seem like they had taken an oath.

Although they did not understand the language the direness of the conversation gave them chills. The private detective was unable to retrieve the bug until early the next day. Afterward, she met with SuejuSoe.

He was sure that Charles was getting bad vibes from him and he wanted the detective, Ashly Skin, to come on to Charles so that he would not pay as much attention to what he was up to. He knew that Charles was lonely and needed some female company. So this worked out pretty good.

Since Ashly was dating Charles she didn't have to disguise herself. Yet he would never let her come with him when he met with the others. He seemed to be fond of her and treated her with the utmost respect. She was not only intelligent but also beautiful, if he could get past the chicken features.

The taped conversations were taken to the Purple Bottom City's leading authority on languages, Dr. Curticle.

Dr. Curticle was absolutely fascinated. She was spellbound. She had no idea what language that was. But she said that she thought that it was in code. That afternoon, the chief cryptographer, Dennis Beerhead, at the Institute for Languages, met with Dr. Curticle. After hearing the tape, he was certain that the language was in some type of code.

"Just where did you get this from?"

"I can't tell you just yet. What can you make of it?"

"I know that it's not like anything that I've ever heard. It isn't exactly code, but I may be able to decipher it in code."

Shaking his head in wonderment, Dennis Beerhead said, "Zoe, darling, you are the only one that I know that can come up with these things no one else ever heard of before. I think that you missed your calling."

"Tell that to someone else. I'm just at the right place at the right time."

"Can I take these tapes with me?"

"No way. I've made copies, you can have one of those."

"When I win the Nobel Peace [comparable to the Nobel Peace Prize on Earth 111], do you want me to mention your name?"

"You had better."

Zoe played the tapes again after Dennis had gone; she was absolutely fascinated. Three days later Dennis called. He was agog with excitement. "Zoe, darling, I've come up with something that you may be interested in."

"Well, don't keep me waiting. Speak."

"I haven't cracked the code to that language, but I've found something in a book that is so old it was written in script. It is over two thousand years old."

"What! What! What! Speak to me."

"It is a language very similar to the one recorded one other time when someone in another dimension accidently landed on this planet. They didn't say much about it but it is out in the dimensions somewhere. They were supposedly telepathic and aren't used for oral communications. Even back then they were a very advanced society."

"This is wonderful news, Dennis, but I want to know what they are saying. I want to know how the test subjects and Charles come to know this language?"

"Those are tall orders Zoe, but if I find out anything else, I will let you know. Come to think of it, I think that I ran across something about Y-Lingepps. I'll get back to you as soon as I come up with something."

"At least I do have something to go on."

A week had gone by before Dr. Curticle and Dr. Beerhead got back together to discuss their findings. It had taken more time than they had anticipated. Decoding an alien unknown language is a whole lots less fun than a picnic.

So far Dr. Curticle thinks that she had stumbled upon something. Scientist don't like to use the word *stumble* because it would make one think that they didn't know what they were doing. Dr. Beerhead wasn't any more about his finding than Dr. Curticle was about hers.

"Dennis, you go first," insisted Dr. Curticle.

"Why? I always thought that ladies were first."

"We are not going by protocol, so you can start whenever you want."

"First, I must tell you the book is in hieroglyphics, plus it is in an alien language. I contacted Reggie Soma in Underground City. Do you know Reggie?"

"I've met him once."

"I ran everything that I had by him to find out what he may know about this. When I played the tapes he freaked out. He told me that he had heard something like this before. He wasn't sure but during the building of Underground City someone unearthed something like an ancient capsule and in its contents a recording of this language was found."

"I went to Underground City to see what he was talking about. I listen to the recording, it was scratchy but it was just as alien as the tape as you gave me. Reggie had a machine that could play the tape at a speed twelve time as fast as a recorder. This machine also could make codes of the message at this speed and play them backward. We did this and were surprised when we really understood what we was hearing."

"Don't stop now, go on."

"The code came out as a warning. It went: OONDI ESPEN ONDI! ONDI!"

"What in the world does that mean?"

Dennis corrected her, "You mean what not of this world does that mean? You told me on the phone that you had uncovered something, give."

"What I came up with was hieroglyphs that I found on some ancient materials before the nova. Hieroglyphs were quite common in those days since writing had not been invented. I think that it symbolizes life after death. It seems that they really believed in this, you could find hieroglyphs in just every tomb that held a mummy. I'm not sure if the god people used them."

"God people, what god people?" asked Zoe.

"You know like Zeus, Dionysus, Osiris, you know, those gods."

"Those are myths."

"Were they really? How do we know if they weren't real? How do we know what they were called myths because they were different and could not be explained? Because their knowledge was eons above our. You know how whenever something comes up that we cannot explain, we usually label it as a myth or hysteria or otherworldly."

"I can see what you mean, but let's not stray too far from the subject at hand."

"Yes, this unknown language," said Dennis, yawning.

"Are you tired?" asked Zoe. "We could continue this at another time."

Dennis yawned again, got out of his chair, and propped against a table, covering his mouth with his hand, and said, "That sounds like something that I can handle. I didn't know that I was this tired."

"You have been working nonstop for six days. I bet that you haven't been eating, have you?"

"No, I must've forgot to."

Zoe got her purse, walked over to where Dennis had propped up, slid her arm through his, smiled up at him, and said, "You are not going to forget tonight because I am taking you to dinner. My treat."

"I don't think my wife would like that."

Somewhat taken aback, she said, "Well, we will just have to bring her along too. I could call her and have her meet us at the Pot Gut Palace."

Dennis grinned, "That won't be necessary because I'm not married."

"You deceitful spook." Zoe smiled, "I already knew weren't married. I was just playing your own game."

"Does this mean that you are not buying me dinner?"

"What do you think?"

"I give up. Let go eat before I faint from hunger." Then he asked in a little boys voice, "Are you going to buy me a drink?"

"Liquids, ma'am, liquids."

As they were walking out the door, Dennis said, "You know that this is something new for me."

"What?"

"I've never eaten in Purple Bottom City before. I don't know what to do."

Zoe smiled up at him and said, "You are in the treat of your life. But there's something I must ask of you."

"I'm listening."

"You must never tell the others underground citizens how great things are up here. We definitely do not want a Spook invasion. Sorry about the Spook thing, I meant an Underground Citizen invasion."

They both laughed hardily as they walked out into the humid midsummer air of Purple Bottom City.

CHAPTER VI

$\mathcal{S}$he was not a normal woman and did not do the things that normal people did. SuejuSoe took another sip of his pepe pop and recalled the first time he had met Ocena Heartburns. He had just left the local gaming house. The Gambit. He had opened the door and there she was. I walked over and stood by one of the miniature water fountains in the courtyard. She was talking to three gentlemen who was falling over themselves trying to win favors with her. Since I was fairly close I could hear what they were saying without listing very hard. I stood with my hands in my pockets trying to look nonchalant. She spotted me and waved. I gave her a three finger wave in return. She stopped talking to the other gentlemen and announced, "A shining star has fallen and it is beckoning for me."

I don't know how to describe her movement; she just floated over to where I was standing and asked, "Aren't you SuejuSoe Suju?" I nodded.

She smiled at me and I smiled back. Extending her hand to me, I shook it. "I'm Ocena Heartburns."

"Hi, Ocena, I see that you already know who I am."

"Don't everybody?" she exclaimed. "Your face is as familiar as Frank Covictus Hangnail," she said jokingly.

"That's nice to know, I hope."

"You know that your face is in the media just about every day."

I smiled, and said, "I don't know because I don't keep up with stuff like that."

Then she looked at me like she could see my very soul and said, "I'm not trying to be nosey, but why are you acting like the world is going to end at any minute? Just what were you thinking about?"

I looked at her and thought, You are nosey, but I didn't say it; instead, I said, "I had no idea that I was acting like the world was going to end tomorrow."

She looked down like she was embarrassed and said, "I said that because you have this weird look on your face like you are trying to hide what you are really feeling."

He was surprised at how accurate she had read him. He cleared his throat and said, "I can easily explain that. I just lost a bundle at the crap table and I was trying to find a way to kick my own ass. The money was gone so quickly I didn't realize how much I had lost. I really didn't expect this. Everyone was telling me how much money that they were winning and no one ever said that they had lost. I just wanted to find out for myself."

"Now you've have found out the hard way," Ocena said. "Welcome to Idiot City, located in fool's paradise. Come on and let me buy an espresso." Taking his hand into hers, she said, "Let's stroll down Dumb Ass Lane to where the other jackasses have gathered."

SuejuSoe didn't have time to give her an answer before she smacked him on the lips. He took it all in stride and did a mocking bow and said "Thank you Miss heartburns. What was that for?"

"Call me Ocena, everyone else does. The kiss was a need I needed to fulfill."

"Thank you, Miss, I mean Ocena. Shall we mosey on down to Idiot City? I bet that I could be the mayor. Mr. SuejuSoe Dumbass, Mayor. Yep, it does have a ring to it."

They strolled down to the Losers and Winners Coffee House. It was half full of patrons, and the look on most of their faces said that they were losers. They ordered two espressos and took them outside and sit at one of the small tables on the terrace. Before I took one sip of my espresso Ocena began telling me the history of her life as seen by her. She had not gotten very far into her story before I realized that was a troubled woman. She was talking about how much she had accomplished in a short period of time. She was a twenty-four-year-old female working in a nontraditional job. She was the owner of Heartburns' Construction & Landscape Inc. You would often see her in overalls and a hard hat, conversing with employees.

We sat and talked for a long time. She talked and I listened. Her saga began when she was in her teenage years. She did not strive for excellence or acceptance; she strove for individuality. She did not want to be like anyone but herself. She did not choose to follow crowds; she would go down a path of her own. She didn't go for fads, crazes, or clothes because they were what was happening. As a matter of fact, she went as far to the left as her peers went to the right, and she was comfortable with her decisions. She thought that most fads were for people who couldn't think for themselves, people who had to be told when, how many, and how long. Oftentimes she would read articles in magazines about style, makeup, and so-called beauty tips and laugh out loud. Anyone with half a brain can see that with all the different women, different shaped, hair, taste, economic status, and traditions these articles could apply to less than 1 percent of the female population. Yet it amazed her how many women believe it could work for them. This is like a one-hundred-eighty-pound woman wearing spandex because it is in style. To her the talk shows, the experts, the commentators were all a joke. The truth is out there, but they had no idea where it was.

As she talked she sounded upbeat, but as she continued you could tell that there was something wrong with the picture that she was painting. There was something dark and sinister lying barely covered and certainly not dead, a monster. A gigantic monster, one she didn't want anyone to see or know about. I could sense all the deep pain, anger, hurt, and sorrow that she had buried so deep no one found out. My heart went out to her.

She looked at me and my heart skipped a beat because I had never seen anyone who looked as serious as she did at that moment. She said, "SuejuSoe, may I ask you a question. I don't mean that, I want to get your opinion about something."

I said, "Sure." What else could I say?

She said, "Tell me, what are the top three things that are wrong with today's civilization?"

"Gee, Ocena, I've never thought about anything like this before."

"You don't have to be right or wrong. This is just a hypothetical, your own personal opinion."

"Okay," said SuejuSoe, "I'll give it a try. Now, let me see, a total disrespect for the law and order, ineffective parenting, hypocrisy, and a breakdown in morality."

"You cheated, that was four. But that's all right. I thought that you would say something like that. But have you ever thought just the opposite. You could keep the ineffective parenting because it's a biggie. A total disrespect for law and order is a by-product of ineffective parenting, so is hypocrisy and a breakdown in morality. Ineffective parenting may not come from your parents but from the parents of your children's peers, parents who give their children too much unsupervised freedom. The thing is kind of like Darwin's theory of evolution, every generation keeps evolving toward a society that is totally lacking the ability to become responsible law-abiding citizens."

SuejuSoe listened and marveled at what she was saying. He had never given much thought to the hypothesis that she had proposed, but the lady was making sense.

She continued, "There are a number of shooters aiming their balls at the net at the same time, some make it, some don't."

SuejuSoe looked at her with a complete lack of understanding on his face. He asked, "What did you just say?"

"What did I just say about what?"

"The ball and the net."

"Aw, I used that as a metaphor. I meant a lot of different things are out there to tempt your child, some may succeed and some won't. Your parents may have raised you with good morals and values and a healthy respect for authority. Your best friend may have been raised with a little less morals, values, and respect, and he may be associated with someone who has less than him. There is something else that I have to put in this bubbling pot, and that is the entertaining industry: movies, news, radio, music, TV, newspapers. They glorify violence, notoriety, sex, and gore. The experts are trying to explain away the existence of God and declare the Bible to be a book of fables. It will take a strong person not to keep his eyes on the very temptation that he prays not to be led into."

SuejuSoe was fascinated, "How do you come up with all these things? You sound like you should be teaching philosophy."

"No, it just really bothers me to see young people throwing their lives away."

"Do you have anyone particular in mind when you say this?"

"Yes, I was thinking about my brother, Iwana, and me."

"I don't get it. You turned out to be a model citizen."

"Did I? But just look at my brother. I forgot to put something else in the pot, and that is the government. How could I forget the government?"

SuejuSoe was perplexed. "What does the government have to do with it?"

"Just about everything," Ocena answered. She continued, "The government creates many of these situations purposefully. For an example, take welfare. In the beginning it was supposed to beneficial, but look what it turned into, it kept the poor people poor. Too poor to really live, it's just an existence and a crutch for many people who are too lazy to work. The worst part is that the people who are on welfare don't recognize this. They think that they are getting over. Another example is how the government lies about everything. UFO sighting, perhaps an alien. Just see how the government explains away everything. They may say something like the so-called alien that was purportedly seen by thousands was a prototype robot being tested by the military for use in germ warfare. They don't seem to care how big of a lie that they tell or how unbelievable their lies are, it's like they are saying since we said it, it is so."

SuejuSoe grinned and said, "You don't care much for authority, huh?"

"I don't have anything against authority. I just hate liars and people who thrive on power and greed and who want to be in charge, and are so corrupt the devil don't want them."

She stopped and looked across the room as though she was looking for someone. Then she looked at me with a frown in her brow. She said, "Listen, I've been going on and on and haven't let you get a word in edgewise."

He answered, "That's okay, I've really enjoyed listening to you. You've given me something to think about that I've never considered before."

A smile lit up her face. "Really? Do you mean that?"

"Of course I do."

"What was we talking about before I got sideswiped?"

"I think that you was telling me about your life."

"Yes, sure, boring stuff."

"No, I've really enjoyed listening. I would like to hear more."

SuejuSoe ordered more espresso, and Ocena continued her saga. She was third out of three children with a dominant mother and a part-time father who was part-time because that was the way her mom wanted it to be. Her dad worked hard building up his business and oftentimes slept in a room he had fixed up in the business. Daddy was kind and gentle and ruled fair and just and in her eyes could do no wrong. When she was small he would bounce her on his lap like a horse. She liked the way he smelled.

Oftentimes she wished that she could put that smell in a bottle and give it to the other girls who had part-time fathers. He always kept a cigar in his shirt pocket and smelled like cigar smoke. She loved to smell cigar smoke; it brought back those bittersweet memories of a childhood that was long ago past. As she was remembering her childhood and her father, a look of melancholy shaded her face. I could tell that these memories had been etched in her memory for eternity.

Nothing satisfied her mom. She learned that early in life. If you were good, it was not good enough. If you were bad, all hell would break loose. She was a small woman, and it bemused her all that bitterness could dwell in a body as small as hers. No one was right but her, and she held a monopoly when it came to God. He would come down and visit her. As the years passed, she made a change. But this is another story. She did not improve with age; she got worse and it amazed her how you could get worse when you are already the queen of pugnacity.

"The only way I survived my early years was to acknowledge what my Mama was, realize that she was not going to change and to go on the best way that I could. I could not ignore her because she adhered to every emotion I had. I could defy her and I did but that was not a smart move to make. She could not forgive, forget, compromise or love. As I grew older I realize that something very traumatic must have happened in her life that had made her this way. But knowing this gave me little comfort. I tried to appease her in every way that I could, but nothing I did made any difference." Ocena went on with her life story, but there was a large place in her mind and heart that she could never let anyone get near and it cost her a price she didn't want to pay.

Ever since the age of twelve, she learned how to manipulate people. She had learned it from her mother. Right after graduation she returned home to work in the family business because her father had had a stroke. Probably brought on by her mother. She had two brothers but they couldn't help. One was committed to the military and the other was addicted to drugs.

When she returned home she threw herself into the task of running the family's business. She didn't give her mom a chance to heap piles of her ideas of morals, guilt, and her ideas of what religion should be. Her mom didn't think that employees should complain. She was working hard, why not them? She paid them well.

"My father's condition deteriorated. All the rumors that were going around surely must have accelerated his demise. I told my dad that the rumors were just that, rumors. But I never knew whether he believed me or not. He knew that I was a controversial person with a nonconformist personality, and he knew that I often did things for no other reason than to shock those who challenge me. He knew that my mother played significant role in the development of her atypical personality. He also knew that I loved him and would do anything in her power for him.

"The death of my father, Grecian Heartburns, changed me. Not in the way a loved one's death usually affect a survivor. I began working seven days a week putting in anywhere from ten to sixteen hours a day. People would marvel at how much the company had grown. I added ten more personnel that was essential to keep up with the expansion of the company. Heartburns Construction & Landscaping Company grew by leaps and bounds.

"Almost everywhere I went I could smell the aroma of his aftershave and cigar smoke. This phenomenon lasted long after the death of my father. I could smell the aroma in the office and in my bedroom. Later I could smell it in my hair. Sometimes I would whisper, 'Hi, Daddy.' Occasionally a single tear would roll down my cheek and I would wipe it away with the back of my hand before anyone would see it. This didn't always work because some of the employees had already noticed. Their hearts, filled with compassion, went out to her. She grieved for her father in a way no one had seen before and this grief went on much longer than normal."

After the company had grown over 50 percent she slowed down a bit and decided to hire someone to manage the company so that she wouldn't have to work so hard. She had already proved to herself and the others that she could do what they had said she couldn't do and did it well. She had wanted to hire a female but second guessed herself and hired a male.

"The management of Heartburns Construction and Landscaping Inc. was taken over by Lymp Dickery. This gave me enough time to resume a so-called normal relationship in society. Although Lymp was very good-looking, articulate, well educated, and available, he was not the one for her. Anyway, a good policy was never date your employees; however, a good rump in the hay was another thing altogether."

Lymp was a business management major from the University of Purple Bottom City and had a degree in marketing. He was tall and well built with defined muscles like he worked out often. Women were drawn to him like a magnet. But for her he was too good-looking to be a good lover. He looked like he was too good-looking to sweat. Sometimes he would catch her looking at him like a hungry dog would look at a bone. It would send chills up his spine. He had to do something about this.

One day after the others had gone he had decided to confront her about this. She came into the office wearing a denim split skirt with a short top and midheel boots. She had her hair in a ponytail and no makeup. Her unadorned beauty stunned him. She entered the office as he was preparing to go home. She said, "Mr. Dickery, I see that you are preparing to go home. Too bad. I wanted to talk to you."

Lymp smiled and said, "I always have time to talk to the boss."

"Is that right," she said, smiling.

"Is there something that I can do for you?"

"All of that depends."

"On what?" he asked, realizing that he had spoken too soon. "Maybe a little, maybe a lot."

"Now," Lymp said, "you have aroused my curiosity." She smiled and asked, "Is that good or is that bad?"

Lymp had left himself wide open for whatever Ocena had in mind. Quickly, he tried to amend this colossal goof-up. He said, "It's getting late, perhaps we should discuss this at a later time."

She came out and flatly asked, "Do you have some place to go or are you avoiding me?" Lymp fidgeted with his briefcase nervously and asked, "Where did you get that idea?"

"From you. You act like you are afraid to be alone with me. Does it have anything to do with all the rumors going around about me?"

Lymp felt transparent, as if Ocena had looked straight through him and saw a truth that he didn't know was visible. He stammered and said, "I admit that I've heard rumors going around about you but you are a fair and just boss and I have no complaints."

"What about the woman? What do you think about me as a woman?"

"You are very beautiful, very desirable, and any man would be proud to have you as a . . ."

"As a what," Ocena demanded.

"I think that I should leave," said Lymp. "That is if you don't mind." She smiled, "I don't mind, go ahead."

As Lymp left the building, Ocena realized that her power trip was over and she had lost. But that was not the end of her story. She needed physical relief, and she was going to get it. No, she thought, I'm going home. She left the plant confused and unfulfilled.

As she walked into the door the phone was ringing. She picked it up and said, "Hello." But a conversation with anyone was something she did not want. All she wanted to do was soak in a tub of hot water filled with milk bath and bath salts. But the polite thing to do was answer the phone. The voice on the other end was her brother Iwana. She really did not talk to him. The only time she heard from him was when he was in trouble or wanted something. "Hi, Iwana, what do you want?"

"What makes you think that I want something?"

"The only time I hear from you is when you want something."

"Since you are going to be uppity, I'm going to hang up."

"Be my guest," Ocena invited him over the phone.

"I just called to see how you are doing since I haven't heard from you in a while."

"That's very sweet of you, but I'm fine and I'm tired and I really want to take a bath and get something to eat. Is there something else you wanted with me?"

"No. Er, sis, I was wondering if you could let me hold a hundred bucks?"

"I knew it. What do you need a hundred dollars for?"

"I've gotten into a little trouble playing poker."

Ocena paused and let her breath out slowly before she spoke. "I see. Have you ever thought about getting a job? Or don't you know what a job is?"

"If you are telling me that you are not going to loan me the money, say so. Because if I wanted to hear someone preach to me, I would go to church."

"So you know what a church is. Have you ever been inside one? I think you should try it."

"I knew that you were going to give me a sermon. I don't even know why I ever bothered you."

"Me neither," Ocena said, Why don't you get a real job that you can pick up a paycheck every.

"Why don't you ask Satan's disciple for the money?"

"You already know the answer to that."

"No, I don't, tell me."

"You know, Mom, she is worse than ever. I'm even scared to talk to her. When she talk at you because she don't talk to you, you can feel hell's fire and brimstone at your back."

Ocena began to laugh because she knew exactly what Iwana was talking about. Plus she knew that he wanted the money. She said to him, "Wanna, I know that you want this money to buy drugs to feed your filthy habit and you know that mom know the same thing. Isn't that the reason why she won't let you come home?"

Iwana said to Ocena with bitterness in his voice, "You know, you are sounding more like her every day. You had better watch out or you may turn into her."

"Thank you for pointing that news breaking item to me. I would kill myself rather than turn out like that."

"I want to know if you are going to loan me the money?"

"No," Ocena said with finality.

Iwana hung up the phone and cursed. "That bitchified slut. Who does she think she is? I should go over there and tell her something." But he didn't because he needed a fix too bad. He will probably have to rob a store or someone to get the money that he needed. It didn't really matter because he had done it before. Besides, what can they do to him, put him in jail? That was no biggie either because he had been there many times before anyway, you could get drugs in the slammer as easily as you could get them on the streets.

After hanging up the phone, Ocena began to get bad vibes. She felt her brother's hopelessness. In a minute, she had to hurry, hoping that whatever it was that had her speeding across the city would wait until she got there.

She was driving up just as Iwana was backing out of the driveway. She honked her horn and he stopped. She knew that he lived with two other guys and it seemed to her that one of them should clean the trash out of the yard and trim the bushes. The place looked like a dump. Paint was peeling off the house; panes were broken out of the windows. They had nailed cardboards across them. The fence had been trampled, and doggy poo was in the driveway along with puddles of oil. The place was not fit for dogs to live in. She wondered how they could live in such filth.

Iwana got out of his beat-up car swearing at Ocena. "What in hell are you doing here?" Ocena looked at him and he was shaking like a willow in a windstorm. His appearance was disgusting.

"I will ask you again, what are you doing here? Where are you going?" she asked.

"What's it to you? Why did you come here for?" Iwana demanded.

"I really don't know now that I'm here. I just got a funny feeling something bad was going to happen."

"So you got into your little o' car and bam! You are here."

"Yes, it was something like that. Where are you going?"

"Oh, me? I going out to rob some stupid hick and get me a fix. Did you come over to chaperone me?"

Taking him by the hands trying to lead him inside, she almost fell when he snatched his hand back violently. She made it to the door and had opened it. The stench from inside almost made her retch. A noxious odor of stale urine, stale cigarette smoke, and pure unadulterated funk overwhelmed her sense of smell. She felt dizzy. She stepped backward trying to get a breath of air that was not totally contaminated by the smell of pure rotten funk.

She pleaded, "Wanna, please don't leave. I've come to talk to you. Please, I've got the money that you asked for."

Iwana stopped immediately. "What did you say?"

She stood waiting for his reaction. He turned around and smiled. He smacked her on the cheek; she stumbled and her stomach flipped over because he plainly and simply reeked of decay.

She knew that drugs were killing him but she also knew that if he should continue to steal and rob he was going to end up dead. After all, he was her brother, and as miserable as he was, she didn't want him to die. She kept hoping that he would straighten his life out and leave those drugs alone. She knew that her brother was a wretched Chickpeo, but what could she do? Her mom had already turned her back on him because he had disgusted her beyond words but she was a pro at being the recipient of slander.

She entered the house and at once decided that the best thing that she could recommend for this place would be to torch it. Protective clothing and rubber gloves would be a necessity to enter this place.

Be extra careful and please do not touch anything. Something was growing on the furniture that should not be there. There were things moving on the floor that could not be squashed with your shoes.

She stepped outside again to breath. A pigsty would be a couple of steps upward from this place. She wondered how a person with Iwana's upbringing could end up living like this. She took out her wallet and counted out one hundred dollars. He said to Iwana, "See, this is the money you wanted, but I will double it if you would come home with me and clean yourself up."

"Why would I need to go home with you to clean up? I can do it right here."

"Okay, show me your bathroom."

"Follow me," Iwana invited.

They reentered the house, but before reentering, she took a deep breath hoping that it would last until she had exited. She followed her brother as he stepped over things lying on the floor and stepped around a pile of things that she could not identify. Too bad, she had to breathe again, she took some tissues from her purse and held them to her nose. They entered the bathroom and she could not believe her eyes. Inside the tub was muddy clothing and algae-covered filthy towels. It looked like it had not been used in years. The commode and washbasin were in the same shape. Carefully she backed out of the room holding her hand over her nose. "So, this is where you take a bath?"

"Yes, it is. Is there something wrong with it?"

"It is filthy. How can you live like this?"

"It takes practice and a good dose of hopelessness and helplessness."

"Lord, I know it does. Do you have any clean clothing?"

"I can't say that I do."

"Okay, get into the car, you are going with me and I'm going to stop and get you some decent clothing."

Iwana smiled wryly, "Still playing the role of the little saint."

Iwana got into the car thinking about what kind of germs and bugs he may infest her car with. Maybe she will sell it.

She pulled into the parking lot of a local discount store and came back out in about thirty minutes carrying two huge bags. She put them in the trunk of her car and resumed her trip home. Iwana was quiet the remainder of the way home.

She pulled up under the parking canopy at her condo, got out, opened the trunk, took out the bags, and entered her condo with Iwana in tow. She told him to sit on a barstool, but he wanted to see what she had bought him. She held up each piece for his inspection and ushered him into the bathroom and gave him orders not to come out until he was completely cleaned up, and if he didn't do it right, she would come in and do it for him.

"Yes, ma'am," said Iwana like a little boy.

He entered the bathroom and noticed that she had left underwear, socks, razor, deodorant, aftershave, a shirt, and a pair of pants lying on the vanity stool. She thought of everything, mused Iwana. First, he would shave with a real razor. He usually clipped the hair off with a pair of scissors. He really didn't care one way or the other.

He remembered why he had become what he was. Satan's angel would never give him a moment of peace. She had criticized him every way that she could. She berated him every chance that she got and let him know in no uncertain way that she despised him because he was not anywhere close to the person that she wanted him to be. He was worthless to her. She also let him know this as often as she could. Only God knew all the names he had called her in his mind.

As he soaked in the tub many unpleasant memories wiggled up out of the grave that he buried them in forever. Dad was cool until his dying day. He will never know why a genteel man like him would marry a bitchy witch like his mom. He could easily see why Ocena continually defied her. He also knew why his brother who was in the military stopped coming home after their dad died. One thing was odd; his mom had doted on him, but he would avoid her every chance he got. Yep! Life was a son-of-a-bitch. Maybe I should start going to church as Ocena had suggested. Yep! Having God in his life to make bad things good and good things better is something he really needed in his wretched existence. He must try it. Damn, he needed a fix.

He got out of the tub and let the water out. There was dirt everywhere. Where did it all come from? Maybe Ocena was right; he hated it when she was right. The residue in the tub was thick enough to plant a turnip patch. He had no idea that he had been so filthy. The clothes that she had bought fit him perfectly. He must thank her but knew that a sermon was in the making.

True to form, the moment he left the bathroom and the moment that she went in and saw all the muck that he had washed off, the title of the sermon began to take shape. "The Evils of Drugs and the Ungodly Effects They Have on Mankind." The sermon didn't last as long as he had anticipated. The old girl must be getting soft. She had made sandwiches, coffee, and chips. I ate without talking, but if I had wanted to talk, I wouldn't have been able to get a word in edgewise because Ocena's mouth was going full speed. Thank God I didn't have to listen. One of his roommates's friends was seeing a shrink and she had accused the shrink of hypnotizing himself so that he wouldn't have to listen to all of his patient's problems and still get paid.

Ocena kept an ongoing verbalization. By looking at her face you could tell that whatever she was saying was important and serious. He was tempted to break his trance and listen to whatever she was saying. On second thought he decided not to.

Gosh, it really did make him feel more human to be clean and full and in a clean place, but he still needed a fix. The intense desire that he was feeling before had diminished a mite, but he still felt jittery. There must some good in him somewhere.

Ocena had gone in to clean the bathroom. She decided to throw everything in the trash. She had disinfectant, deodorizers, sprays, and stuff to shine things with. It took her more than thirty minutes to clean up after Iwana. When she came out of the bathroom, Iwana had fallen asleep on the sofa. She covered him with a light blanket. Then she was free to do whatever she was going to do before she was interrupted by Iwana's phone call and her unnerving premonition. She looked at him sleeping on the sofa, but his sleep was not a peaceful one. The need for drugs kept him jumping and tossing and turning.

When Iwana awoke the following morning, Ocena was already gone. He found a note that she had left on the kitchen countertop. He poured himself a cup of coffee and read the note. "Had to leave early, beginning a new project out on Indigestion Avenue. Will see you later. Cena." He found some bagels and put two in the toaster. He munched on the bagels and contemplated what he was going to do for the reminder of the day. One thing he was sure of, and this came as a surprise, he didn't want to go back to his place.

The phone rang and startled him. It was Ocena. She wanted him to stay put until she got there. He could oblige her with that. But what could he do in the meantime to help pass the time? The thought of getting high toyed with the strings in the back of his mind. But he managed to push it back into a dark crevice and unplug it. Something else would have to come up, but what? I've got it. Cena's stereo was broken and he was going to fix it.

He commenced to fixing the stereo, but those little demons kept beckoning to him. They were very determined, and so was he. He had never fought so hard in his life if you didn't count the time he had fought the temptation to start using the stuff in the first place. I thought that was some kind of super Chickpeo and nothing like a little cocaine could hurt me, and the thought me getting hooked on the stuff was utterly ridiculous. Me getting hooked? That will never happen because my constitution is much too strong. I knew that they said that it was highly addictive, but that didn't apply to me. How wrong I had been. I had lost then but I'm very determined not to lose this time.

Someway, somehow five thirty came; it must have taken the long route, all the way around the wasted walls of duty. I don't know what this means, but I've always heard this saying. He had survived this long, but he felt too sick to celebrate.

Ocena walked in the door and startled Iwana. She took one look and knew that he was in trouble. She helped him to the couch and got a damp towel to place on his forehead and let him lie as quietly as he could in the state that he was in. She wished that she knew more to help him. If only she knew someone to call. Then she remembered Wester'C Ulcer.

She flipped through her addressograph, found his number and began dialing with quivering fingers. Dr. Ulcer's receptionist answered. She asked to speak to Dr. Ulcer and was informed that he was preparing to go home, and she stopped him before he had opened the door. "Dr. Ulcer, a Ms. Heartburns wishes to speak with you. She said that it was important."

Wester'C picked up the phone and said, "Ms. Heartburns, this is Dr. Ulcer, how may I help you?" Ocena told him about her brother's condition and how he was acting. He said that he would come over and take a look at him.

In about twenty minutes he was at Ocena's door. He entered and saw Iwana lying on the sofa. He walked over and took his pulse and checked his pupils and reflexes. Without batting an eye, he pronounced that Iwana was going through cocaine withdrawal and there was not much that he could do for him. He could give him a sedative to help calm him down, but the best thing she could do for her brother was to check him into a detox center. Ocena walked him to the door, and he kissed her softly on the forehead and told her to call him if she needed him and left.

She wiped the perspiration off her brother's forehead and took the towel and rewet it, and placed it back on his forehead and headed to the drugstore to get the prescription filled.

She exited the door and almost had forgotten how humid it was. She made a dash for her car and turned the air conditioner on full blast. She entered the traffic and was soon just another motorist trying to get somewhere.

After my conversation with Ocena had ended and we had parted, I made a vow never to use snap judgment again because I had totally misjudged her. The longer we talked, the more I found out about the real Ocena Heartburns. She was not self-centered and she was not afflicted with self-importance. She was a real down-to-earth kind of person and had weathered many storms and had grown stronger from each one. She was highly intelligent and really cared about people, especially the down and out. Sure she liked to do things out of the norm, but that was her way of saying, hey, I'm me and I don't have to walk in a rut made by someone else to be somebody.

CHAPTER VII

As Charles and SuejuSoe were on their way back from Underground City, they met Ocena and her brother, Iwana, on the Mole train. Ocena had been to see Dr. Wannabelax to see if she could get some pills that were still in the experimental stage for her brother. They had been called miracle pills because they were supposed to stop cocaine addiction in three days. She had tried everything else that she could think of and Iwana was really trying hard to get the monkey off his back.

They stopped at a local coffee house and ran into K'Narf and Pissy Dean. After all the hellos and glad to see yous, they sat down and had coffee. K'Narf, who always said what was on his mind without dressing it up, blurted out, "So, Sueju, how much progress has Wannabelax made on getting Charlie here back where he came from?"

"Not a whole lot. Frankly, I'm disappointed that so little progress has been made."

"But he is trying."

"Like hell he is. They've had a prototype of this thing for years and they are supposed to be perfecting it. It seems that all that they are perfecting is more money for themselves," said SuejuSoe impatiently.

"Aw, you know how those Ghosts are. They are not going to let anything go anywhere until they find a way to recycle it, that would be a major crime."

"I know that they are gung-ho on recycling everything, but they've forgotten about one thing," SuejuSoe said to K'Narf.

"What is that?" asked Pissy.

"They will have to come up topside to test the thing out."

"I don't know, you know those Ghosts have perfected things. They have perfected the taste out of the food and the scent out of flowers. What else are they going to fuck up?"

"Beats me," said K'Narf. "You may have come out better if you had gone to our Institute of Advanced Sciences. It may be purple but it was as good as, if not better than, than the Graveyard's."

"Why did you go to the Graveyard anyway?" asked Pissy. "Never mind, I already know, our illustrious Mr. SuejuSoe Suju."

"Do you have a problem with that?" SuejuSoe asked, looking Pissy directly in the face.

"Come, come now, boys," Ocena said, "let's not let our mouth say things that our bodies cannot back up."

"I don't have the foggiest idea of what you just said," said Pissy. "Maybe you'll get it by the end of the week."

"Or next year," added SuejuSoe. So let's cool it for now."

A man came over to their table and wanted to speak to SuejuSoe. He was bald, his back was wide and this made his legs look short and bowed, and his butt sagged like a loaded diaper. "Mr. Suju, I know that you don't know me, but there is something that I've always wanted to ask you, and I hope that you won't be offended."

"What's that?" SuejuSoe said in an irritated voice.

It's about you and those Graveyard Spooks. Why do you have to go down there so much? With the election coming up, some people have started talking calling you a two faced traitor."

SuejuSoe smiled, showing two rows of perfect white teeth, and said, "Really?"

"Yes." He smiled and exposed his crooked teeth, and said, "Talk is going around about this alien, pointing at Charles, and some people are saying that you don't have the welfare of anybody in Purple Bottom City in mind. They say that they think that you are acting like a pompous asshole, thinking that you are too good to care about the common citizens."

Ocena raised one eyebrow and sighed. Pissy was rolling his coffee cup around and around in his hands. Charles looked at SuejuSoe waiting for the axe to fall.

SuejuSoe spoke. "I don't know who 'they' are who are saying all of these things, but I want you to tell 'them' something. You can tell 'them' that I haven't heard anything from anyone needing help, and as long as 'they' peek at me through the blinds and around the corners, I can't help them. Ask 'them' why don't 'they' set up a meeting and invite me so that 'they' can get to know who I am and to see that I do not bite. I haven't any fangs, and I do not wallow in the mud with swine."

The man looked like he was very sorry that he had spoken to SuejuSoe. He appeared to be nervous and unsure about what to do next. He was wondering if he should say anything else or just leave. SuejuSoe made the decision for him. He said, "Give me a call."

As the man was leaving, he turned and dug his flabby pants out of his ass and farted, and said, "Thank you."

"Now, that is what you call class," joked K'Narf.

"Yes, indeed, that's class, so 'they' say," said SuejuSoe.

"And 'they' know what to say to the right person," K'Narf interjected.

"Yes, and the right person is the preacher man right here," said Pissy.

"What are you talking about?" SuejuSoe asked.

"Nothing," K'Narf answered.

Well, it didn't sound like nothing to me. It sounded like you all are trying to tell me something by saying nothing and I don't like it. That's the coward way out."

"You guys cut it out and let's go. Aren't we supposed to meet with the others in about forty-five minutes?" Pissy said, trying to be diplomatic.

Ocena said, "I need to run a few errand before I get there, so I may be a tad late."

"Women," said Pissy.

"Yes, what about women?" Ocena wanted to know.

"Nothing. I just love them."

"Later."

"Yes. Later."

When Wester'C got to the meeting, everyone was already there. There were Carrie Blister, Pissy Dean, K'Narf Covictus, Arthur Moses, Jelly Belly Jon, and a few others.

The meeting had just begun. Sirrom Belche was reading the minutes from the last meeting. SuejuSoe had the floor; he was acknowledging those who were not on the committee but were volunteering their services. After he had finished, Wester'C took over. "We have called this meeting to strengthen our struggle for getting the right people elected. We do have a way to go. If any of you feel that you may have any input, you can say so now." No one said anything.

Wester'C continued, "It is with the sole desire that we will welcome anyone's thoughts that will shine light in dark corners. Most of all, we must tell the truth at all times. With no exceptions. Do y'all think that this can be accomplished? We must tell our constituents the truth no matter how low-down, dirty, and ugly it is. Tell it anyway. Sometimes we must ask hard questions that will stun the answerer into action. We know that our society is corrupt, and we need to come up with a suitable solution to rectify it. We must ask why the methods that we are using are not responding. I'll tell you the answer, but you won't like it. It's because we have become too civilized.

"Now, I suppose that you are puzzled because you think that there is no such thing as too civilized. Yes, there is, and it is destroying the very fabric and principles of our ancestors who survived the nova and rebuilt this world. One thing is that our justice system is seriously flawed. And we make excuses and say dumb things like it may be flawed but it works. Bull!

"Then, you must ask yourself if it is so good, why does the crime rate continue to escalate?" Wester'C cleared his throat and looked around at everyone in the room expecting someone to say something. No one said a word, so he said, "If there is anyone here who does not agree with what I'm saying I wish that you will acknowledge it. Because these facts are what we are basing our campaign on."

No one said a word. Wester'C continued his narrative. "We have taken God out of everything and replaced Him with idols: false religions, our jobs, our money, clothes, jewelry, social standing, houses, and so forth. I'm not particularly religious, but this country was founded on religious freedom, and our money has "In God We Trust" printed on it. Just because someone else religious practices offend them, their feeling and practices offend someone else just as much. I do know when someone is messing up. You can't pray at the beginning of sport events and other public gathering but, just let a disaster happen, then they are asking everyone to pray. We need to amend capital punishment to suit the crime. Throwing someone in jail that have living conditions better than their homes is not a deterrent. I'm not saying that the police should be brutal. The punishment should be issued by our courts, untainted by corrupt judges and unscrupulous lawyers. The criminal should be made to experience the same pain, fear, hopelessness, panic and every other emotion that their victim experienced. This might make them think before they act."

Wester'C paused, looked around the room, and continued. "To tell the masses just how things are is not easy. But I strongly feel that the people should be the source of power, not the servants that we elect to represent us, when they have another agenda in mind. I don't know when it happened, but those roles were reversed. The elected officials are telling their constituents what they are going to do. This is not the way that it should be, and the people that are elected to represent us should cater to our demands.

"I wholeheartedly agree that entire political system is at a critical stage of decay. To save our world from itself, it is essential that we can get people elected who have the same principles and values as we, so that we can save us from ourselves," K'Narf said.

Bojo spoke up, "This is a new age political arena. People who still adhere to the principals that this world government was based on before all the amendments was put in. There are a lot of people like us who want to change it for the betterment of all.

"Those fat cats and those who want to be power brokers, have made politics a profession and need to be kicked out because they are professional assholes. They have got more shit than Bobo's Bull Farm, and they are unfit to be leaders and shouldn't even try. It's like you plant a seed and the seed began to grow and branch out. The branches get cut all the time by pruning, but the seed, which is the trunk, never gets pruned. So we need to cut the tree at the trunk and did up the roots."

"Can't you see how essential it is that our people get elected? We need to wipe the slate clean and start over," said Wester'C.

"Wait a minute," said Carrie, "we need to stop and step back and look at ourselves, take the time out, and look at how others may feel about what we are trying to do. We need to find out how the doubters, the die-hards, the misinformed, the hopeless, and the helpless see as they view our intentions. These people may think that we are lunatics and pompous assholes trying to upset the windmills of power for personal benefits."

"I've thought of this before. You do have something that I've never considered. Well maybe it had crossed my mind and I stopped it before it did any damage," K'Narf admitted.

"You know, I've done the same thing," Wester'C said.

"I think that we are all guilty of doing this," SuejuSoe added.

"There's nothing else to do but try to erase the tainted state that we have been living by and try to began again, and this is a job of monstrous proportion. Change is never easy, and trying to change something that has been in use for over two hundred years is not going to be easy or pretty. There is going to be a revolution. I personally don't think that this is going to happen all at once because many, many citizens don't see anything wrong with the way things are. They cannot see all the corruption, evil, personal agenda, and all manner of evils written into amendments and addenda that most overlook and don't care about because they just don't know any better."

Ocena spoke up, "I know that this is something that must be untaken gradually. It even frightens me when I think of the massive job that we are up against. We are going back to the original constitution, there's not very much in it that we need to change. It is basically a sound doctrine. It was not until all the amendments started changing the meaning of the original document that things began to fizzle on both ends. Personally, I think anyone who had a smidge of intelligence and can add two and two can see the feasibility our platform can provide."

"Are we trying to get rid of the Mother Court?" [Supreme Court on Earth 111].

"Nooo. We must limit it reach because they make some iffy decisions."

"I can indeed say this is going to take some doing. So let's get on with it."

"Just how?" asked Jelly Belly.

"Now, Jelly, I don't rightly know. But I'm sure that we will come up with something. So we are in the market for suggestions," Wester'C said.

"How in hell are we going to do this?" Bojo asked.

Wester'C stood up, broke a roll of Life Savers, and said, "First thing that we must do is to agree 100 percent in doing this."

K'Narf had a habit of chewing toothpicks and asked in his most serious voice. "Just how are we going to get this done? How are we going to influence thousands of voters that the program that we are offering is much better than the one that they have now. How can we convince them that if we are to continue with the same program we are doomed and a life of distress is all we have to look forward to?"

"I can see that we have our work cut out for us," said SuejuSoe.

K'Narf said, "We sure do and we don't know where to start."

The room got eerily quiet. Everyone was looking at each other for an answer. Charles DeNero spoke up. "I know that I am not of your world, but where I came from we had similar problems. Although they haven't been solved we have began trying to rectify the wrong. If I would tell you that we've overcome discrimination and prejudice and created racial harmony, I would be lying. People on my world are racist regardless of race. They can't seem to help it. Race plays a dominant role in just about everything. The difference between you and him is that all of you are purple. My world had a violent beginning, and things have not gotten much better in some places. In my world there are many diverse races, unlike in your world where there is one race and underneath there is let's say the original race, and both of you think that they are more suitable to rule, not unlike in my world where there are many races that want to rule the world. This keeps us in strife and unrest, there are wars famines and many; many deaths, all for what? There is no peace. The only peace is through military might, who have the biggest and most powerful militaries.

"Pray tell me what does this have to do with convincing voters to accept our platform, said K'Narf.

"If you will let me finish, you may learn something," Charles admonished.

"Okay, then be my guest."

Charles cleared his throat and continued, "As I was getting ready to tell you, this is how we stumbled upon the best way to convince a mass market. First, we went into the communities, in churches, especially the ones with the most negative voters. If we could convince the leaders, they would let us come and address the congregation and surrounding communities so we could tell them how beneficial this would be for them. Secondly, we used the media, radio, TV, newspapers, posters, and pounded the pavement."

"What kind of response did you get?" asked K'Narf.

"I'll tell you this much, an unknown peanut farmer from a place that no one had ever heard of got elected president of the USA."

"I don't believe this," Jelly Belly blurted out.

"I swear. This is the truth," Charles insisted.

"Did it take a long time to sway the public?" Wester'C asked.

"No. Not really."

"This seems like something that could solve our dilemma. But we are going to need some people power."

"No need to worry about that," said Moses. "I can get help from the students if we are willing to pay them something. I can ask them first thing Monday."

Wester'C grinned. He felt sure that things were going to work out. With the suggestion that Charles DeNero had given them, he felt that the platform that they had came up with was going to be implemented and the future would be good. He wished that he could try this out on a limited basis before this thing came out in full force. He was thinking that if it didn't pan out, he would look like an idiot, and he didn't think that he could survive that. He called Charles aside and began to ask him about the questions that were holding his commitment at bay. There had to be a good reason for this uneasy sediment to be tugging at his consciousness. He nonchalantly asked Charles, "Charles, is there something that you left out about the method that was being used to reach the masses? It didn't go all that smoothly without a hitch, did it?"

"It went smoothly. Much smoother than any of us had imagine. I know that you must have doubts, and you should. After all, you don't know me. I'm from another world altogether."

"I know. But I trust you."

"Thank you for your vote of confidence. Then there's the possibility that you all could be suckers in a sucker's paradise. I could be as phony as hobo on a king's throne."

"The jury is still out on that one. I've got work to do."

Charles said, "Yes, sure."

Things were going smoothly and the only bad part was time. They didn't have enough of it. If Moses were to come through with his promise, things would be a lot better. There simply was not enough man power to do all the things that needed to be done. Charles had blended in because he knew more about what they were doing than they did.

Someone went out to get some food because they were working much longer than they had planned. Finally, Wester'C stopped and announced that he was going home because he had some early appointments and he needed some rest. Bojo butted in, That's what all of you doctors say. They must have taught y'all that at medical school."

"What in the world is he talking about?" asked Wester'C.

"Don't mind him he's a reject from the past three generations. I bet that he don't know shit from wild honey," said K'Narf.

"That's one bet that you will lose because I'm looking at shit and there's no honey anywhere in the vicinity," inferred Bill.

"Uh-huh! Somebody must have hit a nerve," said Wester'C.

"Ain't no one in here big enough to get on my nerves. Now smoke that in a peace pipe," bragged Bill.

K'Narf stopped what he was doing and said, "I've got five dollars that says you are wrong."

"Here's five more," said Jelly Belly.

"Listen, I don't want to take you guy's money."

"Bojo, you are not trying to chicken out, are you?" asked Jelly Belly.

"No Lord! I was just trying to save y'all money and a lot of embarrassment."

"You don't have to be so kind. So put up or shut up," said K'Narf.

"All right, we'll do it your way," said Bojo. "My Mama always told me that everything that shines is not gold."

SuejuSoe spoke up in a loud voice, "You guys can cut that crap out. We've got tons of work to be done."

"Does this mean that you don't want a piece of this action?"

"Naw, it's too easy."

"Just what does that mean?" asked Bill.

"It means that I can get on your nerves in less than five minutes."

"Not in this world. Not in my lifetime." boasted Bill.

"Okay. I'll prove it," SuejuSoe began to talk and every word that he spoke he accented it by sucking his teeth. Not only was he getting on Bill's nerves but everyone's else.

Bojo put his hand over his ears along with everyone else and pleaded with SuejuSoe to stop. Bojo said, pulling out his wallet, "Here, man, your five dollars. Here's ten, twenty more.

Everyone was pulling out their wallets, pleading with SuejuSoe to stop. "Stop man stop! K'Narf cried out in agitation. "This is not getting on one's nerves, this is emotional and mental torture."

"Enough already." Yelled Ocena. "I demand that we put a stop to these childish antics."

"Sure, you are right," said SuejuSoe. "Now, let's get back to work. Just remember to never try to jive a jiver."

Bojo went back to work saying nothing to no one. SuejuSoe, WesCter'C and Charles gathered around a large desk discussing a catchy slogan for the yard posters. Wester'C kept glancing at his watch and seemed in a hurry to go somewhere. He spoke, "I'm sorry but the truth is I've really go to go."

"Take off," said SuejuSoe. "It's no biggie."

After Wester'C had gone Ocena came over to where SuejuSoe was and spoke in a hushed tone, "Will I see you later?"

"Can't you see Moses watching you?" SuejuSoe admonished.

"I don't care, that's his problem," she shot back stubbornly.

"You know that that man is in love with you and as long as he feel that way everyone else had better look out."

"Like I said, that's his problem. I'm not vying for sainthood, and Arthur likes to pretend that he's perfect."

"You mean to tell me that you don't have any feelings for him at all?"

"I didn't say that. It's just that I don't like to be taken for granted."

"Can't you tell that he's possessive? Can't you tell that he's crazy in love with you?"

"I know but that night of the prom keeps popping up and he still blames me."

"That happened a long time ago. Y'all should have made some kind of amends or smoothed things over somehow. This don't make sense, and it's sad because I really like the guy."

"We may work something out one day, then again, we may never get over that one night."

"Think back, Ocena, from what I've heard it was you that orchestrated the event of that night. So why don't you take the blame because you are the guilty one."

"Maybe we could get a quickie?"

"You haven't paid attention to a word that I've said. I don't like quickies. I want to make love easy like Sunday morning."

"We'll have to do that at another time and place but in the meantime a quickie is all that I can do."

"Whatever you say. You are a gentleman and I will honor your desires no matter how horny I am."

"Get out of here. I'll see you later."

Later the same night Arthur came over. Ocena let him in and he stood staring at her saying nothing. She felt like an ameba under a microscope.

"Just what do you want from me?"

"All that I want from you is everything. I know that you are not ready to give me this. I want to know if there's a future for us because if there is, I'll wait on you to clear whatever it is that is blocking your ability to commit to me."

"Arthur, every time I see you, you don't have to go through this declaration of your love for me. I already know how you feel about me."

"Yes, but I don't want you to forget that my love for you is eternal."

"Cut that out, Arthur, you know that I love you."

"If you love me so much, why are you spending so much time with SujuSoe? He hangs around you like a shadow, and I hate it."

Framing his face with her hands, Ocena spoke gently. "Darling, please, must I remind you who negotiated this separation."

"I was wrong. Actually, I was having doubts about me committing myself to you especially with you being so public orientated."

"You didn't have to do that. That was something that you choose to do all by yourself."

"Again, I will not deny that I was wrong."

"Being wrong and admitting that you are don't make things okay. They are just words." With her voice rising slightly she continued, "I felt lower than an earthworm when you decided to put our affair on hold. I kept blaming myself. Then I knew that I'd done nothing wrong and all of this was an ego problem. I am not perfect. I won't ever be perfect, and may God deliver me from anyone who is perfect or even think that he is.

Arthur sighed. "I get the picture."

"You know that I'm a nature girl and I believe in the natural order of things. But you are always trying change things to suit the mold that you think it should be. Either you accept me as I am or leave me alone."

Arthur stood up and began to pace. He turned to Ocena and said, "I may have handled this thing wrong, but the mold that you keep saying

I'm trying fit you into it is called society. There are rules and regulations, and people just can't go around doing as they please. Even having sex has rules. You can't go around having sex whenever, wherever, and however you want. Society calls those types of people animals. We are supposed to be able to control those desires and not give in to them. Perhaps we could go back and start over."

"No! No way," she said vehemently.

Then tell me what I can do that will rectify this situation of ours?"

"Stop trying to make me someone that I'm not. I am me. I don't want to be anyone else."

"So I do have a chance?"

"Arthur, my dear love, I've been in love with you ever since I was seventeen, and that is something to behold. You can't just throw something like that away. We have memorable times."

"Honey, can I stay the night? I really need you." He put his arms around her and pulled her close. He could smell the scent of her hair. It smelled of jasmine. She fitted into his arms as though she was made just for them.

He smelled of aftershave and she loved the way he smelled. She put her arms around his neck and kissed him on the lips. He had a smidgen of mint on his breath and she liked that. She could feel the hardness of his muscular, well defined body. It always excited her. There was a growing spot of heat spreading from the pit of her stomach outward, engulfing her entire body. Why could he evoke these feelings in her especially since she had made love only two hours ago with someone else? She must be a slut. There was not another word that she could think of to define it, so *slut* was it. She had never let names bother her before and now was not the time to start. She pulled away from Arthur and sat on the sofa. He sat beside her holding her close to him. They sat like that for a long time.

First thing the following morning, Arthur was up before dawn. He told her that he had to meet some guys on the old Runs Road and he had to be there at six. Ocena pleaded with him, "Please, darling, just one more time."

"I wish that I had enough time but I don't. I'll make it up to you later." He jumped out of bed leaving her to do battle with those unseen demons of lust and desire. The thought that Charles could be right crossed her mind and scared her.

Before Arthur reached Runs Road he sensed that something was amiss. The Rumbling Guts' van was parked out at the intersection of Indigestion Avenue and Body Parts Circle. There was no one in sight. This was not something that they would normally do. The back door was ajar and the ground around the van had been trampled and scuffed.

Arthur shrugged his shoulders and drove on to his appointment. The day was going to be a beauty. The sun had not risen but just looking at the sky there were signs that the day was going to be terrific.

A soft breeze played tag with the wildflowers beside the road. The aroma of jasmine and wisteria floated on the breeze, and this was one of those days that he wished that he could bottle and save for a rainy day.

A feeling of nostalgia tugged lightly at his memory, interrupting his one on one with nature. There was a small lane that was not traveled often to his left. It led to nowhere, just into the forest. He remembered Ocena taking him down that little trail a few months back. They had made love in the forest and it was fantastic. They had taken a blanket with them but she had wanted to lay on the leaves and straws that covered the floor of the forest.

Nostalgia was so intense it made his heart ache. He slowed down and looked down trying to see he didn't know what. But what he wanted was for Ocena to be with him now and they could have an encore.

He remembered how both of them had taken off all their clothing and lain on the forest floor smelling the musty dampness of decaying vegetation. He would never forget that smell, nor how Ocena was so in tune with nature until it seemed as if she had popped out of the ground. But to feel the twigs and straws snapping as they made love seemed like it was put there just for them to make love on. They had run and frolicked in the forest without any clothing on. It didn't matter if someone saw them; it was paradise.

Shaking his head and clearing his memory, Moses continued down Runs Road. Just before he got to the intersection of Runs Road and Elbow Avenue, he spotted something, no, someone, lying in the ditch. He slowed down trying to see what was going on without leaving the safety of his car. He stopped. Lying at the edge of the forest was a body. Going by the clothing that the person was wearing, he knew that it was a member of the Rumbling Guts. Moses peeped out the window and saw a pool of blood mingled with bodies. What happened here? he wondered.

Must have been a gang fight and the Rumbling Guts had lost. As soon as he got to a phone he would notify the police. Wasn't it just like those fuckers marring my perfect morning?

As he neared the intersection and Runs Road, he began to slow down as he looked for a place where he could find a phone. He spotted one at a convenience store. It was still early and there wasn't much traffic. He pulled over and called the police and notified them of the dead bodies. The policeman that answered the phone must have had the IQ of a peanut. He kept asking me dumb questions like "What time did it happen?"

"How in the hell should I know?

"How many bodies did you find?"

"Two."

"Did you find any weapons?"

"No. I didn't look for any."

"Did you who or what initiated the confrontation?"

"No. I guess that they were fighting because the sun came up and someone stepped in someone's foot print. Don't ask me any dumbass questions. You know as much as I know. "Where can we reach you?" You can't.

I hung up the phone and drove away to my appointment. By the time I got to the Rino's Sobut Dude Ranch, I had cooled down from my encounter with the police officer, Sergeant Dumbshit. As I entered the gateway, I was accompanied by the owner, Rino Coldsore. We exchanged greetings and went inside. Coldsore was one of those who came from the Graveyard and didn't go back.

We entered his office, and it was richly decorated with deep leather upholstery and remnants of the old West. We sat down and he poured coffee for both of us. Then he began to speak. "Art, may I call you Art?"

"Actually, most people call me Moses."

"Well, Moses, I know that you are wondering why I asked you out here when we barely know each other. I believe that we can help each other get something done that really needs doing."

Moses raised one eyebrow. Rino continued, "I can see that I've piqued your curiosity. This is what I'm proposing. I've heard about this guy that got here by way of accident and how much he want to go home."

Moses stood up shaking his head in a negative way. "You've got the wrong person. You should have called SuejuSoe Suju. He knows more about it than anyone else."

"That's precisely why I called you. Suju is much too close and much too involved to accept what I'm proposing."

"I'll be a sucker and take your bait. What are you proposing?"

"Dr. Wannabelax is working on stabilizing a portal for travel through the dimensions. Am I right?"

"Yes."

"And, the portal have to be brought up from the Graveyard to be tested. Am I right?"

"Yes."

"Well, where is a better place to do this than out here where I've got lots of space."

"So."

"I'll give them permission to set up the portal on my ranch, you are going to need someone to do it. Yes."

"Yes."

"And if the portal works, I want to go to DeNero's world with him."

"Why would you want to do something like that?"

"According to our history, we were identical to that world and we too had chickens as large as sheep, and since that world has not been decimated, there should still be some there. Yes?"

"Yes. You must be talking about ostriches and emus."

"Whatever, but I would want to bring some back and raise them for a profit."

"I see, and you want me to convince DeNero to let you come along for the ride. Yes?"

"Yes."

"Well, I can see what's in it for you, but what about me? How am I to profit from this?"

"You know that your football team and your baseball teams need new uniforms. They would have them. Plus, I will throw in new equipment for the science lab."

"I'll say one thing, you know all the right buttons to push."

"Is that a yes or a no, or do we have to take it under advisement?"

"I think that you can safely say that."

"Well when are you guys going to meet again?"

"I don't rightly know but I'll keep you informed."

Moses left the ranch and started back to the city. Only now there was the police and ambulances everywhere. They were pulling over everyone. Moses stopped and asked what was going on. A policeman told him that someone had called in and reported two dead bodies. It seemed to him that maybe this was the outcome of two rival gangs' confrontation. A bad one at that. They had found the bodies, and they were allegedly members of the Rumbling Guts. The only other evidence was a van that was abandoned about a mile up the road. There wasn't any sign or any other evidence present.

Then Moses told him that he had reported the incident and if they needed any help to contact him. As he drove away he tried to picture how the incident took place and he thought surely the Stomach Cramps were the culprits. Then he remembered what he had said to the policeman, to call him if they needed some help. Why had he said that to the policeman? He didn't know anything to tell the police. Evidently he had been watching too many television cop shows. Anyway, he shook his head in disgust. "What a blatant waste of life."

When Moses turned on Indigestion Avenue, he encountered more policemen, emergency vehicles, and the news media. He was sure that he knew what was going on, yet he slowed down enough to ask and was told someone had reported dead bodies that they had found.

Moses drove on because he could piece together the rest of the story. There were an abundance of gawky-eyed onlookers, and the police was failing miserably trying to control them. An old woman who was more interested in what was going on then where she was going got hit by a car. Two people were pulled out of a ditch covered with mud and blood, and one of them was screaming obscenities between screams of pain.

Shortly, Moses did pull over and stopped. But before he could sit his car a policeman told him to move along. He drove off but was tempted to park and walk back. Then he wondered why would he want to witness a grisly scene as this one. As he resumed driving home, he felt physically ill thinking about how easily this could happen to anyone, even nonparticipants. Anyone in the wrong place at the wrong time was a prime candidate.

He walked into his apartment and turned on the TV. The scene that he had just witness was on.

He changed channels and it was there also. He clicked again, same thing. "I may as well go to the gym, there's nothing on the tube that I want to see."

Today was Saturday and he wanted to do absolutely nothing of importance. Somehow he just didn't feel like doing anything. The shrill ringing of the phone cut into his thoughts about how he was going to spend his day. It was SuejuSoe.

He wanted him to turn the TV to channel six. "Hey, Moses, check this out." There was an APB out on him. A steaming Moses exclaimed, "What in the name of everything that's holy is going on?"

SuejuSoe answered, "That's why I'm calling you to find out."

"You've got one on me."

"Are you going to call that number and find out?"

"I may as well. I'll clue you in later. I may need you to bail me out."

"Sure thing. Later."

Moses dialed the number with beads of sweat forming on his top lip and nose. The phone rang twice. A voice said, "Purple Bottom City Police, Sergeant Wikket Kneecap, how may I help you?"

"I'm Arthur Moses and I've just found out that you have issued an arrest warrant out for me." Sergeant Kneecap told him to hold on. Another person came to the phone and said, "Chief Regional."

"I'm Arthur Moses, and I've just found out that there is an arrest warrant out for me."

"Yes, that's right."

"Why? What did I do?"

"I need you to come down to the station."

"Why? Should I bring a lawyer?"

"Goodness no, son, I'll explain when you get down here."

"Okay, I'll be right down." Moses hung up the phone and cursed under his breath, "Damn! Why me? Why now?"

Moses walked into the chief of police's office and identified himself. The chief was sitting behind his desk. When he stood up, Moses was shocked. The man was humungous. He must have weighed over three hundred pounds and stood at least six feet six. He held out his hand to Moses and grabbed his hand like a crocodile would grab his next meal. He was sloppily dressed; either he was color-blind or didn't give a darn. He introduced himself, "I'm Retton Gallstone. Please have a seat."

Moses obliged, but he had to free his hand from this crocodile grip. Finally, he let go. Moses sat down and asked, "What about this warrant that's out for me?"

"Aw, don't worry about that, son."

"How can I not worry? I'm the principal of a high school, and how do you explain to thirty-five hundred children plus their parents that the principal has been picked up on an APB?"

"That was issued because you left the scene of a crime."

"And?"

"Well, son, you see that's not the way it's supposed to be done. You see, son, you are supposed to be done. You see, son, you are supposed to give a statement and—"

"I'm listening," Moses interrupted. Then to himself he murmured, Don't call me son.

"You see, son, when you come across something like that, you are supposed to stay there until help or the police arrive."

Moses said under his breath, "You called me son again, fucker." Then he said out loud, "Are you crazy? It was barely dawn and it was dark. Do you think that just because I see a couple of bodies and a trashed van, I'm going to leave the safety of my car? At least it is safer than it is outside, check the bodies, call you and go back and wait until you get there. I don't think so."

"How did you determine that they were dead?"

"I didn't really. As far as I could see, they were not moving or breathing, and at the angle that they were laying, it was a good guess that they were."

"Why was you out there so early in the morning?"

"I had an appointment with the owner of the Rino's Sobut Dude Ranch."

"Was this a business matter?"

"Yes, it was. Now if you are going to charge me with something let me call my attorney and get this thing over with. I'm not going to talk anymore."

"Now, son, it ain't like that, it's because you left the scene of a crime and these questions have to be asked."

Again Moses swore under his breath, "Cheese, dick, don't call me son anymore." Then he spoke out loud. "You mean that you are going to tie up my time just because I happen to stumble up on the aftermath of an accident or crime and at the time I didn't know what was going on?"

"You are the closest thing to a witness that we have."

"I am not a witness. I didn't see anything happen. I feel like I'm be persecuted for getting up early and driving down the road, and being a good citizen by calling in something that looked suspicious.

"No matter how good of a citizen that I am, if I should ever encounter something like this again, I'm going to keep on going."

"Take it easy son, no one is going to arrest you. Everyone already know that the Cramps and the Guts are behind all of this. This was bound to happen one day. I regret that the Terrible Toilet Papers wasn't around."

"So am I. Am I free to go?"

"Not quite. There are a couple more questions I must ask you. Did you recognize any of the victims?"

"How can you ask me something like that? No."

"The next is have you ever been arrested or charged with a felony?"

"No."

"You see, son, that was not so bad."

Arthur's patience was spent. He said in his soberest voice, "Please do not call me son again. I detest it."

"Oh, I'm sorry, son. I didn't mean anything, it's just a habit that I wish that I could break. Again, I'm sorry and you are free to go."

When Arthur got back to his apartment he called SuejuSoe. "How did things go?"

"Like talking to a retard."

"What do you mean, a retard?"

"He kept calling me son even after I asked him not to."

"The chief of police, Retton Gallstone himself. That bozo kept calling me son then said that he was sorry."

A smile played at the corner of SuejuSoe's mouth because he knew how much Moses hated for anyone to call him son.

"Go ahead and laugh," Moses urged. "In situations like this, you'll find out who your friends are." Actually SuejuSoe had compassion for Moses because he knew why he didn't like to be call son.

It all started when he was eight years old. His mom had put his dad out of the house because she was in love with another man. He couldn't see or understand how she could do something like that. This man was married, abusive, and perpetually intoxicated.

Many nights she would sneak him into her bedroom and you could clearly hear them making love, but it always sounded like an animal fight to him. He could clearly remember because many times he was sexually aroused when he heard these sounds. He was too young to understand what was happening to him.

Then Mom could no longer satisfy his lust; he started to get out of mom's bed and get in the bed with his sister. She never cried out or faulted him because she was too afraid of what Mom would do. He knew that his mom knew what was going on, yet she did nothing. She would just lie there until he returned to her bed.

Even when he heard him raping his sister he became sexually aroused and hated himself because these noises were causing his sisters so much pain. It made him feel rotten to the core because these things shouldn't be having this kind of effect on him. He wanted to go in and kill that no-good drunken bum, and he vowed that one day he would.

But that day didn't come. One day in June he wished that he had killed him. He had just came home from summer school and the bum was already there. He came into his room where he was and sat on the bed beside him. He was reeking of cheap whiskey. He began to talk, "Son, I know that you don't especially like me but we can become friends."

"Never." Moses spit out the words as if it had been soaked in bile. He remembered him putting his arm around his shoulders and he remembered how rotten his breath smelled. He almost vomitted. He struggled to free himself of this disgustingly drunk bum, but he wouldn't bulge. He became alarmed and tried to cry out for his mom but he put his big funky hand over his mouth. "Be still, son, and this will soon be over," he had said to him.

Panic took over his entire body. He was more afraid than he had ever thought possible. He took his other hand and took off the jeans that he was wearing and he wondered what he was trying to do.

When he saw him unzip his fly and took out his penis, he still didn't know what was going on. Then words came out of his sewage-smelling mouth. He said, "Now, son, I don't want you to be scared because I'm going to make a man out of you today. It may hurt for a little while but soon it is going to feel good. There's no need for you to struggle because you are really going to enjoy this."

Moses couldn't say anything because he still had his hand over his mouth. He was wondering where his mother was. Why didn't she come and rescue him? Tears began to roll down his cheeks and he began to tremble all over.

The drunken bum took his penis and put it into his mouth and began to gently suck on it. As scared as he was, it felt good. He relaxed a little. Then he told him to take his penis and put it into his mouth. He shook his head violently. "No!" he screamed, "I'm not going to do that."

That was when he forced him to do it. "Amy, you better not bite me either, because I will break your neck, son."

Moses gagged and vomitted. He was telling him what to do, but Moses was in hysterics, thinking that surely he was going to die. This ordeal seemed to last an eternity, and he was thinking that if he got through this there was nothing left to do but kill him. He finally stopped trying to get him to suck on his penis. He thought that the whole ordeal was over but that bum turned him over on his stomach and spread his buttocks and began to force his penis in his rectum. He must have fainted because nothing had ever hurt him so badly. He didn't know what else happened, only that he woke up covered in blood and the most excruciating pain that ever was. He called for his mom but she never came. When he heard those sounds coming from her bedroom he knew why. He decided that he was going to kill both of them.

His sister came into the room and saw what had happened and took him into her arms and cried along with him. Finally, she got calm enough to call the pastor of the local church, Rev. E. E. Scalp. He had trouble trying to understand what she was saying because of hysteria. That alone made him hurry because she was in a frenzy. He came over, took one look, and called the police. When the police arrived they called child protection agency. The bum and mom never knew that the police had arrived.

When they knocked on the door of the bedroom no one answered. They kicked the door in and he was lying in bed on his back and the mom was sitting, straddling him moving up and down. He remembered that he kept screaming, "I'm going to kill them. I'm going to kill both of them!"

They abruptly sit up and acted like that they couldn't believe what was happening. To me they were absolutely loathsome, and if I had me a gun I would have shot them down.

They were arrested and as they were taking them to the squad car the loathsome bum said to me, "Son, you are a damn good piece of fresh meat." He grinned and his toilet-bowl breath escaped through his rotting teeth. He didn't seem to have much reaction to his arrest. I suppose that he was too drunk and too low-down and dirty to have any remorse for what he had done.

My mom was crying uncontrollably, and I didn't know why. I couldn't feel sorry for her because I hated her. It was her fault that all of this had happened. Why did she let that bum move in? Why did she cheat on my dad? Surely she knew that someday something really bad was going to happen and she did nothing. She looked out of the squad car window with tears streaming down her face. I turned my back so that I wouldn't have to look at her.

They took us to the hospital to get checked out. Both my sister and I had been badly damaged.

They admitted us. My sister was twelve years old and had been repeatedly raped by that monster ever since she was nine. My little sister was only six and he had not gotten to her yet. My big sister had a full-blown case of gonorrhea and massive scar tissue in her pelvis where he had torn her because of her immature body was too small to accommodate his huge size.

When we were released from the hospital, our aunt and uncle came and got us. We never did see mom again. Best of all, that bum, Mom's boyfriend, would be behind bars for a very, very long time. My mom got time for being an accomplice. She knew what was going on, yet she never did anything about it.

When I was twelve I told my pastor that my mom was as much of a victim as we were and that she needed deep intense counseling. I didn't care because I couldn't see how she could let what was happening keep on happening.

The trauma that he had experienced when he was a youth had scarred him for life. And it always made him furious whenever someone called him son because the whole nightmare would return. This was the reason why he didn't want anyone to ever call him son again.

SuejuSoe continued, "They must have really roused your dandruff.

"To say the least. That man must think that I have a death wish, staying in that isolated place with the sun just about to rise and dying gang members everywhere. He must think I'm crazy."

"It wasn't that bad, was it?"

"No. It was worst. The man must have had the IQ of a brick. I can still hear him calling me son."

"If you don't cool it, you are going to blow a gasket."

"Your warning came too late. I've already blown one. Listen, I've got to go now, but I will get in contact with you later."

"Okay, bye."

When SuejuSoe walked into the room he heard Bojo saying, "That can't be true."

"What can't be true?"

"Did I hear you say that Moses had an APB out on him?"

"Yes, that is true. I've just got through talking to him. He will be okay, they dropped the bulletin."

"Why?"

"Because he found some dead bodies out on Runs Road."

"Bodies? Who were they?"

"I heard that it was the Stomach Cramps and Rumbling Guts that had gotten into a confrontation and it ended bad."

"I think that it was past due. Those heathens have cheated time for too long. As violent as it was, they deserved it. They was creating hell on Purple Bottom City for too many people. They are maggots."

"That's deep, man. I'm glad that I'm not on your shit list, you could be dangerous, son. "Keep it up. I've got better things to do than hang around with you losers."

"At least we don't go around finding dead bodies in ditches," Bojo said."

"I heard that the Sergeant Kneecap wanted to make Moses a suspect just because he found the bodies and called it in."

"I don't see how Sergeant Kneecap ever got to be a policeman, he's kind of dense when it comes to intelligence. I've had a run-in with him before. All brawn and no brains. He's harmless enough as long as he don't have to make any crucial decisions."

"He's got a job that someone has to do and it may as well be him."

"Ain't that the truth."

On his way out of the door, Bojo stopped and yelled out, "Don't forget we meet at 5:30 at Wester'C's office."

Later that evening in Wester'C's office Jelly Belly, K'Narf, and Bojo were still arguing about their pool game. When Wester'C walked in, they scrambled to their seats and sat down like schoolboys. He smiled.

Arthur Moses was a tad late. When he entered, all eyes followed him. This made him feel self-conscious. He could feel his blood rushing past his ears to his face. This was not his day.

Wester'C asked, "Is there anything that I can get any of you?"

Bojo spoke up, "Do you have any aspirin?"

"Sure, I do. I am a doctor, you know."

Bojo continued, "Beating Jelly Belly and K'Narf was so boring it gave me a headache."

"Will Tylenol do? I seem to be out of aspirin."

"Sure, when you are in the pig pen, you don't ask for bacon."

"Wow, that was deep," K'Narf said.

K'Narf, please don't say anything for a minute," asked Jelly.

"There's no need for hard feelings. Some of us just don't have it," Bojo quipped.

SuejuSoe still had not blended with his surrounding and asked, "Which of us just don't have what?"

"Don't pay any attention to them. They accidently starched their shorts and the friction is giving them orgasms."

"Maybe I should try that," said SuejuSoe. "Man, you lie good enough to be a preacher."

"Or write science fiction," added Pissy Dean.

"Guys, are we going to get anything accomplished here tonight, or are we going to sit here and bull shit each other. I wish that you had brought me some of whatever it is that is making you feel so good," said SuejuSoe. I sure could use it."

"Guys," said Bojo, swallowing the Tylenol, "Have some respect for my headache."

"If you had not bumped your head on the pool table your head would not be hurting."

"Leave the guy alone. He's just getting old. Now let us pipe down and take up where we stopped off last week. So far, we have not gotten a whole lot of negative feedback, and I would say that our grassroots efforts are paying off."

"Man, we have not even scratched the surface of turning Purple Bottom City back to the original constitution before all the amendments were added. Who is there to say what are the good amendments and what are the bad and which one should we keep and which one we should discard? Where do we begin?" K'Narf vented.

"You are right, and everyone agrees with you. I took the liberty of sending out some feelers to our constituents just to see where their minds are on this. Sorry that I didn't notify you, but I didn't think that this was something that was important enough to require a referendum."

"We do have a committee and I think that everything that we do should be run by the committee. By the way, what kind of results did you get from your impromptu?" asked K'Narf.

"There was a surprising number who thought that the government needs a major overhaul. But didn't know where to start."

"I think that I know where to start," said Ocena. "If we start at the bottom then the top will topple."

"Ocena, we are not trying to topple the government, we are trying to get this overload off the people so that things will be more equal." K'Narf hesitated and continued. "If you really thought of It, toppling the present-day government is what we are trying to do."

"We are proposing to separate bad government from good, and trying to determine what's good enough with the present government to leave alone and to cut out all the special interest groups that have change the course of what the original constitution dictates. There are some amendments that are beneficial and there are some that should have never been thought of."

"That's what I'm talking about. Everyone putting their two cents in the pile defining what we are up against and what our next step consist of. Ocena, you are correct in saying start at the bottom since this is such a humungous undertaking."

"No. No. We can just attack the bottom because most of the orders come from the top and flows down to the bottom. Our central government does have a governor who oversees everything. Purple Bottom City is too big for one man. He is surrounded by his cabinet, but there are a lot of false judgment, no judgment, and bad judgment being made. I think that the governor and his cabinet would be the logical place to start."

"This is the very thing that the Underground citizens are looking at. They see a weak government and they think that they can run it a lot better than we can. We also see a weak government, one that is based on a give-in-to-everyone mentality. Whatever some kooks think is upsetting to them, we amend the government to appease them. The principles on which Purple Bottom City was found have been so modified we can't seem to identify with the original."

"We know the original constitution was hard fought and had to be amended. I've read that some time ago in our past our country tried to police the world, all in the name of democracy. But the cost and increase military presence throughout the world was too much strain on one country. We taught these countries how to defend themselves and many were too weak to keep it up and lost ground because some other country want to force their religion on them or they wanted to sit under the same shade that they were sitting under. Fanatics. There was never any peace, no religious freedom, all the civil rights turned out to be civil wrongs. Nothing worked until the nova happened and everyone had to start out on equal ground. I don't think that another nova is in the near future. What I'm saying is that it took a cosmic disaster that destroyed one-third of our world to start at the beginning, how are we going to top that?"

"We are just going to do the same thing in a different way, and the only way that I can think of is through the people," said Bojo.

"And that is goin' to take work, work, very hard work," said Wester'C. And with this in mind I am going to see you later, but before I go, does anyone know the story of Tincan James?"

"Here we go again," said K'Narf.

No one responded, and Wester'C looked around like he was about to pounce on someone like a lion would attack his prey. "Ah ha," he said, just as I thought. If you've never heard of Tincan James, how do you suppose you are going to disassemble a government that has ran amuck."

"I've never heard of Tincan James but I've heard of Tincan Jane," said Ocena. "Now just what did Tincan James do that was so different than Tincan Jane?" Both of them spent years in exile because people that was in power thought that they were too radical and considered then to be threats to humanity because they wanted to build a world governed by the people and do away with fraudulent election bought and paid for by special interest are that what you think we are trying to do?"

"Change, is what everyone is asking for. Just how much change do they want and how far are they willing to go and how much they are willing to do to get this change. Does this sound familiar?"

"Y'all are scaring me," said Charles.

"All I'm asking you to do is think about it and we will continue it at our next meeting."

After Wester'C had gone, soberness penetrated the room. He had given them more to think about than they already had on their overcrowded plates. Because they were not trying to start a revolution in war with arms, but a revolution of change. There goes that word again. Change. Change is certainly needed. But just how far are we willing to go to make a significant change that is not just on paper?

We are not belligerent, and we know that the purple stuff is partially to blame for the way things have turned out. With the increase in intelligence everyone thought that they have the solution to all the problems when in fact they are creating more problems, worse than then the ones we already had. Now that the wild animals were loose it was up to them to corral them, and that made the situation loom.

The situation had hit Underground City like a bomb. They already thought that those Chickpeo freaks were nothing but freaks and didn't know how to run a world, even though it's a purple world. It was time the pros take over and the top and bottom worlds clashed.

The committee had adjourned and was going to meet the following Thursday. This would give them some time to recoup from the wrench that Wester'C had thrown into their half-hashed plans. The thought and ideas did sound supreme because what they were trying to do really needed to be done. That little twist that he threw in about Tincan James didn't help one bit. No one but Ocena had said that she had heard of Tincan Jane and according to her, Tincan James and Tincan Jane are the same person. When males refer to him it is James and when female refer to her it is Jane. This was over one hundred years ago when this character was dubbed. He had tried desperately to change the way thing were, but he didn't have the backing of the people who had fat purses. He almost overthrew the legislative body and was going after the main government when the news media began attacking him mercilessly, with lies and innuendos. Because he was so vocal, threats were made against his life and his family.

Back in those days there were organizations of hatred left over from earlier times. People thought that they went away, but they didn't they just took off their mask and put on another hat and business went on as usual. James/Jane made progress and inroads in getting equality, and representation for the same people that they now fighting for. One night this organization had hired some of their own people to stage an attack on their own people and make it look like James/Jane was responsible. In that attack ten people were killed and many others were injured. It did not matter how high the casualty rate was. They were expendable, and gave their lives so a few could remain in power. They eagerly pointed their fingers James/Jane as being responsible for this attack. What they didn't know was that members of their hate organization were also working with James/Jane trying to undo the very thing that they were trying to do. Their plan backfired, and many of the top leaders got prison sentences. Because of the depth of infiltration of their organization, no one trusted no one, and this was as close to beginning over as it could get. The James/Jane organization was there to pick up the pieces and took over the positions that those who went to prison forfeited. Change began to take shape, and things began to get a lot better and this lasted all of eight years. That is when James/Jane was found mutilated with pieces of him found all over town. It took three weeks for forensics to find out that the body pieces did not belong to James/Jane.

Through James/Jane the whole election process was reformed. There could be no special interest groups getting their candidate elected by buying him into office. Background checks for political aspirants became so strict it deterred all those who wanted to run and had ulterior motives. Term limits were short and mandatory. James/Jane began working tirelessly for the betterment of Purple Bottom City. Then one day the Underground City citizens decided to crawl out of the Graveyard and with the help of dissident Chickpeos began to mess things up.

One day James/Jane vanished.

Thursday, when the committee met again, Ocena was acting very unlike herself. She seemed to be on edge about something. Jelly Belly asked, "Ocena, what's seem to be eating at you?"

She looked at Jelly Belly and asked, "Are you talking to me?"

"Yes, I am. Are you going to answer me?"

"There's nothing wrong with me. Why do you ask?"

"You don't seem to be yourself."

"It's nothing. I just don't want to lose this election. It's too important. Much, much too important. It's like my destiny."

"What are you talking about? You are not even a candidate. Why would you make a statement like that?"

"Because," Ocena explained, "I feel that if we lose this election, life as we've come to know it will cease altogether and there won't be any chance of turning it back around."

Jelly Belly asked, "But why would you feel this way? Is there something that you know and are not telling us?"

She looked around the room as if she was a trapped rat. All eyes were glued to her every move. She got up and began to pace as little beads of perspiration dotted her upper lip. She looked at everyone as if she was seeing them for the first time, and she didn't like how they looked.

SuejuSoe became alarmed. He thought that maybe she was having a breakdown of some kind. He spoke to her in a most patronizing voice. "Ocena, whatever this is that has you so terrified, I'm sure there is a solution somewhere."

She turned and faced SuejuSoe and said in a voice pregnant with contempt. "You are all fools. Mr. SuejuSoe here has been lying to you for months and I've only recently found out."

"Found out about what?" asked Jelly Belly.

"So you do want to know. I suppose that everyone here wants to know."

"Ocena," SuejuSoe called out, "what are you raving about?"

She turned on SuejuSoe and said, "As if you don't know. You lying, low-down snake in the grass. Your time is up."

"What are you talking about?" SuejuSoe asked again with his voice slightly rising.

The room became eerily quiet. All eyes were on SuejuSoe. Ocena continued, "Ask Mr. SuejuSoe why he goes to the Graveyard so frequently. Ask him what those meetings are about. I know that he won't tell you but I will."

"Go ahead and tell them, Ocena," said SuejuSoe, "because I want to know too."

Ocena swayed and slurred her words like she was drunk. "Mr. SuejuSoe here has been plotting with the Spooks to rig the election so that the citizens of the Graveyard would control both Purple Bottom City and Underground City."

SuejuSoe cried out in shock, "What!"

"Do you deny that you have been plotting against the citizens of Purple Bottom City?"

"I most definitely do. This is preposterous. Where did you hear something like this?"

"I overheard Wester'C talking to that professor, Dr. Tinywings, and that journalist that did the story on the Rumbling Guts and the Stomach Cramps last winter. What was his name? Bleu Treet, yes, that's it."

"If that was true, don't you think that Wester'C would have said something about it?" SuejuSoe asked.

She answered pertly, "No, not necessarily."

"But why would he want to do something like that?" asked Jelly Belly.

"I can't say for sure but I suppose it could be a power play of some sort. Why don't you ask Wester'C?"

"I'm going to do just that," said SuejuSoe as he walked out of the office. Jelly Belly called out, "Hey, Wester'C is in here."

"I know. I'll be right back." SuejuSoe did something that he had not done in ten years; he lit a cigarette, reeled from dizziness, and returned to the meeting. He thought to himself, What I really need is a drink.

Ocena sat down hard. Perspiration was rolling down her face. The room was quiet as everyone sat in shock. No words were spoken for at least thirty seconds, but it felt an hour. Finally Jelly Belly said, "That was a shocker." Then he turned to Wester'C and demanded an explanation.

Wester'C was stunned. Where did Ocena get this absolutely erroneous information? How could he explain this to others? He beckoned for SuejuSoe. He came. He asked him point-blank, "What is she talking about?"

"The closest thing that I can come up with is she heard me talking to the governor of Underground City, Dr. Tinywings, and Treet. But we were talking about the possibilities and scenarios and what may happen if Purple Bottom City governments were to emerge. Treet wanted an opinion from me on the feasibility of this happening because he is planning to write a book loosely based on this possibility.

Governor Agnus had asked me to one of their meetings so that I could see that our governments were alike than different. They discussed this possibility. I told them that I would have to get back with them later. I met with them a total of three times before they agreed that their proposition would work."

"How did I get involved in this?"

"They were thinking about you on behalf of the government from Purple Bottom City. The other half would come from Underground City. That is if the two worlds could share a central government."

"Just who informed them that I would have a Lilliputian interest in a farce like that." SuejuSoe swallowed nervously and said, "It must have been me."

"What? What day did you lose your mind? Do you have brain damage?" Wester'C asked SuejuSoe as he strived to keep his voice normal.

"At that time I didn't think that you would mind being referred to as a possibility."

"You got that part right, you didn't think. Because there is no way in this day and age that I would ever take a part in something like that. Now you have people thinking that I'm idiosyncratic."

"I admit that I'm responsible for this entire misconception. Not once did I think that I was doing something unorthodox. I thought that I was being open-minded."

"There you go thinking again. I'm going to let you explain this to the others. For a lawyer your choice of words leaves room for many errors. What you called open-minded, I call gullible. You are too anxious, and because of this, mistakes are made. Come on, let's put this misconception to rest."

In the room where the others were gathered, conversation flowed nonstop. As Wester'C and SuejuSoe entered the room all conversation ceased. Ocena came up to them and said, "I see the traitors are back. Let's see how they are going to explain this away."

SuejuSoe said to Ocena, "Please don't get on my last nerve because you are less than a razor's blade breath away and I really don't want to be rude. There is an explanation for your allegations that is very plausible. Now, if you all will have a seat you will hear the rest of the story."

Ocena sat down and the remainder followed. SuejuSoe began his explanation of what happened. How it happened. When it happened and the aftermath of all the above. When he finished you could feel the tension leave the room. No one in the room could believe that SuejuSoe could have done what Ocena had accused him of doing.

"So you see, Ocena, you can put your anxieties to rest. It was a misunderstanding on your part and I forgive you."

"That's very big of you. Now, crawl back under that rock that you came from."

"I love you too," SuejuSoe said as he gave her a hug.

Contrary to everything that came before and during that meeting, it was more productive than all the others. The meeting was adjourned.

SuejuSoe ended up at The Pot Gut Palace. As he sit down at the big gut bar he was reflecting over who he was, where he was and how he got there. Even though Charles was with him, he felt alone. It gave him chills to think about how easy things could get out of control. He was on his third drink when he seemed to realize that Charles was sitting beside him. He had been so lost in thought until it startled him to see him sitting there.

Charles looked at him and said, "Welcome back."

He looked at Charles as if he didn't recognize him. Finally, he said, "Tell me, what did you think of that little surprise that Ocena sprung on us tonight?"

"I couldn't believe it. I've gone to the Graveyard with you on more than one occasion and have seen you talking with Treet and Tinywings and I haven't seen anything amiss. What Ocena said blew me away. Man, that was freaky."

"Don't I know it. That proves that one can never get too relaxed. You should always keep your guard up."

"I don't think that's a wholesome way to live. Suspicious of everything and body. You would never have any peace of mind when you think that everyone is out to get you."

"I can agree with what you are saying. It seems like you can't do anything pioneering because there are those just waiting for you to make a mistake. It doesn't matter how good your intensions are, they will crucify you. Is life that way where you came from?"

"Sure is. In my world, it seems like the harder you work, the more you accomplish, when you give your all, the less you are appreciated. It makes one want to give up and say fuck it."

"I know exactly what you mean. It's the same in my world too."

"Let's go home before we be misunderstood again."

CHAPTER VIII

*O*cena was on her way to a new job site about twenty miles out of Purple Bottom City's metropolis. She wasn't in any hurry and had other things on her mind. It was exactly eighteen months since she had added the nursery and landscaping business to her construction business. She had a total of sixty-two full-time employees and sometimes as many as twelve part-timers. She treated all of her employees with respect, and they showed their appreciation by giving her the same respect. They had heard many rumors about her, but they weren't going to let these rumors interfere with their respect or their job performance because she was a great boss. She was Ocena Heartburns.

She loved nature and always wanted to be one with nature. She had memorable experiences with nature, and nature always reminded her of her father. A special warm feeling came over her every time she thought of her daddy.

He loved to hunt, fish, and live off the land. Sometimes he would go on a hunting spree and be gone for a week. Knowing this, her mom wondered why he came back. When he went on these hunting trips he would come home smelling as funky as any boar. Her brothers wanted nothing to do with it. Daddy was a gourmet cook when it came to cooking wild game. He loved it, and so did she.

Without realizing it, there were tears rolling down her cheeks. She wiped them away with the back of her hand. This seemed to happen every time she thought of her daddy. She thought that time would lessen the pain, but nothing had changed. She whispered, "Daddy, I love you."

Her tears flowed freely and shamelessly down her cheeks, bringing cleansing relief. She hated to cry because it always gave her a tremendous headache and clogged her sinuses. Come to think of it, the only time she cried was when she thought about her daddy.

She pulled into a spot in front of an unfinished building where she was supposed to be doing the landscaping. She drew out her trusted pad and began to sketch. Landscaping this building lot was going to be a bugger because of the unusual shape of the lot and the unevenness of it, and the tenants did not want the nature of the lot to be changed. She would have to work around obstacles, but she was sure that she could do it. She had a horticulturist on staff, and he had come with the highest recommendations.

Ocena was an even five feet five inches tall and weighed a solid one hundred and twenty-five pounds. People would marvel at how she could handle large bulky items that were twice her size.

She made it look so easy. When there was a job to be done, she would do it. Hard work, long hours, and bad working conditions didn't faze her. She ran the business as smoothly and profitably as it could be done. Her employees respected her, and they would often find her everywhere doing almost any job. Her familiar hard hat with "Cena" printed down the middle was her trademark. She ran the business in a way that would have made her daddy very proud. She was not going to let him down no matter what.

The task before her loomed like a monolith, and it was hard trying to determine where to begin. If there was no beginning, she would have to make one. She opened the door and slid out of the van, a new one that had been purchased for her expanding company. There was nothing to compare the smell of a new car or truck with, except maybe a new book.

She had made a prototype of the places that needed landscaping. This was going to be a mini mall and an office building complex, and the right landscaping could make or break the success of this site. There would have to be some tropical plants with a mini waterfall, and maybe she could get some of those misshapen cedars from down by the forbidden zone. This foliage was so misshapen it was a wonder just to look at it. She was not sure that it would survive in this climate. She would have to check with a local botanist about this. On the left side there was an uneven slope where some type of ground cover would have to be used to halt the erosion. Maybe add three or four clumps of trees, perhaps river birch, flowering cherry, or ginkgo. The final decision would come later. She was busy working from the front of the mall to the south side and the north. The famous jumpsuit that she was wearing had a wide streak of perspiration all the way down her back. She was so into what she was doing she was unaware how hot it had gotten. She returned to the van to get a drink of water and to wipe sweat off her face and neck.

Afterward, she decided to take a short break. She had brought along her ever-present cooler filled with juices, water, and a few snacks. She pulled back the sliding door of the van and sat down. It wasn't long before she began to feel like she was being watched. She slowly scanned the area looking for whatever she could see. She glanced up at that perpetual purple haze that blotted out the sun, wiped the perspiration from her flushed face, and took a pepe pop out of the cooler and began to sip it.

The feeling that she was not alone had magnified. She felt positive that someone or something was lurking somewhere in the nearby woods. She tried to reassure herself that whatever or whoever it was out there had as much right to be there as she did.

She glanced at her watch; break time was over. She really needed to pee real bad, and the bushes was it. She headed for the bushes, stopped, then turned around trying to see if anyone was present, then decided that peeing was as natural as many other things that people would hide to do.

She wiggled out of her jumpsuit and peed. The snapping of a twig had snapped her out of her complacency, and she was going to confront whatever was out there face to face. She was thinking in her seminude state that she would probably shock the shit out of whomever was out there. A smile appeared in her lips as she remembered other times she had shocked people shitless. It was amusing to her. To do the opposite of what people consider to be normal was her trademark. One that she didn't ever want to change.

She pulled her shoes off, and the warmth of the pine needles tickled her feet. It felt good. She put her shoes back on and walked into the forest. The pungent smell coming from decaying leaves and straws brought back a strong remembrance, and tears filled her eyes.

She didn't go far into the woods before she turned and came back. The mosquitoes were ferocious. Once out of the woods, she saw that her clothing was not where she had left them. Alarm began to invade her mind, pushing aside the good feeling that she was experiencing. Danger flags were flapping in her clouded vision. Proceeding cautiously, using skills she had learned from DiAli, a self-styled ninja, she approached the van. She had almost reached the van; then it happened. The strange bearded person jumped from the bushes. It didn't frighten her because she had known for some time that she was not alone. It was the granddaddy of surprises, Rory Cavity.

He spoke, "Hi, Ocena, it's good to see you again. I know that I must have scared you, but I've been watching you for a couple of days trying to get you alone so that I could talk to you."

Her mouth dropped open. "What in the name of Jesus would you want to talk to me about? And I would like for you to repeat what you just said because I don't believe that you said what I thought that I heard you say."

"I came here because I need your help. I saw you coming out here alone and I followed you."

"Well la, la, la, da, la to you," she said as she snatched her clothing from Roy. She noticed that he was still looking at her questioningly, and she asked, "Is there something that I missed?" She turned and waited for Roy to answer.

Roy cleared his throat and continued, "I need you to help me because you are the one and only person that I know who has the independence, clout, and nerve."

"But why should I want to help you?"

"No special reason. I just thought that with your history of defending the down and out . . . you know, I left town in a hurry and in disgrace. I was under tremendous pressure. I felt like I had no choice."

"Tell me about it. Just where in Purple Bottom City have you been all this time?"

"No special place. I've been bumbling around doing odd jobs until I landed one that I stayed with. Now, I want to get my name and life back, but I know that people have not forgotten."

"That's putting it mildly. That episode is probably going down in the history books. Now tell me just what it is that you think I can do for you?"

"You can stand up to anyone and people will still love and respect you or just plain hate your guts. I remember that scandal seven years ago, that was really beautiful. I only wish that I had that kind of guts and confidence to do something like that. Instead, I run away like some scared rabbit. I'm sorry that I've taken up so much of your time, again I'm sorry," he said as he walked away.

"Wait," Ocena called out, "I didn't say that I wouldn't help you. Tell me about whatever it is that's troubling you."

"What's troubling me? The same thing that you said would end up in the history books. What would you have done if it had been you?"

"First thing, I would never have put myself in an uncompromising position like that. Even if I couldn't care less what people would say."

"You see, that's just the type of person that I need to help me. I went to the Graveyard and no one paid any attention to me. I got a job at a pharmaceutical company and always worked at night so no one would see me. I grew a beard and let my hair grow long and changed my name to Michael Hipbone. I started wearing earrings and worked out three times a week for two hours. So you can see, I'm in great shape. Roy Cavity was a scrawny greasy-faced nerd. So to everyone else I'm Michael Hipbone."

She listened to Roy's story about his life in exile and wondered, "What in hell does he think that I can do?"

He wiped sweat off his brow and looked at the sun. She offered him a can of juice. He accepted and popped the top, took a deep swallow, and continued his story.

"When I was eighteen I had my first sexual experience. It was with a fifty-two-year-old woman. I was a delivery boy at a local drugstore and had to make a delivery at her address. She asked me in, and I thought it was so she could pay for her medicine. I was so nervous my entire mouth felt like it was stuffed with cotton. She stood there wearing only a bath towel and it wasn't covering up much. I got an erection instantly. I brushed when she saw it and I could feel the heat of embarrassment painting my face crimson. She came over to where my feet had adhered to the floor and rubbed her hand across my erection and I ejaculated. I never thought that I could have felt shame as deep as I felt it then. My pant had this wet spot which everyone could see. She unzipped my pants and exposed my penis and told me to stay where I was until she got back. I couldn't move if my life had depended upon it. She came back with a towel in her hands and took my penis and began to clean it with the towel. Almost the instant she took it into her hands, I had another hard-on.

"It began to throb and I knew that I was going to ejaculate again. She took it and began to kiss it and tease it. I had never experienced anything that felt that good before and I didn't ever want her to stop. Shortly, she stopped, stood up and took me into her bed room and asked me if I had ever had a woman before. My mouth was still filled with cotton and I couldn't speak. I prayed for some spit so that I could speak again. All I could turn my head from side to side indicating no. She said that today was going to be my lucky day because she was going to make a man out of me. She smiled at me and beckoned me to her bed. I didn't want to go but something told me in no uncertain terms to move it.

"But I couldn't. She said if I was not man enough to be with her, I could just go. I didn't want to stay, but my feet wouldn't move. She lay back on that enormous bed and laughed at me. This made me angry but she kept on laughing. Then she got off the bed and came over to where I standing. Her huge breasts looked like overfilled water balloons, and she smelled like perfume that was somewhat overbearing.

"Her hair was piled up on her head, but loosened it and let it fall down her back. Finally, my feet came unglued and stepped backward. I was desperately trying to pull my pants up and leave. She would caress my penis again and my erection would grow harder, and I got angrier every time she did this. I was in misery and I was afraid. She called me mama's boy and laughed at me. I had had it with her. I was going to show her that I was a man.

"I picked her up and threw her on the bed and jumped on top of her like a savage. I screwed her hard, savagely and urgently. She screamed but I didn't stop. I went harder, deeper, and she screamed again. I finally came. I could feel this release from my toes upward. God! It felt indescribable.

"I was still on top of her when her body began to tremble. She clung to me in desperation, and I looked down at her and she told me that no one had ever made love to her like that and she thanked me.

"As I got dressed she was still lying on the bed trembling. I thought of my boss, Mr. Upright. He was probably cursing me out. I smiled to myself thinking that he would probably fire me for this. But, man, he wouldn't ever believe what had gone on here. I left there feeling like I was the man of the century.

"I can remember this as if it happened this morning. She kept wanting me to come back, but I felt that she may be dangerous. After she had asked me eight times to come back and I refused, she hired two heavy-duty guys to get me.

"One evening when I was on my way home from work these two heavy-guys followed me. Since my house was in a sparsely populated area with woods plentiful, they caught me and dragged me into the woods and beat me up. Then they took terms raping me. I was hurting like everything as if dynamite had exploded in my ass but among all the pain and embarrassment, I was highly aroused and excited. They didn't have to rape me anymore because I became a willing participant. Sex with old lady Lashy just couldn't compare.

"After it was all over, I felt ashamed and degraded because I had enjoyed it so much. Because my parents had told me all of my life that it was one of the worst sins that one could commit, I was thinking that hell was going to be where I was going to spend eternity.

"I never did go see old lady Lashy again, but the two guys that she had hired to beat me up and rape me became my first lovers."

"Why are you telling me all this? I can't do anything about you being gay."

"No. You can't, but there is more to this. Time changes things. Pretty soon me and my two lovers split up because they were being relocated. I think that their boss found out that they were gay and relocated them because he couldn't fire them.

"Our lives went on as normal as could be under the circumstances. I think that all of them found new lovers, but I never forgot about them. Both of them showed up at that media conference, and I had found out that they were in town and we made plans to meet. Somehow, we all had to go pee at the same time, but neither one of us knew that the other would be in the men's room. When we all ended up in the same place at the same time, something snapped. Each one of us had a violent urge to be with each other. So we threw caution to the wind and we had sort of an orgy and we got caught. That's when my problems began.

"I want you to help me clean up my reputation. I want to be Roy Cavity again. I want to know if I've got another chance for a political career, one that I miss so terribly. Is there any way that you can possibly help me?"

"Roy, the best thing that you can do is to come all the way out of the closet and don't go in to any public restroom to have an orgy. Admit that you are gay. In today's society, gays are coming out the closet everywhere, and there are more laws passed in favor of gays than ever before. They hold many high-profile positions in and out of government. These gays do their thing behind closed doors. Find you a steady partner and live a life that makes you happy and forget about the other people. Then again, you could tell them to fuck it. But doing this will put your political ambitions in the toilet. Really." She looked at Roy. "Something is different besides your beard."

"You noticed? I've had some minor surgery to alter my appearance so that I wouldn't look so, you know, Chickpeo."

"Do you have a problem with being a Chickpeo?"

"No, not really."

"I'm no plastic surgeon, so I'm not in any position to give you any real advice on what you should do. But to answer your question on a bias opinion, a lots. You are still Chickpeo. A blind man can point you out."

"I don't want a complete makeover, just enough for people to be unsure of who I really am."

"I see. Now, tell me what it is that you think that I can do for you."

"Do you remember how you got Arthur Moses out of the spotlight when all that todo came up about him banging you? You told the news media that if they printed only the facts, their paper would be one page long. You never admitted to doing anything at all. You said that doing something that God had commanded us to do and making sure that we would do it by infusing us with hormones that screamed not to be ignored was not a crime. Now, which of them was going to challenge God? It was almost like, 'He who is without a fault, throw the first stone.' Everything calmed down seemingly overnight. I knew that people still talk about it among themselves, but then again, most people respected you and hold you in high esteem just because you didn't back down. Right now you are one of the most important persons in Purple Bottom City. If you should run for any office, you would win."

"I still don't know what it is that makes you think that I can do anything about your situation."

"I really don't know that either. I was hoping that you would come up with something."

"One thing that you can do is to start being more assertive. Don't sit back and wait for someone to tell you what to do. It's something like taking a blind step in faith only. I'm sorry, but I don't think that I can help you."

"That's where you are wrong. You have already by just listening to me and treating me like a peer."

"Another thing is you need to get a PA agent, then he or she would really have their work cut out for them."

"I'm glad that you took the time to listen to me. I can't think of another soul who would have done it."

"What about SuejuSoe and Wester'C?"

"Naw. Mr. Right and Mr. Perfect probably wouldn't talk to me. I'm not going around looking for someone to insult me and treat me like I just sprouted horns or crawled out from under a rock. I really don't know what I'm going to do. I guess that I'll see you around."

"Take care, Roy."

"Yes, sure."

As Roy walked away, Ocena was thinking, Now, there goes the king of the pile. She wiped sweat off her brow and resumed working. Roy had gotten her almost an hour behind. She must talk to SuejuSoe when he returned from the Graveyard.

At least she had found out the reason why he did what he did. But the explanation was weak. Nobody's sexual urges are that strong where you would throw caution and self-restraint and the sense of decency into the wind. There are too many places to go besides a public restroom. She stopped abruptly, just listened to me moralizing. I can't go around trying to condemn anyone's actions because I really don't care as long as they are not bothering me. Then again Roy was a hypocrite, one of the worst kinds. He preached morals and lived without morals, and I can say with a clear conscience, he deserved what happen to him. In a twisted kind of way, I feel sorry for him.

Then she smiled when she recalled Roy saying he wanted to make a political comeback. He was never a politician; how could he come back to some place that he had never been? Leave things up to Roy, and you will have a royal fuck-up. Let him dig himself out of his own messes. But I have a feeling that this is one mess that he will never get out of.

I cannot believe he had the audacity to come to me for help. The only way that I would help Roy would be it is the last thing I would have to do to get in heaven. Even then, I would hesitate. She put a sweat band around her head and resumed charting the landscape.

CHAPTER IX

*T*he failure of the portal to the dimensions was hard on the scientific communities of both Purple Bottom City and the Underground City, but there was no one more disappointed than Charles DeNero. He seemed to go into a catatonic state. Overnight, he seemed to become a different person. He wouldn't eat, couldn't sleep, wouldn't go anywhere or talk. If you should ask him something, he would answer yes or no and made no other comment.

SuejuSoe desperately to get him to see a doctor, but he refused. He just sat there like a stature, doing nothing and saying nothing. This went on for six days. Gradually, he began to act normal again. Shortly after this, he began to meet with the test subjects, A and B, communicating in this unknown alien language.

It was time for SuejuSoe's three days at the Graveyard, and he was afraid to leave Charles alone, and Charles had refused to go with him. He had asked K'Narf to keep an eye on him while he was away, but Charles wouldn't have any part of this. But there was no way that he would go and leave him alone.

Wester'C stepped in and talked to Charles about staying with him until SuejuSoe returned from the Graveyard. He only agreed to do this to appease SuejuSoe because he was a grown man and he didn't need a babysitter.

The three days that he stayed with Wester'C was far from ordinary. First, he did not know that Wester'C had a wife and three children. His wife was a former champion ice skater, and two of his children were following in her foot steps and the other one was an exemplary scholar and was a senior in high school at the tender age of thirteen.

All three children took an instant liking to him. In less than an hour, he was uncle Charlie. They wanted him to tell them about life on another world. He relished the attention that was being lauded on him. Never before had he encountered such a delightful family with children who were absolutely fabulous. They made him feel so vibrant, so alive, so in tune with the universe. This was the second time in his life that he had felt the presence of God, and he also realized that the same God was everywhere.

Those three days with the Ulcer family restored his mental balance. The disappointment and shock he had experienced after the failure of the portal seemed as though it had never happened.

The children wanted to follow him everywhere he would go. The two ice skaters put on a private show for him. Their mom joined them; she was really a graceful and superb skater. The oldest joined in, and you would never think that he was anything but a normal well-adjusted child.

The days went by much too fast. He had found another side of Wester'C that he liked much better than the other one. A compassionate, a more humane person resided inside the staunch unflexible Wester'C Ulcer.

By the time SuejuSoe came back from the Graveyard, Charles was more relaxed and in better spirits than he had ever seen. And to think that he had been worried about him. He pulled up into the driveway and got out of the car, but before he got to the door, he heard the sounds of laughter and glee floating across the lawn. The laughter seem to erase the anxiety that he had built up worrying about Charles. He ranged the doorbell, and Mrs. Ulcer answered. She smiled and greeted him. Her smile was framed by an angelic face. She spoke, "Hello, SuejuSoe, come on in."

"Hi, Amy, I came to collect my guest."

Charles came out of the den followed by three enthusiastic children, laughing gleefully.

SuejuSoe was amazed at the change that Charles had accomplished in three days. He grinned. "Are you ready to go home? I meant, to my place?"

"I don't know," Charles teased.

Wester'C's son Chad looked dismayed. "Uncle Charlie, you are not leaving us, are you?" The other two siblings stood holding Charles's hands with sadness painting their faces.

SuejuSoe felt uneasy. He didn't know what was going on. Chad questioned him again, "You are not leaving with Uncle Charlie, are you?"

Wester'C second son looked up at SuejuSoe and asked, "Uncle SuejuSoe, you are not here to take Uncle Charlie, are you?"

SuejuSoe didn't know how to respond to these questions. He looked at Amy, hoping that she could help him out of this dilemma, hoping that she would explain to the children the reason why he was here to pick up their Uncle Charlie. She said nothing. Finally, he spoke, "Children, your Uncle Charlie was here only temporarily until I came back from my trip. I'm back now."

Their grip on Charles's hands got tighter. "You are not leaving, are you, Uncle Charlie?" Chad asked. Charles spoke up, "You guys, I really do have to go. But I'm not going anywhere but to your Uncle SuejuSoe's place. I'll be seeing you again, and we can spend a lot of time together. But both your mom and dad knew that I was going to be here for only three days. Just let me tell you that these were the best three days of my life, and I will never forget them."

"Yes," said Mrs. Ulcer, "your uncle Charlie is not going away forever. You all can spend plenty of time with him."

Chad looked at his mother. A solitary tear rolled down his cheek, and he asked in an unsteady voice, "Mom, do you really mean it?"

"Of course I do," she assured him.

The twins, Connie and Carl, released Charles's hand. All of them surrounded him for hugs and kisses. This affection really choked Charles up. He fought hard to keep tears from rolling down his face. This was a painful separation for everyone involved.

As they were on their way to the car, SuejuSoe said to Charles, "You didn't waste any time."

"Didn't waste any time doing what?"

"Endearing yourself to the Ulcer family."

"I would respond to that statement, but I know that you are kidding."

"I am not kidding. A blind man could see that those children love you."

Charles grinned. "You are not jealous, are you?"

"Damn right, I am. I am those kids' godfather, and they cling to you like a second skin."

Charles smiled his boyish smile. "Some people have it and some people don't."

"I readily admit that I don't know what happened while I was gone, but whatever it was, somebody needs to bottle it and put it on the market."

"D'ja think that it's all that good?"

SuejuSoe paused and cleared his sinuses. "Yes. Even better. It could be a cure for depression." Charles chuckled, "I had a marvelous time with those kids. I never knew that I was compatible with anyone under the age of twenty. I think that maybe I'll . . ."

"I'll what?"

"Nothing."

"Come on, what were you about to say?"

"It wasn't anything important. It was just . . . I was going to say that maybe I'll get married and have some children of my own someday."

"I'm touched," said SuejuSoe. "Maybe I'll try it out myself someday, I think that is what's life is all about."

*****

Later that evening, everyone was supposed to meet at the Pot Gut Palace. They were meeting to confirm plans for the next two weeks before the election day. All the latest polls were in favor of their candidates. Although everyone was glad, they were careful about getting too confident, too cocky. Everyone had an important job to do, and they must get it done; this was not supposed to be a burden on any one person.

Almost everyone arrived at the same time. A room in the back had been reserved for their meeting, and a couple of waitresses were busy taking orders for food and drinks. Ocena entered the room and glanced through the huge double doors and was sure that she had seen Roy Cavity busing tables. She thought, "Naw, that can't be true."

The doors swung shut before she could get a better look.

As the meeting began, SuejuSoe, Wester'C, Arthur Moses, Bojo (Bill Earlobe), K'Narf, Jelly Belly (Jon Dexter), Carrie Blister, and Charles DeNero were present.

"I guess this is just about everyone. Wait. Where is Ocena and Pissy Dean?" asked Jelly Belly. "Where is Mamie? Hold on a minute. We need to wait a few more minutes. There are about five key people missing. Mamie, Magness and Puff isn't here either."

Bojo said, "I knew that Mamie and Puff were going to be a little late. They had to get someone to cover for them until they could return. You know how hospitals are."

Moses commented, "You know Ocena, she is always late. She'll probably be late for her own funeral."

"That may be, but she is needed here now," Wester'C said as he straightened a stack of papers.

Pissy Dean entered the room in a jubilant mood. He joked, "I would have been here on time except I got lost down in Booger Bear Canyon. Then I ran into Ocena, and she insisted that I wait on her until she could pull off her trademark jumpsuit, then we could come here together."

"Well, where is Miss Heartburns?" Wester'C asked. But before he could get an answer, Ocena entered the room with a double gin and tonic in her hand. He looked at the drink that she was guarding and asked, "Is that necessary? We have a lots to cover, and we need everyone's mind 100 percent. Anyway, we are glad to see that you have honored us with your presence."

Not to be one to hold her tongue, she shot back, "Wester'C, it is good to know that you are still as grouchy as hell. It stabilizes my faith in Chickpeomanity."

He began, "Everything makes you . . . never mind."

"You can say what's on your mind, Doc. I feel benevolent today. My horoscope said that I should be nice to a grouch today."

You could see the tension in Wester'C jaws as he clinched his fist trying to remain calm and not get into an argument with Ocena because he had better things to do. He politely said, "Thank you, Ocena, you've made my day. Now we will began our meeting if that's okay with everyone."

No one spoke and he continued, "By your silence, I suppose that's a yes. There is only a month before the election, and we must plan for the final go-round. Carrie, Bill, do any of you have anything to say?"

Bill looked at Carrie then at Wester'C. He was acting like he was trying to get inspiration from one or both of them. He stood up, obviously nervous, cleared his throat, and said, "I feel good about what we've already accomplished, and I think that for the next two weeks, we need to get some heavy-duty endorsements and flood the airways."

Carrie interrupted, "I've already got commitments from our illustrious governor and Senator Albert Gizzard." Bill looked at Carrie like she was a pestering gnat. Carrie ignored Bill's look and continued, "I've even thought about a previctory parade, and I want to know what you think about it."

"I'm not talking about a parade, I'm talking about some high school bands and the candidates riding on a float or in a convertible and our supporters armed with campaign literature, passing it out to the public as they pass. I think that we should do this a week before the election."

"That don't sound bad at all."

Bill took a deep sip of his drink, rubbed his mustache, and agreed that this was a good idea. Everyone thought that this was a good idea except Pissy Dean. Pissy wanted to know if they really needed this kind of publicity. He wanted to know if they didn't think that this was a tad too much. He thought that this would seem like they were flaunting and rubbing their competition's noses in it.

"I don't think a reaction like that will happen. We don't know what the other side is up to," Bill said. "But don't we all want to show aggression and be aggressive? Show that we have leadership qualities. Show that we have intestinal fortitude and are not a bunch of mealymouthed yes people. We want to put the fear of god into the other candidates," Carrie added.

"That was spoken like a true candidate," said K'Narf.

"Let me assure you," said Carrie, "this is not a joking matter, and seriously, K'Narf, you really should grow up."

K'Narf turned slowly around until he was looking into Carrie's eyes and said, "I'm so sorry that I offended you, your madmanship. I guess that I'm not as refined as you, and I didn't have to go around like someone that is. Nor do I have to go around saying things that I don't mean trying to appease people that I don't like."

Wester'C tolerance level had shattered. In a calm voice laced with fury, he spoke out, "This is exactly what we don't need, clawing at each other's throats. We need unity. Any of you who don't think that you are capable of doing this may leave the room now. The way we are always bickering and trying to demean each other is the very reason we are not progressing like we should. We keep talking about the new age politician, if we don't cut out all the bullshit, we are going to be a no age nothing. Am I making myself clear?"

Silence hung in the room, threateningly immense, dangerously like an approaching tornado.

In a whispery voice, Bojo said to no one in particular, "The world is not interested in how many storms you encounter but in whether you are able to bring the ship in."

"What did you say?" asked Wester'C.

"Nothing. It was something my grandmama used to say when things weren't going as planned. It's a quote from someone but I don't know who."

"It's a very appropriate quote for the present time," said Wester'C.

"Since you brought up the new age politicians, what are we going to do about changing the whole constitution back to the beginning except for some amendments? Now would be a good time to cover this."

"I thought that it was understood that we really couldn't begin to implement this until we had all our people in office. We will start in the highest offices, the ones that we are running for now. Then, we will get our people into all the lower offices and before anyone knows what is happening, it will be done. That is, if we stop bickering and agree to keep to the original plans almost like James/Jane."

Jelly Belly stood up and yawned. "Sure we can all agree to agree. Sure we can stick to our original plans and create a new Purple Bottom City government. Is there anyone who doesn't agree?"

By this time Mamie, Puff, and three others entered the meeting and Mamie asked, "Just what is it that everyone need to agree on?"

"To agree to our original plan to topple the present core government and to regress back to the beginning of the Constitution with some amendments intact and to build a new government from there."

"I couldn't have put it any better," said Wester'C. "Good job, Jelly Belly."

"Is that all we missed? I know that more went on. I'm sorry that we are so late, but our replacements didn't show up on time."

"We also decided to have a victory parade a week before the election, and we went over old business. There can't much more we can do tonight, so let's finish up."

Jelly Belly stood up, yawned, and said, "Let's get this meeting over with, I'm going home and having some fantastic sex."

Ocena said, "It thrills me to know that your brains are still in the same place, between your legs."

"Aw shucks," groaned Jelly Belly, "I was going to make that announcement, but now you've gone and done it for me. And I thank you."

"I'm going home," announced Arthur Moses.

"You had better put your boots on," said Ocena.

"Why?" asked Moses.

"I don't think that you can get out of the door because bullshit is already knee-deep," Wester'C said. He then added, "I'm going home too. Y'all can finish up anyway you want to. I've got surgery at 5:30 AM tomorrow morning."

Ocena called out to Wester'C as he headed for the door, "Be careful not to slip up on the bullshit."

This brought laughter to everyone in the room. Within thirty minutes, the meeting was over. They adjourned. Magness, Puff, and Mamie never did find out all that was accomplished in that meeting. Someone would have to fill them in later. Everyone had gone except Arthur Moses. He sat alone with his thoughts. "Was Ocena the woman for him? Is she toying with me or what? What am I doing playing politics? When the election is over, I'm going to make some changes in my life, starting with Ocena." He finished his drink and went home.

The next week, to everyone's surprise, Bill and Carrie eloped. Everyone thought that they would get married someday, but everyone thought that it would be after the election. If they should win the election, the governor and the president would have the same last names: Earlobe.

The preelection victory parade was a huge hit. Besides bands, there were acrobats, elephants, clowns, and local office holders that were on their ticket; in other words, the parade was much larger than anyone had imagined. The next week at the polls, the tally came in a landslide in favor for Mr. and Mrs. Bill Earlobe.

The victory party was so huge, it had to be moved to the grand ballroom of the Excelsior Hotel. President-elect Bill Earlobe, aka Bojo, and governor-elect Carrie Earlobe had made history as the first husband-and-wife team to get elected to the highest offices in Purple Bottom City history at the same time.

At the height of the victory party, trouble began. As if they had not already taken enough, the Rumbling Guts and the Stomach Cramps once again clashed. Only this time, they brought guns: automatic and semiautomatic weapons, critical weapons in the hands of lawless maniacs who had no respect for their lives or any other lives. Actually, they thought that getting killed during a gang fight was an honor.

That night, the Stomach Cramps began to pester all the arriving guests by shooting them with paint bullets. Someone called the police, but by the time they arrived, they were gone. As soon as the police left, they would return. The guest inside were afraid to go out to their cars for fear of an attack by the Stomach Cramps.

Security had been hired just in case something like this might happen. They were halfway expecting some trouble from the Underground Citizens because they had lost the election big time, and they were so positive that they were going to win because they considered themselves so far above the Chief police that there shouldn't have been doubt, any contest. But no one expected any trouble from the local gangs, and this surprised them, but not completely.

As the night wore on, things on the outside got worse. The Cramps had began to disassemble cars and spray-paint others. Once again, the police was summoned. Once again, the Cramps had disappeared by the time they had arrived. A total of fifteen police cars arrived, and many guests chose to leave before something else happened.

Since there weren't any signs of the gang members, all the police left, leaving behind five cars to serve as guards. The guards were outside so that they could see if and when the gang members came back.

It didn't take long. About fifteen minutes, after most of the police left, they returned. Not as openly as they had previously, but in the shadows, out of the view of others. When they saw that some police were still there, they took action. They decided that they would teach the police a lesson and show them that they were not a match for them. They ambushed the police that had been left behind. They didn't have a chance. They were gunned down on the spot.

When the shooting began, panic took over inside. People were running, screaming, stepping over and on each other, trying to find a place to hide. Many people were injured, some critically. But before the stampede was over, the Rumbling Guts shot out a transformer, leaving the area in darkness. The hotel had emergency generators, but the lights were being shot out. So much for the generators. When the police returned and the ambulances arrived, they were ambushed. One ambulance and two police patrol cars were blown up. There were more casualties.

Bill and Carrie had taken refuge in a walk-in freezer. They were trying very hard to leave before anything else happened. More police came, but they couldn't get close because they too were being attacked by the gangs.

A fire broke out at the hotel when someone tried to light a candle when the power went out. It was useless to call the fire department; they couldn't get through because of the automatic gunfire and the explosive devices. A police helicopter hovered over the area, trying to provide light and also to see what was happening. The copter didn't hover long before someone shot it down in a hail of automatic gunfire.

An area two blocks long was under siege and was cordoned off as being impenetrable.

The fires raged on, and the people in the hotel tried to leave. They couldn't escape because the hotel was being held hostage by the Cramps and Guts. Ocena was vexed. Not only had she been trampled, she thought that her leg was broken. Arthur Moses vowed to protect her with his own life. So far, he had not had much luck. He remembered when he was a teenager, he had worked part-time at this hotel and remembered that there was a cellar that had a trapdoor that lead into a drainpipe. This pipe could very well take them to safety. He hurriedly convened with those present— K'Narf, Wester'C, Jelly Belly, Charles and the others— and told them to follow him. As they groped in the darkness and smoke en route to the cellar, Arthur held on tightly to Ocena, helping her and half-carrying her because her leg was broken. He prayed to God that the door would still be there and that they could get it open. As they descended the stairs, the smoke was less dense and they could breathe easier. The air was filled with people screaming, the sounds of sirens, and gunshots. Plus, there were the ever-present sounds of the crackling and roaring fire.

As the group lead by Arthur Moses crawled along the floor trying to reach the cellar or basement, they encountered many people crawling around on the floor completely disoriented. Some were sobbing and praying, completely frozen with fear, too afraid to move. Those who could move followed Moses and the others. If there ever was a hell, they were in the middle of it.

When they finally made it to the basement, Arthur fumbled in the darkness, trying to find the door. People were sobbing because they were afraid that if the fire didn't get them, the gangs would.

As they searched in the darkness for the trapdoor, the guests from the second floor ballroom were running for the door out of the burning building and being shot at like ducks in a pond.

A SWAT team unit was brought in and was making their way to the hotel when an explosion shook the ground for miles around. When the smoke cleared away, only a few members of the SWAT unit were moving, and they were injured.

The explosion was a booby trap set up by the Stomach Cramps after they had shot the four policemen. They had stolen the explosives from the Ace and Ivy Construction Company. The nitro was placed in places that they thought the police would use to reach the hotel. When the SWAT team had reached these places, they unknowingly triggered the explosions. Windows were shattered in every building for blocks. Shards of glass, like small deadly missiles, added to the injured accounts.

Arthur cried out, "Eureka!" Wester'C joined him as they tried to pry open a trapdoor that hadn't been used for decades. The creaking door gave way and slowly opened. A foul order greeted them when the lid was removed, but that didn't faze the refugees. Anything that would lead them out of the burning building and away from those gangs and guns were preferred regardless. A sigh of relief was heard among the crowd. But one thing that smoldered in the dim recesses of Arthur's mind jumped out. He called out, "Does anyone have a lighter or some matches?" No one answered. Arthur swore under his breath. "Goddamn motherfucker, ain't this a blip?"

Ocena cried out, "Wait. I think I have a light." She pulled out her key chain, and hanging on the chain was a miniature flashlight the size of a lipstick. It was given to her as a gag gift, and she always wondered what she could use it for. She found Arthur's hand and put the flashlight in it. He exclaimed, "What in the world is this?"

"It's a flashlight. It's miniature, but it works."

"How do you turn this thing on?" he asked.

Ocena told him, "Just push the little button at the back."

Arthur pushed the button, and it came on, and he was surprised at how much light it put off. He exclaimed, "Well, I'll be a bald-headed dog. It really works."

He directed the beam of light into the direction of the sewer drain. Then he cautioned them to beware where they walked. He really didn't have tell them this because they would walk through anything to get out of there. After approximately fifteen minutes, which seemed like an hour, they came to a drain cover. He looked under the cover, and it had Nose Street on it. Moses told the others that they were at Nose Street, and they were still too close to the melee to come up. They trod on.

In about twelve more minutes, they came to another drain cover. Moses looked under the cover and it said Cheek Cheek Street. Moses was relieved. He climbed the stairwell and exited. When he crawled out of the sewers, he looked up and saw that he was surrounded by a dozen police who had a dozen guns pointed at him.

He was instructed to come up slowly, very slowly. Moses said, "Now wait a minute. I am not a gang member. We—that is, me and the others—have escaped the burning hotel the only way we knew how."

"Okay, okay. How many of you are there?"

"I don't really know. Perhaps twelve to twenty."

"All right, let's get the rest of you out of this stinking hole."

In all, there were eighteen people who had come through the sewers. As they climbed out of the sewers, the night sky was lit up like an inferno. Cars were burning, buildings were burning, and all of it was accented by the lights on the police and other emergency vehicles.

Charles DeNero was in awe as huge purple flames leaped upward toward the semidark sky. He had never seen purple fire before.

Off in the not-so-far distance, the sound of gunshot and the roar of an out-of-control fire filled the air. An all-out battle was raging between the gangs and the police and some poor innocent souls that got caught up in the middle. The police was failing miserably when one after the other fell a victim to the same carnage.

The governor was talking about calling in the Purple Bottom City Nation Military. But the Terrible Toilet Papers came before he could make the call. The chief of police was not impressed. Sure, he had heard rumors of how the Terrible Toilet Papers combated crime and how the other gangs feared them. But all he saw were some young men with a huge ego problem. He resented the Terrible Toilet Papers because the citizenry looked up to and relied on them more than they did the police. The citizenry thought that the police were ineffective and tried to intimidate innocent law-abiding citizens.

The Terrible Toilet Papers were usually the ones who put an end to the Guts' and Cramps's harassment of the citizens. But the chief of police dismissed all reports of this kind because he felt that they were inaccurate. Plus, he just didn't like them.

When the terrible Toilet Papers arrived on the scene, they were given orders that they were prohibited to go beyond their command station. They simply did not obey these orders. They pulled off their garments; underneath, they were all dressed identical. They were dressed in very dark purple jumpsuits. Besides being called the Choir Boys, they were also called the Jumpsuit Boys. Before they did anything, they grouped up and did some type of chant. As they were going through this ritual, the Chief fire and police officers and other onlookers watched, fascinated. Shortly, they disappeared.

In less than fifteen minutes, things began to change. The sound of gunfire slackened. The chief of police had also noticed that things were quieter. He was wondering what was going on. It couldn't possibly be the Terrible Toilet Papers because not any of them was armed. Then again, they never used guns of any type. He would give up his wisdom teeth to know what was going on.

*****

The Terrible Toilet Papers were all schooled in the martial arts. They began their training at the tender age of two. By the age of ten, they had already mastered most of the martial arts. They were swift. They were accurate. They were deadly. They had been schooled in the art of mind control; they could make themselves disappear and become transparent. They had been schooled in and mastered kung fu, kendo, karate, judo, and several ancient arts that have been rarely heard of. They had been trained in meteorology, escape, explosives, disguise, concealment, and possessed a basic knowledge of medicine.

It takes many years and strong mental and spiritual training to reach the state in which rationalization and calculating functions of the mind are suspended so that the mind and body can act as a unit. All of the Terrible Toilet Papers had excelled in this training. Their main purpose in life was to keep the scales of justice balanced and in peace. The leader, called Charmin by those who knew him, was a spiritual man. He did not believe in revenge. He believed in justice. They did not believe in killing

227

unless it was necessary. They believed in rendering their foes useless. Most learn a lesson and straighten their lives up, but the Guts and Cramps are too primitive to learn, so they must put an end to their unlawful practices forever.

Out of nowhere they would attack the Cramps and Guts—*poof!*—and disappear. One by one, the gang members fell. Not many of them saw nor knew what had happened to them.

Within an hour, the only Rumbling Guts and Stomach Cramps that were left were the dead and severely injured. There were no signs of the Terrible Toilet Papers. They never did stick around when they finished a job. They did stop long enough to inform the police and to pick up their clothes, and then they were gone.

The chief of police, his officers, medical technicians, the governor, and part of his staff and the Chief fireman were in shock. They didn't know how twelve young men armed with only tools of their trade and no guns could go into a battle zone like that and do what a slew of heavily armed trained officers of the law could not do. They were amazed at how fast they did it and how fast they disappeared.

Finally, the fire department could enter the area and put out the raging, out-of-control fires. The medical personnel could go in and tend to the injured. The dead were collected and taken to the morgue, and the news media was all over everywhere, interviewing survivors, spectators, Chief policemen, and just about everyone else who was present and willing to talk. A total of fifteen fire trucks had arrived to extinguish the fires, and the news media was in the way, trying to get pictures and live onscreen interviews.

It took more than eight hours to put out the fires. The aftermath of the gang attack had taken its toll. There were at least ten firemen injured by the fire, five more had been shot. Three was seriously injured, and one died. Between the fires and the gang war, a total of seventeen Chickpeos had died.

Twenty-one were seriously injured, and more than thirty were treated and released. A two-block area was destroyed, and damage ran into the millions.

Eighteen gang members were dead, and at least thirty were found tied up and unconscious. The others had fled to parts unknown for now, but they would be rounded up to face judgment.

What a night this had been. A victory party had turned into a bloody gang war and a blazing inferno. Ocena's broken leg had been put into a cast, and Moses took her to his place. Wester'C, Jelly Belly, and K'Narf hung out at Moses's place because the Chief fire and police officers had cordoned off all the streets that lead to their houses.

Wester'C's family was overcome with anxiety because they didn't know where he was or how he was. He called them from Moses's house and told them that he was okay.

Ocena had taken some pain pills and was drowsy. The others sat around and talked about what had just happened. They were simply amazed at the Terrible Toilet Papers. Jelly Belly said, "The Terrible Toilet Papers must be descendents of the gods."

"I can see why you may think that," said Moses.

Charles sat quietly listening to the others and the thought of what was happening in his world invaded his mind. He was wondering if they sent out a search party to look for him. He wondered what the news said about his disappearance. Had they stopped looking for him? What his woman must be going through! Had she found someone else or what?

The violence that took place tonight brought thoughts of home and how much he missed it. It's just as well because Purple Bottom City is probably the place where he will spend the remainder of his life. So he may as well grin and bear it. Why did the violence he experience tonight make him think of home?

"Hey, Charles," interrupted Jelly Belly, "are you channel surfing your way home?" Charles grinned, and Jelly Belly asked, "What do you think of what happened tonight?"

"It was a sight to behold, all right. What I don't understand is why wasn't something done about these gangs before?"

Moses said, "It's always been 'if you don't bother me, I won't bother you.'"

"That's a nice way to put it," said Charles. "But ever since I've gotten here, I've been pestered by the same two gangs. In the meantime, they grow bigger and more powerful. If it were not for the Terrible Toilet Papers, many more people would have lost their lives, and property damage would have tripled."

Jelly Belly said, "What I want to know is, where did they get those names from?"

"Hey," interrupted K'Narf, "didn't the leader of the Stomach Cramps get killed the other week? Moses, you were the one who found him. His name was Malock."

"The leader of the Rumbling Guts is named Pepto," Moses said.

While watching the reporters' on TV, Wester'C said, "I see that they are beginning to let people get through. I better go to the hospital before I go home."

"I guess that it is time for all of us to go home." Looking around, he asked, "Hey, whatever happened to SuejuSoe?"

Ocena said, "I think that he is still at the hospital. He had a nasty gunshot wound to his left side. I think that they admitted him."

Wester'C stopped in the doorway and turned around. Shock was in his face. He spoke softly, "You mean SuejuSoe is in the hospital, and no one bothered to tell me?"

"I didn't know myself," said Jelly Belly.

"I didn't know either," Moses admitted.

Charles said, "I saw him lying on a gurney, but before I could get to him, they took him away in an ambulance. I thought that you all knew."

K'Narf said, "I knew that he had gotten hit when the lights went out. I saw someone reach for a piece of tablecloth and make a bandage for his wound because he was losing a lot of blood. When Moses called out for everyone to follow him, SuejuSoe had already passed out, but he regained consciousness long enough for someone to help him down to the basement so that he could escape through the tunnel. When we emerged from the tunnel and the police was questioning everyone, an ambulance took him to the hospital because he was completely unconscious. I tried to get to him so that I could do something for him. but too many people were in the way, and he was gone before I got a chance to see him."

"Damn! How could I miss all of this?" lamented Wester'C.

"Don't be too hard on yourself," said Ocena. "There was so much pandemonium going on, even the best of us were confused, scared, and panicky."

"Did all of the others get out?" asked Moses.

I can't say," answered Ocena. "With all the smoke, fire, gunshots, screaming, and the pain in my leg, I don't know. I really thank God that we did." She looked at Moses and smiled.

Wester'C was still standing in the doorway when a news bulletin hit the airways. The announcer said, "We interrupt this program to bring you a news bulletin hot off the press. The death toll for tonight's confrontation has increased. Both Bill Earlobe and his bride Carrie Earlobe, our newly elected president and governor, were found dead inside a refrigerated room at the Excelsior Hotel. Authorities believe that they both died from smoke inhalation. We will keep you up dated as this seemingly unending tragedy unfolds."

Wester'C's knees buckled, and he grasped the door to keep from falling. The others in the room sat with their mouths agape, staring at the TV. Wester'C spoke with tears cascading down his face, "Please tell me that they didn't say what I thought I heard them say."

No one answered. No one had to. Tears were in everyone's eyes except Charles DeNero's.

Pissy Dean said, "I had been thinking things couldn't get any worse, now this. I just can't take anymore."

"Yes, you can, and you will," Charles said as he held on to Pissy Dean to keep himself from falling. He continued, "Tonight has been and is still a nightmare. I know that Carrie and Bill were your ticket for a change in your world's government. I moan their deaths too, what I'm saying is, tonight was a son-of-a-bitch but you must not lose faith and give up the hope that you thought the future was going to bring. You all still have each other, and you are still healthy, vibrant, and, alive and can start over. I don't think that it will be as hard as you think it will because Bill and Carrie have already broken the ice, and I think that it is what they would want you to do. They certainly wouldn't want you to lie around licking your wounds and complaining. And as I speak, I want to tell you that before this night is over, more bad news may come this way, and I just want to warn you."

Moses said as he wiped away his tears, "I know that you are right. We should get in control of our emotions even though it hurts so bad. Tears for cleaning the soul is not wasted water."

Ocena said, "Mine are therapeutic. They help to wash away some of the guilt because we couldn't do anything to stop it and the pain and sense of loss because they were one of a kind and we can never replace them."

Charles retorted, "I'm sure that they do. But what I mean is, tears are not going to rectify what is wrong, nor are they going to build a future."

"Point well taken," said Jelly Belly.

Charles continued, "Something is amiss with this whole scenario. I suppose that you are too close and too involved to have noticed. I've been trying to put two plus two together, and I keep getting three. First, what initiated tonight's attack? Could it have been your candidates winning the election in a landslide? Could it be that someone or some other people didn't want this to happen? Or could it be since it did happen, they had to undo it? And since they wanted to erase it, who were the best erasers that they could get without the finger getting pointed back at them? Could they find someone who was just as mean and nasty and who already had a sullied reputation, who no one would think had a motive?"

Wester'C's face lit up like the proverbial lightbulb had just come on. He said, "I can see where you are coming from. Like maybe the whole thing was staged to take out our newly elected candidates without suspicion being thrown on the real perpetrators, then things escalated out of control. Yep, I can see where you are coming from."

When the possible realization for tonight's massacre was finally grasped, emotions swung from one extreme to the other. All that destruction and all those wasted lives, all the pain and suffering. Why? Because someone didn't like the outcome of the election?

Moses said, "It makes a lot of sense. I wonder if anyone else came up with a theory like this."

"There's one way to find out. Let's go visit our local police. They have proven that they cannot protect, maybe they can serve."

"You guys will have to take care of this because I really do have to go the hospital," Wester'C said as he exited the door. "Keep me posted."

K'Narf said, "Let the doc go do his duty. We can take care of this. Jelly Belly, Pissy Dean, Charles. I included you because you came up with the rundown, I know that you are not a part of this but I, we, feel that you could be beneficial, real beneficial. Moses, I suppose that you want to stay here with Ocena and nurse her back to health."

Ocena said, "No, he doesn't. He wants to go right out there with you guys and balance the scales of justice and bring the guilty to trial so that they can get their just rewards."

"You guys heard her. Now let's get this show on the road."

"Hold on a minute," said Charles. "They are just reopening the streets. Don't you think that we should wait a little while? Maybe they have come up with the same conclusion that we have, but I doubt it.

Anyway, I know that all the reports are not in this soon, and they may perceive us as meddling, trying to start up something."

"Right again," said Moses. "We can wait a little while. Knowing our police force, they aren't the swiftest or the smartest."

When Wester'C got to the hospital, he immediately went to find SuejuSoe. He found him on the third floor. He looked down at his friend and said a little prayer then glanced through his chart. He saw that his liver had been nipped by the bullet that had hit him. They had to repair his liver. Inaudibly, he said, "I'm sorry, man." A tear ran down his cheek. He studied his chart further, unaware that he had awakened.

SuejuSoe quietly said, "Say, Doc. Do you think that I'm going to live? Or do you see a problem?" Wester'C thought that he was hearing things. SuejuSoe repeated, "Doc, do you see a problem?" He looked at SuejuSoe and saw that he was awake. A smile spread over his face. If you've never seen joy, you should have seen Wester'C's face at that moment. He came around to the side of the bed and said, "Man, are you all right?"

"Sure, I am. It takes more than a nasty old bullet and a funky old fire to kill me."

"Man, I'm so glad that you're okay."

SuejuSoe asked, "Can you tell me what happen after the Terrible Toilet Papers took over? I must have passed out just before they arrived."

Wester'C was hesitant and didn't know if he should tell him anything or he tell him everything that he knew. Then he thought that he would make a summation. "Many people got hurt, many were killed, and the fire destroyed three city blocks. Ocena got her leg broken." He paused, wondering if he should tell him about Bill and Carrie. He didn't have to wait long. SuejuSoe asked, "How about our candidates?"

"Candidates?" asked Wester'C as he hesitated.

"Yes, you know, Carrie and Bill, our newly elected president and governor."

Wester'C began, "Man, I really don't know how to tell you this."

"Is it that bad?" SuejuSoe interrupted. "You are acting and sounding like they got burned up in the fire."

"It is that bad. I really don't know how to tell you this."

"Just say it," SuejuSoe said impatiently.

"All right." Wester'C paused. "They are dead, and they didn't get burned up in the fire."

"They are what? How can this be? What happened?"

"I don't know. I heard it announced in a news bulletin just before I was leaving Moses's place to come here. They were found in a walk-in freezer that they apparently took shelter in from the fire and shooting."

"Lord, no!" groaned SuejuSoe. "What else can go wrong?"

"I'm going to tell you this and nothing else, I don't want to upset you too much."

"Upset me too much," SuejuSoe said with mockery in his voice. "What in the name of Jesus are you talking about? Don't you know that lying here with part of your liver shot out isn't upsetting? Do you think that all this useless and senseless violence isn't upsetting? Do you think that Bill and Carrie's deaths aren't upsetting? Just how much more don't you want to upset me! Tell me all that you know. I am waiting for you to really upset me."

He said, "This may set your recovery time back, but I know that you want to know. Just before I left Moses's place, Charles came up with a theory. He proposed that the whole thing was staged to cover up the assassination of Bill and Carrie Earlobe."

"Whoa!" SuejuSoe said as he winched in pain. "Did you say assassination?"

Wester'C looked around the room nervously like he expected to see someone hiding in a corner of the room or under the bed. Then he whispered, "You've got to promise me that you won't say a word of this to anyone without exception."

"Okay."

Wester'C began, "The story about Bill and Carrie's death is a sham. But the real reason was that they both had a bullet in the base of their skulls. Somehow, things escalated out of control. The cover story about their deaths was aired because the police didn't want to alert the killer or killers. They wanted them to be confident that no one was onto them. The Stomach Cramps and Rumbling Guts are not scapegoats, they took a willing and active part in everything that went down, and their fates are in the hands of the courts."

SuejuSoe moaned. Wester'C thought that he had given him too many unpleasant facts too soon after his serious injuries. He asked, "Are you all right? Are you in pain?"

"As a matter of fact, I am."

"What's wrong?"

"What's wrong? What's right? Everything is wrong."

The doctor in Wester'C came out, and he said to SuejuSoe, "I have said too much and have upset you physically and mentally. You are not up to processing all what happened tonight. Anyway, there's nothing that we can do right now. You have to get back on your feet. We'll talk later, and I really do have some patients to see."

"Sure, go on, Wes, I'll be okay."

After Wester'C had left the room, SuejuSoe wished that he could reach the phone so that he could call Moses or K'Narf. But he was hurting and movement was very painful. "Lord," he prayed, "please don't let anything else happen."

He slept fitfully the remainder of the night.

*****

Ocena hobbled into the room, and the radio was playing the golden oldies. The Temptations were belting out "My Girl." She smiled because it brought back memories of a life in better times. If only she could bring back those times. Lately, her life had gotten more and more complicated. Dangerous. How could her world be shattered like an icicle that had fallen on the sidewalk? She did not know if it was safe for her to walk the streets. How could violence be so casual? Almost as casual as a walk in the park, but a walk in the park was not casual anymore.

Poor sweet SuejuSoe, what did he do to deserve being shot down like a game animal? I didn't want to see anything get killed. Carrie and Bill were just beginning their married life and political life together, and now they are dead.

She sat down on the sofa, and pain made its presence known. She gasped as her leg brushed against the coffee table. Now Marvin Gaye was moaning "What's Going On?" She picked up her broken leg and let it rest, propped up on a pillow. She nodded as Otis Redding was moaning, "These arms of mine are waiting, wanting to hold you." A knock on the door startled her awake. She hobbled to the door. It was Arthur, the love of her life. He held her gently in his arms; it felt good to be comforted and loved. He asked, "Have you heard anything about the investigation of Tuesday night's massacre?"

"Yes. It's been rumored that some of the gang members have been singing like a songbird."

"I've already heard that. It seem that someone paid the Guts and Bloods big money to disrupt, destroy, and disappear. To cause enough ruckus to camouflage a double assassination."

Ocena pursed her lips, looked thoughtfully out of the window, and asked, "Do they have any idea who is behind this because as long as no one knows, all of us could be in danger?"

"Tell me about it," Arthur said with resignation. "I think that Wester'C and SuejuSoe are in more of a danger zone, but we cannot be ruled out either."

"This doesn't feel good at all, not knowing if your head is about to be blown off."

Moses smiled an insincere smile. His face tried to hide the fear and uncertainty that had invaded their lives. He said, "I'm going to go down to the police station and see if I can find out anything. I came by to see if you are all right and to tell you that I love you, broken leg and all."

She kissed him on the lips and said, "I already knew that but, it is always good to hear."

He walked into the police station, and the first person that he saw Chief Retton Gallstone. He turned to go but not soon enough. He came over and put his hand on his shoulder and said, "Son, I'm real sorry about what happened to your friends. To tell you the truth, I'm sick about the whole thing. I was all for this new government thing, you know the big change."

Moses thought, This Bozo is talking with a smidgen of intelligence even if he did call me son again. He was in favor of the big change in government, and most people had no idea what that consisted of. They just wanted change. He chatted for a minute and offered him a seat in his office that had been cut into and made into one medium office and one smaller office with two cubicles. He closed the door and asked him if he could he help him with anything. This was going to be easier than he had anticipated. Chief Gallstone was willing to talk to him, and he was willing to listen.

He asked, "Could you give me any details about what happened Tuesday evening?"

"I could tell you about as much as we know. I'm most certain that you've heard the rumors about what went down. I don't know what you've heard, but I'm about to tell you something that I don't want anyone to know except those who were directly involved. I've been beating the bushes, and I accidently stumbled on to something. Did you notice how quickly our governor vacated the scene just before the trouble began? Almost as if he knew that something was going down. The fire didn't destroy all the evidence. I wasn't there, but a reliable source said that he saw the governor put something in the champagne bottle that he was about to pour a toast from. Fortunately, no one got to drink any. Just before the shooting began, the governor left as if someone had yelled for him to run. Mr. and Mrs. Earlobe dropped their glasses when they ran for cover. Then you know, a fire broke out."

"No," corrected Moses, "that's not the way it happened. The fire didn't begin until the lights went out."

"Yes, that is right," the chief agreed. "You know the fire burned out of control before the firemen could get to it."

"Uh-huh," said Moses. "I was there."

"Well," continued the chief, "that bottle of champagne still had some in it when the fire investigators came to do their thing. Since someone had already mentioned something about this before, the champagne was tested and came back positive. It contained a neurotoxin derivative."

What!" said Moses. "You can't be serious. Wait, how did they know that those glasses belonged to Bill and Carrie?"

"Fingerprints, son."

"I don't suppose that you could tell me who the informer is?"

The chief answered, "Uh-uh." Then he said mostly to himself, "Something about this just doesn't feel right."

Moses asked, "Did you say something?"

"No," he lied. "I've got to get busy now."

Moses stood up and said to the chief, "Whenever you find out what doesn't feel right about this situation, please let me know. Okay."

"Sure."

They shook hands, and Moses left.

*****

The chief got on the phone and called Kenny Mack, the detective who was in charge of this case. Detective Mack used to be a resident of Underground City, but he chose to live in Purple Bottom City. He mutated but never regretted his decision.

Detective Mack entered the office, and Chief Gallstone was sitting on the edge of his cluttered desk toying with a stress reliever. He asked Mack, "Have you gotten the lowdown on our informer?"

"No, not yet."

"Do you think that he is telling the truth?"

Detective Mack answered, "I think that there may be some truth in what he is saying. I just wish I knew what part is true."

"What got you hung up?"

Detective Mack sat down his coffee and said, "Just like you said, Chief, I keep adding two plus two and I keep getting three."

The chief said, "That's makes two of us."

Detective Mack left the station and drove through the burned-out section of the city. Workers were everywhere, cleaning up the rubble and demolishing guttered buildings. He slowed down and found a place to park, got out of his car, and headed toward the burned-out Excelsior Hotel. He didn't go inside, just stood in the door way and looked around. He turned to go and stepped on something that cracked. He thought that it was a piece of glass, but as he removed his foot, he found a plastic purple rose button. When he picked it up, he could see that even though it was purple, it was not of Purple Bottom City.

Detective Mack returned to the police station and headed for the chief's office. He met him in the hallway, and they returned to his office. He took the button out of his pocket, showed it to the chief, and asked, "What do you make of this?"

The chief took the button and held it under a lamp and asked, "Where did you get this from, and what is it?"

"It's a button, and I got it from the steps of the Excelsis."

"I've never seen anything like this before. What can you make of it? It's not from Purple Bottom City. I am sure of that."

"Where do you think it came from?"

"I can't answer that. I thought that I would take it down to the lab and see what I can find out." As Detective Mack was going out of the door, the chief called out, "Keep me informed," as he maneuvered a toothpick from one side of his mouth to the other with his tongue.

Detective Mack took the plastic-looking button and dropped it off at the lab and took off to parts unknown.

The next day, around 3:30 PM, the lab called. The results of the plastic-looking button were in. The lab report verified that the button was not from Purple Bottom City. They also ran it through the Underground City computers, and it was not from there either. Neither place had any material with the same chemical makeup. No one had any idea where it originated. Detective Mack took a copy of the report and headed for Chief Gallstone's office. Upon entering the office, he found the chief sitting at his desk with his hands folded under his chin forming a pyramid. He always did this when something was going on, and he could not figure out just what it was. He looked up. "Don't tell me you have found something out, and it ain't good, huh?"

"You hit the nail on the head. I have found out something, and it is unbelievable."

"Go on."

Detective Mack put the report in the chief's big bear hands and waited. As he read the report, a pallor came across his face. He brought the paper closer to his eyes as if he couldn't see. He laid the paper down, rubbed his eyes, and looked at Detective Mack. He said, "What can you make of this report?"

"I don't know. What do you think?"

"Hell, I don't have a clue."

Detective Mack poured himself a cup of coffee and sat down. He said, "Chief, something ain't right about this whole thing. I can't figure it out yet, but something ain't right."

"I kinda got the same feeling. It's kinda like trying to shake hands with your image in the mirror."

"I think that I should talk to Mr. SuejuSoe. I think that he knows something even he is not aware of. His alien friend—"

"His name is Charles DeNero," the chief injected.

"That's the one. I need to go talk to him. I wonder just what does he know."

"No can do," the chief said. "SuejuSoe is in the hospital, and he got shot up pretty bad. I don't think that they will let him talk to anyone now."

"Maybe I could talk to the alien . . . I forgot his name."

"Charles DeNero, remember that, son."

"I have it."

"I didn't tell you that I talked to one of their group members, an Arthur Moses earlier. He just wanted to know what we had found out about the massacre. He had an odd theory about this himself. He wouldn't get into it with me. You go on and chase down your ghost, and I hope that you don't have a dry run."

"Uh-huh," said Detective Mack, "either way it will be productive. If they don't know anything, I can cross them off my list. If they do know something, bingo."

"Anyway, I want to be kept updated."

By the time Detective Mack caught up with Charles DeNero, he was getting ready to go to the hospital to see SuejuSoe. He swung his car across the driveway, blocking his exit, got out of his car, came over to Charles, and asked, "Are you Charles DeNero?"

Trying hard to keep control, Charles snapped, "That depends on who wants to know and what do they want with him."

He said, pulling his badge out of his pocket, "I am Detective Mack, and I'm trying to find out who is behind the killings and fire Tuesday night and would like to talk to Charles DeNero, that is if I can find him."

Charles's anger was still simmering, and he exploded. "You stupid idiot, you could have killed me with your sassy-ass aggressive driving. And being a detective, you aren't very observant, how many others have you seen looking like me around here? If you wanted to talk to me, why couldn't you call and make an appointment like civilized Chickenpeople? No. You came here acting like a god. I could have been hurt or even killed. I've been told that our worlds were identical once upon a time, so I guess that your behavior is typical for a man of the law."

Mack was taken aback by Charles's outburst. Now that he had gotten his ego deflated, the man did not look like a Chickpeo at all. He had to do some celestial apologizing. He returned his badge slowly and said in a mild manner, "I'm sorry that I was so pushy. But I really do need to talk to Charles DeNero and SuejuSoe Juso."

"That's Suju. SuejuSoe Suju," Charles corrected. Still fuming, he said, "I'm Charles DeNero. Mr. Suju is still in the hospital. I was in the process of going to see him before your fiasco. Now just what do you want?"

"Like I have just said, I am investigating the deaths of Mr. and Mrs. Earlobe and the others, and I've been thinking that maybe you could help me make some sense of the information that I already have that make no sense."

"You have said a mouthful, but I don't know what you are talking about, and right now is not a good time. I am on my way to see Mr. Suju in the hospital."

"It's really important that I talk to both of you. Do you mind if I rode to the hospital with you?"

"If I said yes I'd mind, would you come anyway?"

"I sure would have."

"That's just what I thought," said Charles. "Get in."

*****

On their way to the hospital, Detective Mack began to talk about the Tuesday night massacre. He wanted to know where Charles was when the shooting began. He wanted to know if he had a good view of the governor and who he was sitting near. Where was he in proximity to the governor? Where was SuejuSoe during this time?

Charles spoke deliberately slow, punctuating every syllable, "Why do you want to know this, and why do you think that I know anything about any of this?"

Detective Mack spoke as deliberately as Charles, "Because you was there and they were there, and I am sure that you've seen things that could have happened but don't remember what it was, and I was thinking that maybe, just maybe, I could jog your memory."

Charles grinned cockily and said, "You have great aspirations. Now that we've got our introductions out of the way, may I inform you that my number one everything is to get back to my world."

Detective Mack said, "I can understand your frustrations being in an alien world, but I'm trying to do my job the best way that I know how. Some very serious crimes have been committed, and I am trying to find out who did it. Or don't they have law and order in your world?"

"They give it their best shot, and it runs about like it does here. Let me tell you that all of this stuff is on my second-to-last nerve. The first one to befriend me when I got here was almost killed. Two others that I have grown to think of as friends are dead, and I barely escaped with my own life. You cannot began to think how this is affecting me. I don't mean to sound like a jackass, but I just don't know what I can tell you."

"I'm sure I can't understand the depth of your frustrations, and I am sure that the depths of my frustrations don't compare to yours. Yet I am frustrated. There is nothing that I want more than to find out who the guilty parties are."

"Perhaps SuejuSoe can shed a little light on the subject. Right now my mind is too numb to think."

"I can understand that. I do have a heart."

When they got to the hospital, they were denied visiting privileges; SuejuSoe was still critical and too weak for visitors. But since he had been asking for Charles, they would let him go in for a minute, as it might lessen his stress and aid his healing. Detective Mack was told that there was to be no questioning. Mr. Suju was sedated because of the pain, and questioning him was out of the question.

He would have to come back at another time when it would be okayed by his doctor.

This didn't sit too well with the detective; even though he stressed who he was and how important all this was, he was denied.

Charles entered SuejuSoe's room cautiously like he was walking in a mine field. He was awake and noticed how scared Charles looked. A smiled creased his lips and he softly said, "It's okay, I won't blow up and I am not going to bite."

Charles flashed an ear-to-ear grin. "I can see that you didn't lose your sense of humor. How are you, man? I mean how are you?"

"I'm tough, I'm going to make it. It takes more than a nasty old bullet to take me out. Just don't make me laugh."

"You know that humor is not my strong suit. I just had to see you. They said that I could only stay a minute. Man, you don't mind if I call you man instead of Chickpeo? I miss you."

SuejuSoe stifled a giggle that was painful. He said, "I thought I told you not to make me laugh."

"What did I say funny?"

"That man instead of Chickpeo."

"Was that all I had to do to cheer you up? You don't know it yet, but there are a lot of dust this—what they are calling it? The Tuesday Night Massacre storm—has kicked up. Bill and Carrie are dead."

"I know. The good Doctor Wester'C informed me."

"I have really got to go before they come and throw me out. You need your rest."

"Okay, Charles. Thanks for stopping by."

Charles exited the room as cautiously and quietly as he had entered.

On his way out of the hospital, everyone he passed stopped and stared. A medical technician dropped a tray of samples, and she walked into a gurney. They looked at him like the alien that he was. He understood. If it was him, he would do it himself. He didn't hurry; he took his time to make his exit.

About a week later after SuejuSoe had returned home, Detective Mack came back to talk to him. He said that he could understand that he was still recuperating and he would not tire him out. He asked him the same questions that he had asked Charles, only this time he hit pay dirt.

SuejuSoe remembered where the governor was standing. He knew where Carrie and Bill were standing and their proximity to the governor. He could remember with clarity up until the moment he got shot. He remembered the searing pain that had gripped him and how hard he had fought to maintain consciousness and how someone had caught hold of him to keep him from falling and wrapped something around him to stop the bleeding.

Detective Mack asked, "Did you see the governor pour champagne for Bill and Carrie Earlobe?"

"I can't say that I did. I saw him holding a bottle, but when the gunshots erupted outside, my attention turned to it."

"Did you see either of the Earlobes or the governor drink a toast?"

"No. I can't say that I did. Because at about the same moment the ruckus began, the shooting started and the lights went out. I tried to find cover, but I didn't have the time. I think I got shot during the first round of fire. I knew that I had been hurt badly and someone was helping me. I fainted and when pressure was applied to my wound, I regained consciousness. Then the fire broke out, and someone was half-dragging me out of the building, and that was my number one goal. I remembered Arthur Moses, may God bless him, telling us to follow him. I was weaker than I thought and I fainted. Someone helped me as we went through a basement and exited a storm drain or something under the floor. Just before it came, my time to go through the drain, I blacked out. That's all that I can remember."

Detective Mack finished writing notes in a pad and said, "You have been a great help. Now I'm going to go and let you get some rest."

"That will take a miracle," said SuejuSoe. "How can I rest when I can't turn my mind off and I keep reliving that night over and over?"

Detective Mack was taken aback by SuejuSoe's outburst of emotions. He felt genuinely sorry for pushing through the door of his mind that he wanted to shut forever, and he said, "I'm really sorry that I disturbed the scab on a wound that ain't quite healed yet. I know that it's painful. Let me assure you that I never would have intruded if it wasn't important. Murders have been committed, lives have been disrupted, and a city lies in ruins, and I feel that you do understand that I am going to turn over every rock and shake every tree and piss in every creek until I catch whoever that is responsible."

SuejuSoe responded, "Detective Mack, I know that you have a job to do. I almost lost my life. It's just that I'm tired and weak from my injuries, but if I can think of anything that may help, I will give you a call."

As Detective Mack was leaving, he pulled out the little plastic-looking button and asked, "Have you ever seen something like this before?"

SuejuSoe took the button in his hand and examined it. He showed it to Charles and noticed that he reacted to it, but he also claimed to know nothing about it. Charles's reaction was not missed by Detective Mack. SuejuSoe said, "No. I've never seen this before. What is it and where did it come from?"

"I wish that I knew." Then he asked, "Mr. DeNero, have you ever seen something like this before?"

Charles answered pithily, "No. I have never seen it before." Yet he couldn't explain or understand why it made him feel so uncomfortable.

Detective Mack thanked both of them and left. As he pulled off in his car, he thought to himself, Something is not right about that alien DeNero. I wonder just how much he knows.

Charles felt physically ill. After he had helped SuejuSoe get settled, he lay down on the sofa and also wondered why that button made him feel so jittery.

Mack's drive back to his office was a troubling one. He knew that he had stumbled upon something, but what? He was not about to let go of it. He decided to talk to the chief again.

When he walked into the chief's office, he was on the phone. That everlasting cigar was grabbed in the corner of his mouth unlit. He acknowledged Detective Mack's presence and motioned for him to take a seat. "Okay, I'll get back to you later," he said into the phone and hung up. Then he turned to Mack and said, "So have you got something to run by me?"

"Something like that."

"Okay," said the chief, "start at the beginning."

"I went to talk to SuejuSoe Suju and that alien DeNero. What I have to say is not concrete, but I think that it is interesting. What I was really looking for was any evidence of the governor's participation. From the statement that I got from SuejuSoe Suju, I can't really say that he did or did not poison the champagne. But when I showed him the button, he couldn't identify it, but when I showed it to DeNero, he definitely had a reaction. When I asked him about it, he denied knowing anything about it."

"What kind of reaction are you talking about?"

"He seem to be nervous, like he was trying to hide something. I think we should call him in."

"Not so fast. I don't have any idea of what you have in mind. DeNero was almost killed too. I know you are not talking about anything like an alien invasion."

"You have got it all wrong. I can't say if what's stuck in my craw has anything to do with aliens. It's just a gut feeling that he know something that he ain't telling."

"We can put a tail on him and see where that leads to. That's the best that I can do."

The next several days, Charles was tailed. Even at Bill and Carrie's funeral, he was tailed. SuejuSoe didn't know for certain, but he felt that something was going on. He asked Charles if there was something that he wanted to tell him. He said no.

Charles was acting nervous and feeling even more uneasy, and he didn't know why. He felt guilty and did not know why. He began to think that maybe he was losing his mind. What else could it be? He had begun to awaken in the middle of the night panting and had no idea why. Only that he was scared shitless whenever it happened. That feeling of dread began to inch closer and closer, and no matter what, he couldn't put any distance between him and that feeling of impending doom. He thought that maybe he should go see a shrink because this was fast becoming a situation that he could no longer handle. Then there was SuejuSoe asking him some dumb-ass questions about him talking in some kind of strange alien language. What was going on? He didn't know anything about any strange alien language. There was no one, absolutely no one, who wanted to know what was going on more than him.

A week later, Charles meet with test subjects A and B. Metor Maam and Baul Steve. They met at an outdoor cafe out on Runs Road. The agent that was following him was shocked when he heard them talking in a strange alien language that he had never heard before. The agent that that had been following Charles before had not told him about any strange language. Matter of fact, he had not told him anything at all. All he was told to do was follow him and to record their conversations. When he reported to the chief and Detective Mack, Mack raised his eyebrows and looked at the chief.

When SuejuSoe found out that the agent that he hired had gone and told the police about what was going on, he promptly fired him. He told him that he had given him specific orders not to talk to anyone but him, and he had disobeyed, and if he could, he would see that he would never work in Purple Bottom City again. Now he knew that he could no longer put it off; he was going to have to confront Charles and do it soon.

*****

The chief asked the agent to tell him exactly what went on. The agent began his narrative, leaving out the part that SuejuSoe had hired him to follow DeNero because he was afraid what may become of him if did. He told how he had followed him out on Runs Road and how he had met up with two other Chickpeos. They began to talk in this strange alien language and their behavior was really strange.

The expressions that they had on their faces freaked him out.

The agent stopped and thought for a minute then said, "To me they looked like robots."

"Explain what you mean when you say robots."

"Maybe I should have said they looked like puppets."

The chief said, "Now, tell me what do you mean when you say that they looked like puppets."

"I don't know how to explain it. To me, they looked like they were being controlled."

The chief and Detective Mack looked at each other, their faces were a question mark and their mouths were open. The chief said, "What can you make of this, Mack?"

"Right now, Chief, I don't know what to think. This just blew my mind. Perhaps DeNero is telling the truth. Maybe he doesn't know anything about any alien language. Maybe he is doing something that he is unaware of himself."

The chief removed his unlit cigar, rubbed his balding spot, and said, "I don't know, Detective, but I'm becoming more inclined to think that this is connected to your button."

"How so? This is far-out."

"No. Not necessary. Just think, a button of an unknown origin. Language of an unknown origin and robotic controlling. Then an alien shows up out of nowhere. Two sub-Chickpeos that were zapped to places outside of our world and came back speaking better than our normal citizens. It all sound kind of otherworldly to me."

"I think that you have been watching too many sci-fi movies."

"Before you make another remark about sci-fi movies, use your mind. You said yourself that DeNero acted like he knew something."

"No. I didn't. What I said was that he had a reaction when I showed him the button. It was very minute, and if I hadn't been looking for it, I would have missed it."

"This could still be significant." The chief told the agent who was tailing Charles to stick with him like a second skin. Then he said to Detective Mack, "Do you think that we should put a tail on test subjects A and B?"

Before Detective Mack could answer, the agent that was tailing Charles spoke up, "Chief, Mr. Suju has fired me."

"What!"

"He fired me because he said that I was supposed to be working for him and was to report to him and only him. If he thought that whatever I had uncovered may have been pertinent to your investigation, he would do the reporting."

"He said all that, did he?"

"Yes. He was really angry that I had not obeyed his orders. He looked at me as though he could strangle me."

"Listen, son, you go on home. I'll get in touch with you at a later time." Then he turned to Detective Mack and asked, "What did I say a minute ago?"

"You were talking about putting a tail on test subjects A and B. But I don't think that it would work because they live too close to XOZ-30 Zone, and most Chickpeos shun going down there."

"That is true. I had forgotten about that. But then again, they could be using it as a base because no one will go down there looking for them. Plus, what we are looking for may not be Chickpeos.

"Who are the they that you are speaking of?"

"The perpetrators. Who else?"

"Oh, yes," said Detective Mack. "Does this mean that we're going to give up on the governor theory?"

Chief Gallstone looked at Detective Mack and sighed, "Don't tax my patience, son. We have got a case to crack, and damn it, we are going to do it."

*****

SuejuSoe was so upset with the detective agency that he ended up back in the hospital. He had wanted to know just who gave them the authority to go against his orders. And whose idea it was to change agents when he had specifically chosen one and not another. The possibility of suing the agency still played in his mind.

The agency said that the agent that he had been using had an emergency and had to go out of town for a short while and they didn't think that it would hurt for a substitute to fill in for a few days. They were adamant that they did not give the substitute agent permission to go to the police or to reveal to anyone what was going on.

The trouble was the substitute had always wanted to be a policeman but couldn't cut it. He wanted to come up with one case, just one case, to show PBC's finest that they had really missed out on a good one when they wouldn't let him back in the academy.

The man was unstable and people didn't really feel comfortable around him. Some said that he made them feel like he was reading their souls. The anxiety that they had experienced being around him made him think that he was powerful. Nevertheless, he managed to get hired by the Purple Bottom City Detective Agency, a private for-hire agency. Their motto was no job was too low for them to go or to high for them to spy.

SuejuSoe and the head of the agency were talking outside the burned hotel. The conversation was so intense until he cut himself on a shard of glass and didn't know it. In a couple of days, his temperature went up and he was rushed back to the hospital where he was diagnosed with septicemia. He surmised that if he had not been so occupied with the unscrupulous private detective, he would have paid more attention to his surroundings and would have not gotten hurt. But that was just one man's opinion. He was most anxious to get back to work, but he was still a little weak. Charles had begun to get on his nerves because he had yet to adjust to the fact that he probably would have to spend the remainder of his life here and would never get back to his world.

Then there was something strange and distant about him. Sometimes he acted like someone else, and at times, he acted like something else had taken over his mind. Then he had stopped talking to him. The first thing that entered SuejuSoe's mind was that Charles had found out about the tail that he had put on him. He was afraid to ask him about it because he wasn't sure that this is what was bothering him, and if he did ask, he would know what was going down, and if he didn't already know, he would then. If he would ask him a question, he would answer yes or no or maybe, and that's all he would say. Actually, SuejuSoe thought that he was having a breakdown. He decided that he would talk to Wester'C about this.

*****

Wester'C said, "You've given me a lot to digest. Not to mention that some of is eerily otherworldly. I don't know what you expect me to do or say. You have put a lot on my plate, and I don't like any of it. Why did you wait so long to say something about this?"

"I waited because I had to be sure that what I was seeing was real and not conjured up by stress." He crossed the room and got a tape out of the table drawer. He put it in the stereo and pushed the Play button. The sounds that came from the tape was definitely alien to him. He stopped the tape and looked at Wester'C. "Well," he said.

Wester'C looked at SuejuSoe like he had gone berserk. "Just what was that you played?"

"That, my friend, was a conversation between Charles and the two test subjects from the portal."

"Where did you get it from?"

"When Charles first began to meet with these two, I hired a private detective to follow him if he was to meet up with the test subjects and to tape their conversations without them being aware of it. It took some doing on my part, but I was determined. He has no idea that I've done this."

"What tipped you off and made you suspicious of his doings?"

"It was not one particular thing. I had been spending a lot of time with Charles, and slowly he began to act like he wasn't always there. He became secretive and somewhat withdrawn. At first, I thought that he was reacting to being in an alien world surrounded by as he often called us, purple chickenpeople. I felt that it was more than that. After the failure of the portal, one day, I heard him talking to test subject B in an alien language. I asked him about it, and he said that he didn't know what I was talking about. I heard them talking another time in the same alien language, and again, he denied it. That's when I hatched this plot."

"You dirty dog. This is really heavy duty. Have you ever confronted him about any of this?"

"Sure, I did. He denied knowing anything about either one."

"Do you think that Charles is not who he says he is, or do you think that he is not telling the truth about his arrival or what?"

"Man, I don't what to think anymore. This whole situation is taking a toll on me. I really don't believe that he is an evil and destructive alien. I think that he is basically telling the truth."

"Are you going to confront him with the evidence yourself, or do you want some witnesses to be with you? I could get in touch with the usual gang to give you some support."

"I don't know if we should do that. He would think that I had betrayed him, and he wouldn't trust me anymore."

"Pray, tell me," asked Wester'C, "how are you going to get any answers to this enigma unless you confront him?"

"Because I don't know what he would do or how he will react, you know, how he will handle it." Wester'C stood up, looked around and asked SuejuSoe if he had some coffee, poured himself a cup, and sat back down. He took a sip and said, "I think that it's time for him to piss or get off the pot. After all, he is an alien to us, and we really don't know what he is capable of or how much he can be trusted or if he can be trusted at all."

SuejuSoe said hesitantly, "I suppose you could be right."

"You know darn well that I'm right. You are a lawyer, and you know that I'm right."

SuejuSoe said in a small voice, "Lawyers have been wrong lots of times."

Wester'C began talking like he was trying to reassure a terminal patient, "Now, SuejuSoe, we can go about this any way that you think best. I'm sure that an amiable solution can be obtained without too much damage. But I must insist that we must find out one way or another. Besides, he may be a permanent citizen of Purple Bottom City."

SuejuSoe was hesitant, but he reluctantly agreed with what Wester'C had proposed.

The meetings of the PBThree, as they had been dubbed, escalated. Their purpose was still unknown. The secrecy that they had once kept had gone lax. Wester'C, Arthur Moses, and SuejuSoe had witnessed more than one encounter, and they were absolutely awed by the spectacle. It seemed as though their bodies hosted an unseen presence and was operating without their will or knowledge.

The big question was in two parts: who were the intruders? if there were intruders, what did they want? Somehow, a plan needed to be devised to find the answer to these questions without risking unknown repercussions.

One day, while driving through the burned-out section of the city, Chief Gallstone witnessed one of their rendezvous. More strangely was that when the rendezvous was over, all three took something like the plastic button that Detective Mack had found and promptly swallowed it. The chief exclaimed, "Sweet mother of Jesus! What in the name of the Almighty is going on here?"

The trio parted, but the bizarreness continued. They acted like they had just woke up and didn't know where they were or who they were.

The chief witnessed this for a few minutes then drove back to the station and summoned Detective Mack. Detective Mack was already in a meeting with the Purple Bottom City Steering Committee, Number 111: Jon Dexter, 'Bojo', Wester'C, Ocena Heartburns, K'Narf Covictus, and SuejuSoe. When the chief heard this, he joined their meeting.

When he walked in, they were discussing the very thing that he had just witnessed. He was livid. Addressing Detective Mack, he said, "So you have been holding out on me. I thought that you were supposed to keep me informed on everything. Why haven't I been told about this?"

"If you give me a minute, I will explain. If you think back awhile, you will remember us discussing this very same topic."

The chief paused and searched his memory. Shortly, he conceded. He had discussed this before but not in depth. He composed himself and said in his usual voice, "Just what is going on?"

Detective Mack said, "Chief, you know everyone that is here, don't you?" The chief indicated that he did.

Detective Mack looked at the chief and said, "Chief, these people came here with some information that you simply must hear. Personally, I don't know how to handle it."

"Okay, fill me in," he said.

When their stories had been told, the chief told one of his own. He told them what he had just witnessed. He told them about seeing Charles DeNero and the two test subjects having a meeting of some sort and how unnatural their actions and stance had been. "They acted like they were being manipulated like a puppet. When their meeting was over, it seemed as if all the essence had left their bodies and they were totally discombobulated. It took a few minutes before they returned to normalcy and they didn't seem to know where they were or why they were there."

SuejuSoe spoke up, "I think that is why whenever I asked Charles about anything, he denies it. It is because he is unaware of what is happening."

"Could be," said Wester'C, "he is being used, but by who is unknown and why is unknown." Detective Mack was the only one who had made the connection between the unknown object, the plastic-looking button, and the possessions. He was 80 percent sure there was a vital connection between the two.

The chief added, "I saw all three of them swallow something like that button when their meeting was over. It seemed like some type of ritual."

SuejuSoe asked, "Do you think that that little button has anything to do with the invasions, I mean possessions?"

The chief pondered a minute and said, "Now that it's been said, I'm inclined to agree with that theory. But what I want to know is how are we going to get to the bottom of this? How can we capture whatever is causing this?"

"I don't know how we can capture something that we can't see, and if they have these kind of powers, do we want to capture them? Something that's that powerful and alien—if we could capture them, what are we going to do with them?" asked Detective Mack.

Moses asked, "Don't they have some kind of gadget that can detect electrical energy output?"

"Sure they do," said the chief.

"I want to know where we can get our hands on one," Moses said. "It could be a useful tool."

The chief said, "You can try the Institute of Unexplained Phenomenon or perhaps the Paranormal Institute of Purple Bottom City."

"Hell's bells," exclaimed K'Narf, "I don't know how those things work." He looked around and asked, "Does anyone know how those things work?"

Jelly Belly said, "Hey, wait a minute, aren't those things made for catching spooks and ghosts and stuff like that?"

The chief said, "Yes. That could be the case, but to answer Mr. K'Narf's question, I'm sure that they will send someone who can work it. I'm sure that they don't just let any bozo monkey around with it."

"Oh, Chief," Wester'C called out, "do you have any suspects other than Charles, the test subjects, and the governor, or are you still checking out other leads?"

"Hold on now," said the chief. "Who said that those were suspects for the Tuesday Night massacre? No, son. We already know who did the act, we are just trying to find out who put them up to it." The chief got out of his chair and stretched, looked at Wester'C for a minute, then said, "We are still searching under rocks and behind trees. We are not quitting. I just feel in my soul that all this is connected somehow."

"I'm glad about that because we could be barking up the wrong tree because those suspects could be totally innocent."

"Mr. Wester'C, I mean Dr. Ulcer, I'm glad that you pointed that out because something is going on out there, and whatever it is has got to be checked out. We kinda zeroed in on those, but there are other possibilities out there."

"I have decided," said SuejuSoe, "to confront Charles and find out just how much he does know."

"If you ask me for my advice, I'll tell you that I wouldn't do that," the chief said. "Because they could take countermeasures."

"I've thought about that," SuejuSoe said. "But it could bring everything out in the open."

"Go ahead and give it a try. You may be able to work a miracle, and please do let me know the outcome." the chief said as he unwrapped a new cigar and ushered them out of the door.

*****

The next day was their day of reckoning. Wester'C, Ocena, Moses, K'Narf, and Jelly Belly met at SuejuSoe's place. They were in luck because Charles was there. SuejuSoe didn't know exactly how to approach the subject with him. They all sat in SuejuSoe's living room sipping espresso when Charles asked, "How did your meeting pan out? Are y'all any closer to catching the big bad boogie man?"

SuejuSoe grinned and said, "I'm glad you brought this up because there is something we want to discuss with you."

"Me? What do you want from me? I don't know anything about this."

"Maybe you do." SuejuSoe smiled.

Charles agreed to participate, and SuejuSoe and Wester'C began asking him what he knew about test subjects A and B. Charles answered, "Nothing."

He was asked if they ever had a meeting together. Charles looked at SuejuSoe strangely and asked, "What?"

"I asked, have you and the test subjects ever met together?"

"With all due respect, SuejuSoe, but just what in hell are you talking about?"

"Please answer the question, Charles."

"I'm not about dignify that with an answer."

"You don't have to," said SuejuSoe as he inserted the tape into the machine. "Just explain this." Charles turned and watched the tape. He saw himself with test subjects A and B talking in a language that he had never heard before in his life. His mouth flew open in shock. He couldn't believe this. He turned toward SuejuSoe and Wester'C, unable to talk. He stammered, spit flew from his mouth, and he felt faint. Ocena helped him sit down and gave him a glass of water. He gulped it down and spoke haltingly, "When? How? What is this?"

Wester'C said, "You mean, you don't know?"

"I don't know anything about this."

"What language are you speaking, and where did you learn it?"

Charles yelled, "I have told you that I know nothing of this."

Shortly after the interrogation began, Ocena began to feel uneasy. She had a feeling of being watched. She looked around trying to see if anyone had noticed how weird she felt. She had noticed that SuejuSoe and Moses seemed as uneasy as she was. She whispered to them and told them how she was feeling. That was when they admitted that they had sensed the same thing. Yet no one had any explanation why this was happening.

As the possibility of being possessed by an alien being came up, everyone present could sense a diabolical presence. Wester'C had been especially sensitive to this presence. He was rendered speechless and began babbling like a baby.

Everyone turned to Wester'C and was alarmed. They gave him water to drink, but he was still unable to say anything comprehensible. Everyone present was in distress to some degree with the exception of Charles DeNero. Charles didn't understand what was going on, and he felt extremely confused and didn't know what to do. His agitation overwhelmed him, and he screamed. Instantly, everything reverted back to normalcy.

The quietness that ensued was very eerie. Everyone was completely bewildered because no one knew what was going on. They looked to Charles for answers, but he was as perplexed as everyone else. Shortly, Wester'C voice returned to normal. He said, "Does anyone here know what just happened?"

From the look of shock on their faces, he knew that they didn't have any answers. This time, Wester'C addressed Charles. He asked, "What can you tell me about any of this?"

Charles asked, "Why are y'all asking me these kinds of questions? What makes you think that I might have anything to do with this? I am as confused as any of you, probably more so."

This time, SuejuSoe grabbed Charles by the collar and demanded that he tell them why he and test subjects A and B had been secretly meeting for the last two months. "Why were you meeting? What language were you speaking in? Answer me, Charles, because I want to know," SuejuSoe shouted.

"SuejuSoe," Charles began, "you better take your hands off me. I won't be this nice not one minute longer. I have already told you I don't have the faintest idea what you are talking about."

SuejuSoe walked over to a chest and took out a huge envelope and took out more tapes and pictures. He put another tape into the machine, and as the tapes wailed out an unknown language, he passed around pictures of Charles and test subjects A and B. Charles listened to the tapes and looked at the photo and was astonished that it was really him. SuejuSoe became more agitated. "I have tapes and pictures, and you sit there and tell me you don't know what's going on."

Charles looked at SuejuSoe and the others like they were the devil. He wondered how SuejuSoe could say these cruel things about him. He thought that these Chickpeo were his friends. How wrong he had been. Feeling alone and despised, he would tell them just what he thought. He looked at each of them and saw the looks of suspicion shrouding their faces and he said to them, "When I ended up here, I was an alien in a really alien world. I had nowhere to go and no one to turn to. Then you, SuejuSoe, befriended me, took me into your home, and treated me like I was your brother. You gave me a sense of belonging, and I responded to those feelings, and now you are accusing me of betrayal. I have told you over and over that I don't know anything about what you are accusing me of and you don't believe me." Charles began gathering his belonging and preparing to go, but before he left, he turned to them and said, "I cannot explain what you have here on tapes and pictures. I can't even remember ever doing this. Perhaps I am evil and don't belong here, so I'll be going and I just want to tell you"—he pointed at SuejuSoe—"and the rest of you, thanks."

SuejuSoe interrupted, "If you feel the need to go, go. But before you go, why won't you tell me us about these meetings, these pictures, and this strange language?"

Charles said to all present, "Let me say to all of you, I have told you everything that I know about this, and since I don't know anything more, I can't tell you anymore, and the way you are treating me, if I did know anything, I wouldn't tell you. I could tell you where to go and what to do when you got there, but I'm too much of a gentleman."

Ocena looked at Charles and saw the pain he was experiencing. She took his both of his hands in hers and said, "I believe you. I don't understand how any of this is happening, but I believe that you don't know anything about it. Only a short while ago, this room was visited by something unseen. I felt its presence." And she turned to the others. "You all felt it too. This controlling presence could be controlling you as it tried to control us, then erase your memory of whatever happened."

Charles looked at Ocena and thanked her for saying that. Wester'C said, "I did experience an uninvited presence, and it emitted evil vibrations. I could sense a feeling that I had never felt before, and I never want to feel them again ever. I didn't have the strength to resist its will. If Charles had not screamed, I don't know what would have happened."

Charles said, "Thanks for saying that, and I want to thank all of you and especially you, SuejuSoe, for putting me up." He opened the door and was preparing to make his exit when Wester'C said a little too loud, "Wait! Where are you going?"

He turned around and looked him straight in the eye and said, "To get away from all of you. To a motel or a flophouse or maybe live in my car till times get better. I may even go to the Graveyard. Why would you care?"

"No, wait. You can stay with me and my family."

Charles looked at Wester'C and said very somberly, "Gee, thanks, Wester'C, but I cannot live with anyone who thinks that I am out to get them and don't trust me. I hold no ill feelings toward you, it's just that I think that I've overstayed my welcome."

"But you don't have any money, how are going to make it?"

"I may go and sell my story to the media. I'm sure they will pay me handsome for the story of a stranded alien. They would pay for the inside scoop on a genuine alien, period. As a last resort, there are homeless shelters, soup lines, and the government."

Ocena spoke up, "There's no way that I'm going to let you go out there all alone. You can come stay with me and stay as long as need be."

Moses looked at her like she had lost her mind. He gave her a look that could split mountains, but he didn't say a word.

Charles said okay and that he would wait in her car until she was ready to go. As he exited SuejuSoe's place, everyone looked at SuejuSoe as if he had sprouted horns and a tail. They looked at him as if he had just committed the ultimate sin. Things were quiet for a short while. Finally, Ocena asked Moses and K'Narf if they had felt a presence. They looked at each other and admitted that they had also and that they had been influenced by it.

SuejuSoe looked at the floor, wishing that it would open up and swallow him. He felt too ashamed to look them in the face. He felt like a pile of shit. He should have believed Charles. Now, he supposed that he would never trust him again, and it was all his fault. As he was preparing to apologize for his misgivings, the alien presence returned with a vengeance. It was much stronger and omitted a smelted coppery, sulfury odor. Everyone in the room could feel the presence and smell its odor. Tensions ran so high in that room that you could strum it. No doubt this entity had been listening in on their conversation and didn't like what it had heard.

Everyone in the room had been rendered powerless. They could no longer move or speak. It seemed to be testing them to see just how much it could do to them without killing them. When it discovered that they were extremely inferior compared to them, it slackened their tongues so that they could speak. But first it would acknowledge its companions. It said in a heavily alien monotone, "We are from a world outside of your dimension, the world Xzppi. Your world signals us to come here, and we are unsure of your intentions and would like for you to tell us."

All in the room sat, staring at nothing and hearing heavily accented words being spoken but saw nothing, telling them that they had signaled them. Now they wanted to know why they were summoned.

Before anyone spoke, Charles came floating through the door. He was in the prone position. He floated into the room and was placed on the sofa beside Ocena. When Charles sat on the sofa, he began to speak in that same strange alien language. Everyone sat and stared at Charles doing nothing and saying nothing. It began to make a noise; no one could determine if it was laughing or was in critical pain.

An unseen voice said, "That was hilarious." It seemed as if each time one spoke, the smell of sulfur grew stronger. They laughed a lot, and the room became suffocating.

The only thing that Moses could think of was, "Can you reveal yourself to us so that we can see what you look like?"

"Under these circumstances, I don't think that that would be wise," one of the entities said.

"Why?" Moses asked.

The being spoke in the language of their world. No one knew what was being said.

Moses spoke again, "Why don't you show us what you look like, and please speak in our language so that we can understand."

Charles spoke up, "I know what they are saying." All eyes turned to Charles. He continued, "They said that they cannot reveal themselves in their true forms because they couldn't survive under the purple skies. Their world is a dark world, and only in darkness can they materialize."

Charles noticed everyone looking at him. He shrugged his shoulders and said, "Don't ask me how I know, I just did."

The voice spoke again, "That's right. He has no idea how he can speak our language, but I'll tell you this much, he is the first reason why we are here."

Charles bolted, "I didn't have anything to do with you. I don't even know who or what you are."

"But you did," the sulfur-smelling entities said.

"How?" Charles asked, feeling like the universe's biggest idiot.

By this time, the room was chokingly thick with the odor of sulfur, and they had decided to exit so that they could breath. The entities moved to block their exit but saw that they were in great distress and permitted them to leave. Wester'C was in more distress than the others and had just about passed out. He had to be helped out of the house. Once outside, it took a while before the odor subsided enough for them to breath normally. The distance between the entities and them had to widen because of their inability to coexist. They did not come any closer but spoke louder. The voice was saying, "We were dimension channeling when you"—indicating Charles—"got in our way. We dropped you off in a place that was suitable to sustain your physiology and continued our journey. We programmed your aura so that we could keep an eye on you while we were gone. Although we weren't here, you were aware of our presence but you didn't know it was us. But your quest to get back to your world in the ill-conceived portal sent the test subjects right into our path again. This is when we decided to find out what was really going on. When we found out what you all were attempting to do, at first, we started to take him back to his world and let that be the end of it. But that would've been too easy, so we decided to stay a while just to appease our curiosity."

Charles stood there shocked. "You mean to tell me that you can get me back home to my world?"

"That is very simple to do," the voice said. "But let me continue to tell you how you summoned us. We were on our way to our sister world when that riffraff ran smack into us. One was sideswiped, and the other hit us head-on, this knocked us off our course. We picked him up and sent him back to you. Since your dimension travelers saw us in our true forms, they will always have a sense of not belonging to any world."

Another entity said, "When we first scanned this world, we were unsure that it was inhabited. On our second scan, we detected two different life-forms. On a closer scan, we discovered that the task of uniting both worlds politically was in the progress, and this was an unpopular venture. We called it the doomed split-world syndrome. Some in your underground world are serious practitioners of channeling, and we believe that it is through them that we were summoned, but we are not a perfect entity and we could be wrong. Perhaps it was you." As he spoke, the superfunky odor of sulfur and a thousand rotten eggs hijacked the surrounding air. Wester'C vomited.

Everything seemed as if it was moving in slow motion, and the alien's words seemed to turn into rocks that you could catch them in a bucket. As the words hit the bucket, they seem to be saying, "We found ourselves to be in the middle of a political campaign. It was hard for us to pass up, we had to do something. Political events in our realm hadn't happened in over one thousand of your years. It was all fun and games up until the victory party."

A different tone of voice was heard, we assumed it to be feminine. "We can tell you something that has been troubling you for a spell. The person who is behind the killings and fires is not Roy Cavity."

SuejuSoe looked at Wester'C, who looked washed-out from his bout of vomiting, then at Moses and said, "Roy Cavity! We never suspected Roy Cavity because he is too dumb to put together a tic-tac-toe game."

The entity spoke in an irritated voice, at least that's what everyone took it to be. "I didn't say that Roy Cavity did anything. We didn't use Roy because he was so willing to be used. He wanted us to give him power so that he could use it to become a top-heavy VIP in politics. We could sense his total lack of intelligence and did not have anything to do with him. Like we've already told you, there are those in the bottom half of your world that makes channeling a religion, and they are in touch with other from spirit worlds. These individuals want to control the top and the bottom of this world, and they have power and are extremely intelligent and dirty as a volcano is hot. You want your guilty parties? Go to the Underground City and look under the most prestigious names that you can find."

During the time that they were listening to the voices, they were in a semishocked condition. The voices were telling them about themselves;

they were in awe about how much they really knew. They were in awe about how they could manipulate others and their surroundings.

Charles asked the voices how he was responsible for bringing them to this world when he didn't know this world existed.

They answered in unison, "Yes. You brought us here." The sound of all of them speaking at once sounded like a clap of thunder.

"But how?" Charles asked as he prayed that they wouldn't all answer at once.

"Because you got in our way. We were dimension traveling when you got in our way. We brought you to a world where you could survive and left you. Had it not been for that silly, primitive portal, we would have never returned except to return our uninvited voyager. You kept interfering in our affairs."

Charles voice began to get louder. The voices cautioned, "Be careful not to offend us because we have no morals. No sense of right or wrong according to your worlds. If we don't like someone or something, we get rid of it. In our world, there are no laws. There is nothing that any of you could relate to."

"You mean to tell me that you put me through all of this because you thought it would be fun?"

"No!" a voice thundered. "We did it because you got in our way."

Charles trembled slightly, but he was too angry to be afraid. Just to think that he had been through this because something wasn't paying attention to where they were going. He began to speak, but the entities silenced his voice, a voice that was screaming to be heard but was mute.

"Now, let us finish telling you what you want to know. The being Roy Cavity wanted to be as much help as he could be to us. He couldn't see us as you can't, but he prayed to us because he thought that we were gods and could answer his prayers. We told him that we were a malevolent being. He didn't care as long as we could help him get control of Purple Bottom City. During the ordeal with Roy Cavity, he was under the impression that we were some kind of spirits that he had paid a medium to conjure up especially for the purpose of getting him control of your world. He confessed to us that there was nothing that he wouldn't do to achieve this. We never let him know that we were anything other than what he wanted us to be. He paid for the gangs to start a melee so that he could get inside and kill the newly elected president and governor."

Wester'C finally got up enough nerves to speak, and he said, "How can we believe this, Roy Cavity didn't have enough intelligence to coordinate a diabolical plan like this. The man was next to a moron."

"Your memory is short. Remember, I told you to look at Underground City's highest echelon. They played a major role in derailing your plans for a reconstructed constitution. They also wanted to rule Purple Bottom City, and they always have, ever since they crawled out from under the ground and saw that you had survived, thrived, and prospered. They feel superior to you."

SuejuSoe said, "I've already known that, but you are not guiltless. You did your share of adding fuel to the fire with controlling people and adding confusion everywhere you could."

An entity spoke, "I don't know what you mean, adding fuel to the fire?"

"It's an expression that we use, meaning making a bad thing worse. You kept throwing out clues that kept us wondering and making decisions based on false clues. By the way, what are the little buttons for and what do they represent?"

"Buttons?" an entity asked. "What buttons?"

Before this question could be answered, Detective Mack and Chief Gallstone drove up and saw everyone standing around outside seeming to have a serious conversation with no one. They exited their auto and asked, "Would it be too much trouble for me to ask what is going on?"

SuejuSoe held his hand up, indicating for him to be quiet. This irritated the chief, and he began in his most authoritative voice, "What—"

His voice was silenced. He looked around like he was expecting an answer to come from above. Again, he tried to voice his frustrations. Again SuejuSoe held up his hand. A vein popped out on the chief's forehead, pulsating like he was going to have a coronary. SuejuSoe said very calmly, "Chief, we have company, more aliens that have seemingly unlimited powers. If you promise to be good, they may let you speak again. You cannot see them, but I'm sure that you can smell them. I am going to take down my hand, and I'm sure that you will be able to speak again."

When SuejuSoe removed his hand, the chief and Detective Mack seemed thunderstruck. They could now smell the funky, rotten-egg, sulfury odor that surrounded them. Then they heard alien-sounding voices coming from nowhere. Chills ran the gamut of Chief Gallstone's back and he had began to perspire profusely. The unlit cigar that he kept in him mouth fell to the ground. Detective Mack looked at the chief and saw the shape he was in and tried to recover some control of the situation. He said, "Somebody just tell me what is going on."

SuejuSoe spoke up, addressing the entities, "These are members of our police community. They too were working on the murders and the aftermath of your meddling."

Detective Mack saw Charles standing among the others and was puzzled. He asked, "Did these aliens come from another world different from Mr. DeNero's?"

"The answer to that is a most definitely yes, then again, it is a no."

"Say what?"

SuejuSoe began trying to explain, "You see, they are not only from a different world, they are from another galaxy."

An alien voice spoke, "We are from a world that no one knows exists. There are no physical forms of any kinds. We live in what you may call a spirit realm."

Detective Mack jaw dropped lower because he could not believe what he was hearing and could not believe that he was having a conversation with an unseen funky-smelling entity. He said, "I need to know what this is about."

SuejuSoe began again, "These aliens dropped off Charles in our world after they had abducted him from his world. They say that he got in their way while they were surfing the dimensions and dropped him off here because this world was compatible with his physical constitution. When they arrived, they were fascinated by our political process and they decided to stay around to see what would happen. When we were trying to get Charles back to his world with the portal, the test subjects bumped into them and were partially transformed. They could communicate in their language and were healed of some of their mutations. Because the entities could not unveil their forms and survive in this world, they used Charles and the test subjects as substitutes."

Detective Mack said, "Go on. I'm sure that there is more to tell than this."

An entity spoke, "We had just finished telling them about Roy Cavity and his part in murdering the newly elected president and governor and their partners in crime."

263

Upon hearing this, the chief broke out of his silence and asked, "What are you trying to tell me? Are you saying that you know about everything that have been going on."

"That is the condensed version."

Charles DeNero said, "All of this is good, but I want to know how and when am I going to get back home? You all can finish what you started after I'm gone."

"That's true, but do you remember swallowing a button of some sort?" asked the entity. "That was a transmitter so that we could keep up with your whereabouts. If you should leave without returning the transmitter, we could track you anywhere and you could feel our presence mentally and physically and you would never have any peace of mind."

"How am I supposed to return the transmitter? I am ready, and you are more than welcome to get it back."

The entity said, "Walk forward ten paces and turn to your left, then walk to your right three paces, stop, and bend over."

Charles followed their instructions, and the transmitter appeared in his hand. He took it, held it out, and the entity took it, held it up to the light of the purple sun, and it exploded, emitting a small shower of brightly colored prisms. He was amazed at the display and wondered what would have happened if it had not been retrieved. He thought, I have got to be careful around these aliens, and he wondered what to expect next.

It seemed as if this was the climax of the mystery of events that had plagued Purple Bottom City for the past few weeks. At least, this gave them enough to go on to finish up by themselves. They felt confident that the Terrible Toilet Papers would round up the rest of the Rumbling Guts and the Stomach Cramps. It seem that the most pressing thing for them to do was to rid their world of the aliens and Charles DeNero.

They wanted to see what the entities looked like in their natural forms, and Wester'C brought the subject up again. He asked the voices, "Could we see you in some natural form or something similar?"

The entities said that they could, but it would have to be dark, completely dark. But since their sun didn't completely set, they didn't think it would become dark enough for them to show themselves without causing great harm to themselves.

Moses said, "Out on Runs Road down by Booger Bear Canyon, it gets the darkest around nine o'clock. I believe that it would be a safe place for them to materialize."

"Booger Bear Canyon!" an alien entity voice boomed. "Just what is a Booger Bear Canyon?"

"It's just about the darkest place in Purple Bottom City," Moses answered. "It's a bit depressed, and light can't shine directly into it."

The entities pondered over this proposal and agreed to meet them at nine o'clock. Then there was silence. No one heard anything for about ten minutes and guessed that the entities had gone. SuejuSoe asked, "Did something just happen here, or did we experience a mass hallucination episode?"

K'Narf said, "Don't ask me because I don't know. I am not sure of anything that happened here."

Wester'C asked, "Do any of you know the significance of what just happened?"

"Can't say that I do," said SuejuSoe.

Ocena took Moses by the hand and shook her head. Moses said, "I'll take a stab at it. We've just found out that beings from an unknown universe dropped Charles DeNero on our doorstep so that we could babysit him until they decided to come back and take him home. Then, we find out who murdered Bill and Carrie. We found out about an alien language that had been driving our professionals insane trying to decipher. We found out that Charles was telling the truth and that we are powerless against the visiting entities because they have powers that we can only imagine. We also found that Roy Cavity isn't as dumb as we previously thought."

"I'll say that you covered that pretty good," Wester'C said in a voice that had not lost its nervousness. "I still can't believe this has happened."

"Yeah," said Ocena, "you can have nightmares the remainder of your life."

"I won't doubt that at all, we all may because there is no telling when one of these invisible entities may decide to drop in on us."

"Chief Gallstone, what is your take on all of this?" asked Ocena.

The chief, not fully composed after the ordeal, said, "If I had not been here and seen and heard, mostly heard, all this, I wouldn't have believed any of it. Even after witnessing it, I still don't know if I believe it. I had no idea that anything like this could exist, and this makes me feel uneasy that we are so vulnerable."

"That's right," K'Narf agreed. "We won't ever know when we are alone."

"We may as well go and see how much work we can get done before tonight's rendezvous. I can hardly wait to see what they actually look like," said Moses.

Charles said, "I don't care what they look like. They could have gotten me back home first. I didn't ask to come here. I had a good life where I was and I want it back."

"Don't be sore, Charles. You must admit it is an adventure that you won't ever forget and can't ever repeat. You are going to be with us tonight, aren't you?" asked Moses.

"Just who are the 'us?'" inquired Ocena. "I've never said that I was going anywhere to meet creatures that I cannot see and have already told us that they were evil in the middle of the night out on a dark road. You have to be out of your mind! They could zap us to another world like they did Charles, and there isn't anything we could do about it."

Moses looked at Ocena like he was seeing her for the first time. He framed her face with his hands and looked deeply into her eyes. He said, "I can't believe you said that, you are not the adventurous woman that I fell in love with. Your daringness added to your charm. I knew that I would never grow tired of you. You were always flirting with danger, teasing disaster, and daring anyone who was foolish enough to challenge you. Now you are telling us that you are afraid of what some invisible evil being may happen to look like. Oh, please . . ."

"And the same to you," Ocena said as she exited the door.

"I'll bet that you'll be there," Moses called out to Ocena as she walked over to Charles's car and got in. "Because I dare you not to come."

She said, "Ha!" and kept walking.

Charles stood with his mouth agape like he couldn't believe any of this was really happening. All he could think about is the fact that he still could go home. That thought had been etched in his brain. Just to think that all of this actually happened because he was in the wrong place at the wrong time.

SuejuSoe called Chief Gallstone and Detective Mack and asked them if they were planning to be out on Runs Road tonight. The chief seemed genuinely pleased to hear from them. K'Narf nudged Moses and whispered, "The devil is gone astray."

Moses said, "Huh?"

"Never mind," said K'Narf.

266

"Chief," Wester'C began, "I think that you should prepare yourself for a major shock if you are going to witness the entities' materialization."

"How so, son?"

"You have already witnessed some of their powers, who knows how many more that they have that we know nothing about. How can we know that we can trust them? I brought along my little black bag just in case."

The chief looked at Wester'C then Moses, Ocena, and K'Narf. Their faces were solemn. A little bell in the chief's mind went off, telling him to beware because this was for real. He unfolded his arms and sat upright. Searching their faces again, he said, "Y'all are serious, aren't you?"

"Yes," they said in unison.

The chief said, "Well, let's get on with it."

Wester'C began to relate what had happened earlier. He recounted every detail. The chief and Detective Mack sat listening, mesmerized by what they were being told. Some of the narrative sounded like it came straight out of a science fiction movie. It was hard not to laugh out loud, but the look on their faces told him that they were not kidding. When Wester'C got to the part where they were told that Roy Cavity, along with the powers that be in Underground City, were behind all the murders and melee that happened at Thursday night's massacre, the chief lost his composure. He jumped out of his seat and began raging like a maniac. Then he was told that Roy Cavity was power-hungry and vengeful, plus he wanted to rule Purple Bottom City and was willing to do anything to make this possible. He wanted the citizens of Purple Bottom City to pay for ruining his life.

The chief said, "Just hold on one gall-darn minute. Who did he say ruined his life? Because the last time I recalled, he did that all by himself, and may I say that he did it very well."

"Nevertheless, that is what the entities told us. He craved power and would stop at nothing to get it, and if the aliens could give this power, he would do as they wanted."

Moses added, "The entities said that Roy Cavity had paid the Stomach Cramps and the Rumbling Guts to disrupt the victory party so that he could get in and murder Bill and Carrie and get away with it."

The chief almost choked. Moses continued relating what the entities had told them. The chief reluctantly sat back down knowing that there wasn't anything that he could do. The part about how the entities had used Charles and test subjects A and B bodies because they could not used their natural forms on this world without dying, he didn't understand. He told him about how the entities had intercepted the test subjects from the portal path and used them as host agents. He related how the entities could control others' minds, bodies, and thoughts. When he finished talking, no one could tell if the chief was in shock or stark-raving mad. He slowly got out of his chair, looked at everyone in the room, and balled his hands into fists so tight until the veins in his neck and temporal region began to pulsate dangerously. No one spoke to him because he was a huge man, and no one wanted to be the recipient of two fists the size of hams. He was given all the room he needed to cool down.

Shortly, he spoke, "I know what you have told me is the truth because I don't know anyone who could lie like this. It was real neat how the aliens wrapped up the mysteries of the massacres and murders. If Roy Cavity is the guilty party, why isn't he being arrested?"

Detective Mack said, "Chief, as we speak, an APB has gone out for his arrest. I have information that he has escaped to Underground City and is being hidden by the powers that be."

"This story is too far-out not to be believed. Now you tell me that the unseen visitors are going to reveal their physical forms tonight, huh? Since they have so many powers, maybe we could ask them real nicelike to intercede one more time and go to the Underground City and get Roy and his powers-that-be cohorts to finish the job."

"That sound like a dandy idea, Chief, but I don't think that they intercede in affairs of other worlds."

"I see," said the chief, still somewhat lost in thought. "It was just an idea. Now you tell me that they are going to reveal their true world forms tonight. I simply cannot miss out on this."

*****

As the hour, everyone's nerves were on high alert, and banal chatter was kept at a minimal. They went in three cars, with the chief leading the way. SuejuSoe warned them that since the entities could read minds, they must be extremely careful about what they are thinking about.

The ride to Booger Bear Canyon seemed ever scarier than it usually did. The shadows seemed taller, and it seemed to be unusually quiet. If you didn't control your imagination, you could swear that the trees were moving.

While they were waiting for the voices to arrive, a single thought began to materialize in Detective Mack's mind. He was thinking that if the voices could not survive in light, perhaps that could be a way to contain them: by hitting them with the full force of the high beam of the car lights. In an inaudible voice, Detective Mack related his thoughts to the chief. Wester'C caught a whiff of the conversation and warned them that the voices had powers that couldn't be imagined and asked why they would want to contain them. He warned them not to do anything unless they initiated it. The chief wanted to rebuff him but decided not to.

The wait was an unnerving one. Time seem to crawl by, and the fact that the voices could already be there observing them wasn't helping either. The chief asked, "Didn't the voices say that they were evil and didn't live by any law?"

Wester'C nodded his head, indicating yes.

"So," the Chief asked, "why do you think that they will keep their promise?"

Wester'C answered, "Because they feel that they don't have anything to fear from us. They think that we are inferior beings and we fear them."

"Never underestimate the power of a one-eyed cat." Detective Mack said to no one in particular. Moses asked, "Why did you say that?"

"No special reason, it just seems to fit the occasion. My mama use to tell me that."

"What does it mean?"

"I honestly couldn't tell you."

It was now ten past ten, and there wasn't any sign of the voices. SuejuSoe wanted to leave because he didn't think that they would show up.

Wester'C said to give them ten more minutes. They sat back and waited, each one entertaining their own private demons.

SuejuSoe was thinking about how he hadn't taken time out to form a meaningful relationship and the fact that he was getting older and didn't have a wife or children. He had married his career. But if he should survive this night, he was going to actively seek him a mate and cut down on some of the meetings and committees. He had a girlfriend, but she was not the type of person that he wanted to settle down with.

Arthur Moses was thinking about the same thing that he always thought about, Ocena Heartburns. He wanted to marry her, but she kept putting things off. He wondered how he could get her to commit. He had gone through hell, floods, and ice for her, and he felt that he deserved her and was going to have her. Nothing more. Nothing less.

Wester'C was reflecting and thanking God for his blessings. His family, friends, work, health, and the fact that He had always watched over him. Life had been good to him because he had came from very humble beginnings, and to say that it was a struggle would be putting it mildly. But he persevered. He just hated what had happened to Charles earlier, but he couldn't go back and erase what had already happened. Dang it, it must be hard for him being treated like that. When you are an alien in an alien world, it's hard enough, but to be falsely accused of things that you know nothing of is a cesspool. Then there were Bill and Carrie Earlobe's murders, all he could do was ask why.

K'Narf Covictus was thinking, What in hell am I doing out here? There are a number of places that I would rather be. He wondered if he was letting the others taking him for granted. He wondered if he was really helping or was this something he had convinced himself that he was doing. He wondered if his girl really cared for him or if she stayed with him because he made her feel important and she could socialize with the so-called elite of Purple Bottom City. Then he thought, What am I doing out here in the middle of nowhere in the middle of the night waiting for some unseen voices with overbearing egos who are too ugly to show their true form in daylight? Now here he was out here in the middle of nowhere, not knowing if they would come and, if they did, what they may do to them. Damn! I must be crazy.

Detective Mack was trying very hard to keep his mind on the matter at hand but was having a hard time doing it. Last night had given him good memories. He wished that things would hurry up and be over because he wanted an encore.

Charles DeNero was thinking, I don't care what happen tonight because I am going home and anything can't top that.

The chief was going over a list of what he should do if the voices should show up. He could not imagine a being that was invisible. He wanted to beat the hell out of them for trashing his town. So they say they were evil; that could be a bluff or a downright lie. If it was a bluff, he was going to call it. He was going to tell them.

A voice asked, "Just what are you going to tell them?"

The chief was momentarily horrorstruck. He blurted out, "What did you say?" All eyes turned to the chief.

"Who are you talking to?" Wester'C asked.

The chief was embarrassed. He said, "I thought I heard someone say something."

The voices said, "You did."

"See, there it goes again."

"We don't hear anything," said Wester'C.

The chief became agitated. "Who is saying these things? Why don't you show yourself?"

The voices said, "So you want to kick our asses for trashing your city, huh?"

The chief didn't answer.

"So you say that we think that we are superior. I am going to give you a demonstration to prove to that we are as bad as we say we are. A demonstration that you'll want forget."

"Hey, Chief, what's going on?" SuejuSoe asked.

The chief answered in an agitated voice that wavered with fear. "Some voices are speaking to me, I think that they are going to show me that they are superior to us." He grimaced and continued, "You don't think that I'm going crazy, do you?"

"No," Charles spoke up. "I have been hearing them for a short while. Evidently, you have been thinking negative thoughts about them."

Wester'C asked, "What have you been thinking about? I warned you, remember."

The voices spoke to the chief, "Just shut up and take your punishment. I can see that you have a passion for cigars. When I get through with you, you will never want to see another cigar."

The chief looked at Charles and said, "Please tell them that I'm not losing my mind. You can hear them too. Somebody, please help me."

The chief saw ten lit cigars in front of him. He couldn't move. He could not talk, and he felt a sinister presence. It felt like pure evil. His pulse and heart rate doubled. He thought that he was having a heart attack. He was caught by the hair and pulled out of the car and suspended in the air. The chief was screaming, but no one could hear him. They turned him upside down and put cigars in his mouth and nose as far as they could. The chief couldn't breathe. He vomited. The voices took his vomit and put it back into his mouth and forced him to swallow it again. The chief vomited blood, cigars, and other unidentified stuff just before he passed out. The voices let him drop to the ground. Then a female voice took over. She removed his pants and underwear and took his penis and began caressing it. The chief began to regain consciousness. It didn't last long before he was flipped over by unseen hands, and an unseen penis was rammed up the chief's anus. I call it this, but I am only guessing because I didn't see anything and am only going by his reactions.

Everyone witnessed what was being done to the chief, but they were unable to do anything. They couldn't move.

When the voices finished with the chief, he was covered in vomit, cigars, blood, and bowel movement. The voices said that they were going to make sure that the chief remembered who was superior. They unlocked his vocal cords so that he and the others could hear him scream. A blood-curdling scream pierced the quietness of the night and made the others cringe in fear.

When the chief had stopped screaming, they picked him up by the hair again about ten feet off the ground, then let him drop like a sack of cement.

The voices released the hold that they had put on the others and decided that they would reveal their true forms as they had promised. Slowly their forms took shape. Their faces were oblong, with a translucent horn in the middle that gave off pulsating puffs of maladroit energy. They had no mouth, eyes, or ears. Their bodies were transparent and covered in luminous hair that glowed in the darkness. You could clearly see their big illuminated heart beating. The size of their hearts was overwhelming; it must have taken up one half of their chest cavity. I will call it a chest for a lack of another word to describe it. Anyway, it was huge.

Wester'C could not take his eyes off them. They were indeed grotesquely horrifying. The very sight of them could make a being freeze in their tracks.

They began to laugh. A harrowing, demonic laugh.

In their need to show their superiority, they had forgotten about the chief. The chief had crawled to his car and turned the high beams on them. They squirmed and screamed in their evil language as best as they could, scattered their seeds of evil, trying to turn each of them against the other. But before they could do that, Ocena showed up and saw what was happening and hit them with the high beams of her car. The voices vaporized. All that was left behind was the pungent smell of burning sulfur and seeds of evil that could never germinate.

There was one scream that surpassed all others, and that was the scream Charles DeNero let go when he found out that his only hope of getting back home was gone. He had gone from desperation to desire to hope and finally devastation. He no longer wanted to live, but he didn't want to die either. But he couldn't think of one thing to keep him from giving up. Everything that had happened to him from his abduction to his abandonment was not his fault, and he was a victim. "Help me, God," he prayed.

It took a while before they could stop shaking enough to drive. They put the chief in the backseat of his car, and Wester'C did what he could for him. He was glad that he had taken the time to bring his little black bag. They took him to the hospital. On arriving in the ER, he went to work on him. They had to clean blood, vomit, and feces off him before they could work on him. A doctor asked Wester'C, "What in the world happened to him?"

Wester'C answered, "Nothing in this world. Something out of this world."

The doctor said, "I don't understand."

"And I don't think that you ever will," Wester'C added.

The doctor hunched his shoulders and began to work on the chief. He was in a catatonic state, unable to respond to simple questions. His rectum would need quite a few stitches and so would his penis. A tube had to be inserted in his nose and stomach because his throat had been ruptured from the force of jamming cigars down his throat. He needed stitches in his nostrils. He lay upon the table looking like a harpooned whale, a huge man on the table in total defeat. Wester'C wondered why big guys didn't take advice from normal-sized guys. He was absolutely, positively sure that he had told the chief that the voices could read and control minds. He just didn't listen. He said a prayer for him.

They had scheduled the chief for emergency surgery because pieces of cigars were embedded in his lungs.

Two weeks had passed, and the chief had yet to speak. The doctors said that it would take a while before he could talk because of his vocal cord injuries. His mind was in shambles.

Detective Mack had arrested Roy Cavity, and he swore up and down that he had nothing to do with any of this. He swore that he was being framed because he had an alibi, and it would prove that he was nowhere in the vicinity when all this took place. The Guts and Cramps shot down his alibi, and Detective Mack stated that Roy Cavity would never see the light of day again outside the walls of a prison.

Charles DeNero was past devastated because he couldn't get back to his world. All those questions that he had on his invisible list of things that he had wanted to ask and find out about later didn't seem to matter much anymore. He really wasn't interested in those things anymore. He had to learn to adapt to a life that had been forced on him because he was trapped in this purple world where he would probably spend the remainder of his life. He decided that he was not going to get upset because that was not going to help matters. He had to get his life in a new order. First, he needed an income, so he would have to find a job. This was going to be harder than he anticipated because SuejuSoe had shown his true colors as a chameleon. He could change to fit in any situation. He had no ally in him. He wouldn't enlist the help of Wester'C because they actually believe he was capable of doing those things that he was accused of. He decided that perhaps K'Narf, Ocena, and Pissy Dean were the only ones he could turn to for any help. His summation of life on this purple world was that it sucked, and it was having a physical effect on his heart. He was pounding and was perspiring profusely, but he needed to maintain control and make the best of a very bad situation. It wouldn't be a walk in the park, but it wouldn't do any good to cry over spilled purple milk.

Bill 'Bojo' Earlobe and Carrie Blister, two political activists, sat at a table in the AuHu Bar and Grill watching other Chickpeo and a few Graveyard people.

Bojo was looking at Carrie who was deep in thought. He took a sip of his espresso and said, "A quarter for your thoughts." Carrie answered, "No way. My thoughts are far more valuable than a dinky old quarter. Give me twenty dollars, and I may take it under advisement."

"No can do. Advisement have been sold out for months."

"In that case, I'll take it under consideration, and I'm coming back to Purple Bottom City. What do you want to know?"

"Where on Earth were you? Tell me, and I'll buy you another espresso."

"Okay. You are on," said Carrie.

"Spill."

"Well," she began, "I know that the Elite Political Committee wants either you or me to run for congress or president, and I'm not sure that I want to run. There are so many things to consider, and it would take up too much of my time. It'll set me back for years. On the other hand, I think that you will be the number one candidate of choice."

"Are you through? I certainly hope so because that is the biggest pile of crap that I've heard. So you think that your time is more valuable than mine," Bojo snapped.

"Listen," said Carrie, "I didn't it mean that way. What I meant is that you are more qualified than I am, plus you will do a better job."

Bojo spoke in his unique voice sounding like a snake oil vender. "Get real, woman, are you trying to set the wheels of equality counterclockwise?"

Carrie said, "I don't want to hear anything about turning back the hands of time. I actually think that you think that if I should run, I would get elected, and you just want know how to handle that, especially if you should run and lose. This doesn't have anything to do with the equality of the sexes. Sure, I think that what I do is important. I love my job, and I don't want to give it up, especially to be fighting an ongoing battle among corrupt politicians who don't care about anyone but themselves and power, how much they have, and how much they can get."

"So you don't think that bringing unity, honesty, and dignity to our government is not an important job."

"I didn't say that. Sure, I do."

"Didn't you just tell me that you thought that your job was too important for you to consider running?"

"No, I didn't," said Carrie. "I said that what I'm doing is important."

"More important that what I do?"

Carrie pulsed her lips and answered, "No, not necessarily, but it equals to it."

Bojo sat quiet momentarily and said, "I wondered why I haven't married you, now I remember."

Carrie ignored what he was saying and asked, "Are you going to buy me dinner, or should I just order my own or just get up and go home?"

Bojo was about to speak but instead called for a waitress an ordered two steak dinners. Carrie said sarcastically, "At least I won't starve while I'm sitting here being important."

Bojo murmured, "With the help of Jesus, maybe I will last through the night."

"What's did you say?" Carrie asked. "Are you sitting over there using the name of the Lord in vain, or are you saying it because you actually believe in God?

"Surprise! Surprise!" said Bojo. "Actually I'm not religious, but I do believe in God, heaven, judgment day, and miracles."

Carrie said, "What more is there to believe in? I've never known you to go to church."

"That's where you are wrong. I go to church fairly often I just don't feel the need to broadcast it." Carrie shook head in disbelief and continued, "How did I miss this? You never talked about religion to me, Why?"

"I don't know. I guess it was just never crossed my mind. Anyway, I don't want to lock myself into a religious mode. I call it simply being saved. Religion can be a lot of different things to many different people."

"For a long time, I've wanted to ask you to come and visit my church, but I didn't know that you attended church, and I was afraid that I would offend you."

"Actually, I've been to your church."

A surprised Carrie gasped and asked, "When?"

"I guess about a year and a half ago."

"How did I miss this?"

"I don't know," answered Bojo.

Carrie quipped, "Now don't go copping an attitude with me, I'm just asking questions. Why didn't you come back?"

"When I left the first time, I didn't have any desire to return."

"Why, what happened?"

"I don't know," answered Bojo. "I'm not a soothsayer, and you'd have to ask someone much wiser than I." He hesitated, "I don't want to say bad things about those who are supposedly servants of the Lord, but your pastor was as fake as a three-dollar bill, and he turned me every way but on spiritually.

"When I first recognized him as one of the guys who was a regular shooting crap in the backroom of the Pot Gut Palace, I couldn't respect him as being a man of the cloth after that performance he put on.

"That man knew more four-letter words than a rummed-up sailor. Then I also recognized him as the womanizer that the guys that I played golf with were talking about."

"You are kidding?" a shocked Carrie asked.

"No. I wish that was so."

"When did all this happen?"

Bojo said, "Let's not talk about this."

Carrie had stopped eating and had her fork suspended in the midair. "Why, what don't you want to tell me?"

"Nothing. I just don't want to talk about it. But to answer your question, it was about a year . . . never mind, I've already told you."

Carrie said as she resumed eating, "You do know that this is hard for me to believe, don't you? I've heard some rumors about this, but I've never taken them seriously. Golly gee, why haven't you told me about this before now?"

Bojo said, "It's not important."

"Like hell, it is," Carrie said in a voice pregnant with controlled anger.

"Really," said Bojo. "After all, you are not going to church to worship the preacher. Even if the preacher is screwing up. We are supposed to do as he teaches not as he does."

Carrie wiped her mouth and said, "I suppose that would make logic in a mad world. Just the same, I don't think that people like that should be in the church except if they are trying to get their souls saved. I don't think that they should be allowed in a pulpit. This goes for every denomination and every person that works in the field of serving God. For some other god and the devil, that would be perfect. They threw out the mourner's bench, brought it back, and I think that they got rid of it so that the unsaved would not be embarrassed for people to know that they are not saved. I know they will give another explanation, but they don't always tell the truth. Or haven't you noticed?"

"I'll leave that up to the congregation and God."

She took a prolonged look at Bojo and said, "You do have a strong belief in God, don't you?"

"I suppose," said Bojo. "While I'm at it, let me confess to you and testify to the Lord about my beliefs. I believe in God, the Son, the bush burning, the parting of the Red Sea, Noah, and the Great Flood and the resurrection."

"Personally, I've never felt the need or the desire to make an announcement like a lot of people, you know they are always going around saying things like 'when I go to church Sunday or I am going to Sunday School.' I just go. It's a private thing."

"How did I miss this? I thought that I knew you so well."

Bojo said, "Baby, I don't want to hear you say 'how did I miss this?' anymore. When I was growing up, my mama made us go to church and Sunday school whether we wanted to or not. We didn't just didn't go to church and Sunday school, we had to memorize half of the Bible or else."

"Or else what?" asked Carrie.

"Or else you get your brains beat out. I didn't think that I would have to put it in words."

Carrie smiled and said, "I too remember getting a lot of 'or elses' when I was growing up too, and I didn't talk about the 'or elses' either. I can smile now, but it still isn't funny. Did they stop when you got grown?"

"No. Did yours?"

"They couldn't because they were etched in my mind."

For a while they ate in silence. Carrie was halfway through the meal when she complained, "I should have ordered seafood."

"Is there something wrong with your dinner?"

"No, it is delicious, too delicious."

"Then what's the problem?"

"My weight. How do I say this? I need to go on a diet. After tonight I'm going to diet and exercise. I don't suppose that you have noticed?"

Bill shook his head indicating that he had not noticed, but he had and he was not about to say anything. Carrie's butt looked like two basketballs in a sack. Whenever they made love her juicy butt just bounced them into orgasmic heaven. There was no way he would say anything negative about her weight because he could still remember hearing her tell old lady Dessie to butt out.

Every time Dessie saw her she would make a comment about her weight. Carrie got tired of this. The very next time Carrie ran in to her, she told her how the cow ate the cabbage. She said to her and her cohorts standing in the middle of a local supermarket isle that in no uncertain way did she need any old withered-up, used-to-be-lard-asses, blue-wig-wearing busybodies always in her face telling her that she had gained weight. Didn't they know that she, better than anyone else, knew this and she didn't need anyone always in her face telling her this? Especially when their own bodies looked like modified diarrhea guts and the rest of them looked like a constipated turd and some of them had asses that were flabby as a bowl of chitterlings. She looked around, and people in the supermarket had stopped whatever they should have been doing and were watching her. She told them that she could watch her own weight and didn't need them to watch it for her.

She told them, "I don't give a halfhearted hunk what you say I look like. You withered old has-beens and those of you who never were need to shut the fuck up and stay out of my business." She turned around and said to no one in particular, "If I were you, I'd be busy losing some of that lard of your own butts and getting rid of some of that ugliness that you carry on your faces like a demon mask and in your personalities like an overburdened ass. You need to pray that God will send you someone wise enough to discover a way to press some of those fucking wrinkles out of your flabby ass skin and find a way to erase some of your ugliness. Maybe y'all just need to get fucked. To all of you who have not been up in my face at least twenty-five times, I'm not talking about you." Then she walked away. Many of the onlookers gave her an ovation. To say that people talked, they did and did often. This little capsule of truth circulated all over town. A lot of people wished that they had said it themselves because it needed to be said. It seemed that the only business that a lot of people had was someone's else, especially the busy church bodies.

From that day onward Bojo made a vow to never say anything about Carrie Blister. Not now. Not later. Not ever.

Out of the blue Carrie jarred Bojo out his remembering by saying, "You know, I wonder if homosexuals are born that way or if they choose their sexual preferences. I kinda think that they are born that way."

"Carrie, you must have mad cow disease the way your mind is jumping around."

"Tell you what, I'll bet you ten to one that they are."

Bojo shook his head, "Uh . . . uh . . . uh . . . that is one bet that I will never make. I think that you are trying to make me feel as dumb as a box of rocks. Aw, what am I talking about? You can't measure the intelligence of rocks."

"You are talking logic and I'm talking fallacy."

"What you mean is bullshit. I can tell you one thing, I'm not a genius but I can solve most problems on a day scale. Then on the other hand I am not a perfectionist, a fool, a prude or purist or a saint but gays are one pill too big for me to swallow. Sometimes I find myself wondering what it would be like to screw a fag. Not often, you know, just every now and then. I wonder if someone would let me watch."

"Ain't this a blip! You are a sick man. You better hold on tight because you are about to fall into the macabre. I've got a friend that is gay, do you want me to ask her if she will let you watch her make love? Really, I never thought those kinds of things ever crossed your mind."

"No, not women, you know, guys," said a nervous Bojo. I want to know how it feels to have a dick in your ass."

"Now this is a BLIP!" Carrie said quietly. Then she added, "I'm sure there are more than a few who are willing to oblige. My mama always told me to live and learn. Today I've found out that my man wants to have a tryst with a fag."

"Cut that out," Bill whispered. "Someone may hear you and get the wrong idea."

"I'll tell you one thing, I've got a friend that is gay, and other than sexual preferences she is just like the rest of us."

"I'm not in this new age stuff, and I've always been told that God doesn't like fags and it is hard for me to embrace the principle of the homosexual. I can tell you this much, if someone should ever catch me with my pants down and my butt banging away, it will be with a member of the opposite sex. For the love of Peter, I for one cannot understand why a man would choose a shitty ass over some juicy pussy. Even sorry pussy is better than that."

"I can see that we are talking about our illustrious Senator Roy Cavity. Before you light into Roy, there is something I want to ask you. Why are we so down on homosexuals when fornicating and adultery are just as much of a sin? Remember, the Bible said that no sin is greater than another sin. Sin is sin, and the wages of sin is death. Even murders get more respect than the gay people. They are at the bottom of the barrel. As a child of God, who are supposed to love everybody, I just don't understand."

That scandal of Roy Cavity was still on his mind. He just couldn't see how Roy could put himself in a noncompromising position like that. To say that he was dumb as a dodo would be giving him a compliment. To even try to explain something like that was political suicide. No suicide, period.

It was true that Roy Cavity was laden with troubles and with grief. He was a bitter man who had never done anything outstanding or good in his entire life. It was brought out how antihomosexual he was. What was not said was the fact that Roy had been chosen to serve the remainder of Kato Fingerwrist's time after he had a massive stroke. It did not say that the only reason that he was chosen for the appointment was because the governor was banging his sister. Everyone who knew anything about Roy Cavity knew that something was wrong with him. He disappeared and no one heard from him again. His mail piled up so high until some kind soul did a humane deed and burned it.

Carrie put her fork down and wiped the corners of her mouth. She was a pretty woman but not a classic beauty. She had that type of beauty that started to fade at an early age. Whenever she would walk by heads would turn. She was good-looking and she knew it. She looked at Bojo and asked, "Are we having dessert?" Then she answered herself," I was really kidding because one thing that I don't need is dessert."

Bojo felt relieved because he had been thinking the same thing. "No, not for me."

"Where were we before the Roy Cavity saga began? Yes. Homosexuality. Now where was I?" Carrie mused."

"I think that we were talking about God and religion," Bojo answered. "But before we lay Roy Cavity to rest I want to know how a man of his statue let himself get into a predicament like that? He must be dumber than people give him credit for. Roy had no sense of rationality."

"I don't know what I would have done if someone had caught me with my pants down to my knees and my penis in the crack of another man's butt in, of all places, a public restroom. What would I have given to have seen that?"

"What part?"

The whole thing. Plus, his face when he realized that he had been caught. I wish that I could have read his mind to know what he was thinking about."

"That's just it," said Carrie, "he wasn't thinking, he was reacting." She pushed her chair back from the table.

"Sometimes it seems like homosexuals are an entirely different species."

"Yes," said Bojo. "If someone ever caught me with my pants down I will be taking a dump or with a member of the other sex."

"Then that will be the day you die. Because I will kill you. You are indeed a sex fiend and have an insatiable appetite. I mean that every time I see you, you want to satisfy your lust and call it love."

With a broad smile on his face, he said, "Girl, what are you talking about? I only want sex on days that have 'd' in them and twice a day on days that have 'y' in them."

"And you want to know why I'm tired all the time."

Bojo paid for their dinners and they went outside giggling. Their relationship was a special one. Bojo said shyly, "Uh, tell me, how did you know that our governor was banging Roy Cavity's sister?"

"My precious love, didn't I tell you that I have friends in high places? They sit high and look low, real low."

"I can see that."

Bojo was thinking to himself, "Do I love this woman or what?" He walked along beside her and said to said to himself, This is sooo good.

When they got back to Carrie's place he was feeling sorta like he always felt, horny. He was wondering if he should approach this subject since he had been talking about it only minutes ago. Besides, Carrie had given him a title, Dagasteena. I guess that I will live up to my reputation, king of the studs. That sounded nice. She couldn't resist him because he had this hold on her and she loved it.

Their lovemaking was always fantastic, and she could bounce him into orgasmic heaven any place and any time.

He sat in a huge chair in Carrie's living room, a chair, that he always said was his but wasn't. It didn't bother Carrie because she was hoping for the day when he would move in and claim it. She poured two drinks and came over and sat on his lap. She sipped her drink and he sat his on the coffee table. He reached under her sweater and unhooked her bra and held her breast in his hands. She murmured. He stopped, took a sip of his drink, then continued to tease her breast They became tense and rigid and sat up proud like a soldier standing at attention. He liked that. He held her breast in his hands and lightly nibbled on the nipple. She gave a low throaty moan. Then he ran his hand under her skirt. She had on a pantyhose. God, how he hated pantyhose. Nothing to worry about; she stood up and dropped her skirt and pantyhose in a heap on the floor. He didn't take off his clothes because she liked to do that herself. When she returned to her place on his lap she could see that he was greatly aroused and his erection seemed to grow in rigidity. This didn't give her all the time that she wanted to undress him, so she began right away. Bojo was masterful at controlling himself, and she was counting on that. She began by taking off his tie and shirt. Every piece of clothing that she removed she would cover with burning kisses of desire. He loved the way she would nibble on his breast and neck and suck each one of his fingers before she would remove another piece of clothing. By the time she got down to his under wear, he was on fire and he could wait any longer. They lay on the plush carpet and consummated their love. He had an offbeat rhythm that she could not synchronize and this made their lovemaking all the more intense. Carrie came. She came again. They lay on the carpet stuck together by juices of their lovemaking and plain old sweat.

Shortly, they both went into the bath room to clean up. Taking a shower was their choice of hygienic restitution. They showered together lathering each other and rinsing each other off. But the mist of their lathering, desire over took them again. Carrie wrapped her legs around his waist and clung to his neck as he penetrated her again and they made love in the tepid water as the pulsating shower rained down on them.

They stepped out of the shower spent. Carrie looked at Bojo and asked, "Will you marry me?" Bojo looked at Carrie like he was not sure he had heard her correctly. "Say what?"

Carrie looked at him with love shining in her eyes and he knew that he had heard her right, but he didn't have the answer that she wanted to hear so he decided to stall. Carrie said, "Will you marry me?"

Bojo said, "Precious, nothing would make me happier, only now is not a good time with all this campaigning we are going to do."

"I know that. I don't mean right now. I just realized that I can't live without you in my life."

"And you won't have to because I feel the same way about you."

"Really," Bill, please don't say this because you think that is what I want to hear."

"I wouldn't do that. I thought that you knew me better than that."

"Does this mean that we are engaged?"

He inhaled deeply and exhaled through his teeth. He wasn't actually lying because he would probably marry her some day. He said, "But of course, my love."

As he reached for his clothes, Carrie said, "Don't go home. Please stay with me tonight."

An excuse popped into Bojo mine but quickly fizzled out when she kissed him on the lips. The towel that was wrapped around them fell to the floor as he took her into his arms and put her on the bed.

The next day Bojo and K'Narf met at the Pot Gut Palace. K'Narf was a kind and giving person, but a lot of people thought of him as a shady dealer. He knew this but wouldn't let it bother him because he knew where his heart was and that was for the betterment of all citizens. He had dedicated uncountable hours of his time to the community and had given his last dime to help someone who he thought was worse off than him. He was not a rich man, a far cry from being one, and at the rate he was going the poor house was much closer than his friends thought. He was Bojo's friend, and Bojo knew that he would never find another like K'Narf. He trusted him with his life.

When they found a table and sat down, the first thing that Bojo said was, "Carrie asked me to marry her last night."

"Somehow, that doesn't surprise me any. What did you tell her?"

"Least as I could. I blamed it on the coming election."

"Well what are you going to do?"

"Marry her."

"Congratulations, man, you are getting one hell of a woman."

"Thanks, man. When it happens, I want you to be my best man."

"You've got it," K'Narf said as he congratulated his friend.

"Another thing, K'Narf, I want you to be my campaign manager since I've decided to run for president. We simply can't let those spooks get even a fingernail in the door of Purple Bottom City."

"You've got it. When did you decide to run?" I think sometime between three o'clock this morning and now. I haven't even told Carrie. "What are you running for?"

"President, I suppose. Another thing I want to ask you." Bojo paused, as if he was afraid to ask. He smiled nervously like a little boy and said, "I want you to be me when I can't be me."

"I don't think that you should be running for anything because you have lost your mind. Just what do you mean when you say that want me to be you when you can't be you?"

"That was the imposition that I was afraid to ask of you."

"I don't know what that means."

"I don't know either. It's just that anything that I can't do you will be there to back me up. I may have to think of things as they come up and you will follow suit and you may have to be in the lead sometimes and I will follow suit. Okay."

"I don't know what you call it but this could be imposing, but what are friends for?"

"Your first official duty is to call Mamie and tell her to notify the committee and set up a meeting ASAP. I'm going to call Carrie and tell her of my decision."

"You've got it."

After Bojo left K'Narf he headed for his office. He needed to modify his schedule to make room for his campaign. He had to adjust his case load because the next ten months were going to hectic and tiring, very tiring.

K'Narf made a call to the local media and requested they attend the next meeting of the Concerned Citizens for Government meeting. He did not tell them what the meeting was going to reveal.

Bojo finally caught up with Carrie and asked her to meet him for lunch. Carrie agreed but insisted that cut it short because there was something that she had to do. They met up at the Left Over Purple Place. They both ordered a salad and grilled fish with mustard sauce. Bojo was pouring dressing on his salad when they both began to speak at the same time. "I've got something to . . ." They stopped. Bojo insisted that she should go first.

She said, "Baby, I know that we've been through this before and I've come up with excuses, but just after you left this morning I made a decision to run for governor. Please don't be angry."

Bojo began laughing. Carrie was confused. "What's the matter? Did I say something funny?" It took a while before he could contain himself. Finally, he said, "I was going to accept the committee's nomination to run for president."

"You did what?" asked Carrie.

"I'm running for president," he answered as he grabbed her around the waist swinging her around, kissing her on the lips.

"You mean that you are not angry?"

"No," he answered enthusiastically, "I'm delighted."

He stopped twirling her around and she sat down because she was feeling dizzy and he winded.

After she had rested a few minutes she said, "Do you know what this means?"

"Sure. Both of us are running for political offices. Number one and number two."

"No, that's not what I meant. I mean what this means for us."

"Can't say that I do. What are you talking about?"

She leaned closer and spoke quietly, "It means we won't have much time to be together for a long time."

Bojo smiled and said, "You know what they say. 'Love will find a way.'"

"Does this mean you love me?"

"More and more every day. Later tonight I will tell you everything that you always wanted to hear from me but never asked."

"I'll be waiting with a lollipop. Since I don't have a baby for you to kiss, I will bring you a lollipop."

"Okay. Make mine cherry."

She giggled, "I've already given you one cherry. A girl has only one."

He smiled and smacked her on the lips and said, "I'll see you at the meeting."

*****

Later that night when the CCBG met, both Carrie Blister and Bill Elbow announced their decisions to accept their nominations and be candidates of their choice. This pleased the committee because they felt that both of them were new age politicians and adhered to their policies of government reform. They felt that Bojo and Carrie both had name recognition and didn't have to start at grassroots. They felt that they were the kind of people who didn't mind running things. They were educated, had impeccable backgrounds, and had the ability to look back and visualize the future. Plus they didn't like the way Purple Bottom City was being run. Those weak leaders who wanted to let Underground City get to make a bid to run their world and PBC as one when they didn't know anything about it. They didn't like the way Purple Bottom City was being run on the backs of those who could least afford it while the rich was getting richer. They were adamant about getting all those rich people out of office who made a career of keeping the poor people poor and the rich people rich.

What surprised them most was that so much media and concerned citizens came until the police and firemen had to come and disperse the overflowing crowd.

That it is impossible. Somewhere in this world or out of this world this could be a common sight. Should I leave the rest of my life up to fate? Naw! I don't believe in fate either.

CPSIA information can be obtained at www.ICGtesting.com
Printed in the USA
LVOW12s0514250215

428177LV00004B/10/P